MARY WEBB

poet, mystic and lover of nature was born in 1881 in Leighton Cressage, Shropshire, the county where she spent most of her life, which she passionately loved and about which she wrote in all her novels. Educated mainly at home, she began writing at the age of ten, and her verse and prose were published in many papers and magazines in both America and England. *The Golden Arrow*, her first novel, was published in 1916. *Gone to Earth* followed in 1917, with a collection of short stories, *The Spring of Joy*. Her other novels were *The House in Dormer Forest* (1920), *Seven for a Secret* (1922), *Precious Bane* (1924) and, posthumously, *The Armour Wherein He Trusted* (1929).

In 1912 Mary Webb married a schoolmaster, Henry Webb: they moved to London in 1921, living in Hampstead until her early death in 1927, her short life one of struggle against illness and near-poverty.

Admiring contemporaries – who included Rebecca West, Walter de la Mare, Arnold Bennett – described her as a 'strange genius' and 'one of the best living writers'. But despite the fact that *Precious Bane* was awarded the Prix Femina Vie Heureuse in 1925, it was not until six months after her death, when Prime Minister Stanley Baldwin read and publicly praised *Precious Bane*, that her work began to reach a wider public. But though she enjoyed a posthumous success, it is only in recent years that a new generation has recognised again the unique magic of a novelist whose literary achievement stands firmly in the tradition of the Brontë sisters, and of Thomas Hardy, but whose style and voice is nevertheless utterly her own.

Virago also publish *Precious Bane*, *Gone to Earth* and *The House in Dormer Forest*.

Mary Webb

SEVEN FOR A SECRET

With a New Introduction
by Michèle Barale

Virago

Published by VIRAGO PRESS Limited 1982
Ely House, 37 Dover Street, London W1X 4HS

First published in Great Britain by Hutchinson & Co. 1922

Virago edition offset from Hutchinson 1922 edition

Introduction copyright © Michèle Barale 1982

Printed in Finland by Werner Söderström Oy,
a member of Finnprint

British Library Cataloguing in Publication Data
Webb, Mary, *1881-1927*
    Seven for a secret.—(Virago modern classics)
    I. Title
    823'.912   PR6045.E2

ISBN 0-86068-333-8

To the illustrious name
of
THOMAS HARDY,
whose acceptance of this dedication
has made me so happy.

I saw seven magpies in a tree,
One for you and six for me.
    One for sorrow,
    Two for joy,
    Three for a girl,
    Four for a boy,
    Five for silver,
    Six for gold,
    Seven for a secret
    That's never been told.

Old Rhyme

CONTENTS

		PAGE
INTRODUCTION		ix
I.—GILLIAN LOVEKIN		9
II.—ROBERT RIDEOUT		19
III.—AUNT FANTEAGUE ARRIVES . . .		25
IV.—GILLIAN ASKS FOR A KISS . . .		38
V.—ROBERT WRITES TWO LETTERS . .		50
VI.—TEA AT THE JUNCTION. . . .		61
VII.—GILLIAN COMES TO SILVERTON . .		71
VIII.—GILLIAN MEETS MR. GENTLE . .		82
IX.—THE HARPER'S FORGE		88
X.—THE BURNING HEART		96
XI.—ISAIAH ASKS A QUESTION . . .		109
XII.—AT THE SIGN OF THE MAIDEN . .		116
XIII.—ROBERT SAYS " NO "		127
XIV.—" DAGGLY " WEATHER . . .		134
XV.—ISAIAH HEARS A BELOWNDER . .		140
XVI.—RALPH ELMER COMES TO DINNER .		150
XVII.—TEA FOR FOUR AT THE " MERMAID'S REST "		158
XVIII.—THE GIFTS OF RALPH ELMER TO GILLIAN LOVEKIN		170
XIX.—BLOOM IN THE ORCHARD . . .		182
XX.—ROBERT PLEACHES THE THORN HEDGE .		188

PAGE

XXI.—BRIAR ROSES   194

XXII.—WEEPING CROSS 203

XXIII.—ISAIAH SAYS " HA ! " 210

XXIV.—A HANK OF FAERY WOOL .   .   . 216

XXV.—THE BRIDE COMES HOME   .   .   . 225

XXVI.—A.B.C. AT THE SIGN OF THE MAIDEN . 230

XXVII.—" IN A DREAM SHE CRADLED ME ".   . 237

XXVIII.—FRINGAL FORGETS TO LAUGH   .   . 248

XXIX.—SNOW IN THE LITTLE GYLAND   .   . 261

XXX.—ROBERT AWAITS THE DAWN.   .   . 268

XXXI.—" NOW WHAT BE TROUBLING THEE ? " . 274

XXXII.—" SEVEN FOR A SECRET THAT'S NEVER
        BEEN TOLD "   284

INTRODUCTION

The *Bildungsroman*, a tale of the growth and development of a young person, has almost exclusively told the story of a boy: David Copperfield, Ernest Pontifex, Stephen Dedalus, young Werther, Tom Sawyer. Those novels which describe the maturation of a young girl are few, and most frequently detail the life of a woman in some way exceptional: Moll Flanders, for instance, or Emma Bovary, or Becky Sharp. Mary Webb's *Seven for a Secret* can most certainly be read as a *Bildungsroman*, as a novel which tells the story of Gillian Lovekin's growth and maturity. It is a novel which shows how a callow and selfish young girl, a girl who could use everything and everyone to satisfy her curiosity and vanity, becomes a woman able to love selflessly. And it is a novel which, in detailing Gillian's history, does not omit the part which the erotic plays in all maturation. In this presentation of adolescent female sexuality, Webb is unusually honest and admirably realistic. It is a frank, overwhelming sexual curiosity which impels Gillian's early behaviour. But it is a wiser Gillian, a Gillian no longer physically or emotionally virginal, who has come to understand nature's great mystery of regeneration and life, a Gillian who can, therefore, love without selfishness. For Mary Webb, this mature knowledge redeems Gillian, bringing her from darkness to light, healing completely the scar which was her mark.

But Mary Webb was unwilling to create a young Gillian whose narcissism makes her despicable to the reader. Instead, we cannot help but enjoy Gillian's vitality, her desire for independence, her flirtatious attempts to wield power. She seeks escape from the farmhouse of her father, despite her love of the Welsh moorlands and her pleasure in the "incipient splendour" of the common things of her life, because she would have a larger world to experience and because she would herself be larger: wiser in the ways of the world. Robert Lynd, in the introduction to the 1929 edition of the novel, characterises Gillian's quest as being of little worth: "She has, when we meet her first, no real ambition, except to be a greater Gillian Lovekin and to escape from the farm that is too small a stage for her." But Lynd's claim of—"no real ambition" is far from correct; Gillian Lovekin, despite the crassness of her yearnings or the confined terms of her desires—confined and crass they well might be since she has never been but twelve miles from the farm—wants all that is to be had. She wants the power of self-definition and the power, as well, that comes from others' acceptance of this definition. Gillian Lovekin wants to shape herself rather than be shaped by the dictates of her father, a man who is loud rather than wise, or by the proprieties of her aunt, a woman who defines a lady as distinguished by her lack of any presence whatsoever: "You can tell a lady, because nobody ever knows she's there."

Mary Webb certainly had sympathy for Gillian's longings for "a sparkling band round my head, and sparkling slippers on my feet, and a gown that goes 'hush! hush!'", shallow though such longings are. Webb understood in her creation of Gillian that her character's adolescent desire for a multitude of admiring young men, for the adulation of the crowd was a childish desire for just another sort of glitter and sparkle. But she also understood that the roots of such a desire were not to be dismissed. Gillian's vision of herself is far from infantile; rather, it is "the vision desired by all humanity—the vision of a secure small nest of immortality built upon the crumbling walls of time. She wants to go on

being herself even when she is dissolved in nothingness."
Gillian, like all of us, would cheat death. She wants to use her
"art"—her as yet unlearned music—to achieve fame and
power and thus attain a sort of immortality. Mary Webb, in
other words, created in the character of Gillian Lovekin one
whose maturation reflects the deepest levels of human maturation. We do not only see a country girl marry in haste,
repent in leisure and finally discover who it is that she has
loved all along. We see, too, something that is larger; in
Gillian's quest for self-definition, autonomy, power and,
ultimately, immortality, we see something mythic.

It is, of course, not at all expected to find the mythical in
the story of a young country girl. Although we have a literary
tradition which allows for the intrusion of the mythical in the
story of the young boy—Stephen Dedalus—not even so compelling a figure as Maggie Tulliver of George Eliot's *Mill on
the Floss* has led the reader into the strange literary grove
wherein the life of one small girl suggests those tales that
chart the growth of human consciousness and culture. I do
not wish to lay too heavy a burden upon Webb's novel; it is
not the undiscovered masterpiece of twentieth-century liter-
ature. But neither is it merely a piece of once-popular fiction,
interesting only from an historical perspective. *Seven for a
Secret* is an intriguing novel, tightly written, ambiguously
resolved, and purposely didactic: the author wishes to make a
point. And her point is that the young girl is prompted to
dream and act by those same human impulses which spur a
young boy.

These are, then, human desires rather than gender-related
actions. Both sexes are impelled in their early history by a
need to deny mortality; both sexes seek power over their own
lives and over others in an attempt to overcome death's
power. But, as Mary Webb demonstrates, power and love
cannot coexist. Ultimately, if love is to be experienced, the
power of self-determination must be willingly forsaken.
Thus, in what was doubtlessly read by her contemporaries as
a pleasantly passionate novel about life and love and the
relationships between the sexes, Webb reflects Sigmund
Freud's revolutionary presentation of the dualism of love and

the will to power, Freud's belief in the warring forces of love and death. In what most of her contemporary reviewers considered a gentle, pantheistic mysticism, Mary Webb presents, in fact, a facet of mystical apprehension which is at equal ease with beauty and terror—with the Dionysian. Regeneration and motherhood, murder and brutality are presented at the novel's end as having equal value in life's terms; nature makes no moral distinctions in the world of this novel.

Seven for a Secret was written in 1922 and reissued in 1929 after the author's death two years earlier at the age of forty-six. It is Webb's fourth novel and has been criticised as tired and even melodramatic in plot, as reflecting yet again a theme common to Webb: the contrast of sacred and profane love. To view the novel as merely reflective of a contrast is, however, to ignore the novel as the story of growth, as *Bildungs-roman*, and is to see Gillian Lovekin as a puppet created to enact a rather thin melodrama. If, instead, the novel is understood in terms of the mythic references and images which are woven through it, the novel then seems an example of authorial craft, and more, of authorial courage. Webb took the life of a not terribly unusual moorland girl and through mythic imagery made that life—filled with all the details of farm and middle-class existence—comment upon the meaning of human love, sexuality, culture, art and death.

Despite Mary Webb's reputation, both contemporary and posthumous, as the sweet apostle of nature, the lyrical poet of joy, *Seven for a Secret* gives evidence of Webb as a writer who did far more than trip lightly through the tulips. She contemplated, instead, with a total lack of squeamishness, the meaning of human value in amoral nature. She had no apparent difficulty maintaining love—passionate, sexual, and spiritual—as the supreme value even while admitting that only reproduction has value in nature's larger scheme. She could accept the notion that human understanding is filled with ellipses, accept the possibility that even our most noble, most beautiful gestures are without ultimate meaning—and still not appear cynical, not appear despairing, not appear to value the human gesture any less. While Mary Webb was certainly not Thomas Hardy's literary equal in terms of style or complexity, like him she did not flinch from portraying the world as she perceived it to be, both beautiful and terrible at once.

Early in *Seven for a Secret*, just after she has declared her intent to win money, gown, suitors and applause, Gillian stands in her father's pasture. She has been trapping rabbits in order to make enough money for music lessons. While she was standing there, the dead booty at her feet, splashed with blood, "the sheep stirred about her like uneasy souls, and the rabbits lying at her feet might have been a sacrifice to some woodland goddess". Gillian is described in terms of the moon; she is "sharp" and "silvery" and "cutting". Webb further compares Gillian to a ruthlessly pursuing falcon, supple, sure and powerful. Neither in her posture nor in these comparisons is there the least aspect of feminine gentleness. Rather, the effect is one of sharp cruelty and bloody death. Gillian, when we first see her, is a forest goddess, Artemis of the silvered crescent moon and killing arrow. But as the novel progresses we see Gillian change from huntress into the all-giving mother, from Artemis to Demeter.

Whether or not the reader is pleased with the change in Gillian, is comfortable with a Gillian become a "sobbing little creature", it is certain that myth's makers would shape slim archers to maternal fullness. For Mary Webb such change—the loss of Gillian's hard-won self-identification—was not the product of ultimate capitulation to all those patriarchal forces which Gillian had earlier fought. Rather, it was the natural capitulation which we all are nearly helpless to refuse in the face of nature's power. It is not that Gillian loses, but that ever regenerating nature wins. As must all the figures of myth, Gillian submits to her destiny.

But destiny, as the novel's very title implies, remains an eternally mysterious force. Almost as though she is aware that her novel's end might pose a problem—"But the reader must by this time be indignant"—Mary Webb assures us that the end we have seen is merely partial. But what more there is to tell she cannot, for to do so would require an explanation which is beyond the ability of language. She has told us as much of the story as she is able; the rest is to be learned "out in the early summer morning, listening to the silence" where one knows that "there is more, that in and beyond the purple earth and silver sky there is a mystery so great that the knowledge of it would be intolerable, so sweet that the very intuition in its nearness brings tears". The secret, like the Eleusinian mysteries, is not to be contained in words or even captured totally in a story. With the perception of the great tellers of tales, Webb understands that the story she narrates has reverberations beyond the page. She knows that language, even at its most artful, cannot fully grasp life.

Just as silence seems to be the very heart of mystery, so too speechless Rwth, in a most provocative way, is at the very heart of this novel. In a literal way, Rwth remains a mystery throughout much of the story. Both Robert and Gillian seek to discover her unknown background and her relationship to Ralph Elmer. But revelation of her history serves to make Rwth's character yet more mythic: she is the lost child renamed, left speechless, deprived of her birthright, forced to wash floors, mocked, beaten—and alone capable of perfect spiritual love. If her figure seems a familiar one to us, it is because it is one common to English folktale, to fairytale.

But while Rwth's character suggests a folktale heroine such as Cinderella, it suggests as well the classical figure of Persephone, the abducted daughter, whose descent into the dark earth causes winter, but who reappears with spring. Rwth is like Persephone, goddess of rebirth, daughter of the Great Mother Demeter. What happens to her enables love to bloom, marriage and children to come about. The Persephone who returned from the underworld, though brightly beautiful, though strewn with flowers, was the possessor of awesome memories. Having seen the secrets of the dead, Persephone now knew all the terrible things, all the mysteries. And Rwth, in her youthful innocence, has perhaps a single reward, suggests Mary Webb; she is freed from the boundaries of reason and language and can grasp, as can no one else, "the secret that's never been told".

Michèle Barale, Colorado, 1981

CHAPTER I

On a certain cold winter evening, in the country that lies between the dimpled lands of England and the gaunt purple steeps of Wales—half in Faery and half out of it—the old farmhouse that stood in the midst of the folds and billows of Dysgwlfas-on-the-Wild-Moors glowed with a deep gem-like lustre in its vast setting of grey and violet. Moorland country is never colourless. It still keeps, when every heather-bell is withered, in its large mysterious expanses, a bloom of purple like the spirit of the heather. Against this background, which lay on every side, mile on sombre mile, the homestead, with its barns and stacks, held and refracted every ray of the declining sunlight, and made a comfortable and pleasant picture beneath the fleecy, low, cinereous sky, which boded snow. The farmhouse was built of fine old mellow sandstone, of that weatherworn and muted red which takes an indescribable beauty beneath the level rays of dawn and sunset, as though it irradiated the light that touched it. It was evening only in the sense in which that word is used in this border country, which is any time after noon. It was not yet tea-time, though preparations for tea were going on within. Among the cornricks, which burned under the sun into a memory of the unreaped August

9

tints of orange and tawny and yellow, redpolls were
feasting and seeking their customary shelter for the night,
and one or two late-lingering mountain linnets kept up
their sad little lament of " twite-twite-twite " in the bare
blackthorn hedge. Blackbirds began to think of fluffing
their feathers, settling cosily, and drawing up their eyelids.
They " craiked " and scolded in their anxiety to attain
each his secret Nirvana. From the stubble fields, that
lay like a small pale coin on the outspread moor, a flock of
starlings came past with a rip of the air like the tearing of
strong silk.

The rickyard lay on the north side of the foldyard ; on
the south was the house ; to the east it was bounded by
the shippen, the cowhouses and stables. To the west lay
the orchard, and beyond it the cottage, which in these
lonely places is always built when the farm is built. The
whole thing formed a companionable little township of
some five hundred souls—allowing the turkeys to have
souls, and including the ewes when they lay near the
house at lambing time. As to whether the redpolls, the
linnets and the starlings should be included, Gillian of
Dysgwlfas was often doubtful. They sang ; they flew ;
and nobody could sing or fly without a soul : but they
were so quick and light and inconsequent, their songs
were so thin and eerie, that Gillian thought their souls
were not quite real—faery souls, weightless as an eggshell
when the egg has been sucked out. On the roof of the
farm the black fantail pigeons, which belonged to Robert
Rideout of the cottage, sidled up and down uneasily.
All day, troubled by the clangour within the house, they
had stepped at intervals, very gingerly, to the edge of
the thatch, and set each a ruby eye peering downwards.
They had observed that the leaded windows stood open,
every one, all day ; that the two carved armchairs with
the red cushions, and the big sheepskin hearthrug of the
parlour, had been brought out on to the square lawn
where the dovecote was, and beaten. They had seen
Simon, their hated enemy, slinking round the borders
where the brown stems of the perennials had been crisped

by early frosts, miserable as he always was on cleaning days, finally sulking in the window of the cornloft and refusing to enter the house at all. All this, they knew, meant some intrusion of the outer world, the world that lay beyond their furthest gaze, into this quiet place, drenched in old silence. It must be that Farmer Lovekin's sister was coming—that Mrs. Fanteague who caused cleanings of the dovecote, whom they hated. They marked their disapproval by flashing up all together with a steely clatter of wings, and surveying the lessening landscape from the heights of the air.

Most of the windows were shut now, and a warm, delicious scent of cooking afflicted Simon's appetite so that he rose, stretched, yawned, washed cursorily, shelved his dignity and descended to the kitchen, where he twined himself about the quick feet of Mrs. Makepeace, urgent between the larder and the great open fire, with its oven on one side and gurgling boiler on the other.

By the kitchen table stood Gillian Lovekin. Her full name was Juliana, but the old-fashioned way of treating the name had continued in the Lovekin family. She was stoning raisins. Every sixth raisin she put into her mouth, rapturously and defiantly, remembering that she and not Mrs. Makepeace was mistress of the farm. When her mother died Gillian had been only sixteen. Her first thought, she remembered with compunction, had been that now she would be mistress. She was eighteen on this evening of preparation, and just " out of her black." She was neither tall nor short, neither stout nor very slender ; she was not dark nor fair, not pretty nor ugly. She had ugly things about her, such as the scar which seamed one side of her forehead, and gave that profile an intent, relentless look. Her nose was much too high in the bridge—the kind of nose that comes of Welsh ancestry and is common in the west. It gave her, in her softest moods, a domineering air. But her mouth was sensitive and sweet, and could be yielding sometimes, and her eyes had so much delight in all they looked upon, and saw so much incipient splendour in common things, that they charmed you and led you in a spell, and would not let you think her plain or dull.

She liked to do her daily tasks with an air ; so she used the old Staffordshire bowl (which had been sent from that county as a wedding present for her grandmother) to dip her fingers in when they were sticky. The brown raisins were heaped up on a yellow plate, and she made a gracious picture with her two plaits of brown hair, her dark eyebrows bent above eyes of lavender-grey, and her richly tinted face with its country tan and its flush of brownish rose. The firelight caressed her, and Simon, when he could spare time from the bits of fat that fell off Mrs. Makepeace's mincing board, blinked at her greenly and lovingly.

Mrs. Makepeace was making chitterling puffs and apple cobs.

" Well ! " she said, mincing so swiftly that she seemed to mince her own fingers every time, " we've claned this day, if ever ! "

Gillian sighed. She disliked these bouts of fierce manual industry almost as much as Simon did.

" I'm sure my A'nt Fanteague did ought to be pleased," she said, making her aunt's name into three syllables.

" Mrs. Fanteague," observed Mrs. Makepeace, " is a lady as is never pl'ased. Take your dear 'eart out, serve on toast with gravy of your bone and sinew. Would she say ' Thank you ? ' She'd sniff and she'd peer, and she'd say with that loud lungeous voice of 'ers : ' What you want, my good 'oman, is a *larger* 'eart.' "

Gillian's laugh rang out, and Simon, who loved her voice, came purring across the kitchen and leapt into her lap.

" Saving your presence, Miss Gillian, child," added Mrs. Makepeace, " and excuse me making game of your A'ntie."

" Time and agen," said Gillian, pushing away the plate of raisins, " I think I'd lief get in the cyart by A'nt Fanteague when she goes back to Sil'erton, and go along of her, beyond the Gwlfas and the mountains, beyond the sea——"

" Wheer then ? " queried Mrs. Makepeace practically.

" To the moon-O ! maybe."

" By Leddy ! What'd your feyther do ? "

" Feyther's forgetful. He wouldna miss me sore."

" And Robert ? My Bob ? "

She looked swiftly at Gillian, her brown eyes keen and motherly.

" Oh, Robert ? " mused Gillian, her hands going up and down amid Simon's dark fur.

She brooded.

" Robert Rideout ? " she murmured. Then she swung her plaits backwards with a defiant toss, and cried : " He wouldna miss me neither ! "

She flung Simon down and got up.

" It's closing in," she said. " I mun see to my coney wires."

" It's to be hoped, my dear, as you'll spare me a coney out of your catch to make a patty. Your A'nt Fanteague dearly loves a coney patty."

" Not without feyther pays for it," said Gillian. " If I give away my conies as fast as I catch 'em, where's my lessons in the music ? "

She opened the old nail-studded door that gave on the foldyard, and was gone.

" Gallus ! " observed Mrs. Makepeace. " Ah, she's gallus, and forever 'ankering after the world's deceit, but she's got an 'eart, if you can only get your fingers round it, Robert, my lad. But I doubt you binna for'ard enow."

She shook her head over the absent Robert so that the strings of her sunbonnet swung out on either side of her round, red, cheerful face.

" If I didna know as John Rideout got you long afore I took pity on poor Makepeace (and a man of iron John Rideout was, and it's strange as I should come to a man of straw), I'd be nigh thinking you was Makepeace's, time and agen. Dreamy—dreamy ! "

She rolled and slapped and minced as if her son and her second husband were on the rolling board and she was putting them into shape. But John Rideout, the man

of iron, remained in her mind as a being beyond her
shaping. After his death she had seen all other men
as so many children, to be cared for and scolded, and
because Jonathan Makepeace was the most helpless man
she had ever met, she married him. She had seen him
first on a market day at the Keep. Tall, narrow, with
his long hair and beard blowing in the wind, his mild blue
eye met hers with the sadness of one who laments : " When
I speak unto them of peace, they make them ready for
battle." For the tragedy of Jonathan Makepeace was
that, since he had first held a rattle, inanimate matter had
been his foe. He was a living illustration of the theory
that matter cuts across the path of life. In its crossing
of Jonathan's path it was never Jonathan that came off
as victor. Jugs flung themselves from his hands ; buckets
and cisterns decanted their contents over him ; table-
cloths caught on any metal portion of his clothing, dragging
with them the things on the table. If he gathered fruit,
a heavy fire of apples poured upon his head. If he fished,
he fell into the water. Many bits of his coat, and one
piece of finger, had been given to that Moloch, the turnip-
cutter. When he forked the garden, he forked his own
feet. When he chopped wood, pieces fled up into his face
like furious birds. If he made a bonfire, flames drew themselves out to an immense length in order to singe his
beard. This idiosyncrasy of inanimate nature (or of
Jonathan) was well known on the moors, and was enjoyed
to the full, from Mallard's Keep, which lay to the north,
to the steep dusky market town of Weeping Cross, which
lay south. It was enjoyed with the quiet, uncommenting,
lasting enjoyment of the countryside. On the day Abigail
met him, it was being enjoyed at the Keep, where the
weekly market was, and where people shopped on ordinary
occasions, reserving Christmas or wedding or funeral
shopping for the more distant Weeping Cross. Jonathan
had been shopping. Under one arm he had a bag o
chicken-food ; under the other, bran. Both bags, aware
of Jonathan, had gently burst, and a crowd followed him
with silent and ecstatic mirth while he wandered, dignified

and pathetic, towards the inn, with the streams of grain and bran making his passing like a paperchase. She had heard of Jonathan (who had not ?) and this vision of him was the final proof that he needed mothering. She told him briskly what was happening, and his " Deary, deary me ! " and his smile seemed to her very lovable. She wrapped up his parcels and listened sympathetically to his explanations. There was " summat come over " things, he said. " Seemed like they was bewitched." She did not laugh. She had a kind of ancient wisdom about her that fitted in with her firm, rosy face, her robin-like figure. She knew that the heavens were not the same heavens for all. The rain did not fall equally on the evil and the good. Here was Jonathan, as good as gold, yet every cloud in heaven seemed to collect above him. As he ruefully said, " Others met be dry as tinder, but I'm soused." Realizing that war with the inanimate is woman's special province, because she has been trained by centuries of housework—of catching cups as they sidle from their hooks and jugs as they edge from the table—Mrs. Rideout decided to spend the rest of her life fighting for Jonathan. She had done so for twelve years, to her own delight, the admiration of the country round, and Jonathan's content.

Robert was ten years old when she married Makepeace. His heavily-lashed eyes, which had a dark glance as well as a tender one, and of which it was difficult to see the colour because of their blazing vitality, his forbidding mouth with its rare sweet smile, were so like his father's that she would ponder on him for hours at a time. To John Rideout she was faithful, though she married Makepeace. And as Christmas after Christmas went by, and still Jonathan was alive and well, she triumphed. She loved him with a maternal love, and when Robert grew to manhood, Jonathan took his place. Abigail would look at his tall, thin figure with pride, remembering all that she had saved him from during the past year.

Now, while Abigail worked in the farm kitchen, Jonathan was very unhappily putting a tallow dip in his horn lantern, in order to harness the mare and go to the station across the moor to fetch Mrs. Fanteague. The tallow candle refused to stand up, bending towards him like the long greyish neck of a cygnet, pouring tallow on to Mrs. Makepeace's check tablecloth. Jonathan thought of the things that the harness would do, of the gates that would slam in his face, and the number of times he would drop the whip ; he thought of the miles of darkly sighing moor which he must cross in order to bring back Mrs. Fanteague and her sharp-cornered box (always by the mercy of heaven and in defiance of material things), and he sighed. Abigail would have a sup of tea ready for him when he got home. "*If* he got home," he amended. With a fatalism which shrouded his character like a cloak, he regarded the worst as the only thing likely to happen, and whether he stubbed his foot or fell from the top of the hay-bay, he only said " Lard's will be done."

As he opened the stable door, a goblin of wind puffed his light out. The door slammed and pinched his fingers. He had no matches. Time pressed, for no one ever kept Mrs. Fanteague waiting. He lifted up his voice.

" Robert Rideout ! Robert Rideout ! " he called.

His thin cry wandered through the foldyard to the rickyard, and brought sleepy eyelids half-way down. The echoes strayed disconsolately into the vagueness of the surrounding moor, which, at sunset, had darkened like a frown.

Robert did not appear.

" Off on lonesome ! " commented Jonathan. " What a lad ! Oh, what a useless, kim-kam lad ! Never a hand's turn. Allus glooming and glowering on the yeath !"

" What ails you, stepfeyther ? " asked a deep and quiet voice. " What for be you blaating by your lonesome outside the dark door ? "

Jonathan sighed with relief, settling himself like a sleepy bird in the strong, secure presence of Robert Rideout. He stood with his white hair blowing, wringing his hands like a frail prophet of disaster, and told Robert of the long day's mishaps.

" Ah ! It's allus like that when mother's off at farm,"
said Robert, fetching out the mare, who nestled her nose
softly into his rough coat. Horses never worked so well
for anyone as for Robert. When he milked the cows,
they gave more milk. No ewe, it was said, would drop
her lambs untimely if he were shepherd. The very hens,
obliged by hereditary instinct to " steal their nesses,"
would come forth with their bee-like swarms of chicks
when Robert went by, revealing their sin and their glory
to his eye alone.

" Ready ! " said Robert. He gave Jonathan the reins
and whip, tucked a sack round his knees, saw to the lamps,
and opened the gate.

" Leave a light in stable, lad, agen we come—if we
come."

This was his customary phrase. If he only went to
call the ducks from the pond, he bade his wife as fond a
farewell as if he were going on a voyage. It was most
probable that he would fall head foremost among the
ducks and that the weeds would coil themselves about
him and drag him down. It was curious that no one
ever thought of stopping Jonathan doing these responsible
tasks. For instance, he went to " lug " Mrs. Fanteague
back because he always did so. Things happened ; but,
so far, the worst had not occurred. There is a vein of
optimistic fatalism in the country which always hopes
that the worst never will happen. Besides, there was
Mrs. Fanteague. Coming home, she would be in command.
Even now, when she had not so much as alighted on the
windswept wooden platform of the branch line station at the
Keep, her presence, advancing solidly beyond the horizon,
comforted him inexpressibly. There was also Winny,
the mare. She would look after him. She understood
him very well. When he jerked the off rein, she swerved
to the near, and vice versa. She knew every stone, every
bit of uneven road, every stray scent that crossed it, fine
as a thread of cobweb, all the walking gradients and the
slippery bits. She knew the place where the road ran
beside the railway line for half a mile, just as you came

to the Keep—where, if Robert had been driving, she
would have been "nervy" and relied on him, on his
voice and his firm hand on the rein—where, if anyone
else had been driving, she would have run away. When
she had Jonathan in the trap, she did not run away ; she
allowed herself no starts or tremors. If he had left things
entirely to her, nothing would ever have happened. The
animal world, as if to make up for the unkindness of the
inanimate, was kind to him, and as the stocks and stones
rose up and confounded him, the living creatures comforted him, motherly and consoling.

" I'd come and send you a bit, stepfeyther, only I mun
see to sheep."

" Good-bye, lad, and God bless you," said Jonathan.
" I'll be right enow when the mar' gets going."

But as they swung out on to the moor, he turned and
glanced at the comfortable lit windows of the farm and
shook his head sadly and murmured : " Lard save me to
lug Mrs. Fanteague back."

CHAPTER II

ROBERT RIDEOUT

A SHARP young moon sidled up over the dark eastern shoulder of the moor, entangled herself in the black manes of the pines which swayed a little in the rising night wind, slipped through them like a fish through a torn net, and swam free in a large grey sky which was beginning to tingle, between the woolly clouds, with a phosphorescence of faint starlight. In the last meadow that sloped up, rough and tussocky, to the splendid curve of moorland, Robert found the sheep, uneasy beneath a dubious heaven. They lay with their dim raddled bodies outlined by crisp, frosty, faintly luminous grass. The presage of lambing-time was already in their eyes.

"Coom then!" said Robert. "Coom then!"

They rose with a faery crackling of herbage, and prepared to go whither he should lead them. But as he turned towards home, a voice, sharp and silvery as the young moon, cutting the deep boding silence like a sickle, cried from the other side of the bare hazel hedge :

"Bide for me, 'oot, Bob?"

He turned, unsurprised and unhurried.

"What ails you, Gillian, child, nutting in November? Dunna you know the owd rhyme?"

"Say it!"

> "Nut in November,
>   Gather doom.
> There's none will remember
>   Your tomb."

" You made it," she cried.

He laughed shyly.

" What for do you go to think that-a-way ? "

" I dunna think. I know. You made it, somewheer
in that black tously head of yourn. I do believe you've
got a cupboard there, like Mrs. Makepeace keeps the
jam in, and you keep the tales and songs and what-nots
with little tickets on 'em, and fetch 'em when you want
'em."

She jumped down from the hedge-bank, and two dead
rabbits in her hand swung across her apron and dabbled
it with blood.

" I'se reckon," said Robert, surveying her with amused
eyes, " as you'm a little storm in teacup, and no mistake.
What's come o'er you to ketch the conies ? You're like
nought but a little brown coney yourself."

She threw the conies on the grass, flung back her plaits,
set her hands on her slim hips, and said : " I've got to
catch 'em. I'm bound to get money for lessons in the
music. You know that."

" What for's it taken you to want the music ? "

" I mun sing, and play a golden harp like the big man
played at the Eisteddfod."

" What then ? "

" Then I'll buy a piece of crimson scarlet stuff and make
me a dress, and put the harp in the cyart along of A'nt
Fanteague, and go into the world and play to folks and
make 'em cry."

" What for cry ? "

" Cos folk dunna like to cry at a randy. Even at the
Revivals they only cry when the preachers shout mortal
loud and the texts come pit-a-pat, pit-a-pat, and knock
'em silly. If you can make 'em cry when they'd liefer
not, you know as you've got power over 'em."

" You'm a queer chyild."

"Where did you get that song you learnt me yesterday?"

" Foot of the rainbow."

" Did you make it ? "

" Did I make the moon ? "

" If you wunna tell, you wunna. You're pig-headed, Bob Rideout."

" I'm as I was made."

" I'm sorry for you : but I'll sing the song.

> " I took my little harp in hand,
> I wandered up and down the land,
> Up and down a many years.
> But howsoever far I'd roam,
> I couldna find the smiles or tears
> Of whome.
> And every quiet evenfall
> I'd hear a call,
> Like creatures crying in their pain,
> Come whome again ! "

" Not so bad," said Robert. " Only you dunna make it coaxing enough at the end."

" I dunna want to. I want to startle folk. I want to sing till the bells fall down. I want to draw the tears out of their eyes and the money out of their pockets."

" Money ? "

" Ah ! Bags of it. I canna be a great lady without money."

" What ails you, to want to be a lady ? "

" I want a sparkling band round my head, and sparkling slippers on my feet, and a gown that goes ' hush ! hush ! ' like growing grass, and them saying, ' There's Gillian Lovekin ! ' in a whisper."

" Much good may it do ye ! "

" And young fellows coming, and me having rare raps with 'em, and this one saying : ' Marry me, Gillian Lovekin ! ' and that one saying : ' I love you sore, Miss Juliana ! ' and me saying : ' Be off with ye ! ' "

" So you wouldna marry 'em ? "

" No danger ! I want to hear the folk clapping me and joining in the chorus like at the Eisteddfod—and my heart going pit-a-pat, and my face all red, knowing they'd cry when I made 'em, and laugh when I made 'em, and they'd remember Gillian Lovekin to their death day."

" Lord save us ! You're going to learn 'em summat

seemingly, Jill. You're summat cruel when you're set
on a thing. Curst, I call it."

"And when I went to sleep, nights, and couldna bear
to forget I was me for ten hours ; and when I went to
sleep for good and all, then I wouldna take it to heart so
much, seeing as they'd remember me forever and ever."

She drew up her slim body, which had the peculiar
wandlike beauty given by a narrow back, sloping shoulders
and slender hips. The scar on her forehead shone silver
and relentless in the moonlight. The sheep stirred about
her like uneasy souls, and the rabbits lying at her feet
might have been a sacrifice to some woodland goddess.

Robert looked at her, straight and attentively, for the
first time in his life. Since his coming to the Gwlfas
twelve years ago, he had taken her for granted. Now he
saw her. His dark and dreamy eyes, so well warded by
their lashes, his brooding forehead and his mouth, that
was large and beautiful, the lips being laid together with
a poise that partly concealed their firmness, all seemed to
absorb her.

In just the same way he drank in the beauty of the
countryside, the strange, lovely shapes of trees and rocks.

While she stood there and thought of her future as she
had planned it, she slipped into his being like a raindrop
into the heart of a deep flower. Neither of them knew
what was happening, any more than the sheep knew
whence came the unease that always troubled them
before snow.

Robert was as simple, as unselfconscious as a child,
without a child's egotism. He saw the landscape, not
Robert Rideout in the landscape. He saw the sheep, not
Robert Rideout as the kindly shepherd in the midst of the
sheep. Mountains did not make him think of himself
climbing. He did not, as nine hundred and ninety-nine
people out of every thousand do, instinctively look at
himself when he came to a pond. There was nothing of
Narcissus in his soul. He seldom wanted to imitate
birds, but rather to listen more intently. So now he saw
Gillian with the inward eye, heard her with inward hearing,

drank her into his soul, but never thought of himself in
relation to her. He saw her slender waist without his
arm about it, her mouth unkissed. His eyes lingered on
shoulder and breast almost as men's eyes dwell on a
Madonna, and to him the full-length portrait of Gillian
was exactly as she herself saw it—alone, self-wrapped,
self-complete.

Perhaps he was dreamy. Perhaps he developed late.
His father had been just the same, only without Robert's
poetry. He had not married Abigail till he was forty-
five, though he had met her in his thirtieth year. Abigail
had begun by laughing at him. But through those fifteen
years she heard the deepening passion in his voice, until
his least word could set her in a flutter.

Gillian was not sufficiently interested in Robert even
to laugh at him. She had seen, in her childish fashion,
the vision desired by all humanity—the vision of a secure
small nest of immortality built in the crumbling walls
of time. She wanted to go on being herself even when
she was dissolved in nothingness. She wanted to make
men and women hear her, love her, rue her. In the dove-
grey, cooing silence of the farm, any mental absorption
gained double force. So, while Simon purred, and Isaiah
Lovekin made up his accounts, and Robert chopped wood
outside, and Jonathan went through the vicissitudes of
his day, Gillian built up this dream, in which she was
always in the foreground, bathed in light, and masses of
vague faces filled the background. When Mrs. Fanteague
came from Silverton bringing news of the world and a
great feeling of gentility, her dream became so vivid
that it kept her awake at night.

Robert, with a long sigh, relinquished her as a bee leaves
a flower. And like a flower, self-poised but fragile, she
seemed to shudder a little in her recovery.

He turned to lead the sheep home, and they followed
him with crisply pattering feet.

Gillian picked up the rabbits with one of her supple
falcon swoops. Disturbed by Robert's unusual manner,
she found relief in singing, and as she wandered after the

sheep in the moonlight, watching her shadow with impersonal curiosity, she chanted to a tune of her own in
a high treble that re-echoed against the bluff of moor :

> " I saw seven magpies in a tree,
> One for you and six for me.
> One for sorrow,
> Two for joy,
> Three for a girl,
> Four for a boy,
> Five for silver,
> Six for gold——"

And down in the hollow by the low-voiced brook,
Robert, in his rich, quiet voice, finished the song :

> " And seven for a secret
> That's never been told ! "

CHAPTER III

AUNT FANTEAGUE ARRIVES

WHEN you came towards Dysgwlfas Farm from the sheep fields, it looked larger than it was, because the house was long and narrow, and the loft, with the granary and the room where the roots were kept, had been built in one with the farm. Beneath the granary was the high, square archway, called the Drifthouse, that led into the foldyard. In front of the house was the garden, where the dove-cote stood, and a stony path, lichened at the sides, led up to the house from the double wicket with its arch of privet.

The pattering feet of Robert's flock passed this gate and went on to the foldyard. Gillian, following in the leisurely and dreamy manner she had acquired lately, pushed open the wicket and went across the crisp grass to the parlour window. Looking in, she saw by the light of the well-trimmed lamp and the leaping flames that her father had come home. He was a person who could not come home without everybody knowing it. He had, as his sister—Mrs. Fanteague—said, a presence. The house re-echoed with his voice, his step. When he sat in his armchair by the fire it became a throne, and the parlour became an audience chamber. If anyone came in, he said " Ha ! " and they felt found out. In his buying and selling of sheep, this " Ha ! " did more for him than any amount of money. He said it so loudly, so knowingly and so judicially that every flaw in the goods offered leapt into fearful prominence, and the

25

seller, however case-hardened, could see nothing else, could feel nothing else but a desire to go away with his detected enormity, and hide. Very often Mr. Lovekin had not seen half of the things his interjection implied, but that did not matter. The legend of his acumen was about him like the protecting leaves of winter broccoli. Nothing but the best was ever offered to him, and he procured the best at reasonable prices. Hence he was becoming rich, although he had inherited a derelict farm and a debt. His father had possessed neither a presence nor a voice nor a " Ha ! ". He had not stood six foot six with shoulders to match, nor weighed eighteen stone, nor had a patriarchal beard that flowed to his waist. He had been a much more industrious man than his son ; known more about sheep ; deserved success. He had failed lamentably. His son, riding about the country on his cob, penetrating the remote, precipitous hillsides where fat sheep were to be had for little money, had become a personality and a power. His lightest word was received with respect ; a seat near the fire was kept for him on winter afternoons in the inn parlours ; auctioneers had been known to wait to begin a sale until his large figure was seen looming in the assembly.

Whatever may be the ideas of civilization, in wild places physical perfection still dominates, as in the days of Saul. It may be that, as the fight with natural forces is more imminent in the country, it is more obvious that the biggest man is likely to last longest, and staying-power is greatly admired by country people. It may also be the instinct for hero-worship, the desire to have something big set up as a sign, something large enough for legends to accumulate round.

How much Isaiah Lovekin guessed of his own incipient godhead did not appear. He never commented upon it. He never spoke much. Perhaps if he had done so the spell would have been broken. He simply profited by it, accepted it, grew fat on it. Sometimes there might seem to be a roguish twinkle in that dark eye of his, but it was difficult to find out what it meant. Usually his monumental reserve was unbroken even by a twinkle, and, like some stately promontory, he accepted all that the sea of life brought to his feet. Nobody ever questioned his position, nor doubted his ability to live up to it. Only in his daughter's eyes sometimes there was a fleeting look of something half-way between mockery and motherhood. It had been there even when she looked up at him from her cradle, when she had been nothing but a bundle and a grey glance, lying so low at the feet of an immense, overwhelming being. Everybody had seen the look, compounded of pity and laughter. Isaiah had turned to his wife, as if for protection. Mrs. Fanteague had said : " That's no Christian child ! She's a changeling. She'll never live." Mrs. Makepeace was sure it was only a tooth coming. Certainly Gillian had managed to live, changeling or not. It was Mrs. Lovekin who died, finding it too difficult to be the wife of a Deity.

Gillian, having watched her father sitting before the fire, splendid, happy and idle, until her high nose—flattened against the window-pane—was very cold, suddenly hooted like an owl and drew back.

No ! He did not jump. If only she could have made him jump ! She kicked off her clogs, went into the kitchen, and startled the sleeping Simon instead. Mrs. Makepeace had gone, and the kitchen—shining, tidy, smelling of wet soap—was inhabited only by Simon and by the gentle, hesitating " tick-tack " of the clock.

" Quiet ! " said Gillian. " Oh, dear sakes, I can hear the leaves a-falling on my grave ! I'll even be glad to see A'nt Fanteague, Simon, for she do make a stir, O ! "

She washed her face and hands at the pump, and tidied her hair at a little glass on the wall. Then she went into the parlour, singing in her high and delicious voice :

> " Five for silver,
> Six for gold,
> Seven for a secret——"

" Ha ! " said Isaiah, and she became silent, wondering in a kind of hypnotized way what she had done.

" So you've raught back, father ? "

" Ah."

" Bin far ? "

" Over the border."

" Whiteladies or Weeping Cross ? "

" Weeping Cross."

" Bought anything ? "

" A tuthree."

" Seen anybody ? "

" Who should I see ? "

" I mean, anybody fresh ? "

" How you do raven after some new thing, Gillian ! "

" But wasna there anybody but the old ancient people as you always see ? "

" There was a dealer from beyond the mountains."

She clapped her hands.

" I wish I'd been there !　Was he young ? "

" Middling young."

" What was his name ? "

" Elmer."

" Could he ride without a saddle ? "

" I didna enquire."

" Oh, I wish I'd been there ! "

Isaiah smoked in silence.

" If I'd been there d'you know what I'd ha' done ? "

" Not even the Almighty knows that."

" I'd ha' come walking up to him in my new frock that is to be, slate-coloured blue like the slatey drake, and my hair done up, and beads in it——"

" Beads ? "

" Glass ones, shiny like diamonds."

" Oh ! "

" And I'd ha' bowed like parson's wife at the Keep. ' Pleased to know you, but no liberties allowed.'　And I'd ha' dared him to ride full gallop without a saddle."

" Oh, you would, would ye ? "

" And if he was thrown and killed, I'd say : ' One fool the less ! '　But if he did it proper, I'd jump up in front and I'd say : ' Kind sir !　Take me out in the world and learn me to sing, and I'll be yours forever, beads and slatey frock and all ! '   And if he beat me, I'd say nought : but if he couldna ride, I'd laugh."

" Just as well I didna take you."

" Take me next time, father ! Do ! "

" Decked like a popinjay, and being gallus with the fellers ? No ! Here you stop, my girl."

" Father ! "

" Eh ? "

" When I've learnt to sing proper, I can go out into the world, canna I ? "

" No."

" Why ? "

" You mun bide, and see to the house."

" But Mrs. Makepeace could do that. And if you'll let me go, I'll come back when you're aged and old, with the palsy and the tic doloreux, hobbling on two sticks and tears in your eyes and nobody to love ye ! I'll come in a carriage, with silver shoes and a purse of money, and maybe a husband and maybe not, and I'll walk in with a sighing of silk and pour out money on the table, and bring you oranges and candied peel and sparkly wine and a fur coat and summat for the tic doloreux ! "

" Thank you kindly."

" So you'll take me next time ? "

" No."

" Well, then, I'll ask A'nt Fanteague to take me. So now ! "

" Best make the toast, and see if fire's alight in the guest-chamber, and look to the oven, for I smell burning."

Gillian collapsed, departing almost in tears to the kitchen that was so quiet, and the guest-chamber that was quieter still. She drew up the sullen fire in the grate, which was damp from disuse, and in its fugitive light she surveyed the large white bed with its Marcella quilt, the chill dressing-table, the clean cold curtains, the polished oilcloth icily gleaming. There were no sounds except the crackling of the fire, and the wind soughing a little in the chimney. For the first time in her life Gillian

was glad her aunt was coming. Aunt Fanteague lived
in the great world, at Silverton itself. There would be
plenty of pianos and singing masters there, and young
men who could ride without saddle or bridle and accom-
plish feats of daring and danger at her command. Having
drawn the fire up to a roaring blaze, she ran downstairs
to make the toast. Turning a hot red cheek to her father,
she said :

" I wish she'd come ! "

" You do ? Ha ! "

" I'm feared it's happened at long last."

" What ? "

" Why—Jonathan."

" Oh, Jonathan'll turn up all right, peart as a robin.
Accidents he may have, but that's all. And your A'ntie's
along of him, you mind."

" Yes, A'ntie's along of him. Maybe she'll bring me
a present."

" Maybe you've burnt the toast."

" Hark ! The wicket's clicked."

Gillian was out of the room and the house in a twinkling.
She submerged her aunt in kisses, while Jonathan
trundled off to the yard humming, " Safe home, safe
home in port."

" What you want, Juliana," said Aunt Fanteague,
" is control."

She entered.

" *Well*, Isaiah ! " she said.

She always said this on entering her brother's house.
It expressed, among other things, her exasperated disap-
pointment that the place was no better kept than it had
been last time she came.

" Ha ! " said her brother. But instead of feeling
found out, Mrs. Fanteague behaved as if she had found
him out.

" I see the big white stone by the wicket has not been
put in place yet, Isaiah," she said. " Twelve months
ago come Christmas Jonathan knocked it out bringing
me home—and I thank my Redeemer it was no worse !

Twelve months, Isaiah! Fifty-two weeks! Three hundred and sixty-five days! How many hours, Juliana ? "

" Oh, A'ntie ! "

" Where's your book-learning, child ? "

Mrs. Fanteague sat down in the large chair opposite Isaiah—the chair that had been so well brushed and polished—and Gillian standing between them was like the young sickle moon between two of the vast immemorial yew trees on the moor.

" You're late, sister ! " said Isaiah.

" And well may you say it ! And well may I be late ! What Jonathan wants is two guardian angels forever beside him, and he on a leash, with nothing else to do but walk along quiet under the shadow of their wings. It was into the hedge this side, and into the hedge that ! Never a stone but we were on to it—and into the hedge agen ! Then my box fell off, and how it kept on so long only the Redeemer knows—for Jonathan tied it. When we got well on to the moor, what must the man do but drive into the quaking slough, and there we were ! "

Isaiah smiled into his beard. After all, they had arrived. People always did—in the long run—when Jonathan drove them.

" Is it froze over ? "

" It is not, Isaiah. Look at my boots ! Out I had to get. He trod on my umberella. Then I dropped my reticule and he trod on that. The mare wouldn't stir. So I said the Nunc Dimittis " (Aunt Fanteague was High Church) " and took the butt-end of the whip to her, so after a bit we got to the road agen, and I didn't mind the other things near so much. But, seeing as you won't leave this God-'elp place, what you want is to let young Rideout drive. Now there's a man ! Nothing said, but the thing gets done. If you'd send Rideout, your sister's bonnet wouldn't be torn to pieces with hedges and the whip— for when Jonathan thinks he's slashing the mare, it's your sister he's slashing, Isaiah, every time ! "

Isaiah looked at the fire. A twinkle seemed to tenant

his eyes for a moment. Perhaps he was thinking that if he sent Rideout there would be nothing to discourage Mrs. Fanteague from coming very often.

" And how's poor Emily ? " he said

" Poor Emily's as usual, Isaiah."

Emily was, for the time, dismissed. Mrs. Fanteague was untying her bonnet strings. She was large, though not so large as Isaiah. When her bonnet, which seemed to have been built with bricks and mortar, not merely sewn, was off and lay in her lap, the likeness to Isaiah became more obvious. She had the same fine head, massive but low brow, and solid features. Her hair was built up just as her bonnet was, and looked like sculptured hair. In it she wore massive combs and five large yellow tortoise-shell pins. Her dress had the look of being held together only by the ferocious tenacity of its buttons, which were made of jet. Not that she was fat, but she was large of bone and well developed, and her dresses were always tight-fitting, after the style of a riding habit. Pinning her collar together was a big square brooch of wedgwood china depicting a cross, a young woman and a dove. The symbolism of this had never been explained to Gillian, though she had often enquired. It remained, like Isaiah, mysterious, capable of many constructions. Cuffs, knitted by Emily and trimmed with beads, finished her sleeves, and a well-gathered skirt came down to within an inch of the ground. She gave the impression, as she sat there, of being invulnerable, morally and physically.

" Would you like to wash you and change your boots, A'ntie ? There's a good fire in the guest-chamber."

" There is, is there ? Well, you're tempting Providence, for coal's coal and it gets no cheaper. But I don't say it isn't pleasant."

" And I filled the boiler, so there's hot water to wash you."

" Juliana, you're improving ! "

Praise from her was infrequent. If she had known the reason of the improvement, perhaps she would have withheld it.

" Dunna forget the cooling tea and a man that's sharp-set for his'n," said Isaiah.

They departed in a whirl of black skirts, coloured skirts, reticules, bags and bonnets.

Isaiah smiled at the fire. He knew very well why Gillian bestowed such affectionate care on her aunt.

But as Aunt Fanteague did not know, and as she had, like many rocky natures, a great, though concealed, craving for affection, she was touched. She was glad she had brought Gillian a present.

" When I unpack," she said, as she instinctively moved the dressing-table to look for dust underneath, running her finger over the polished surfaces, " there might be something for a good girl."

Gillian flushed, partly with pleasure, but mostly with annoyance at being treated in so babyish a way. Was she not Miss Juliana Lovekin, of Dysgwlfas ? But it was not politic to show her annoyance. As the most practical way of getting nearer to the desired fairing, she began to uncord the box, which had been carried up the back stairs by Robert. It was the same yellow tin box in which Mrs. Fanteague's bridal raiment had been packed when she had left the farm on that long-ago summer day with the man of her choice.

This phrase was literally true, for Mr. Fanteague had had no choice in the matter. The box still looked wonderfully new, considering that Jonathan had fetched it once or twice every year across the moor. It had lost much less of its early freshness than Mrs. Fanteague had. Gillian's firm, pointed fingers undid the knots, and at last the lid, painted blue inside, was lifted to reveal tissue paper, the black silk Sunday dress, best bonnet, gloves, and braided cape which Aunt Emily's nervous fingers had folded. Underneath lay a small packet.

" I must tell you, my dear, it isn't new," said Aunt Fanteague. " But it's jewellery. And I know the vanity of your heart, Juliana."

" Jewellery ! Oh, A'ntie ! "

" You can undo it, if you've a mind."

Gillian most certainly *had* a mind. She undid it. And
there lay a small cornelian heart with a golden clasp
through which a ribbon was to be slipped. It was wonderful—a fairy gift. It had colour, which she loved, and
romance, and it was her first ornament.

"A'ntie! When you're ancient and old, when there's
none to comfort ye, I'll mind this locket! And howsoever far away I am, I'll come to ye! I will that! And
I'll try to keep my nails clean, too, because you say they
werrit ye. See! Dunna it look nice agen my frock?
Have you got ever a piece of ribbon I could tie it on with?"

Aunt Fanteague found a bit of black velvet, took up
the candle, and said it was time to go down.

"And now," said Isaiah, "let me hear the news of
poor Emily. She's well, you say?"

"I say that poor Emily's as well as can be expected
in her peculiar situation."

"Does she eat and sleep?"

"She eats but poorly, and dreams."

"Dreams, A'ntie? Oh, I wish I could dream! What
does she dream?"

"She dreams of angels."

"Ha!"

Isaiah had a great idea of looking after his women-
folk. He always asked particularly after their physical
well-being. If that was satisfactory, nothing else mattered.

"Ha! If she dreamt of a babby, it 'ud be better!
That's the dream for Emily! Always was!"

He gave his rare, tremendous laugh—the laugh which,
as legend said, had once frightened Dosset's bull so much
that it had omitted to toss Isaiah.

Mrs. Fanteague rose.

"Toast there may be, and cooling tea, and a welcome
of sorts inside, and a cold wind drawing over the moor,
but out I go, Isaiah, if you speak indecent. Before the
child, too!"

"I amna a child, A'ntie! And I like to hear about—
A'nt Emily."

"Sit down, sister. I'm mum."

Mrs. Fanteague, after suitable hesitation, sat down.

" How old *is* Emily ? " asked Isaiah, who was not good at dates.

" Emily's forty-one."

" Well, it's not past praying for, then. You mind when Bob Rideout was born, Abigail was forty-three. And you couldna find a stronger, lustier——"

Mrs. Fanteague arose again.

" Oh, sit down, sister ! I'm dumb as a corpse ! "

" Is poor A'nt Emily still in love, A'ntie ? "

This romance of Emily's was a perennial source of interest to Gillian.

" Yes, my dear."

" And does Mr. Gentle still call ? "

" Regular as clockwork. More regular than any new-fangled clock."

" But they inna going to get married ? "

" I don't know, my dear."

" What does A'nt Emily think ? "

" She wouldn't consider it ladylike to think anything till Mr. Gentle spoke."

" And dunna he ? "

" No, my dear. Not like that. He says it's blowing up for rain, or there's a peck of March dust, or what a sight of apple blow, or as it was a pleasant sermon. And he reads. We're doing Crabbe now. And once he said he liked lilac, when Aunt Emily had a lilac dress on. But that's all."

" Ha ! " said Isaiah, and buried his face in his cup.

" Oh, A'ntie, how awful ! "

" No, my dear, it's very pleasant."

" Awful for poor A'nt Emily ! Coddling about year after year ! I'd want Mr. Gentle to fall down on his knee-bones——"

" He's a little bit rheumatic, Juliana."

" He should ha' done it when he could. To fall down on his knees and say : ' I love ye ! ' And get up quick and kiss me till I couldna breathe."

Mrs. Fanteague looked at her brother accusingly.

" Like father, like child ! " she said.

" And then for him to say : ' Fix the day ! Fix it ! Fix it ! ' And me all in a fluster, like the ducks when I catch 'em. And away to church. And into the trap. And off to the station ! And him saying : ' You be mine forever and ever.' Only I dunna think Mr. Gentle would do. Can he drive and ride without a saddle ? Durst he walk along the top of a waggon o' hay when it's going quick, like Robert does ? "

Mrs. Fanteague smiled. It was not easy for her to smile, because her face had set in other lines.

" Juliana," she said, " if ever you see Mr. Gentle, you'll understand. No words of mine can make you. Mr. Gentle's one that never has a speck on him, and never loses his dignity ; he's a real polished gentleman."

" Oh, dear sores ! I shouldna like him. He'd kiss so soft."

Isaiah came to life.

" What d'ye know about kisses, my girl ? Has Robert been playing the fool ? I'll give him the best——"

" You wouldna find it so easy ! Robert's strong. But he hanna kissed me nor wanted to. I never thought of it afore you said."

She began to look dreamy.

" I'd like it to be said as Gillian Lovekin married young and had a very sweet nature, like they said about Great-Aunt Amy Lovekin."

" Did you take them pastries out of oven ? " enquired Isaiah.

" O dearie, dearie me ! "

She fled to the kitchen, returning slowly.

" Spoilt, I suppose ? "

She nodded.

" Fetch 'em ! "

They came. Twenty-four cheese-cakes and some pastry " fingers," all of ebony-black.

" How much stuff went to 'em ? "

" Pound o' flour, half dripping, three oranges, sugar, two eggs——"

" What 'ud that cost, sister ? "

" Well, as you've got your own fowl, maybe about a shilling."

" Fetch a shilling, Gillian."

" Oh, father ! Not a coney shilling ? "

" Ah."

" But that's a music lesson, father ! "

" Fetch it. It'll learn you not to get dreamy and moithered like poor Emily. You be glad I'm too lazy to leather ye."

Gillian retired to the kitchen in tears. Her aunt, coming out to " dry " while she washed-up, was prepared to comfort the weeping penitent.

But instead of a penitent she saw, when she entered, two pillows placed in chairs at the table. One was dressed in Isaiah's best coat and hat, the other in Gillian's summer frock, a lace curtain for a veil, and the cornelian heart.

" It's A'nt Emily's wedding breakfast ! " said Gillian. " Mr. Gentle's spoken at long last ! "

CHAPTER IV

GILLIAN ASKS FOR A KISS

AUNT FANTEAGUE was to stay a fortnight. She had been at Dysgwlfas a week before Gillian found courage to think of asking her about the visit to Silverton. Now she was desperate, because, when she got up at seven and peeped into the outer world, the sky was soft and woolly with snow, and a few flakes already wandered past the window—which meant that Aunt Fanteague would hasten her departure lest, as she said, " a worse thing befall her." At Dysgwlfas people were often snowed-up for a week at a time, and Christmas drew near, and it would never do for Mrs. Fanteague to be away at Christmas, for then poor Emily and Mr. Gentle could not keep the festival together, since they would be unchaperoned.

" This day, if ever ! " said Gillian, breaking the ice in her jug and wondering, as she washed her face, how she would break the ice in Aunt Fanteague's mind.

As she lit the kitchen fire she thought how lovely it would be to live at a grand place like the Drover's Arms at Weeping Cross, where the Farmer's Ordinary was, of which her father told her carefully censored tales when he came back from fairs and auctions.

While she sat by the sudden blaze made by an armful of heather and chips, and drank her cup of tea, she read the serial in the weekly paper her father took in. It told how a young and innocent girl, not very much prettier than herself, went to London and was betrayed, and lived in luxury and sin, and then died. She thought it would

38

be almost worth dying in order first to see and hear and experience all the wonderful things the heroine saw and heard and felt. "Betrayed!" What food for curiosity! What depths of horror! It recalled old tales, and detective stories (of which Robert possessed two), and Judas Iscariot. It was wicked, deliciously wicked, and it implied a sort of vicarious wickedness in the betrayed one. It had a thrill. She had lived, this girl, for nearly a year in a "palatial suite" somewhere near a place called Piccadilly. Gillian supposed that this was where the pickle came from, which occasionally varied the home-made red cabbage. She went to theatres. She wore satin, jewels, swansdown. She was called "Madame." She was kissed. She went about in a motor-car marvellously upholstered, with the man who betrayed her, who was over six feet tall in his (expensively) stockinged feet, and had a long drooping moustache and a fur coat. Gillian was sure he could have walked about on the most toppling load of hay without the slightest inconvenience. Delightful Iscariot! There he was, within a few hours' journey of Silverton. If once she could get there, she would only have to step into a train, and in such a little while she would be in London. The rest, no doubt, followed mechanically.

"Ask her, I will, this very day! She may say she's deaf. She may read a book. She may walk out of the room. But I'll ask her. If I can get to Sil'erton, I can get to London."

She surveyed herself in the kitchen mirror.

"I'm not so bad. And if I learn to sing that'll be one to me, for this here Julia couldna sing a note."

While she stirred the porridge, she saw a vision of herself in the slate-coloured dress (that was to be), with a feather hat made of the slatey drake, walking in high-heeled satin shoes past shops full of yellow, square bottles of piccalilli.

"Dreamy!" said her father, as he knocked the earth from his boots and came in to breakfast. "Now look lively, my girl, for the sooner I start the more chance to

get back early.　It's white-over now, and I've got to get
a hundred sheep back afore night."

" Is it set in for snow, Isaiah ? " asked Mrs. Fanteague.

" Ah."

" Then I pack.　I'll catch the last train from the
Keep."

" A short visit, sister ! "

" Weather's weather, Isaiah.　If I stay, maybe the
thaw won't come till after Christmas.　And Emily'd be
all alone."

" There'd be Mr. Gentle, A'ntie."

" Aunt Emily wouldn't dream of asking a gentleman
to the place in my absence," said Aunt Fanteague.

Gillian opined that there were a good many different
kinds of women in the world, for what could be more
different than the minds of Emily and Julia ?　And she
herself was like neither.

Isaiah swallowed his breakfast, went to the door and
shouted for Robert.

" Be I to come, sir ?　Or stepfather ? "

" No, I must make shift, for Jonathan must take Mrs.
Fanteague.　I'll ride the cob, and call for Dosset's lad—
he's got a pony.　He'll give me a hand with the sheep."

" I'd sooner Robert drove me," observed Mrs. Fanteague.

" Robert's got to stop.　The threshing-engine may come
any minute.　If it does, Jonathan's no manner use."

" Mother says, would you kindly send her as far as the
Maiden ?　Mrs. Thatcher's took bad.　They want mother
to bide the night over."

" And welcome.　Jonathan can send her."

Isaiah looked at Robert, hesitated, then stepped out
into the foldyard.

" Oh, Rideout ! " he said, with less than his customary
ease, " no offence, but you'll bear in mind as my girl's
for none but a farmer, or higher."

Robert smiled.　His smile was slow, sad, a little ironical,
but sweet.　His eyes did not always smile in unison with
it.　They did not smile now.　There was criticism and
a spice of mockery in them.

"Nothing less than a lord, sir!" he said. "But what is to be, will be."

"Whatever's to be, it's not to be cowman-shepherd, seesta?"

"Ah! I see, sir. And if so be I'd raised my eyes to your little maid, I'd lower 'em agen. But I want no woman."

"What do you want, lad?" asked Isaiah, with some compunction.

"My time to myself, sir," replied Robert, and turned towards the stable.

"His time to himself and he wants no woman!"

Gillian laughed as she washed the dishes, having listened at the kitchen window.

Robert had not, previously, seemed worth captivating. She took him for granted. Now, as she watched his sturdy and independent figure cross the fold, she became conscious of him as a young man to be enslaved.

"Good-bye, sister!" said Isaiah. "There's a box of them winter pears, and the red apples you like, and Gillian can gather some eggs for ye, and Robert'll get you a couple of fowl. Tell Emily to dream what I said!"

With a shout of laughter he swung into the saddle.

"Good-bye, Isaiah," said Mrs. Fanteague. "God willing, I shall see Silverton shops to-night."

"A'nt Fanteague willing, I shall see 'em soon!" thought Gillian.

"Shall I give you a hand, packing, A'ntie?" she asked.

"No, child."

"Shall I kindle a bit of fire in your room?"

"I'm not so nesh as to need a fire to pack by, my dear."

"Could you sit by this 'un then? I want to ask you summat particular."

"Oh."

"A'ntie! Let me come and bide with you a bit! Please, A'ntie!"

"For why?"

" To learn to make that grand Simnel cake, and bake a ham the old-fashioned way, and plain-sew."

" And go shopping and look for a young man ? "

" Oh, A'ntie ! "

" Well, maybe it ud liven up poor Emily. I'll con sider it."

" Not too long ! Life goes over. ' Nut in November nut for doom.' "

" Who told you that ? "

" Robert."

" Do you like that young man ? "

" Oh, all right ! He's nought but cowman-shepherd, though."

" That's right, child. Never demean yourself."

Aunt Fanteague became ruminative. There was a young organist at Silverton, also a bachelor doctor and an unmarried curate. Aunt Fanteague dreamed. How surprised the ladies who now despised her would be ! If it was the curate, she might even be asked to decorate the pulpit instead of doing the two dark windows by the door. If it was the doctor, the little doses of bromide for Emily after Mr. Gentle's visits would be prescribed free. If it was the organist—well, it had better not be the organist.

" Well, my dear, if you're a good girl, and your father raises no objection, you shall come for a bit in the New Year !"

" Oh, A'ntie, I do love you ! "

" That you don't, Gillian ! But so long as you respect me, I ask no more."

" How long can I come for ? "

" That depends."

" A month ? Two ? Three ? "

" Maybe a month."

" When, A'ntie ? "

" When the snow's gone. January, maybe."

" I'll buy some cashmere with my coney money and make me a frock. And I'll kill the slatey drake."

" Don't bedizen yourself, Gillian. You know what poor Emily says of a lady."

" What ? "

" You can tell a lady, because nobody knows she's there."

" But slatey colour's as meek as mice, A'ntie ! "

" It's according as it's worn. Now write me the label while I pack."

As Gillian wrote the label, she thought how it would look,

" Miss Juliana Lovekin. Silverton."

" Miss Juliana Lovekin. London."

She preferred the last.

After dinner, Jonathan, with resignation in his manner, brought round the trap. The eggs and fruit were packed in. Mrs. Makepiece sat on the tin box at the back. Jonathan observed :

" It's snow for our pillow to-night, Mrs. Fanteague, ma'am. Ah ! that's what it'll be, snow for our pillow ! "

Mrs. Fanteague waved resignedly, and they drove away through the thickening snow.

" Please God, take care of A'ntie so that I can get to London soon ! " prayed Gillian.

The simplicity with which people express themselves when there is no one to hear but the Almighty must often entertain Him.

" Robert ! " called Gillian. " Robert Rideout O ! "

" Well, Miss Gillian ? "

" What have I done to be treated so stiff ? "

" Nought."

" Well, then, come your ways in. We'll have a randy, same as we always do when they're out."

" We didn't ought."

" Didn't ought's in Dead Man's Yard. Come on ! We'll make toffee. There's all the market butter. We'll play ' I spy ' all over the house. Then I'll help you to milk. Then we'll have tea. You can finish outside while I get it. They'll neither of 'em be back before

seven or eight. It'll be cosy as cosy. We'll pretend it's
our house and I'm your missus."

Robert flushed and turned away, suddenly shy, perhaps
because of Isaiah, perhaps because of his consciousness of
Gillian in the meadow.

" No ! " he said.

" Yes ! I'm going away come New Year."

He turned quickly.

" Where ? "

" To Sil'erton. I'll tell you at tea. Now for the toffee ! "

She was going away. This would be the last time of
childish romping. When she came back she would be
a lady. She might be engaged—even married. He
could put in longer time at the wood-chopping to-morrow.
He scraped his boots and came in.

" Butter first ! " said Gillian. She ran to the dairy
where the round yellow pats—all decked with swans—
lay on their clean white cloth. Into the saucepan went
two pats, for Gillian never believed in doing things by
halves.

" You stir ! You're an old steady-goer ! " said she.

Robert scrubbed his hands in the back kitchen and
stirred. They were nice hands, large and dependable
and strong. What they undertook, they finished. The
animals on the farm loved them. People with whom he
shook hands at market felt a kind of promise of protection
in them, and they would have trusted him with their
lives or even their bank-books. They were hands that
might have helped to make him a great surgeon. The
local vet. had noticed them, and had offered to take
him into partnership. But Robert refused. He did
not like to see creatures in pain oftener than he could
help. Also, he had his dream to dream on Dysgwlfas
Moor—his dream, which was that of Dysgwlfas itself.
Day after day, in the early morning or after his work was
done, he brooded upon the waste as it lay beneath his
gaze, self-wrapped, conning its own secret, dreaming of
itself and its dark history, its purple-mantled past and
its future clothed in vaporous mystery. The colour

that comes on the heather when it is in full flower, which
is like the bloom on a plum, was in his dream. The
rumour that runs, in warm, dark spring evenings, from
the peering leaf down the veins of the stalk, to the waiting
flower sleeping in the root—a rumour of rain and misty
heat and the melodious languors of a future June ; this,
too, was in his dream. Wave on profound wave of beauty
broke over him, submerged him. The wonder and terror
of it came to his soul with a keenness that darted from
the colours and perfumes like a sword hidden in roses.
Far beyond the rim of blue was still the moorland—the
secret moorland, with its savage peace. There the curlews
cried, eerie and lonely, in spring. Thence the wind drew,
urgent, vital. And always, whether he was at market
or chapel, in the farm or the inn, which lay alone out on
the moor, he heard—whatever the weather or the season
—as it were a long way off, and far down in his consciousness—the roar of the winter wind over the bleak, snowy
acres of Dysgwlfas. He was aware that an almost vocal
sympathy existed between the place and himself. There
was something he must do for it, but he could not guess
what it was. Also he felt a vague portent in the winter
country. There was something waiting for him there
in the future—some deed, some high resolve. Was it
Death ? It was mysterious as death, he thought. All
his days he walked in this dream, which did not hinder
his deft hands nor his quick feet, and continually
the country spun more threads between itself and
him.

He would sit dreaming by his mother's fire as if he had
been fairy-led, or, as Jonathan said, as if he had been
" comic-struck." And now Gillian was finding a place in
his dream. Softly, relentlessly as a leaf-boring bee, she
was impressing herself on the purple twilight of his
unwritten poetry.

As to what all this meant he was doubtful. He must
bide his time. He could always do that, without being
either lethargic or futile. And when the waiting was
over, he could act.

At the present moment it was time to act, for the toffee was ready.

"Dunna forget to put the tin in cold water, Gillian!" he reminded her.

They played "I spy" till it cooled. Then it was milking-time. There was laughter in the cowhouse and milking was soon done. Then, with one of her weird owl cries, she ran across the dark fold into the kitchen.

It glowed, for Robert had made up the fire. She set the table with the best china, brought out cranberry jelly, new bread, lemon cheese, visitor's tea. She put on her best frock, put up her hair, and picked a scarlet geranium from the window to wear in it. She would be as gay, as pretty and as kind as she could. It wasn't nice of her father to tell him he was only a cowman. And perhaps, if she looked really pretty, Robert would kiss her! That would be good practice for the future. Isaiah had forbidden all "May-games." Kissing was certainly a May-game. But then—Robert had such a nice mouth. Now that she considered it attentively, it was remarkably nice.

She went to the door. Snow was falling thickly now, whirling softly, coming in large flakes. She could see Robert's lantern in the stable, and his shadow on the white wall.

"Bob!"

He came, smoothing his roughened, snowy hair.

"Now! I'm missus. You're maister."

"I'm cowman-shepherd," said Robert. "And you're the maister's daughter. And only a farmer's good enough, but you might consider a lord."

"Oh, Bob! You *are* unkind. I didna say it."

"You think it. You know right well you'd never marry a farm labourer."

"Maybe, if—if the labourer was called—Robert Rideout O!"

"You're a jill-flirt, my dear, and that's all about it. Gillian jill-flirt!"

"Pretend, Robert!"

"There's danger in pretending."

She sulked.

"This is a good tea," observed Robert. "And I'm sure it's very charitable of you, miss!"

"Don't you dare mock me!"

"I amna. I'm enjoying meself."

He stretched comfortably. His lean, strong, pleasant face was happy in the firelight. His boots steamed. The snow-wind soughed fitfully in the chimney. Gillian, demure in the dignity of having her hair up, poured out tea and did the honours.

Through his lashes Robert observed her ; saw her lovely, wilful, remote ; wanted to conquer and possess.

"I'd thank you not to look at me so fierce!" she laughed.

"I'd thank *you* for some more tea," said Robert, "and some of that nice cake."

"Oh, Bob! You hanna come to see me a bit! You're after what you can get!"

"Ah! That's the tune of it!" said Robert, lying splendidly. "Jelly, please, mum!"

After tea she sat on the hearthrug and told him her dreams—some of them. She told him how she would dress when she sang at an Eisteddfod, and as she looked up, lit with new beauty, he suddenly found out what it was he wanted to do. Pennillions! He would make pennillions about the moor, and in the midst of them should be Gillian Lovekin. He did not know quite what pennillions were, nor how to make them, but he could learn. He could walk over the mountains to the abode of some Eisteddfod singer, and learn. Here was the way to express all those strange things, those wild and dim and tender thoughts, that invaded his soul and would not let him rest. When he had given them house-room, when he had made garments of song for them, they would not cry out on him so. And secretly, unknown even to herself, Gillian should be the bright centre of these dim pictures, the flower in the rocky cavern of his poetry.

"Seven for a secret!" he murmured.

" Now then ! No talking to mommets ! What is it ? "
cried Gillian.

" Nought—nought."

One must not make love to the master's daughter, nor
enthrone her in a poem, nor make poems. He reflected
with amusement that the time in which he would make
songs in his mind would be paid for by Isaiah ; that the
moor all round the farm, which had inspired him, was
Isaiah's ; that their central beauty would be Isaiah's
only child.

" It'll take a deal of overtime to make up for all that,
I doubt ! " he thought. His smile stirred Gillian's
curiosity.

" Tell ! Tell ! "

" No. I canna tell ye."

" Summat you're going to do ? "

" Maybe."

" For me ? "

" In a sort of a way it'll be all for you."

" Oh, Bob ! "

" Now say all about what coloured gowns you'll get
when you're a rich lady."

They sat in the firelight, happy, gay. Anyone looking
through the snow-fingered window would have thought
them lovers, not knowing the barriers of class and wealth
between them.

Seven o'clock.

" I mun go now, Gillian. Thank you kindly."

" We shanna have another time like this before I go
away."

" Never, maybe."

" Robert ! "

" Well ? "

" Pretend ! "

" What ? "

" Pretend we're—" she whispered.

" Pretending's no good."

She held up a glowing cheek. She was bent on
adventure.

" You can take one, Robert ! "

But Robert's face was hard. It smiled no more ;
there was no sweetness in it. She did not guess that it
was his hardest battle yet.

" When I want a kiss," he said, " I'll ask for it."

He was gone.

Gillian flung herself on the hearthrug, raging, sobbing.

" Oh, I *wanted* him to kiss me ! I wanted to know
what it was like ! I'll pay him out for this ! Oh, dearie,
dearie me ; suppose they're all like Robert ! "

She was in despair. She could not think how the
innocent Julia (who never dreamt of asking for kisses,
but always screamed and said, " Unhand me, sir ! ")
had had love affairs.

" I don't believe Julia was all that much prettier than
me ! " she sobbed. " But seemingly it's them as don't
ask don't want, and them as do ask can't have ! "

CHAPTER V

ROBERT WRITES TWO LETTERS

THE Makepeace kitchen was even more miraculously neat than most country kitchens. The saucepans and frying-pans looked as if they could never by any possibility have been used. The tiles had the soft polish given by daily washing with milk and water. The open grate shone smooth and immaculate as a fine lady's shoe. The check tablecloth of red and blue revealed, when folded back for culinary operations, a table of honeycomb whiteness. The lustre jugs, the Broseley plates and Coalport teapot gleamed from the dresser. The eight-day wall-clock of inlaid oak, with the soothing tick and the chime that sounded as if it were made of pale gold, was rich with satiny polish. Everything seemed to be there to satisfy Mrs. Makepeace's love of cleaning. Things were cleaned not because they needed it, but because it was "their day." The result was that Jonathan and Robert appeared as wild hill men of some earlier race strayed into the trim residence of an elf.

They sat, on an evening in mid-January, one on each side of the fire. Mrs. Makepeace was at the farm, helping Gillian to pack. The thaw had come, and the path from cottage to farm was full of large dark patches where the snow had melted. The jessamine bush by the door showed bright green points, and the lingering afterglow was green beyond the window.

Robert looked across the room into the pale sky, and

the pelargonium with the white eye, that stood beside
the one with scented leaves against the muslin curtain of
the lower half of the window, returned his gaze limpidly.
There was something of Gillian, he thought, in its wistful
boldness. He called it, to himself, " peartness " and
" bashfulness," and he began to make a poem about it,
humming beneath his breath as he whittled thatching
pegs. The sticks for these lay in a pile on the rug, which
was one of Mrs. Makepeace's own manufacture—of bright-
coloured wools with the word " Welcome " in the centre.
They were using their pocket-knives, of large and practical
make. The potatoes for supper simmered gently, hanging
above the fire, and a stockpot on the hob gave out a good
herby odour.

Jonathan paused in his work and looked at Robert for
a long time, his mouth a little open.

" So she's going ? "

Robert nodded.

" The missus 'ere," said Jonathan, with a backward
jerk of his thumb towards his wife's sacking apron hanging
on the door, " gave me so to understand."

Jonathan was so used to being watched and guarded
by his wife that he lived in a perpetual sense of her
imminence. Whether she was away at market, when the
door was tenanted by her apron and sunbonnet, or at the
wash-tub, when her cloak and hat were there, she was
always present to him.

" Ah ! She says, ' When they shake their wings, it
goes hard, but they wunna come back till they break their
wings.' "

On the upper half of the window Robert saw a picture
of Gillian in the slatey dress, which was real to him
because she had described it, lying as he had often
seen a wild duck lie, with one broken wing trailing out
beside it.

" We mun see to it as she dunna."

" I reckon it'll be me to drive her to the station to-
morrow-day, Bob ? "

" No ; me."

Jonathan fell into a seemingly mystical contemplation of his pegs. The clock registered a quarter of an hour.

" Flocks, hill pasture, a new shippen and a sight of money in the bank, so they do say ! " he remarked.

Robert came out of a dream of wild duck and rose-coloured pelargoniums.

" Money ? What money ? "

" Money as young Gillian Lovekin'll get when the maister goes."

" Money," said Robert, going on with his work, " is nought but dung."

" Dear sores, man ! It buys all but Paradise. And some say it buys even that."

" Can it buy love ? "

" So they do say ! " Jonathan chuckled.

" Where did they say that ? "

" At the public—the ' Naked Maid.' "

" I dunna like that name. Why dunna they say ' The Mermaid's Rest,' like the sign says ? "

" Well, lad, there she is over the door, shameless as the Woman o' Babylon, mother-naked to the waist. We call 'er what she is. I'm thankful she's got some decent scales. She's not so ondecent as Eve in my poor mother's Bible. It's little wonder to me as Adam went wrong. Now if Eve had bought a calico chemise and a pair o' stays and a tuthree petticoats and a nice print dress and apern, there'd ha' been no such May-games with serpents and apples and what-not. Maybe their eldest would ha' bin a decent lad and brought up a family close by the old people, and there'd never ha' bin niggers then."

" Why ever not ? "

" Cain's love-children were the beginning of the niggers."

Where Jonathan had gained his Scriptural (and apocryphal) knowledge was a mystery. This, and the legendary lore of the countryside, formed the basis of the tales for which he was famous.

" Paint the wench out, I say, or paint a bodice in. It draws the eye like that. It's bad for the lads. For till they get married and find out what a poor ornary thing an ooman is, the lads think she's summat grand and curious."

Suddenly, in the midst of the dream of wild duck and pelargoniums, Gillian's face swam up on the green sky with the pale, lissom body of the mermaid on the sign. Robert got up, threw the pegs on the floor, and walked up and down the little room. Two strides and a half. Turn. Two strides and a half. Turn. He must stop this garrulous old voice, or lead it elsewhere.

" Tell about the mermaid coming first ! " he said.

" Washed ashore at Aberdovey. Ah ! That's what came to pass. High tides they get at Aberdovey, time and agen. This was a spring tide like none's seen since. A mort of queer shells and seaweed came in on that tide, and coloured fishes and sea flowers from countries far away. And her. There she lay in a swound among the green weed, and a fisherman found her and went nigh mad with love. So she wiled him and she bewitched him, and she sang at him :

" ' Back to the sea, fisherman ! Back to the sea ! ' "

" ' No danger ! ' says he. And he kisses her.

" ' Put me in fresh watter, then,' she says, ' so long as it *is* watter.'

" ' What'll you give me ? ' he says.

" ' My love for one night ! '

" ' But you're a cold mermaid. You canna love ! '

" ' I'll come mortal for one night ! '

" So she came mortal for one night. And in the grey dawn he chucked her into the river. And she swam upstream to the top of a mountain, and crept across to the spring of another stream, and so to another agen, and at last she was at Dysgwlfas inn, just where the little gyland goes down to the stream. And she sang at the inn-keeper, and wiled him away. Some say they went down to Severn, and so to the sea. But they never heard tell of the inn-keeper agen, only they found a bit of old sea-money in the shallows. Some say as she was seen on the moor with a shepherd that knew a charm to keep her mortal for ever. But anyway, a sign-painter put her on the sign-board, and there she be."

"She was Gillian!" thought Robert. This braving of circumstance, this luring of men, this boldness and elusiveness, were all Gillian, and the starting-out to-morrow to conquer the world was very like the mermaid's journey. Would he might be that shepherd at the end! He knew so well what she wanted, and he was powerless to give it her. He could only put his soul into a poem and enthrone her there. Would she care? He snapped his finger and thumb.

"Not *that!*" he said, and began to love her.

"Laws, lad! you nearly made me cut meself!"

Jonathan whittled always in fear of ultimate dissolution.

Quick steps came through the slush. With a scraping and rubbing of shoes, Abigail came in, and immediately began to get supper ready.

"Well, missus! Packed and labelled?" asked Jonathan.

A noticeable stillness came upon Robert. His brown hands lay motionless on his knees. His eyes waited on his mother's face.

She was hindered in her dialogue by the supreme necessity of watching Jonathan. No guardian angel with a sinner, rifleman with a target or cat with a bird, could have been more tense and absorbed than she was when Jonathan wielded a knife. Each time he picked up a stick and began to hack bits from one side to make a firm stay for the cord she leaned a little forward, working her mouth with each cut, unable to speak. Then, as he relapsed into the less dangerous task of marking out a slight groove round the stick, she would relax. Finally, when he flung the peg on to the heap, she would sigh, smile, and take up her parable. So it was only in scattered sentences that Robert heard how the new dress fitted; how Miss Gillian had bought a pink ready-made blouse, three white nightdresses—not unbleached, such as she usually wore—shoes with heels, and a veil; how lovely she looked in the toque made of the slatey drake; how she had taken six rabbit skins to the chief draper at Weeping Cross, and had them made into a muff and tippet ; how she had laughed like half a dozen woodpeckers, and sung like twenty throstles ; and how they had finally made some paste and fastened on the label :

> Miss Juliana Lovekin,
> Passenger to Silverton.

Ah, how sad the white eye of the pelargonium ! Almost it seemed to Robert that a dew had fallen in that quiet room, for he saw it through tears.

" A fine mingicumumbus ! And only to go to her a'ntie's ! " observed Jonathan.

" Going opens the door to the world," said Abigail, turning the stockpot upside down over an immense basin, and proclaiming supper.

Robert hummed very softly :

> " And howsoever far I'd roam,
> I couldna find the smiles and tears of whome."

" What a kimet——" began Jonathan, looking at him open-mouthed. But at this point he cut himself, and Abigail took command. She had everything at hand. No trick of an unkind fate could surprise her. She had simple disinfectants, ointments, clean needles for thorns, soft linen, bandages, even a bit of iron for cauterizing, in case some mad dog should seek out Jonathan and bite him (which Abigail was sure would happen if there were even one case of rabies in the West Country). While she bound him up, she made him feel like a wounded hero, so that a glow came over him, and he enjoyed his troubles, and the idea that he was clumsy was never allowed to enter his mind.

Robert looked at the heap of pegs beside Jonathan. They would take him till midnight with his own. It did not occur to him to leave them undone. There was the task, just as in potato setting or haying, and, if one was incapacitated, the others must do more.

" What time'll she start, Mother ? "

" The noon train."

" Then I'll please to ask you to give me bite and sup
as soon as I've milked. I'll just put on me market coat
and wrap horse rug round me."

" You're set to take her then ? "

" Ah."

With a safety-pin in her mouth, Mrs. Makepeace looked
at her son across Jonathan's bandaged hand. Her eyes
were keen with love—futile love, for she could not help him.
She would have liked to " cosset " him as she did Jonathan,
but she knew it was useless. He looked back at her with
those deep eyes of his—brooding and sad, stern and a
little mocking—and his secret, which she had guessed,
but had not certainly known, leapt across the quiet
room.

" Drat the girl ! " thought she. " I didna want it to
be this way. 'Twas she should ha' loved first. Now
here the lad'll sit and mope like a bird with a shot mate.
Nowt said. Nowt done. Oh, deary me ! Canna you
hold still a minute, Jonathan, my dear ? "

Jonathan, who had been enjoying his cut very much,
looked up wistfully, like a child in fault, at this sudden
irritability.

" Mother, is there ever a bit o' writing paper in the
place ? " asked Robert.

" Ah ! There's a sheet or two left from the box Mrs.
Fanteague sent me Christmas was a year."

She fetched it.

" A pen, Mother ? "

But no pen could be found. They were not a writing
family. Isaiah kept the farm accounts, Robert's songs
were in his mind only, and when Abigail wrote on the jam
covers she borrowed a pen from Gillian.

" There's a drop of ink, but the pen's lost," she said.

Robert lit the lantern and went out, returning soon
with a quill from the poultry house, which he cut into
shape. His mother's mouth did not work when he used
the knife, nor did she watch him. Was he not the marrow

of his father, that man of absolute, though quiet, competence ?

Robert put the quill and paper on the chest of drawers beside the shell box and the Bible in readiness, and went on with the pegs.

As Mrs. Makepeace washed up she thought : " So it goes ! Nowt said to her. Nowt said to me. It'll be a wonder if the Lord Almighty gets a word out of the lad. He'll just eat sorrow. Now, what's that letter he's set on writing when we've gone upstairs ? "

She fetched the candlestick.

" Time for us to be going, my dear."

" Which was what Lord 'Umphrey said when the Dark Coach came for the Lady Rosanna Tempest," remarked Jonathan. " ' Time for us to be going,' he says. And in she got. And off they druv. And clap went all ! For Lord 'Umphrey was the owd lad himself, and none saw 'em after."

" It's raining soft and quiet," said Abigail, opening the door and looking out into the night.

" Heavy going to-morrow, Mother."

" Ah, Bob ! " she sighed.

As she knelt in her unbleached nightdress and the red woollen shawl that John had given her, she made an extra prayer for her son.

" O Lord ! Let Miss Gillian and Master and everybody bend to my lad's will like corn to the wind. Amen."

But whether this prayer was addressed to Christ or Jehovah or a pagan god it would have been difficult to say.

As soon as he was alone, Robert set out the writing materials and began his letter. It was very short. He addressed it to " Mister Gruffydd Conway, by the kindness of Mister Cadwalladar, Grocer, The Keep."

With his face bent over the letter, his dark, slightly wavy hair and well-shaped head outlined against the white wall, he made a pleasant picture. When he lifted his wide brows to glance at the golden-sounding clock, the yellow, figured face seemed to congratulate itself as though it were feminine and had charmed these grey eyes.

Robert was glad when the letter was done. He drew
a mug of beer from the cask in the larder and went on
with the pegs again. These done, he fell into a deep cogitation, while the low firelight shone up into his face,
accentuating the strong jaw, the fine lines about the eyes,
the slightly hollow temples, the decisive nose. So he was
to sit, alone and brooding, on another winter night not
so very far away, while the clock ticked low as if in awe,
and the red firelight tinted his face like that of the Roman
soldier in Gillian's picture. Perhaps even now, in the
silence, the future spoke ; perhaps even now his very
self was aware and ready.

She was going from him. Should he ask her to write ?
Of what use were letters ? Either you had a person's
very self beside you or—nothing. Of what use would it
be to him, wanting her laugh, her stamp of rage, wanting
her there to watch and plan surprises for, of what use to
have a letter, stilted and formal, saying she was well and
A'ntie sent compliments ? Also, she would not be allowed
to write to him when her family were aiming at the Church.

" All as is, is this," he thought, " the way I feel to the
child must be the secret that's never been told."

He pondered.

" No reason I shouldna know she's well," he thought,
" and things going pleasant."

He wrote another letter. This was addressed to :

> " Gipsy Johnson,
> > " The Caravan on the Fair Ground,
> > > > " Silverton."

Gipsy Johnson travelled into Wales by way of the
Gwlfas every spring, returning in the autumn, and living
through the winter at Silverton. He was one of Robert's
friends. Robert had a silent, unstressed, lifelong friendship
with a good many people. Each spring and autumn
he and Johnson smoked a pipe together by the gipsy fire,
saying little, asking few questions, but conscious of mutual
trust. There was very little that Johnson did not know
about Silverton and the country where lay his beat.

Also he had the key to that curious express system which, in lonely places, can bring news almost as quickly as the telegraph wires, running over the land like secret wildfire—the Mercury of democracy. Under his eye Gillian would be safe. That desire of hers to go to London alone, of which Robert knew, could not be carried into practice without Johnson's knowledge. It was a desire that must be decisively treated, Robert had decided. Of what use was parental authority or the aphorisms of aunts or the mild shockedness of a Mr. Gentle, when dealing with a girl like Gillian? His lips took their forbidding line and there was a flicker of amusement in his eyes. He and Johnson were the men for that job, for they could meet wiles with action, and boldness with superior knowledge of the situation, and they were not polished and would have no qualms about using force if necessary. At the idea of himself daring to dictate (though silently) to Miss Lovekin, Robert threw back his head and laughed soundlessly. Yes. He and Johnson would carry it through.

" Dear sores! If she went flaunting in her innicence to that wilderness o' men, she'd soon be trod under foot," he thought.

He wrote :

" DEAR FRIEND,
        " Master's girl's coming to Mrs. Fanteague of the Lilacs to stop a bit. Please to keep a glim on her. Leave me know all's well time and agen. Send quick if you hear tell of her travelling anywhere. Hoping all's well as it leaves me.

                                        "ROBT. RIDEOUT."

He lit his pipe and sat looking at the envelopes with some complacency.

" That job's jobbed," he reflected. He went to the window. Velvet-dark night leant against it with an almost palpable weight ; it was as if the glass might fall inwards at any moment. He drew back the bolt and went out, stepping straight into the breast of a great cloud that lay

across the Gwlfas like a grey bird. Through the fold,
under the drift-house, he went, on to the little lawn in front
of the farm, where the mossy grass was spongy, and white
fragments of snow lay to the north. He stood by the
pigeon cote. Yes! There was her lit window—pale
yellow, like a Lent lily. Once he saw her head outlined
against the light.

He threw a pebble. It struck sharply on the glass.
He threw it as if it were a signal of distress, because of
the sudden pain of knowing that to-morrow there would
be no bright Lent lily there. She opened the window
and leant out. She had a white shawl on. Underneath
he could see in the flickering candlelight a sleeve with
frills—one of those new, extravagant nightgowns, no
doubt.

And it was only for two old ladies to admire! Oh,
dear!

" Good neet ! " he said abruptly. For now that she
was there he could think of nothing to say. He had
ceased to be the usual human word-coining machine, and
was just a surge of wild instincts and desires.

A ripple of laughter fell.

" And you called me up out of my beauty sleep to say
' Good neet ! ' as crousty as can be ! ' "

" You werena asleep."

" What's kep you up so late ? "

" Writing letters."

" Letters ! I didna know you could ! "

" I can do whatever I set mind to do."

" Where be they ? Who to ? Can I see ? "

Robert slapped his chest.

" They be in my pocket. They be to friends o' mine.
You canna see 'em. But they consarn you."

He laughed.

" Oh, you aggravating man ! "

She slammed the window.

The Lent lily faded.

" Well, God bless ye ! " said Robert, as his heavy boots
went " sook, sook " across the lawn.

CHAPTER VI

TEA AT THE JUNCTION

MORNING came coldly over the sodden moor, where part-ridges ran across the deep cart-tracks with the glee of creatures released from a spell. For the present winter had withdrawn like a slow wave, and the green places shone like stained glass with a light behind it. The farm glowed in deep jewel reds ; the ricks took the colours of ripe barley ; Robert's face was red beneath its brown. The wind came from the north-west and was sharp and glassy as an iceberg. Gillian's cheeks tingled as she climbed into the trap and waved a gay farewell to her father, and she was very much amused at his evident perturbation on seeing who was to drive her. Rich as a dark pink rose with a touch of brown in it, she shone through the new veil, beneath the feathers of the defunct drake. The brown-grey rabbit fur suited her. Joy suited her. She had washed her hair with the farmhouse shampoo of beaten egg-yolk, and it gleamed with lustrous softness. Her gloves were of suède. She liked her shoes so much that she would not have the rug over them. The cornelian heart added its touch of elegance. Gillian was, she felt, a real lady.

"Well, if ever ! " breathed Robert, after a mile in silence, during which he had stolen many sidelong looks.

" It inna so bad, is it ? "

" Bad ! You're the Queen of May, Miss Gillian."

" Miss ? "

" Ah, you've got to be Miss Gillian now."

" Miss always I shanna be ! "

Robert suddenly slashed at the mare, to her everlasting surprise. It had never happened before. What had come to this dear master ? What had she done ? Indignant, half in revolt, she made the cart spin past the last fields of the farm. They were opposite the gyland now. These neighbouring fields always seemed to be tentatively asking each other's protection against the wild that lay, vast, purple, and silent, on every side.

To hide the sudden fury that possessed him at the thought of Gillian's marriage, Robert pointed with the whip to the long, narrow cover of stunted larches and birches called the " Gyland," which rose steeply on the other side of the brook beyond the first of the Mermaid fields.

" Unket ! " he said. " Real unket, that place is."

" Ah ! "

Gillian had not noticed his confusion. She was engrossed in the thought that this evening she would be out in the world.

" It's a place," said Robert, still looking at the dark, snow-strewn cover, " where summat 'll come to pass. Summat unket."

" What for will it ? "

" I dunno. But I feel it in my bones."

" Tell it ! It's like a tale of frittening."

" It's like as if there were places where the Lord o' Darkness comes borsting through, and they bear the mark before and after. Like as if good's thin there—only a croust—and he can come through easy. All the while afore it, the place bodes it. All the while after, it minds it. So it's different from other places forever and ever."

" I like that. It's right nice and 'orrid."

" I dunna like it. It's got summat to do with you and me."

" Oh, Robert ! What way ? "

" I dunno. Some way. You mind how you fell out o' cradle and cut yer forehead ? "

" Ah, I fell out o' cradle. I was dreaming about where I came from—a green place with mountains and chiming

rivers where I was before I was born. I woke up all of a
sudden, and it was dark, and there was a sough o' wind,
and wildfire in the window, and I knew summat beyond the
glass was jealous of my dream."

" And you only five summers ! "

" Ah. I couldna put words to it for a many years.
But I knew there was somebody crushing and crushing at
the farm to get at me and the dream. And in the morning,
Mother said she noticed a great crack in the chimley
right to the ground."

" And you'd had the dream before ? "

" Ah ! Every night, when Mother rocked me, the
dream came. Always the same. Little round hills like
Gwlfas Pyatt, and some a bit bigger like ' the green hill
far away,' and all round 'em at the back, sharp-pointed,
high black mountains, and bright streaks of silver down
'em, that was rivers."

" And it was a good dream ? "

" I canna tell you the good of it. It was like all the
best things—like the feeling of sliding on good ice, and
riding down hill with a wallop, and neesening, and the good
feeling of Lord's Supper, and paddling in the brook, and
having dinner at the ' Ordinary ' (only I don't never),
and finding a vi'let in winter."

" But it broke ? "

" Ah. It broke like gossamers when the soughing
came in the chimbley. Then the bad spirits put a mark
on me, and I'm a child of hell."

" No."

" Ah ! I canna help it. Whenever the good dream
comes, the bad'll break in. As soon as I begin to see them
shiny meadows and green, mossy mountains, I'm feared."

" Dunna be."

" But if those devils came crushing in agen, I'd die."

" They shanna. I'll keep you safe."

" You ? Oh, Robert ! You binna strong enough."

" I be, because I——"

" Because what ? "

" Oh, gerron-with-ye, mare ! " said Robert very crossly

The mare's moist dark eye came round—for he drove without blinkers—as if in reproach.

"And maybe that's what the dark feel of the gyland means. Maybe they'll break through there and kill my dream."

"There's summat waiting there, I make no doubt. We mun just bide and see."

"Do ye like my dress, Robert ? "

Green hills and granite mountains must recede before such a weighty question.

"It's middling tidy."

"I'd like to give you a clout in the ear, Bob Rideout ! Only 'middling tidy' ! "

"But I canna see why you mun go and kill the poor owd drake. Owd drake and me was allus friendly."

"I wanted a hat that colour."

"If you allus kill to have, you'll go to the land o' silence raddled all o'er."

"I dunna care."

"Mind the day dunna come when you'll sup sorrow for it."

"I shall get preaching in Sil'erton, thank ye kindly. Look ! There's public. What a lost and forgotten place it looks. I canna bear the way the sign creaks, winter."

"It's unket, like the gyland. But it's a grand place enough, with all the upsy downsy rooms, and the great guest chambers, to say nought of the attics. It's bigger than Thatchers want."

"Father says, if Mrs. Thatcher dies, Mr. Thatcher 'll leave."

"That'll be a big change. Thatchers ha' been there many a long day."

"I wonder who'll come ? "

"Ah."

"Maybe somebody young as'll give a Christmas tea. I'd like to go to a Christmas tea at the public."

"Likely you will some day."

"I wonder what Mrs. Thatcher felt like when she came walking over the heath in her bride-dress, and

Mr. Thatcher's arm in her arm, and the blush roses in blow, and none in all that great place but him and her ? And I wonder what Mr. Thatcher felt like ? "

" I can pretty well guess."

" Say ! "

" I wunna."

" You're talking very choppy. You ought to read the book of good manners A'ntie lent me. It says nought about chopping the words like worms under a spade."

She pulled out her handkerchief and played with it. Whiffs of scent came from it, lace edged it ; all this forbidden sweetness was unbearable. At the top of the long road that swept in a grand switchback of gradually descending country from the " Mermaid's Rest " to Mallard's Keep, Robert pulled up short.

" Now look you, Gillian, no more o' that ! No more about kissing and weddings and what-not. Flesh and blood wunna stand it."

Gillian's face was gleeful. So flesh and blood wouldn't stand it ! Aha ! He wouldn't kiss her, but none the less he thought her pretty. He was obstinate, but he had been obliged to ask for mercy.

" I tell ye," went on Robert's angry voice, " another word and I'll drive down there dang-swang, and dash us to pieces at the bottom and lie in one grave."

" Oh, Robert ! Why won't flesh and blood stand it ? "

Robert gave her a look, a fierce, swift look like a ray of concentrated light. Then he set his face towards the Keep again.

" Oh, coom on, mare ! We'll miss that borsted train ! " he said.

They continued for some miles in silence. At last, after many lonely hills and valleys, they climbed the last steep hill to a Pisgah view of Mallard's Keep. There it lay—the end of delight for Robert. There it shone, its clustered roofs, square church tower and miniature railway station all sloping up a hill with the inconsequence of a card house. Beyond were meadows, steep woods, blue distance, purple distance, smoke-coloured hills, and

more hills so pale as to fade on the sky. All about them
plovers ran in the mangold fields and wheeled in the air
with their wistful winter cry. A luggage train like a toy
drew out from the distant station with no sound, and a
puff of white smoke floated like a bubble against the dark
woodland. The acrid scent of burning weeds came up
from an unseen fire somewhere in the meadows below
the road. A thrush, balanced on the top twig of a fragrant
fir tree, sang with piercing sweetness. Robert looked,
listened, sighed. His broad shoulders were a little bowed,
and looked pathetic. When a man is young and his pulses
strong ; when desire is swift and eager, and all things
subservient to it ; then it is very easy to take, very hard
and bitter to renounce. They might have been driving to a
fair or a harvest dance or a Christmas supper as a betrothed
couple, or even to church to have their banns called.
(Oh, thought forbidden ! Oh, sweet thought !) It might
have been the gate of heaven, that little, huddled, shining
town. It was, instead, the gateway of despair. They
were going to no feast of fulfilment. It was not golden
September, but cold, early spring ; nothing begun, nor
likely to begin—no possibility of any harvest for his love.
"Oh, dang it ! " he said.

An idea came to Gillian. It would be fun ! It would
be doing a kindness to Robert also. It would be Christian,
as Christian as one of Aunt Fanteague's prayer-meetings—
nearly.

"Robert ! Would you like to come as far as the Junction
along of me, and us'll get tea, and I'll go on by the last
train ? "

"Oh, my dear 'eart ! " murmured Robert.

"I canna hear what you say, Robert. Tell it out !
I dunna like churching-mice."

"I darstna."

"Well, but darst you come ? "

"Well," said Robert, staring defiantly at the far blue
hills, "I dunna see why not."

She clapped her hands.

"We'll have some fine May-games, Robert O ! There's

a shop at the Junction where they sell cornets in summer
—made of biscuit with pink ice inside. But they wunna
have 'em in winter. Oh, dear ! "

" There'll be buns," said Robert, " and plum cake,
likely, and brandy-balls and liquorice."

" Ah, but liquorice is for children."

" Hoity-toity ! you *be* grown-up and grand ! You'll
be getting altogether marred for us poor folk when you've
been in Silverton a bit."

" Well, Mr. Rideout, it wunna be you as has to live
with me, so you needna mind."

Off they went, hell-for-leather down the hill, for Robert's
patience was exhausted. Not a word did he say as they
rushed on, nor as they climbed the steep main street, nor
as they drove over the cobbled inn yard where he unharnessed and stabled the mare. Without a word he
shouldered Gillian's box and turned towards the station.

The road twisted back for a few yards, and they faced
towards Dysgwlfas. There it lay, so faint, so blue, the
one long, wavering line that meant so many miles of
folded, seamed and tumbled land. There was his home.
There he must bide until he had fulfilled his task, silently
laid upon him by the silent moor. He must drag its heart
out, mingle it with his own being, make it into something
lovely and unfading. The soul of Gillian Lovekin also
should be mingled with it. He had no knowledge, no
words, no books, yet he would do it.

" Ah ! " he said to himself, as he brooded on that faint
far-hung ridge. " I'll get the guts out of the place. I
will that ! "

" O, look ye ! " cried Gillian.

There, about a mile away, between two hills of bare
larches, which shone golden in the afternoon sunlight,
was a puff of white smoke—the train.

" Look sharp, or we'll miss un ! " cried Gillian.

When they came to the station Robert discovered that
he had not one penny in his pocket. Here was a pretty
pass !

" I amna coming," he said sulkily.

" I've taken your ticket ! " laughed Gillian. " Come you shall ! "

She commanded, scolded, implored. It was useless. At last the guard prepared to wave his flag. Robert stood stolidly on the platform. Gillian was in despair. Her afternoon's fun was to be snatched from her. Suddenly she was lonely. She leaned out.

" Oh, please, sir ! " she cried to the guard. " Could you and porter give my 'usband a leg up, for he's all of a kim-kam with the rheumatics ? "

Before Robert could collect his wits he was hoisted into the carriage by four kind, brawny arms and received by Gillian.

The flag waved. The whistle blew. They were alone.

" Dear to goodness ! " said Robert, red and wrathful, " If I *was* your 'usband, my girl, I'd learn you not to make such a gauby of me ! I would that ! "

But Gillian only laughed.

" Oh, deary me ! I hope nobody knew us ! What ud father say ? But I got my way ! "

" Ah ! you got your way by a nasty, sneaking woman's trick. I wish I could get mine as easy," remarked Robert, with a sudden blaze of passion in his eyes.

" And what met that be ? "

" Ah, maybe that's the secret that's never been told, Miss Gillian."

With a wild and gloomy expression he turned his back on her, and did not look at her again until they had passed the three wayside stations set in the woods, and were nearing the Junction. He was afraid, desperately afraid, of forces undreamed of within himself, of a savagery that slept within his own soul, bound, but strong enough to break any shackle.

As they drew in to the Junction he turned to her.

" Gillian Lovekin ! " he said. " I warn ye, dunna play too many May-games with me. I tell ye straight, I canna stand it."

From her corner she looked at him and quailed a little.

Then she jumped out on to the platform in a flurry.

"Come on!" she cried. "Now for the buns and the cake and the tea O! Darby and Joan at the Junction!"

Robert was obliged to laugh. And although the forbidding expression came back to his face afterwards, Gillian felt that she was forgiven. They came to the one tea-shop in the single street. Its small, rounded window was full of brandyballs and bulls' eyes, green canisters of tea with gold hieroglyphics on them, buns, ginger snaps, leather boot-laces, thimbles and oranges. Inside was a broadly smiling lady in a white apron, who said:

"Pleasant weather for sweet'arting," and made Robert angry again.

But when the tea came—it was perfection. There were cakes of many shapes; there was a brown teapot with raised forget-me-nots on it; there were pikelets and jelly, and pink willow cups and a large cake with icing that stood on a doyley smelling of mice.

When they had finished it was time to go to the station. On the way they looked into shops, and Gillian saw a picture of a Roman soldier standing in a glare of light. Underneath was written: "Faithful unto death."

She went in and asked the price. It was three and sixpence, or, as she thought of it, two rabbits and a half. She bought it.

"Look! It's like you, Robert!"

Robert looked into the face of the soldier. He brooded so long that the approaching whistle of the train took them by surprise, and they had to run.

"For you!" she said, as they reached the platform. Then, as she looked at his rough coat, his dark hair and eloquent, proud glance, she was suddenly homesick. She leant out.

"I'll see Severn to-night!" she said, with bravado.

"What do I care if you see a score Severns?"

"I want to see it—smooth and green, with swans on it."

"I canna abide swans."

"Robert!"

"Well?"

"There's nobody in this carriage but me."

" So I see."

" If you've a mind—"

" Gillian Lovekin ! your name ought to be Gill-flirt ! "

" But, Robert ! "

Robert looked at the flushed cheek, the smiling mouth ready to droop, the eyes that shone with the radiant tints of the feather hat.   Then without more ado he turned and rushed up the platform with long strides.   When he came back there was only the flutter of a handkerchief from the receding train.   But on his way home Robert took many refreshing peeps at the picture of the soldier.   It comforted him, in the suddenly realized emptiness created by that fluttering handkerchief, to dream that there might come a time when he would stand amid the red ruin of his life defending the helpless, childish soul of Gillian.

CHAPTER VII

GILLIAN COMES TO SILVERTON

THE country grew dimmer, grew dark, in the short journey. It only took three-quarters of an hour, but to Gillian it was like a whole day. Once she saw the far hills dark against the afterglow, once she caught a glimpse of a brook lit by reflected radiance. Then came straggling houses, a village church, houses clustering thicker, roofs all huddled together, a square church tower, two silver spires, a great bridge across the Severn—Silverton. They ran into a bay of the long station, and there stood Aunt Fanteague in her best mantle and her well mortised bonnet, very severe.

" We missed our train," remarked Aunt Fanteague. When she used the first person plural, things were very wrong.

" I'm only a country girl, A'ntie," said Gillian. " Silverton 'll soon learn me to catch trains." She thought of the London express.

" I've met the train twice," said Aunt Fanteague, half inclined to be mollified.

Gillian gave her a great hug.

" It ud serve me right if you hadna kept any tea for me," she said, " and I clemmed."

" No one shall clem in my house, Juliana."

" Oh, A'ntie, you *are* good."

They walked out of the station yard, up the hill, with bright shop-windows on both sides. The cake shop at the top of the hill was a blaze of light and gay-ribboned chocolate boxes.

71

" Not even London," said Gillian, " could be better than this."

" Oh, London ! Well, I've never been there myself. Silverton's good enough for me. Where there's a church, and a doctor, and a butcher's, and the other shops for the necessary, and a good wool shop, and reasonable coal, it seems to me there's no need of London."

" But folk tell a sight of tales——"

" Oh, tales ! They'll make tales out of nothing. Now if you went to London what ud you find ? "

Gillian opened her mouth to say: " A lover," but remembered in time.

" You'd find churches and butchers and the other shops, maybe a better wool shop, but less reasonable coal. That's all."

" Oh, deary me ! "

" But you can ask poor Emily."

" Has A'nt Emily been to London ? "

" Why, yes, my dear, you needn't scream. She went to her operation."

If she had said coronation, Aunt Fanteague could not have spoken more respectfully. They left the bright street and took their way up a narrow alley of ancient black and white houses. The moon was up, and it threw the deep shadows of old romance. Never a dark brooding shade of a gable without the possibility of a Romeo for every Juliet. Bells began to sound. They rang the chimes. A mellow bell said a word that sounded like " June " six times. As they crossed the square, the shutters were being put up. More black and white gables leaned to Gillian, more shadows lured her. Up another narrow street, down a little hill.

" Here we are," said Aunt Fanteague. The rumbling of the out-porter's barrow followed them down hill. They had come to a little brown house, between a high, red garden-wall and another brown house. There were two windows up and two down, two gables, black oak beams let into the brown stone, two hollow white steps, a bright knocker.

They knocked, and there was Aunt Emily. She stood pensively under the pale light in the narrow hall, while the cuckoo-clock, a little behind the times, struck six.

Aunt Emily kissed her.

" It's years since I saw you, dear," she said. " Why, you've quite grown up ! "

" You saw her just before your operation," said Mrs. Fanteague.

" Yes, yes, sister."

Gillian understood that the time of the operation would be an inexhaustible topic ; would perhaps provide her with much useful information.

The box arrived.

" Now, Emily, you take the child in. She's starved and clemmed. I'll see to the box."

Aunt Emily led the way.

She was tall and thin, and she seemed to have too many bones in her face, so that when she spoke, you expected them to click together. She had a lined forehead, a pointed chin, a wistful mouth and eyes that always seemed to have just stopped crying. She was dressed in grey, with a small lilac bow. Her hair was slightly grey and was knotted at the back and covered with a net, not built up like Aunt Fanteague's.

In the parlour the table was set for tea, and the fire of reasonable coal burned brightly. There was a piano which was a musical box. There was an oval case of stuffed willow-wrens ; there were two glass-fronted cupboards of china, a whist table, and several framed lustre paintings on velvet ; a cabinet portrait in a plush frame signed Hubert Gentle ; a piece of coal which was supposed to contain a diamond, and which caused much future trouble to Gillian. (She was unable, after some weeks, to tolerate its bland assumption of priceless worth, so she proved it with a pocket knife. In the manner of coal, it fell to pieces. There was no diamond, nor was there now any coal ; and it was an heirloom. Not only that, it was a faith. She felt, on the day when she faced Aunt Emily across the fragments, really a child of hell.)

There were innumerable photographs on the walls, all a little mottled, a little yellow. They seemed to be of people who could never really have lived. The ladies wore chignons, the gentlemen wore whiskers. All wore stiff and curious clothes. She was told they were the Aunts' grandparents, her great-grandparents. She was glad she had never known them. On the mantelpiece were vases of everlastings. In a corner was a painted drainpipe (sunflowers on a brown ground), containing bulrushes. On one wall was Landseer's *Fidelity*, on another *Highland Cattle*, on another a still life study by Aunt Emily in youth (apples, Michaelmas daisies and vase), and on the fourth, *Wedded*. On the piano were some sacred songs.

" As you're a traveller, I know sister will excuse you sitting down as you are," said Emily. " Do you take milk and sugar ? "

" Everything, please, A'ntie ! "

That was it ! She wanted everything ! She would take milk and sugar and all the rest of life. She would bear anything, even pain. Only never, never would she be like Aunt Emily. She would rather die. The atmosphere of the house oppressed her. It was so quiet. She was used to her father's " Ha ! " and Robert's tramp in the yard, and a sound of shifting cowchains from the fold, and stampings from the stable. She was used to the smell of strong tobacco and beer. Here was only a faint scent of camphor. She thought even the bread and butter tasted of camphor, as if it had been cut for a tea-party of the mottled people on the walls, a long time ago, and preserved. But Gillian was hungry again by this time, so the camphor and the seed cake, the quince conserve and the little cakes were all equally delicious. She wished Robert could enjoy it too. What would Robert be doing now ? She saw again the dark moor, the winding road with snow water lying in every uneven place, the vast and cloudy sky, the cart with Winny trotting briskly, ears pricked for home, and Robert's figure, stooping forward a little in one of his customary attitudes of easy power, holding the reins in his large, capable hand with a look of carelessness which would have been swiftly belied if the mare had stumbled.

When she looked at the brilliant tints of Aunt Emily's apples, she saw that quiet picture. While she heard the coals fall with a tindery sound into the white ash on the flawless hearth, she heard also Winny's splashing trot, the creaking of the harness, the rattle of the whip-holder, which had always been loose. Aunt Fanteague was a long while on the stairs, for not only must she go into the ethics of overcharges, but she also had to enquire as to the absence of the out-porter's little boy from Sunday School, which was held under one of the silver spires. She also had to hear, in a loud, mysterious whisper, that the reason was that the missus had had an increase, and that all had been " collywessen " in the house. She then had to look out some comforts for the porter's family, and give him many injunctions. So Aunt Emily and Gillian had a long time together.   They had not met for some years, because Aunt Emily had not felt equal to the journey to the Gwlfas.

Sometimes, beyond the shutters, muffled footsteps would go up or down the hill, and Gillian thought they sounded as steps would sound if she was in her grave, and had a flagstone over her, and was wakeful. Suddenly she felt sorry for Emily, sitting there so still, eating so little, getting ready for the dreams that would come in three hours. It was not in Gillian's nature to be sorry for people, and when she pitied, she despised. Why had Aunt Emily become like this ?   Why hadn't she run away with Mr. Gentle ? Looking again at Mr. Gentle's portrait, she wondered less. But she had the native courtesy which is in most country people, however rough they may be.

" He looks to be a very pleasant-spoken gentleman," she said.

" His likeness to Charles the First of blessed memory," said Aunt Emily, " is considered to be very striking."

" Was that the one that had his head—— ? "

"The likeness is the only resemblance," said Aunt Emily, rather stiffly.

Gillian wondered if, should Aunt Emily so far forget herself as to ask for a kiss, Mr. Gentle would behave as Robert had behaved. Could Mr. Gentle blaze into sudden anger, with a look underneath that made you hot and cold ? She did not think so. Her thoughts wandered to Aunt Fanteague. There was and always had been a mystery about Aunt Fanteague. There was a Mr. Fanteague; but where he was, what he did, who cooked his meals and made his bed, nobody seemed to know. He was as mysterious as the Trinity.

"A'nt Em," said Gillian suddenly, flinging herself on the rug by the grey knees of Miss Emily, "A'nt Em, do tell about Mr. Fanteague ! "

Aunt Emily gasped.

But the necessity of answering was taken from her. Mrs. Fanteague stood in the doorway.

"Mr. Fanteague, Gillian, is a spark that runs among the stubble," she said, and with that she poured herself a cup of tea, and closed the subject. "A spark among the stubble ! " It sounded nice—better than Charles the First. She would like to meet Mr. Fanteague. Since her early years all mention of him had been hushed and frozen. She and Mrs. Makepeace simmered with curiosity. Apparently this was not to be satisfied.

"Maybe, if I'm right nice to Mr. Gentle, I can get it out of him," thought Gillian.

She was too much on her best behaviour to get up and look at his portrait, but she could see it fairly well from her chair, for her sight, like her supple movements, had something in it of the falcon. She took the opportunity of Mrs. Fanteague going to fetch hot water to say : "I do want to listen to Mr. Gentle reading."

"It's his evening to-morrow," confided Aunt Emily. "He never misses. Not in all these years. Colds he may have. Once it was measles that he caught in the Sunday School. (I compare him to the brave leper Missionaries, for though it was not dangerous, it

was just as sacrificial.) And once it was earache ; but
he came."

Gillian clasped her hands round her knees and said,
without any sarcasm :

" It must be grand to have a lover ! For a chap to be
mad after you ! "

Aunt Emily hastily reached a palm-leaf fan that hung
on the wall. She was very much embarrassed.

" Mr. Gentle would never be mad after anything,"
she said. " And I don't call him my lover, nor anything
so forward. I call him my gentleman friend."

" I suppose it inna very likely as Mr. Gentle could ride
without a saddle ? " Gillian asked.

" Juliana ! " said her elder aunt, returning, " you must
keep in mind that whatsoever your Aunt Emily and me
was used to in times gone by, we're used to good manners
now—stirrups and saddles and good broadcloth—a paid
pew in church—no feckless ways like at the Gwlfas."

" But it inna feckless to ride bareback !—you've got to
get ever such a grip of the knees ! "

" You mustn't talk like that when Mr. Gentle's here,
child. And now I'll show you to your room. You can
unpack ready for bed. We're early folks. We go to bed
at nine, nights, except on Mr. Gentle's evenings, and then
we allow ourselves till ten. One evening I shall ask the
curate and his mother. He is a very earnest young man ;
one that found his God before he lost Him, and never left
the narrow way."

" Oh, deary me ! Never no fun at all ! "

" To play the devil's game, Juliana, is not fun, but death."

" Afore I die," said Gillian, as she brushed her hair
(which filled her with despair because it never would be
anything but plain brown) before the grand swing-mirror,
" afore I die, I'm in behopes to play the devil's games
once anyway."

Aunt Fanteague sat down on the bed and raised her hands
to heaven.

" Juliana ! I counsel you to read two chapters in the
Bible to-night instead of one. Travelling's turned your

head. Best not come down again. I'll bring you some
bread and milk in bed. There's ' The Dove in the Eagle's
Nest,' you can read when you've read your chapters."

" It's a dove's nest I'm in," thought Gillian. " I'd
liefer it was an eagle's."

She wandered round the small, clean, bristling room.
Three texts, girl and swan, kittens in basket, all framed in
cut cardboard. An entertaining screen made of Christmas cards. A wallpaper with blue roses on it. A book-
shelf with " Peep of Day," a Bible, a " Lady's Companion,"
that had belonged to her grandmother, and had always
been considered a great treasure, for her grandfather had
" looked high " for his wife, and had married the school-
mistress from Mallard's Keep. There were also some bound
copies of the " Quiver " in the seventies. Gillian thought
there would be some good reading in these. She was
fascinated most by the dressing-table, for it had a china
set of dishes and boxes painted with unearthly flowers,
culminating in a kind of china antler on which Gillian's
rings (if she had possessed any) were supposed to hang.
She looked at her bare brown fingers. What a long way
it seemed to that desired day when she would stand before
a glittering audience with rings of all colours on her white
hands, and sing them into an ecstasy. Well, she had
gained one step. But had she? Looking round the
pictured walls, listening to the silence, broken only by
slow chimes, she had a sudden flash of perception that
this was further away from her dreams than the Gwlfas
was. She realized that place is nothing—or at least
very little. Aunt Emily's visit to London helped in this.
When Aunt Emily had been in London, she had really
been further away from it, from its glittering savage soul,
than she had been when she walked the old streets of
Silverton in health. A hospital ward was not London,
though in the centre of it : nor a prison, nor a nunnery,
nor any place which had been made, either subtly or
openly, into a cage. Gillian did not think all these things
in any consecutive way, but the realization was borne
in on her—and she knew that if she married the curate

or anyone else whom her aunt should choose for her,
she would be in a cage even if he took her to London.
There was, then, no choice. It must be the way of the
girl in the story—or the Gwlfas.

"They're poor old kim-kam things," she reflected.
"And Aunt Emily's as soft as an unshelled egg. But I
mun stop a bit, and learn some music and find a way to
get to London town. And I'll have some May-games with
Mr. Gentle. I can just see 'im singing ' She is Queen of
the Earth.' I shall write to Robert one of these days.
I'll buy me some scented paper and then, maybe, Robert
'll kiss the letter."

Mrs. Fanteague, entering with the bread and milk,
found Gillian dutifully reading the Bible.

"Breakfast is eight prompt," she said. "And then,
when you've given me a hand in the kitchen, I'll take you
to see the town, Juliana, and you can buy a cake for tea.
And mind, what you want, Juliana, is steadying, and to be
brought to Jesus, and to mind and say isn't instead of inna."

"Yes, A'ntie."

Mrs. Fanteague departed, with an injunction that the
light was to be out in ten minutes.

Gillian shut the Bible, put it away, took from beneath
the pillow an ancient Bradshaw which she had found in
the parlour, and began with much puzzling to· look out
the trains to London.

She would have been very much surprised if she had
known that Robert's friends (minions they would have
been called in romance) would soon be watching every
outgoing train, unobtrusively, while they went about their
work, and that Mrs. Fanteague's little day-girl would to-
morrow be in the confidence of Gipsy Johnson, and would
find the Bradshaw in the morning and would report her
every movement.

She would have been surprised, also, if she could have
looked beneath the sloping roof of Robert's attic, where
the door was so low that he had to stoop, though he was
only of average height. There beneath the flaking
whitewash Robert went to and fro in the small place, by

the light of the moon and the tallow dip. On the mantelpiece leaned the Roman soldier, and before him lay
Gillian's old hair-ribbon. In his stockinged feet went
Robert, for boots were not allowed on the white attic
stairs, and slippers were at the Gwlfas unknown. And
as he walked, he chanted to himself the poem he had
thought of on his journey home.

" Is she a cruel wench, Gillian of the Gwlfas ?
  The birds ask, the creatures of the moor ask me.
  Is she cruel ? She strangled a bird to bedizen her,
  And her red cheeks are comely with our blood.
  Is she hard of heart, Robert Rideout ?
  I'll answer the birds and the creatures of the Gwlfas.
  Ah ! She's hard of heart to-day. She's had no sorrow—
  Nowt but a scar on the brow. When her heart's wounded
  She'll love you, all you birds and creatures of the Gwlfas.
  She mun sup salt tears afore she's raught free of evil.
  Her life mun be wounded. She mun be brought low.
  Can you bring down the pride of a woman raddled with blood—
  Of a heart like weathered granite on the steeps of the Gwlfas ?
  Only the blazing sun of midsummer can crack the granite,
  Only love can find the way into a young gallus heart.
  I, Robert Rideout, would cleave her soul asunder.
  I'd take her in a net of love and make her suffer.
  Never should she go flaunting in the plumage of her sisters
  Out in the world where folk lose their souls.
  I'd lief love her till she's blind and deaf to herself,
  Until she canna-d-abear herself and is dead to herself.
  And when she lies at my feet beseeching the cowman-shepherd
       for his love,
  When her pretty hair is spread on the floor of our kitchen,
  I'll speak unkind to her even a little longer.
  But at long last, oh birds and creatures of the Gwlfas,
  I'll suddenly snatch her into my arms and take her breath with
       kisses.
  Gillian, Gillian, Gillian Lovekin !
  Gillian, Gillian, Gillian Rideout !
  It's bad to be cowman-shepherd when you love a rich woman—
  A woman with well-raddled sheep on the hills and money in
       the bank.
  I'd lief give one of the sheep to every old widow in the country,
  And a pound of her money to every orphan,
  And when she'd got nought left but a virgin's garland
  I'd up and ask her for that.
  So she'd be a beggar. Then I'd make her queen of Dysgwlfas,
  And I'd work twenty hours out of twenty-four for Gillian,
  And sleep in her arms the other four.
  And Gillian would be twice remembered after she was dead,
  In my pennillion and in the children I'd give her."

By which it will be seen that tea at the Junction is very
intoxicating, and that young men who live on the moors
are sometimes quite as foolish when they are in love as
young men in towns, and that Robert was not so chill
and curt a being as he led people to suppose, and
that he badly needed some lessons on the making of poetry.
Away in Silverton the first milk-cart rattled down the
steep street, and Gillian woke to her town life, hearing
the chimes ring six. At the Gwlfas Robert came to himself. It was time to feed and water the horses, so he
put away his picture and his ribbon and the memory of
his passion, and tip-toed downstairs and out into the
cold, realistic world of a January morning. Going the
rounds with his lantern, he smiled ironically at his foolish-
ness, knowing that his pride would never allow him to
tell Gillian his secret. He would not even write down
his poems, for fear someone should see them. Not until
he was as old as Isaiah, and had a white beard and a chill
pulse, not until he had made his poem perfect through
decades of loving work, would he let anyone hear it.

" She'll be peeking through blind now, no danger,"
he thought. " Mighty angered her'd be if her knew about
Johnson."

He laughed as he milked, and remembering that they
were Gillian's cows, or would be some day, and that
Gillian could not stay in Silverton for ever, he even
went so far as to hum a little air to the obbligato of the
trickling milk, like a very contented basso-profondo bee.

CHAPTER VIII

GILLIAN MEETS MR. GENTLE

GILLIAN heard the day girl taking down the shutters and talking to Gipsy Johnson at the front door. He was a strange messenger of love, with his curious medley of garments, his rings, his dirty face and unmistakable aroma of the real nomad. Gillian looked out of her window. Gipsy Johnson looked up. In one dark glance he had photographed her on his mind ; wherever she was, in whatever company or dress, he would know her again. Gillian thought, "There's a poor forsaken gipsy, like them as passes, spring and fall of the leaf." She threw him a penny. He stooped with servile haste and picked it up. Round the corner he laughed very softly. There is one quality in life that gipsies appreciate more than ordinary country folk—irony. The girl was virtually his prisoner. She was his friend's girl. She was to be kept safe for his friend with her will or without it. He cared nothing for that. He might be giving her the heart's desire, or the dregs of hell. She threw him a penny, and undisturbed, unconscious, she hung her cornelian heart about her neck, and ran down to make the toast.

"Can I learn the piano proper, A'ntie ? "

"Yes. I'd thought you'd best make the most of opportunity. Lost time ticks in hell. Never waste time. If poor Emily'd learnt she'd have done great things in the world, I make no doubt."

"Can I begin to-day ? "

" I'll think about it."

" Who'll learn me, A'ntie ? "

" There's a very nice lady——"

" A lady ! "

" You cry out as if you're hurt, Juliana."

Gillian bent lower over the toast. Those dreams of a pale young organist with flowing hair and delicate fingers, who would fall in love with her, but whom she would scorn—where were they ?

" She's own cousin to Mr. Gentle. They're a very gifted family."

So Gillian went, after breakfast, with her Aunt, and had her first music-lesson. And when she had wandered through the market and seen the shops and helped her aunt to make apple dumplings and had dinner, she began to long for evening and Mr. Gentle. At least he would be someone to experiment with. She went up to her room and put on the pink blouse for tea. The gas lamps were being lit, and purple dusk was gathering. She had read the Parish Magazine from cover to cover. She had practised her scales. Down she ran, vivid with excite- ment. When she flushed and her eyes shone, her scar and her high nose were forgotten. Tea was in the parlour in honour of Mr. Gentle. There were rock buns and cream buns and many delights. Aunt Emily wore lavender poplin with a lace collar. Her hair was done so as to disguise its greyness. She wore a cameo brooch, and had scent on her handkerchief. The three women hurried to and fro, altering a spoon here, a plate there, rearranging the bunch of laurustinus on the table, poking the fire. If Mr. Gentle could have seen them, he would have been much embarrassed. He was so very unassuming, in spite of his royal appearance.

Steps ! A halt ! The bell ! Gillian was in the hall in a flash.

She opened the door. There stood Charles the First.

" Come in, Mr. Gentle," said she. " I'm A'nt Emily's niece, as maybe you know."

Mr. Gentle made a most beautiful bow.

" I am indeed honoured and delighted, Miss Lovekin ! "
he said.

The bald spot on his head was apparent when he bowed.
But when he stood up Gillian saw it no more, and forgot it.

" Emily ! " said Mr. Gentle, and he bowed again. " I'm
glad to see you so well ; if I may say it, so charming."

Mr. Gentle did not speak the language of Silverton. He
had a small library of his grandfather's books : therein
he read indefatigably, and therein he found his phrases.
As Mrs. Fanteague said, even if he lacked words, looks
would carry him through. He wore a very high Glad-
stone collar, a made tie, a white waistcoat and a cut-
away coat. He had cuffs.

Gillian knew that he would have thought Robert very
common, for when asked what he would have, he said
he would take a little preserve. Robert would have said :
" Jam, thank you kindly," and ladled it on to his plate.

Mr. Gentle did not seem to care whether he had any or
not. It amazed Gillian.

" How many songs can you sing, Mr. Gentle ? " she
enquired.

" Well, Miss Lovekin, I have six in my portfolio, but we
usually content ourselves with two. Two is our limit, I
think, Emily ? "

Emily said yes.

" But to-night let's have 'em all ! " begged Gillian.
" And if you're hoarse I've got some liquorice as Robert
bought me."

" Who's Robert, dear ? "

This from Emily, who felt that she had a corner in
romance to-night.

Mr. Gentle looked roguish.

" Oh, Robert's only cowman-shepherd," said Gillian.

Mr. Gentle's manner showed that the liquorice of a
cowman-shepherd could never soothe the larynx of a
Charles the First.

" If Emily will accompany me, I will sing ' Queen of
the Earth ' as a beginning," he said.

Emily would.

Mr. Gentle's voice trembled a little ; it was slightly falsetto. The pathos of it, of Emily, poor sad Emily, as Queen of the Earth, of Mr. Gentle as a lover—poor Mr. Gentle, who in all his fifty-five years had never felt the divine fire, never been tempted to swerve from good manners—was entirely lost on Gillian. For many years had he sung this, not even meanwhile making Emily queen of his own home. To Gillian they were enigmas. She was impatient. She evolved an amusing plan. It occurred to her when Mr. Gentle was singing: " Oh ! that we two were maying."

She would make Mr. Gentle sing it as a duet with her. He should take her up the river in a boat. Emily should not come. She would see if she could make Mr. Gentle flush as Robert had flushed, make him angry, make his hand tremble as Robert's had done at the Junction. If she were Aunt Emily she would soon make Mr. Gentle propose. It was silly of Aunt Emily.

" Maybe if I get 'im to tell it over to me, he'll tell it over to Aunt Emily after," she said. But in her heart she knew that she was mean. What business had she to trouble this middle-aged man, this forlorn woman, both content to stay for ever in their backwater ?

Conscience, like a tolling bell, warned her : but she would not hear its plaintive note. She hardened herself as she had done when she cut off the head of the slatey drake. She was a child of sin. Was she not scarred ? She would play the devil's May-games with Mr. Gentle, with Robert, with anybody. Only in Robert there was something obdurate, a hardness more adamantine than her own, but of a different quality. Mr. Gentle sang all his songs. The last was " Annie Laurie," to which he played his own accompaniment. While he sang his eyes dwelt on Gillian. Aunt Emily did not know, because she always listened with hers shut.

Mrs. Fanteague yawned a good deal during the singing, and said very promptly after " Annie Laurie " :

" Now for our reading."

They were in the Fourth Book of Crabbe's Collected

Works. Mr. Gentle read very mellifluously. While he read, Gillian plotted how she would make him fall in love with her. If there had been a pale musician, anybody, except the unapproachable curate, she would have let him alone. Even now, when she looked long at him, she quailed. But she decided to victimize him.

Crabbe was over. The tray was fetched by Gillian from the kitchen. After supper, all being much more flippant —for, as Aunt Emily said, cocoa is very heartening—they played round games.

They played : " This is the one-horned lady (or gentleman) very genteel, come to enquire of the two-horned lady."

Those who answered a question correctly wore a spill (made by Emily during the afternoon), which was stuck in their hair. Mr. Gentle put his behind his ear—a thing he would never have done before cocoa. He ended with a great sheaf of spills, and Aunt Emily said with pride that he always did. He was so well-informed.

Helping Mr. Gentle on with his coat, under the demure hall light, Gillian said :

Mr. Gentle, will you take me on Severn ? "

Mr. Gentle thought perhaps he might—some day.

" Not Aunt Emily ! "

" Not Emily ! "

Mr. Gentle rubbed his head in perplexity.

" Not Emily ! What will your Aunt Fanteague think of that ? "

" We'll just go off early, afore breakfast, some day when the mornings be lighter."

" But I never—— ! "

" Ah ! but you will for this once, Mr. Gentle ! It'll be grand on Severn ! "

Mr. Gentle sighed. He never rose before nine, and he hated rowing. But this vivid creature pleaded so ! Her eyes were so imploring ! Her smile was so sweet !

He was not young enough to resist her.

For youth is hard. It is not true that temptation is worse for young men. It is the middle-aged men, wistful with loss or unfulfilment, prone to melancholy, reverential of youth, glad of any music to sing them out of remembrance of the gathering silence—it is they who find it hard to say No.

Robert Rideout would have snapped out " No," and have done with it.

Mr. Gentle hesitated, and while he did so, Gillian laid her hand on his arm and he was lost.

" Some day—some day, Miss Juliana."

" The first sunny day, when the weather's lightened up a bit ! " said Gillian firmly.

Mr. Gentle, looking rather miserable, assented, but he added that it was likely to be a long winter, and a very cold, wet spring.

CHAPTER IX

THE HARPER'S FORGE

SHARP light struck out from the shutterless window of the round lambing-hut, built of turves and roofed with furze by Robert himself. It was warm inside, even without the heat of the rough brazier of live coals resting on four large stones. Shafting slightly upward, the light struck across the frozen grass of the moor, where it sloped towards the sky-rim. The hut stood in a hollow, and beside it was the low roof of thatch supported on larch boles and surrounded by hurdles, where the ewes were.

Robert sat by the table in the restricted lantern light, reading a letter. Sometimes he got up and stooped over a lamb, lying dank and limp beside the brazier—come through the door of living, with only just its life. Sometimes, when a low note of pain sounded from the shippen, he would go out, and the wide moor would become an ebony frame for his small, round, daffodil-coloured light. Then, sitting down again, he would rest the patched sleeves of his stained coat on the table and muse upon his letter. It was from Gruffydd Conwy, at the Forge Cottage of Trewern Coed, over the border, and it was to invite him to come, on the first Saturday when he was free, and talk with Gruffydd about pennillions.

Robert, who was always practical when this was necessary, counted the ewes that had not yet lambed, and decided that he could be spared on the next Saturday. He was rapturous to be nearing the knowledge that would enable him to cage his thoughts swiftly and permanently. He whistled and hummed to himself, and sometimes sang aloud, and his voice went tenderly rolling under the grey-moth dawn towards the eastern horizon, beyond which Gillian lay, rosily sleeping in her white nightgown. His poet's heart conjured her : his eyes beheld her : his arms ached for her. Could desire have penetrated that young hard heart of hers, he would have drawn her from her bed, from the house, the town, over the dim fields like a white heron, into his arms. But she was like the maiden in the glass coffin, and not even the faintest tremor of his deep, hidden passion could penetrate to her soul.

He was glad of these nights of watching ; they sapped his strength a little, and by lowering his vitality and making his passion less physical, less throbbing, they brought life into better focus, and drew back his peace, as dusk draws again, over the wild sunlight of the plain, quiet folding mist. He stamped the brazier coals to blackness with his nailed boot and went, with a lamb under each arm, along the path that smelt of earth and rime and winter hay, to his mother's cottage.

Standing outside the back door, as his custom was when his boots were muddy, he whistled a blackbird call to his mother, who came hurrying out and gathered the small ugly creatures into her arms.

" Jim Postman's been," she said, " and brought tidings as Mrs. Thatcher passed away last night."

Jonathan came to the door. He was going to market, and had therefore been shaving, and had therefore cut himself. He stood with the razor in one hand, and a lump of rather dirty cotton-waste in the other, looking like a picture of an attempted suicide.

" New folk, new folk," he said. " There'll be new folk at the ' Maiden ' now, and I dunna like new folk. When I catchen sight on a new face I smell trouble."

" I smell burning," said Mrs. Makepeace, as she ran to the oven.

" Be that 'am done, mother ? " he inquired with keen interest.

"Ah! It wur in all night. But it mun cool afore we get our teeth in it."

"We met not live to eat it!" said Jonathan sadly. "Poor Mrs. Thatcher hasna. New folk! New folk! God 'elp us!"

"Oh, what a poor God-'elp you be, Jonathan," remarked his wife, peeling the "rough" pastry from the cooked ham, and keeping an eye on the lambs, lest a hot cinder fall on them.

"You mind the tale o' the New Folk at the 'Maiden,' a hundred year ago," continued Jonathan, unperturbed. "Took the place all of a pother. No arglin and barglin. No banting of the price. No coddling about with the agent, choosin' this bit o' paper and that bit o' paper for the walls. Took it out of hand, just when the bird's-eye was in flower on the door-sill. Come trooping in, they did; some say as they come by a great coach as nobody ever see in these parts afore or since; but I'm of opinion as they come in a hearse. Howsoever, in they came. And Maister's great-grandmother was the one to put fires for 'em. And it was her and an old ancient man as welcomed 'em. In they came, and went straight to the oak cupboard as is built into the kitchen wall. And one of 'em—a very owd-fashioned looking gentleman—stooped down and wrenched away the boards o' the floor, as was loose, and they lugged up a great wooden box. Maister's great-grandmother didna know what was in it, only from the weight it seemed to be she thought it wasna money. And with that, with no more ado about it, the four gentlemen picked up the box, and heaved it up on their shoulders, and the two ladies puck up each a can'lestick and they took off. But the thing as made Maister's great-grandmother fall down in a swoon was how they went. For they walked straight through the kitchen dresser, plates and cups and all, and through the wall, box and all. And the thing as frittened the old lady worst was the way the blue willow-pattern of the dishes shone through the gentlemen's greatcoats. Ah! there's frittenen at the 'Maiden,' no danger.

Much good may it do the new folks, whosoever they
be."

" There isna nobody in these parts as 'ud care to take
it on—a wold meandering place the like o' that," said
Mrs. Makepeace. " I doubt it'll be left for the ghosses for
a spell."

Robert, eating his breakfast, saw the old house left to
the ghosts, heard the strange sighings and groanings of a
winter's night there, and thought how fair a place it would
be if he and Gillian owned it. Never, he supposed, in any
place but one like this—half lapsed into Faery—would
he and Gillian love one another unhindered. It would
be grand to gather her up, angry or laughing, and stalk
away with her to the old inn, and to speak a charm, and
behold ! inn and all would sink into Faery, and he and
she—alone of the earth-born—would live there undisturbed, drawing pewter measures of the tiniest capacity
full of nectar for elves.

" What'n you chuckling at ? " queried his mother.

" Nought, nought," said Robert, with his mouth full.

" What a lad ! oh ! what a lad ! " Jonathan held up
his hands in protest. " Allus chumbling things over in the
mind of 'un, and that forgetful as I never see."

Robert rose abruptly.

" I'm going to take the day off, Saturday, stepfeyther,"
he announced, " so give an eye to the sheep, oot ? "

" What'll Maister say ? "

" Maister can say what pleases un."

" Where be going, lad ? "

" I be going to see a mon, over the border, Mother.
You'll see to the lambs, wunna you—the while I do the
jobs ? "

He was gone.

" Now what work's he after, going off on lonesome ? "
pondered his mother. But she knew it was quite useless
to ask. For no migratory bird, with its journey mapped
secretly in the recesses of its subconsciousness, could be as
secretive as Robert when he did not choose to speak.
Sometimes she used to wonder whether Robert's father

could have made him speak. Then she would sigh ; for
the older Robert grew, the more like his father he became,
and the more absolutely she loved him. In her courting
days she had been so dominated by the dark beauty of
John Rideout's eyes that she had clung to the door half-
fainting when he left her, and in her most rebellious, most
loquacious moments he had only to turn his glance full
upon her with a " Well, wench, what ails thee now ? "·
and her heart would, as she said, " turn in her," and the
words and the anger would fall to silence. So whenever
Robert did or said anything to remind her of these moments
—moments of precious reality not known before nor since—
she was grateful, and she would brush aside the wishes
of the unfortunate Jonathan, as she brushed the fowls off
their perches when they roosted in the wrong house.

So when Saturday came, there was a wallet full of bread
and cheese and a bottle of home-brewed for Robert, and he
had no opposition to meet but Isaiah's " Ha ! " which,
though very loud, was soon over. And at the time when
the early bells were ringing in Silverton—for there were
two " high " churches where there was an early service
of some sort every day—and when Gillian was putting
in the last hairpin and thinking how nice it was not to
get up at six, Robert set out across the moor.

The blinds were all down at the " Mermaid's Rest," and
it saddened Robert to think of the stout, gay, motherly
woman clinking her glasses no more. He looked away
to the little coppice, the unket place, still unket though the
snow was gone. A flash of water at its foot, a flash of
bright moss-green on its side, a dreaming yellow in its
larch boughs where the knops were swelling towards the
leaves—why, then, was it so grievous ? It must be what
he had said to Gillian : evil had broken through there,
or would—a horror, strong and fierce as some great beast,
would split the solid earth and raven through the land.
And again, like a warning bell, came the intuition that he
would see it happen, that he must wrestle with something
stupendous, even here at the gates of home.

He strode on across the rolling brown of heather and

dead bracken and bare wimberries. Plovers mourned softly, always a little withdrawn, and a hawk was present in the air above him for a time, and then was gone. The solitariness of hill and moor in winter is oppressive to some natures. It did not trouble Robert. No voice of shepherd or of sheep, no chirp or lark-song ; only the snow-fed brooks rushing over their rocky beds, the plovers withdrawn like souls in trouble, the hawk silent as a leaf. A man's country. Nothing soft or feminine was here to remind him of Gillian, except one white cloud that trailed softly half across the pale sky and had a spring-like presage in it—as if it were made of white narcissus or snowdrops, close packed like market-bunches of flowers. He would have made Gillian a posy like that, if he had been able to marry her, a posy packed so close with sweetness that you could not tell flower from flower (the subtleties of art were unknown to Robert : if he had known them he would probably have rejected them). He would have tied it firmly with strong string and encircled it with cut paper, and it would have been so large that both small hands would have had to hold it. And up the church she would have marched, gallus as a fairy, until she came to him, waiting there, caring not a pin for anybody. And then he'd have turned right round and given her a look, the look that he had to conquer and deny every time she was near him, and ten to one she would have dropped the posy plump at parson's feet.

Robert laughed aloud, and forthwith, being surrounded by so many kindly square miles of loneliness, he began to sing :

" Gillian, Gillian, Gillian Rideout ! "

And the plovers, glancing in the light, answered him between their silver wings with silver cries, and alighting here and there on bright green patches amid the heather, uplifted their crests and ran gleefully, hearing afar the step of the old magician, Spring, who sent green fire through the darkest places, and inebriated them with vitality and drove them to love, and gave them for a little while the freedom of the house of life.

And Robert, forgetting that he was only cowman-shepherd, and that Gillian was away, and that there were young men of position in Silverton, young men whose blood he longed to shed, uplifted his voice and sang :

" She's lying on the white cloud as if it was a bed of flowers.
    If she was asleep, I would kiss her.
    The flowers smell as sweet as a May morning,
    And their petals are as white as milk.
    But her hand's sweeter to kiss and her arm's whiter.
    She's like a golden plover running in the black yeath—
    But when I reach out my hands, she minds her as she's got wings.
    I've a mind to buy a pair of silver shears
    And clip one wing ever so little,
    So you couldna fly away from me forever and ever,
    Gillian, Gillian, Gillian Lovekin !

" My 'ouns ! " he remarked, as he sat down to have his dinner at mid-day. " It's about time I went to see owd Conwy, it is that ! "

He faced to the East and thought of the Junction as he ate his bread and cheese, and it was borne in upon him that distance counts for very little, states of mind for very much. Isaiah's state of mind, for instance, was more powerful than all the miles between here and Silverton, between here and London. Isaiah's state of mind, impinging on his own, putting him on his honour and firing his pride, was the only thing that kept him apart from Gillian. Without it, he thought, it would not have taken him long to fetch her home. How many hours to Silverton, with his old stick for company and a song in his heart ? And then ? Well, then he would have her ambition to fight, the longing for the world ; " and she hankers after them things summat cruel," he thought. Still, there are surprises in love, raptures, agonies, that can wash away ambition like a shell on the shore. If not one wave, then another, the tenth wave, maybe. If not—then another ten. In time, the most landlocked shell must go. But there was always Isaiah. There was Gillian's money. There was the opprobrious word—cowman-shepherd.

He turned westwards again. It was the renunciation of fact for dream, and of life for poetry. He would set

his whole mind on the mastering of this strange thing—
poetry—this creature so unlike the creatures he had
hitherto mastered and tended—this unbiddable creature,
mysterious, white, wonderful, the fallow-deer of God. He
thought of a fallow-deer, because there was a carving of
deer on the high mantelpiece in the " Drover's Arms " at
Weeping Cross. So, like the young huntsman in the old
legend, he set forth to follow the pale enchanted creature
through the whispering forest of life forever.

CHAPTER X

THE BURNING HEART

TREWERN Coed was a typical border village, not quite sure of its nationality, mingled in speech, divided between the white, blue-roofed cottages of Wales, and the red thatched ones of Shropshire. It lay in a hollow of the hills that were round it like a green-clad arm, and a broad shallow river washed its gardens. From far away Robert descried the forge cottage with its shed, and as he came up the road he heard the sharp sound of the hammer and saw the sudden tempest of sparks within when Gruffydd laid a heavy hand on the bellows. A tall man stood in the open doorway of the forge ; Robert's eyes dwelt on him for a moment, and left him. He was not Gruffydd. He wore a fine greatcoat, smart leggings, and boots cleaned with blacking instead of dubbin. Some gentleman. Certainly not Gruffydd, the wild, the rough, Gruffydd who, when he played on his harp looked, it was said, like an otter tearing the heart of a victim. In the red-lit shadows Robert saw the cause of the stranger's presence—a big chestnut cob that had cast a shoe. He looked round liquidly at Robert, knowing him to be a friend.

" 'Noon," said the stranger.

" Evenin'," said Robert, for any time after twelve is called evening in Shropshire.

" Why, lad," cried Gruffydd in his musical, roaring voice, which, seemed, when he sang, to send out spark-storms of melody at the will of the mighty bellows in his chest,

" why, thee's the mon from Gwlfas, inna ye—as wrote me a letter and wanted me to learn ye in the music ? "

" Ah, I be, sir," said Robert.

The two large, rough-hewn personalities looked at each other, were aware of each other. The man in the doorway watched them.

" It's the pennillion, inna-d-it, the little pennillion as goes well to the strings ? "

" Ah."

" But you must sing 'em in the Welsh whatever, and I mind you said you have no Welsh, lad ? "

" No. But I shanna sing 'em to a harp. I canna play it."

" Oh, the little pennillion is married to the harp," cried Gruffydd. " What for would you separate 'em ? "

" I shall only sing 'em a bit to myself, like, going to and agen on the farm. And maybe when I'm old I'll write 'em in a book."

" Twenty mile to come. Twenty mile to go," murmured Gruffydd, " to sit in the smithy cottage and learn a pennillion. But he dunna want to play it, an' he dunna want to sing it. What woman's brought this upon you, lad ? I see well as it's the easement of the making of pennillions that you clem for. Hark ye :

> *Out of the white ash seven little blue flames ;*
> *Not so terrible is the heat.*
> *Out of my burning heart seven pennillions ;*
> *And my heart is eased."*

Robert flushed. The stranger laughed awkwardly, as if expostulating at emotion. But Gruffydd took no notice of him. Throughout the interview he treated him simply as the cob's attendant, and not at all as a personality. To ease his shyness, Robert turned to the stranger and said :

" Far to go ? "

" A good step. Nice bit of grazing country hereabouts."

" Ah."

" Cheap ? "

" Pretty fair. In some of the lost and forgotten places it's nigh to be got for the asking."

" Silverton's a good way off, I suppose ? "

" A tidy step. It's a good way from our place, and we're twenty mile from this."

" What place 'ud that be ? "

" Dysgwlfas."

" Dysgwlfas. I've heard the name somewhere. Why, surely, that's where Lovekin, the sheep-farmer, lives ? "

" Ah, that's my master."

" Good land there ? "

" Ah, and cheap."

" Thought so. Trust owd Lovekin to find a comfortable place and stick to it. Never saw the marrow of Lovekin's sheep for quality."

" Dealer yourself ? " queried Gruffydd from beneath the cob, as he blacked over the newly shod hoof.

" Ah, I do a bit in that line."

" Live or dead stock ? " asked Robert.

" Live. Buy to sell agen. Do a bit of farming as well."

" Come far ? "

" Dolgelly way."

" Good pasture ? "

" No fault to find with the pasture. Markets very middling."

" No rails nigh to your place ? "

" No."

" That's one thing Maister's allus pleased about," said Robert,—" being so nigh the Junction."

For the life of him he could not keep down the flush and smile that the name conjured ; and Gruffydd, leading out the cob, smiled into his beard and observed to his recording memory, that the young chap from Gwlfas had a girl at the Junction.

" I've a good mind," said the stranger as he flung himself into the saddle with supple ease, " to pack my traps and come over the border to your place—it grows good sheep."

" And what ud the missus say, losing her folks the like

of that ? " asked Gruffydd, blowing up the fire to finish his interrupted work.

The stranger, half round in the saddle, faced the light of the forge fire. In his eyes, sparkled with dull red, there rose for a moment a curious look, not exactly shy, not exactly sullen, not quite brutal. It tenanted his face for a moment, then the harsh lines round his mouth slipped into a smile, and the look was gone.

" Missus ? I know better than to take a missus," he said. " A housekeeper's my choice, all the time—a working housekeeper, not the aunty-praunty, change-of-an-afternoon sort, and ' The Last Rose of Summer ' on the piano. Someone as can keep at it ! "

Gruffydd chuckled.

" Do they give you warning pretty frequent ? " he asked.

" No. The one I've got I've had for five years, and I don't expect any change."

" Well, you're a wunnerful man, indeed," said Gruffydd, with the caressing gentleness that always preceded his most scarifying remarks. " A wunnerful man you be. Any children ? "

" No."

" Ah, you'll wear the name out, no danger ; but it's fine for you, Mr. What's-your-name, not to be werrited wi' brats. You met be obleeged to part with a penny a day to keep 'em—oh, dear me ! "

The stranger's face was dark red with anger, but not a word did he say.

Robert was sorry for him, and remarked, as he chewed a bit of wheat out of his pocket :

" If ever you come our way, I'm sure mother'll be pleased to give you a glass of homebrewed, mister."

" Thank ye kindly," said the stranger. " It's a good country. No houses though, I doubt ? "

" Well, dang me," said Robert, " if that inna rum. To-morrow as ever is they be taking poor Mrs. Thatcher to the churchyard, and the ' Mermaid's Rest ' 'll be to set."

" 'Mermaid's Rest?' Why, surely, that's the old public off the road from Weeping Cross to Mallard's Keep? "

" Ah."

" I was past there once, I mind it well. I got a quart there. Queer, seafaring sort of a sign. Don't they call it the ' Naked Maiden ' ? "

" Ah."

" That's the inn for the fellows, no danger."

" Oh, there's few as passes."

" I could bant them a bit in the price, could I ? "

" The rent, like ? "

" No, I don't rent, I buy."

" You'd get it for a song," said Robert.

" Thank you kindly. I'll bait there to-night if they'll take me in."

" And glad to, I reckon, if you dunna mind a corpse in the house."

The dealer laughed.

" Corpse ? No. Dead sheep don't blaat. Can I come along with you when you go ? "

He liked Robert; why, he could not tell. Perhaps it was a certain simplicity, that gave an impression—not at all a true one—of gullibility and workableness. Perhaps it was the same thing that made the cob nuzzle against his coat. Whatever it was, he liked Robert much better than Robert liked him.

" I shanna be coming back till well on to night," said Robert. " Wouldna you sooner get on ? The weather 'll break afore midnight, likely."

" No, I'll wait. I mislike trapesing over the miles without a soul to speak to. I'll wait at the public."

" A'right."

" My name's Elmer—Ralph Elmer."

" Mine's Robert Rideout."

Said Gruffydd afterwards, as he fetched his harp from the corner of his kitchen, where it stood reverently shrouded :

" Cag-mag. That's what he deals in. That's what he is. Cag-mag."

Robert, with the consciousness of facing slumbering power that comes to even less sensitive people than he in the presence of a great personality, accepted and recorded the remark, and then as the first notes sounded and the great voice of Gruffydd filled the cottage with masculine sweetness—stern, gracious, irresistible—he forgot all about it.

Not until their talk was over, and the illustrations to the talk, twanged out with a sweet monotony in the fire-lit dusk, had fallen silent, did Robert have a thought to spare for anything in heaven or earth. Then Gruffydd's wife came in, stealing softly from kitchen to parlour, where the fire was lit in honour of Saturday afternoon and Robert, with the tray of blue willow china and the big brown loaf, and the skep-shaped brown earthenware honey-jar—and he remembered the time.

" You mun sup," said Gruffydd, " for if there's one thing the music and the little pennillions do for me it's to give me a bellyache of emptiness. I mun eat after I've sung. It stands to reason in bird and man."

So Mrs. Conwy poured out the good strong tea and the liberal cream, and cut bread and butter, and looked softly on the two men—motherly at Robert, wifely at Gruffydd—and spoke a little, but not too much, for she had the gifts of sympathy and of silence. And it was not till the quiet of the countryside was deepened by layer on layer of night, and the rolling fields and the moor were silvered by moonlight, and the owls were questing, that Robert drew the back of his hand across his mouth and rose with :

" Thank you for me, Mr. and Mrs. Conwy."

" Come agen, lad, come agen," cried Gruffydd, with the ready kindliness of the artist.

At the inn by the ford, with the reins over his arm, stood Elmer, in the countryman's attitude of tireless patience.

" Ride and tie, shall we ? " he said, pointing to the saddle.

" Thank you kindly, I'm sure."

" You have first go."

He watched narrowly while Robert swung into the saddle, and his manner became more cordial.

" You're used to riding," he said.

" Ah, time and agen."

" You look to me as if you'd learnt to ride bareback."

" That's gospel," said Robert.

" What for ? "

" Well," said Robert, with a chary smile, " there was a wench, and she thought as a fellow was no good if he couldna ride the worst horseflesh bareback."

" So you did it ? "

" Ah."

" What did she say ?   Gave you what you wanted, eh ? "

" She said nowt, for she knew nowt. And I didna want nowt."

Elmer roared.

" Not much give an' take in these parts," he remarked. " Does she live hereabouts."

" No."

" Where then ? "

" I take no account of her doings nor her place of residence," said Robert loftily. " If you dunna mind, I'll canter on a bit and come back. The cob's a bit fresh."

He was away into the silver country, which looked as if the light had congealed upon it in great lumps and ingots. Elmer mused as he walked on alone. It was a good country, better than the mountain-folded hamlet of which his holding was a lost outpost. His home life, too, would bear mending, though no power on earth would have made him say so. This fellow with the pleasant smile, it would be companionable to have him in for the evening, especially when Rwth was in one of her sullen moods. He would have red curtains in the bar parlour, and plenty of brass and pewter (what was Rwth for if not to clean it ?) and some good whiskey. Sometimes, he would ask old Lovekin, and pick his brains, and sometimes Rideout and he would have a randy and a good laugh. Rideout looked as if he could laugh, for all his grave innocence of bearing ; he—Ralph—would try some of his bawdy stories on him. And there was always the enormous jest of living at the sign of the Naked Maiden. It was a good centre too. He could reach more of the big fairs and auctions on his cob than he could now, and he could go to the Junction for very distant ones.

He began to whistle between his teeth, not loudly, like a bird, as Robert did. He sped on with the lissom, elastic grace, a little like the grace of a weasel, that marked all his movements. Now and then he switched his brown gaiters and his breeches of Bedford cord with his riding whip (refused by Robert) and there was something in the way he did this that conjured up a vision of a far away Rwth, savage, sullen and tearful, suffering instead of the leggings. If an owl swooped low over a hedge, or a bat squeaked close by, Ralph's pointed ears seemed to prick slightly, his keen, pale eyes, which had nothing liquid about them, but were hard, like pebbles, were focussed shrewdly on the intruder and then impatiently withdrawn.

Robert came galloping back.

" Your turn now, mister," he said.

" You can say Elmer, if you've a mind," said the other, and behind his harsh manner was the wistfulness of the wilfully lonely soul, of the selfish soul which will not trust itself in the deep seas of humanity, and is left high and dry on the gritty shore, and is sometimes afraid. " Or Ralph," he added, to his own surprise.

" Bob for me, then, but if you'm going to be a friend of the gaffer's, I dunna see as we can call each other the like of thatn. It ud mortify the owd mon."

" We'll say nought when he's there, then. Old folks are bad to cross. But when we're alone, my lad, I'll learn you a thing or two, see if I don't. Maybe we'll get a piano at the ' Naked Wench ' and get some girls in."

He slapped Robert on the back, and took his turn in the saddle. Robert, walking stolidly on, hoped that Gillian would stay in Silverton a long time. He had not hoped this before. Now he did, intensely. The sparks that came into Elmer's cold eyes at the mention of the randy, would flash into Gillian's in a second, and ignite God knows what fire in her wild heart.

" Lord only knows what'll come to pass if they meet," he thought. " I wish I'd kept a still tongue. Send him a stiff price as he canna pay." And half consciously, as he walked with his ungraceful ploughman's gait over the aromatic crushed bracken, his left hand crept beneath his Sunday sleeve, beneath his coarse blue and white shirt, to the muscle that came and went obediently, hard and full as a cricket ball, between his heavy shoulder and his mahogany coloured elbow.

So, turn and turn about, they traversed the twenty miles very quickly. When they came to the top of the slope leading down to the Mermaid's Rest, Robert was riding, and Elmer saw him outlined on the pale sky, not graceful, but broodingly strong. Below him, the inn with its huddled roofs, its bright, pale-green square of winter cabbage and dark blur of orchard, its small windows gleaming forlornly, its whole air proclaiming that within it held not a revelry, not a bridal chamber, not a new born child, but corruption. Dimly aware of discomfort of soul, Ralph turned to the surrounding country, and his gaze travelled over it. There, lower than the inn, one field away from the browny-white ribbon of road, lay the unket place—a long inky smudge with a long silver streak of water below. He stiffened a little, like a dog at a new scent, pricked his ears slightly, stared. And out of nowhere, like the faint lament of a sheep from cloudy heights, came the knowledge that this place was prepared for him, had always been waiting for him, quietly and unobtrusively, and would not let him go until what must be had been accomplished.

Weirdly, alarmedly, he turned his eyes upwards to Robert's moonlit face. Robert was looking at it, too. No sound came from the vast, surrounding country, the mysterious sky, the death-enfolding homestead. Even the two men, so alive, so real, with the bright blood in their cheeks and the sweat of their galloping still in their armpits, even they held their breath, staring into one another's souls, but seeing only the unket place. Then suddenly, as if at the releasing of a spring, Elmer withdrew his eyes, unpricked his ears, loosened his taut muscles, laughed with a curious forced dismalness, and said :

" Who's for the ' Naked Wench ' and a measure of whiskey ? "

All was dark at the inn.

" Tabor on the door," said Robert.

Ralph knocked, and hollow sounds ran down the passages. Then a wild head appeared at an upstairs window, and Thatcher said :

" Who be that, drumming on door ? "

" Me," said Robert. " Here's a chap wants a shake-down and a mug of beer or summat, and he dunna mind payin' for what he wants. And seein' the expense you've been under, I thought you wouldna mind."

" You're kindly welcome, sir," said Thatcher, " and if you inna afraid of my poor missus 'ere, you can take pot luck, and I'll give you my bed—for that's all we've got, saving the little uns' bed. Rideout here knows as the sticks of furniture's gone bit by bit, for times be bad."

" Where's the body, then ? " asked Robert.

" On the palliasse on the table in the parlour," said Thatcher. " It wouldna do to have her upstairs wi' the little uns about. Yo can see her if yo've a mind."

Robert, with country courtesy, accepted. They went into the parlour, up three crazy oak stairs from the flagged kitchen. On the table, covered with a sheet, lay the stone-still figure. In her folded hands Thatcher had put a bit of silver honesty. " For an honest woman she was, and a tidy," said he with a heavy sigh. " And it's bad to be left with a two year child, and nobody to do so much as a bit o' washing."

" Ah."

" I mun find another, I reckon, but I shanna better poor Minnie. When your time comes to choose, Bob, take care you dunna go for a gallus eye and a flaming cheek and a white bosom. Watch 'er, my lad. Watch 'er for a tuthree week, a tuthree month. See 'er on a

Monday at the wash-tub. See 'er with a chyild. Harken at 'er chaffering at market. Drum 'er up early in the morning and see if she flies into a tantrum. If she does— go wi'out 'er."

Robert, standing beside the shrouded figure of the perfect wife, saw, conjured by love in the close, death-scented place, Gillian the desired, the radiant : Gillian, whose cheek flamed, whose eye was gallus, whose bosom —ah ! he must not think of that—Gillian who would have failed in every one of those examinations.

" I'll get Mr. Elmer's supper for you, if you've a mind," he said eagerly, " and I wish there was more I could do. You needna bant the price," he added, " he can pay for what he wants."

Elmer was smoking by the dying fire, sitting in a corner of the settle. Robert brought in an armful of chips, and the fire roared in the wide chimney ; then he helped Thatcher to make a bed for himself on the floor upstairs ; he opened the huge cupboard of black oak that filled a recess in the kitchen, and brought out a rough repast. Elmer was not dainty. He tossed off glass after glass of the weak whiskey, looking round the room with an appraising eye, noting the pewter measures on the dresser, the bread-oven built of brick, in a corner, the built-in cupboards, the soot-encrusted, solid beams.

" It'll weather a tuthree storms before it's done," he observed, removing his pipe and spitting into the fire.

" Ah, it wunna built for a day."

" Who baits here mostly ? "

" There's a tuthree come by to fairs and market, and there's a minister comes by of a Sunday, and gets his dinner, and there's two farms over yonder where the chaps come from, evenings, and stepfeyther and me come, and now and agen a waggoner lugging lime or summat from the Keep, and gipsies and a pedlar or two, and a carrier, Fridays. That's all as I mind."

" But in the old days it must ha' bin a prospering place ? "

" Oh, ah ! Folk all travelled by road then, and it was

twenty mile from any dwelling, saving our farm. There was a mort of folks came by then—the coach tuthree days a week, and carriers and run-away couples and dear-knows-what. Highwaymen, they seyn, too. Larders and cellars was kept full then. And our maister's grandfeyther was used to say it was a sight to see on a frosty night, when the landlord and the maids and men turned out for the coach. They'd hear the horn whining acrost the moor, and the coach ud come spanking up, and then there'd be a to-do. They'd all got to be thawed and fed."

" Good money flying about then, I bet," said Elmer. " But I've a mind to see if I can't beat up a bit of business, though them days are gone. Rwth can be barmaid, and Fringal can see to things when I'm away."

" Who be they ? "

" Rwth's my housekeeper. Fringal's my man."

" There'd be three of you to keep the ghosses out, then."

" Ah."

" And when you wed——"

" I shan't."

Again the peculiar look of the afternoon was in his eyes.

" I thought maybe you'd got your eye on someone," said Robert, wistfully. If only Elmer would marry, he need not be so afraid for Gillian.

" I've no mind for a wife. Argling and bargling : this not to her pleasure, that not to her mind. Rights of bed and board : grumbling if there's no brat, grumbling if there's too many. You're not your own man if you've got a wife, Rideout."

With a suppressed, agonizing power, a great flood of longing rose up in Robert's heart—longing for that very argling and bargling, that grumbling, those divine rights of bed and board. Again, very delicate and vivid, Gillian stood before him—flushed, as she was in her tantrums. Oh, God ! to hear her grumbling—grumbling at not having any children !

He dashed the bottle down on the table by Elmer. " Here ! help yerself," he cried. " I'm off."

As he strode through the meditative night, he felt sick

with passion, frantic with longing, with tenderness. And
with the acute intuition of the poet he saw that Gillian
would assuredly come back; that she would meet Elmer;
that Elmer's philosophy of self would go down before the
passion she would arouse; that maybe she would be his.

When he came to that, Robert stood still in the middle
of the moor. A faintness and weakness melted his heart,
his limbs. He trembled like an animal that has seen a
spirit.

"Oh, Lord," he whispered huskily, "it's coming. I
can see it, I can hear it. Blackness of darkness! And
I fetched the chap here, fool that I be."

The farm and the cottage, the huddled ricks, the great
crossed and twisted boughs of the orchard, riddled with
moonlight, slept. The black-purple moat of shadow
slept beneath. Only the white owl went her soundless
way, like a pale spirit of evil, incandescent with phantasmal
sin.

CHAPTER XI

ISAIAH ASKS A QUESTION

LONG before daylight, Robert lit his candle and wrote a letter to Gillian.

" MISS GILLIAN,
    " I wish to acquaint you as poor Mrs. Thatcher's gone, thinking you met like to send a wreath or summat for the grave. All very quiet and lonesome here. Nobody comes by in a week of Sundays. Mother heard tell at market as the May Fair at Silverton was to be summat odd this year.
    " With respects, and I keep the picture on the mantel shelf.
                                        " ROBT. RIDEOUT."

With a slightly grim, slightly gratified smile, Robert addressed the letter in his firm handwriting, that recalled stiles and five-barred gates and solid fencing, and put it in his pocket till the postman should come by on Monday. Downstairs Abigail was early about, for a Sunday funeral in which all were free to partake was something that did not happen every day. She was glad her black merino was so respectable. She had pinned it up under her apron. Jonathan's black coat was airing by the fire, and Jonathan himself, sleepy after a night in the lambing-hut, sat on the settle, persuading his crêpe hat-band to lie smoothly round his hat. Mrs. Thatcher would have been gratified if she had seen the stir that her funeral

was making—in lambing-time, too, the most absorbing
season of the year at the Gwlfas.

" That black-faced ewe's dropped three lambs," said
Jonathan as Robert came in, " and two mean dying."

It was obvious that he did not dream of opposing them.
If they meant to die, they would, for all Jonathan would do.

" Where be they ? "

" Along of the rest.　Her's in such a taking, her wouldna
let me shift 'em.　Where be going ? "

" To shift 'em."

He was gone.

" What a lad !　What a restless, never-to-be-plazed
lad !　Why dunna he leave 'em ?　They mean dying,
any road."

" Robert wunna let 'em die."

" Where'd the ship a' been yesterday if it hadna been for
me ?　What a lad !—Maundering off on lonesome in
lambing-time ! "

" Well, it inna often as the lad takes dog's leave, be it ? "

" It minds me of the tale of poor Joey Linny, poor
soul.　He was used to go wandering about, and onst he
come unbeknownst into a triple fairy-ring, and they got
'im.　Ah !　they seyn it were like that in times gone.
Folk burnt witches then, and ducked 'em and dear knows
what.　And things was different.　Any road, the fairies
cotched poor Joey Linny, and away-to-go.　But they
seyn as now and agen at thrashing-time, of an evening,
when it's a bit wild and wet, you'll see a white, peaky face
at the windy, with a bit of wispy hair flying in the wind,
and it cries :

Ninny, Ninny,
Poor Joey Linny !

That's what your Robert'll come to, mark my words."

Mrs. Makepeace laughed.

" I reckon they'll be after you first, Jonathan, my
dear," she said.　" They'd find our Bob too lungeous
for 'em."

When the breakfast things were washed up, dinner
put to simmer, the fire " douted," Jonathan arrayed,

and the safety-pin removed from Mrs. Makepeace's dress,
they set out. Robert, returning with the rescued lambs,
after seeing to the ewes, sat down to his late breakfast
in great content. He considered that his letter would keep
Gillian where she was till May ; that between now and
then a roving, devil-may-care fellow like Elmer, just come
to a new country, would surely pick up a sweetheart, and
all would be well. Whatever happened, Robert was quite
determined that Elmer should not marry Gillian. When
he had finished his jobs and put on his Sunday clothes, he
sat down to think over all that Gruffydd had told him about
the making of poetry. There was a knock, and Elmer
came in.

" Can't make anybody hear at the farm," he said.

" No. Maister's at the funeral."

" Aren't there any other folks ? "

" No."

" No missus ? "

" He's a widow."

" Any children ? "

" One."

" Girl ? "

" Ah."

" Where's she ? "

" Away."

" For good ? "

" Ah, I'm thinking it's for good."

" Well, if it's all the same to you, I'll wait till he comes."

" Ah. Bide and welcome."

They went round the farm, talking in a desultory way.
It became clear to Robert that Ralph intended to buy
the inn. He was going to see the owner to-morrow, on
his way home. To-day he wanted to see Isaiah to bespeak
some lambs.

They were in the sheep fields when they saw the gig far
off, like a bright, clockwork toy on the immensity of the
moor. They awaited it at the wicket.

" Ha ! " said Isaiah, and Elmer not only looked found
out, but flinched.

Isaiah had his measure.

His " Ha ! " had never failed him. It was a good
touchstone. As a woman says risky things to gauge
the men of her acquaintance, so Isaiah said " Ha ! "
Because Elmer had flinched, he had to pay more for the
lambs than they were really worth. If he had only looked
found out, he might have had them for about the correct
price. If he had been undisturbed, he would have got
them at a bargain. " The battle to the strong " was
Isaiah's motto. Still, he did not object to Elmer. He
reverenced his money. He had a vision, as he sat opposite
to his guest at dinner—served by Mrs. Makepeace—and
helped him as lavishly as he liked to help himself to thick
red slices of undercut, lumps of fat, and slabs of pudding,
of all Elmer's money being gently, quietly, but irrevocably
transferred from Elmer's bank to his.

He sat at the end of the table, mountainous behind the
mountainous beef, with the carving knife and fork in his
hands, and considered Elmer across the clean Sunday tablecloth with its severe appointments—two vegetable dishes,
two jugs of beer, bread, cheese, sauce and gravy, cruets.
Isaiah liked the necessities of life to be plain, plentiful
and permanent, and he cared for nothing else. Observing
Elmer's face, with that vague hint of underlying weakness
somewhere, he came to the conclusion that Elmer would
eventually become a necessity—if he turned out well.
He would, if he turned over money quickly, did up the
" Mermaid," owned a few horses and many sheep, make
a good match for Gillian. Particularly did Isaiah wish
this when the two or three weak lines showed through the
general hardness of his new friend's face. A pleasant,
harmless fellow, Isaiah judged him, with capacities for
dissoluteness checked for monetary reasons. A man who
would always go for the main chance, the paying thing.
A sensible man, and one that might with judicious
" Ha "-ing, be made quite biddable. Healthy, too. Isaiah
did not want Gillian's children to be sickly. It transpired
during the meal that Elmer's people lived somewhere in
the Midlands, and were very respectable and of good

standing. Lastly—the emotional reason always came last
with Isaiah—it would mean that Gillian would be near
him, only just across the moor. It was surprising what a
gap her departed laughter and footsteps had left in his
life—in spite of the fact that he was far more comfortable
with Mrs. Makepeace in calm and undivided control of his
digestion.

" You'll be lugging a sweet'art along of you out of Wales,
no danger ? " said Isaiah tentatively.

Ralph looked up with a startled expression.

" Oh, no," he said hurriedly. " I don't care for the
Welsh."

" And what for not ? " ·

" Too small, too stocky, too sallow."

" You favour size ? "

" I like a girl with a fresh face and a little waist—
a bit of colour about the place—and not too tall, nor yet
too little. But I never look at 'em. I'm not a marrying
man. Too expensive."

" Ha ! But if you did, it ud be one with a bit of colour
and a little waist."

Isaiah smiled upon Ralph. He had so exactly described
Gillian.

" Pudden ? " he said, and helped Elmer lavishly to
the honest, solid mass of raisins and suet, eggs, treacle
and flour, called " Sunday Pudding "—perhaps because
only in the vast leisure of Sunday could it have been
digested.

" I allus liked a trim waist and a fresh colour myself,"
mused Isaiah aloud. " My missus had 'em, and there
wasn't a tidier wench in the countryside when I took her
to church."

A faint illumination came into Elmer's eyes.

" I suppose your girl takes after her ? " he queried
politely.

" Ah."

" Pretty then ? "

" Middling pretty."

" But away ? "

" Away for a bit.   A tidy bit, I shouldn't wonder."

" But she'll come back ? "

" Ha ! "

Elmer jumped, and by jumping revealed to Isaiah the thoughts which the " Ha " seemed to have been pointing at.

Isaiah went on composedly with his dinner.

" She's with her aunties," he vouchsafed. " And there she'll stop for a while. Plenty of young fellows there, seemingly, as likes a slim waist and a fresh colour."

" Is she walking out with anybody ? "

" She knows better. She'll bide at home till her dad says ' walk out.' "

Elmer laughed softly. In the laugh was the secret glee of youth in its own freemasonry. This middle-aged man might be the best sheep breeder anywhere round, he might be a terror for making money, but with regard to his own daughter, Elmer judged him a fool. He'd soon see whether old Lovekin's daughter would bide at home if he—Ralph Elmer—said " walk out."

" But you're not a marrying man," said Isaiah slowly ; and Elmer blushed up to his hair at the implied discovery of his inmost thoughts.

Isaiah was pleased with him for blushing—it was a confession of his own power. And what a foil for Rideout ! Once those sparks were well lit in Elmer's eyes, Isaiah judged that most things—cowmen-shepherds included— would go down before his eagerness in attaining his desire.

" Well," he said, " we'll have our bit of a smoke and a nap now, and then I'll show you the lambs. . . . Can you ride well ? " he added carelessly.

" Ride ? I should hope so. I haven't met what I can't ride yet."

" Ha ! "

They established themselves by the fire with pipes and newspapers. After half an hour Isaiah looked up.

" If you take the lot," he said, " you can have the lambs for a shilling per head less than what I priced 'em at. And I priced 'em dirt cheap, God knows."

" Thank ye kindly," said Elmer ; and while Isaiah dozed, he smiled into the fire. The question about riding had revealed to him not only Robert's secret but Isaiah's. It was Lovekin's daughter who had inspired Robert to ride with daring. Robert then was in love with her. Isaiah was enquiring for someone else to ride into his daughter's heart. That is to say, Isaiah did not want a cowman for son-in-law. And the girl ? Evidently the girl's ideal was a fellow just like himself.

He smoothed his thin, jutting jaw, his sleek hair, his long, thin legs in their smart cord and leather, smiling a little with pleased vanity.

" Damn it ! " he thought, " I'd like to oblige 'em all, walk in and win the girl, waist and colour and bankbook and all—only——"

A dark, gloomy, harried expression suddenly swept over his complacent face, like a cloud distilled from wild black mountains sweeping its heavy shades over a prosperous dairy country.

CHAPTER XII

AT THE SIGN OF THE MAIDEN

" WELL, Mother," said Jonathan, coming in soused with rain one wild early morning at the end of February, " this be Febriwerry-fill-ditch and no mistake. A sight for ducks ! You'd best moble up afore you go to the house."

" Inna Mr. Elmer moving in to-day ? " asked Mrs. Makepeace, as Robert came in.

" Ah, dang it all. And it's me that's got to go and give a hand."

" Well, it's to be hoped that housekeeper of hisn's got a good stout coat on 'er back, and not the sort of Welsh gotherum as Miss Gillian favours," said Mrs. Makepeace, and her brown eyes softly observed Robert. " And, talking of Miss Gillian, Maister had a letter from her yesterday."

Robert was very busy doing up his leggings.

" She's been gallivanting on the river," continued his mother, " and some gentleman along of her, and—oh, no, Bob, she's not drownded."

" Engaged to be married ? " said Robert.

" You breathe that word ' married,' " said Jonathan, " as if it was one and the same as drownded. Yo mind me of the tale of Chamfrey Parrish—old Sir Chamfrey Parrish of Boltings End. 'E mun ha' bin a caution ! His daughter was to be wed, and they sent a sight of bidding letters and ordered the feast and the fine clo'es. But old Sir Chamfrey would have all the men's coats (they was poor relations, and he gi'd 'em their coats, like) lined with black. They was bottle-blue coats on top. And all the women's cloaks as he gi'd was rose-colour, but he made *them* be lined with black, too. And his daughter met cry, and the folks met look glum, but it was wear 'em or away-to-go. Well, Miss Matilda was ready and the bridesmaids was ready to follow 'er, and the chaps lined up in their bottle blue. And there come one running, and he says, ' The groom's shot isself with his feyther's blunderbus ! ' They was in a taking then, all but old Sir Chamfrey. And he says : ' Turn your coats ! ' 'e says. And they whispered a bit and fidgeted a bit, and somebody ups and says : ' But you couldna *know* he'd do it ? ' And Sir Chamfrey turns round very quiet-like and says : ' I knowed Matilda ! ' he says. Eh ! He must ha' bin a caution, must old Sir Chamfrey."

Mrs. Makepeace, who had been slowly persuading the oven door to shut without sound, now clapped it to with some relief. She never interrupted a story of Jonathan's ; she always laughed in the right places ; but a sorrow was in her heart for the man who had never told a tale in his life and would listen to the tales of others with a quiet, ironical slow smile.

" Engaged to be married, Mother ? " said Robert, like a man half-stifling in deep water.

" Neither engaged, nor like to be, my dear. But the poor gentleman took a chill, and he's very bad, and Miss Gillian blamed for it, seemingly, along of being so venturesome, 'ticing him on the water in cold weather."

" But, Lord love you, Mother, what a little nesh thing like Gillian can do, a great strong fellow can do, surely," said Robert.

" He inna strong, nor young, lad, and you'd best mind how you call her Gillian afore maister."

But Robert, whistling like a tree full of birds, had gone out into the driving rain.

With the rain slashing his face, and the wet heather thrashing against his legs, and a day's work for a man he did not like before him, he yet whistled every one of Gruffydd's tunes that he could remember. There was a

rift of rainy blue afar ; the voices of lambs were uplifted
with tremulous young eagerness, Spring was on her way
here, she only tarried a little in the mountains of the
South, and Gillian—Gillian—Gillian was *not* engaged to
be married.

Robert set his hands on the high fence between the
Gwlfas fields and the moor, and was over in a flash, because
Gillian was not betrothed. As he went he made a little
song :

> Spring's asleep over yonder
> In the mountains to the South,
> With a rose on her mouth,
> And Gillian's asleep in the East.
> There's ice on the pool, in the fold
> Man and beast wander,
> Starved wi' cold.
>
> Spring'll call us to mind
> And the wood lark'll sing
> Bits of green grass'll spring,
> There'll be yellow-gold on the gorse,
> Wheat pricking through the loam.
> But there's one'll be winter-blind
> Till Gillian's raught home.

When he had made it, he sang it, and the plovers, equally
intoxicated, answered him through the grey walls of rain
that stood up on either side of him like the walls of a glass
corridor.

There was no sign of Elmer or his belongings, only the
wreckage of the Thatchers' move, bits of straw and paper,
broken glass and boxes, dead plants in pots, and forlorn
stalks of cotton grass that grew along the fence. Robert
had the key, which Elmer had left with him. He went in,
gathered up the rubbish from the kitchen floor, and made
a fire. He was very handy.

" Now," he said, " when they come it wunna take two
shakes to open a box o' china and get 'em a cup o' tea.
That poor wench'll be starved with cold if she's anywhere
near as nesh as Gillian. If Gillian was—if *I'd* the say in
what she wore, I'd buy her a great thick pilot coat like
Mr. Mooney's uncle's at Weeping Cross when he come
back from the sea. Ah ! I'd lap her up in that, and a

tuthree rugs and——" he stretched out his arms—" and these," he said. "Dear-a-me, where did I put them matches?"

Silence in the old hostel. Only the whistling of the windlestraws, the distant gnawing of a rat. (And what is more desolate than the daylight gnawing of rats and mice ?) The windows, washed with water, were like the windows of an under-ocean castle, with the grey swell of the heavy, stirless sea threatening to cave them in.

Robert fetched the well-pail full of water, and a discarded broom, and sluiced the kitchen flags. Then he sat down before the fire on a sugar-box to smoke and wait. At last there came a faint sound, a slight disturbance of the apparently permanent silence and loneliness. It grew, resolved itself into a thudding, a rattling, but no voices. A dour homecoming, with no voices, no laughter, no pleasant give-and-take nor merriment nor cajolery !

" Well ! " thought Robert, " they're very mum. Still on, it be only the feller's housekeeper and the odd man. It inna a bride as comes whome."

The sound resolved itself into a blur of darkness, two pricked ears, breathing, steam, and Elmer's voice :

" That you, Rideout ? "

" Ah."

" We're as late as bitter apples," said Elmer. " We've had the devil's own luck, and the waggons got stuck a mile back in that bit o' slough at the brook head. But they're coming along now. This " (with a sideways nod) " is Rwth. She's dumb."

" Dumb ! "

" Ah. She's a foundling—a dumb foundling. I gave her a job out of pity. She's a pelrollicky creature, and feckless. But I keep her. She'd be on the roads else."

" On the roads else," repeated Robert, stupidly. And still he stared and stared at the woman in the gig. Still he felt, as he put it, that his heart had turned to water.

Dumb ! And of so great a lostness in the enormous world ! No people. No voice. No love. No anything. And there she sat, with the atmosphere of lostness so thick about her that it was almost impossible to speak

to her. As soon shout " Ahoy ! " to a lightless boat, as
Mr. Mooney's uncle had once done—shout " Ahoy ! "
to a boat full of silence and see it (as Mr. Mooney's uncle
swore he had done) silently manned with ghosts. In the
vast nonentity that this woman inhabited, what was a word ?

The windlestraws bent to the rain, the heather sighed
beneath it. Still Robert looked at the woman whose
abode was silence. What was it ? She was, as Elmer
said, feckless. She was pelrollicky. Her dark, wispy
hair hung about her face forlornly. But her face ! Carved
in some fiercer mould than the faces he knew, carved out
of dark, riven granite, tortured, grim and wild—yet
somehow beautiful. And her eyes ! Yes ! There lay
the secret. It was in her eyes. Black ; not velvet-black,
but that rarer thing, clear lucent black, like moonlit
ebony water in a mill-race. Clear black, with the pupils
like velvet, lashed heavily with coarse lashes, thickly and
heavily browed, and much too large for her colourless face.
Such was the savage, the anguished savage, who went by
the commonplace title of Elmer's housekeeper, and who
now prepared, at the sharp word " Down ! " (uttered as
if to a dog) to climb out of the trap and begin her duties.
Robert half lifted her out. She was very small, shorter
than Gillian and much thinner, for though Gillian was
lissom, she was plump.

She looked at Robert as he lifted her down, and some
indecipherable message went up from the great black eyes
to the kind grey ones. Then she turned and went into
the silent house.

" This is Fringal," said Elmer, with another sideways nod.

Fringal from the back of the trap, where he appeared to
be clinging like a monkey, looked up from the boxes and
hampers he was unearthing, and nodded slightly, with the
spryness of a wagtail. He was rosy, shrivelled, gay and
toothless, but the gaiety never went beyond a certain
limit. He was like a park where the wanderer is continually
met by signposts saying : " *No Road*," and " *Trespassers
will be Prosecuted*," so that he soon learns that the park
he is free to explore is very small.

" He's the old man of the mountains," said Elmer.

" Welsh ? " queried Robert of Fringal.

Fringal doubled-up with laughter, quite silently.

" No. He isn't Welsh," said Elmer. " I don't know what he is. He laughs if you call him Welsh. Rwth's Welsh. She makes him laugh."

Robert silently thought that Fringal was more laughable than Rwth, who was fitter for tears than mirth. But he did not find either Elmer, unloading his most cherished possessions before his new house, nor Rwth, nor even Fringal amusing. To think of the three of them shut up in the dreary house for the night positively made his flesh creep.

" Is there any crockery there ? " he asked. " Tea-things and that ? "

" Whatever for ? "

" I'll make her a cup o' tea," said Robert, with the slight surliness he could not keep out of his voice when speaking to Elmer.

" Let her make you one, more like," replied Elmer. " She's *working* housekeeper."

" No danger ! "

Robert's irony was lost on Elmer, who was unloading boxes for Fringal to carry indoors.

Robert went in.

She was kneeling before the largest box, fiercely yet controlledly wrestling with the strong cord. She had taken off her cloak, which Mrs. Makepeace would certainly have called Welsh-gotherum, and her thin shoulders stood out beneath her colourless print gown.

" Here ! " said Robert, " loose me do it for yer. Yer arms are no but sticks, child."

She relinquished the cord, gazing at his hands, master-fully at work. She knelt back, her coarse small hands clasped, her anomalous hat dripping water on to her shoulders, and slowly lifted her eyes from his hands to his face. He had opened the box.

" Well ! Here bin the very thing I was alooking for— now we'm got a bit o' crockery we've come whome proper, lass ! " Robert spoke lightly to hide the almost un-

bearable desire to weep that this creature brought. He
had never felt like that before—never so much like that.
The dreadful grip of Pity, more clinging, more lasting than
the grip of Terror ; the immense, wild pity that drove
Christ to Calvary and has driven men mad, was upon
Robert Rideout as it had not been ever in fold nor lambing
shed. He had felt it there. He had felt it through
all the dark, bitter things that are beneath the pleasant
life of farms as they are beneath the pleasant life of the
world. But he had not seen anything like this woman
before. She had, as it were, rolled up into herself the
endless, silent agony of dumb creatures. Their dumbness,
too, was hers. Only she could reason. As Robert said
to himself : " She can put two and two together. She
knows to things. She inna kimet. There be the trouble."

And as he unpacked cups and saucers, he muttered :

" Not enow of words, it's jeath, that is, a burning
sorrow and not enow o' words."

All the while these dark, lustrous eyes were upon him.

" Where be kettle ? " he enquired. " Fetch un, oot,
child ? "

She obediently rose and went out into the rain to fetch
the kettle from the trap.

" Now, take your hat off, for it's like nought but a bit
of clogged troughing," said Robert, " and then you go and
put these cups under pump, oot, to get straw off 'em."

Impassively she did all he told her. Her obedience
seemed to him to be like the obedience of a well-beaten
dog. His attempt at jollity rather failed before it.

" Theer ! " he said, " now we'll lay tea, and you can
sit there by the table and pour out for us."

She sat down in the place indicated. Her heavy, stolid,
rather dazed expression did not alter. She did not attempt
to warm her blue hands at the fire. He noticed that her
teeth were chattering. Yet she sat, erect and constrained,
exactly where he had said. It was unbearable. There
was a smarting at the back of his eyes. He was not used
to pain like this. In his mother's cheerful house pity
could not clutch you, though she might have drawn near

without. But here ! Here the water washed the windows, and twilight brooded through these morning hours, and the sad grasses sighed outside the door, and out of the dusk beyond the fire there looked upon him from the eyes of a woman the soul of the creation that groaneth and travaileth in pain—the soul of the crucified.

He got up, knocking over the box he was sitting on, and went to her.

" Hark ye ! " he said. " Dunna do what I tell ye, nor go where I tell ye, for the dear Lord's sake ! Dunna shiver when I come anigh you ! Why, you're starved wi' cold—and I dunna wonder with them cloes. Here, lemme rub your 'ands."

He rubbed them so hard that it must have hurt her. Gillian would have cried out. Not so this creature. She watched wonderingly as his large hands went quickly up and down hers, and when he had finished and stood up asking, " Thawed a bit ? " she lifted her eyes to his with a new expression in them. He knew the expression. It was trust, faith. It was more than he guessed—for it was the beginning of adoration. As he stood there, anxious, benevolent and harrowed, with those dwelling eyes upon his face, he noticed a change beginning at the corners of her mouth. And suddenly, timidly, radiantly, she smiled.

He turned to the door.

" Whenever be you coming for your tea ? " he asked with some irritation. " It's cooling while you wait."

" Coming—coming——" called Ralph from the barn, whence came expostulatory cacklings of released poultry, and whence came also Fringal, in a silent paroxysm of laughter.

Elmer came in.

" Well, Rideout, you've made it into a reg'lar home, sweet home," he observed. " Whiskey ? "

" No. Give it her."

" She dunna drink whisky. Workus brats ! Lord, where'd the country be ? Taxes ! "

Fringal was convulsed at these economics.

" Give it her," commanded Robert, and he reached his hand for the bottle.

Elmer withheld it.

" Well, if you wunna, you wunna," said Robert. " All the better for me. It's whome for Bob Rideout and his own work by his lonesome for Mr. Elmer."

Elmer stared a moment ; laughed ; realized that Robert meant it, and relinquished the bottle.

Robert poured some out, added hot water and gave it to Rwth.

" Don't you drink it ! " commanded Elmer. " I want it, and Fringal here wants it, and it'll scald your innards."

" Oh, my dear sores ! " exclaimed Fringal, his face seamed with mirth, " it's very temptuous ! I could fancy a taste indeed, for it's soggin' wet."

" Give it Fringal ! " said Elmer. " If you get fond of the bottle, my girl, who's to tend the bar ? "

" Drink it," said Robert composedly.

She drank it, coughing, and Fringal was again convulsed. Then she gave the cup back to Robert, and once more she smiled. Elmer's mouth was a thin, hard line. Robert handed him back the bottle.

" Theer ! " he said. " Pity's served, so you can take the rest."

" Much obliged, I'm sure, for my own whiskey."

" Your own ? " queried Robert. " What's your own ? I mislike the sound of it."

" That's because you've *got* naught of your own," said Elmer. " What's my own, you say ? Why, this inn and those waggons coming along, and this whiskey and the sheep in the meadow——"

" And this girl ? "

" Why, yes—who's else's is she ? "

" Anybody 'ud a'most think," said Robert slowly, with his eyes steady on Elmer, " as you was married to her."

Elmer's eyes narrowed, as if to hide their expression, and suddenly Fringal's jaw dropped slightly.

The black eyes in the dusk of the corner seemed to hold the three men as in a mirror.

Then Elmer laughed uproariously.

" What, married to that ? " he cried.   " To that Moll-Mawkin ? "

But all day as they worked, Robert saw those narrowed eyes and the stubbly dropped jaw of Fringal, and heard the silence lapping about them in those moments of tension.

" Mr. Elmer ! Mr. Elmer ! " cried a hoarse, lost voice from the storm, " be this Mr. Elmer's at the sign o' the ' Mermaid ? ' "

A heavy rumbling drew near ; stopped ; seemed as if it had never been.   It was as if the wheels had come to the inn at the world's end and would never need to go any further.   Two waggoners, clad in mud-spattered corduroys with sacks over all, stood at the door.

" Well, you've lugged it out at last then," said Elmer, " heavy going, ain't it ? "

" Ah ! heavy going and heavy weather."

The waggoners looked mistrustfully at the black-windowed house, so eerie and lone on the savage moor.

" Bin a death here ? " asked one.

" Well, yes."

" I thought as much."

" Any place 'ud look poor-favoured in this weather," said Elmer.   " And there's no inn but knows death one time or another."

" Ah ! I dur' say.   But we mun be shifting things.   We mun be getting along."

They intended to be far away before nightfall.   The place began to look kinder when some of Elmer's furniture was in.   It was commonplace, but good, and it seemed sufficiently self-complacent to stare down a ghost.

" Mr. Elmer ! Mr. Elmer ! " came a second lost voice, and two more waggoners, also clad in sacks and corduroys, appeared.

The seven men, with shuffling and deep breathing, carried in the heavy things, and Rwth unpacked boxes and swept up the mud and straw.   The horses, with tarpaulin over their steaming flanks, munched hay, standing in the downpour of water as if they were really the dark enchanted steeds of naïads in the land under the lily roots.

The sign of the Mermaid swung and creaked in the rising wind. Smoke bellied from the chimneys. The house took on an air of habitation. But Robert, looking at it with disfavour, remembered a song of Gruffydd's about an inn at the world's end.

" Ah ! that's it," he thought. " The inn at the world's end. That's what it's like. I never seed it till now."

As he drove in the staples that were to uphold the polished cupboard in the parlour, he felt somehow as if he were driving nails into a coffin.

And out of the tumult of rain and rising wind, came a third lost voice : " Landlord ! Landlord ! Be this the inn o' the Naked Maiden ? "

It was a gipsy runner, lean, breathless, drenched.

" I mun speak with Robert Rideout," he said.

Robert came to the door.

" Darst ye come out in the rain ? " said the runner. " I munna mouth it afore folk."

Robert led the way to the barn.

" I'm from Johnson," said the man. " I'm to tell you Gentle's dead, and Emily's mad, and Gillian's off to Lon'on, and you're to come."

Robert felt that he was in no danger of stagnation.

" To-night ? " he said.

" No. Johnson 'e says to-morrowday. Her's wrote to her dad for money. It'll come to-morrow. To-morrow's the funeral. Whilst they're at the funeral her'll take the express."

" What time's the funeral ? "

" Noon."

" Tell Johnson I'll be at his caravan at sun-up to-morrow. And now take bit and sup, and I'll stand the reckoning."

They went in. And stranger than ever now seemed the kitchen, with its long shadows, its barrel of beer by the fire, the rugged waggoners, the lean gipsy, Elmer, the old man of the mountains, himself, and the silent, tragic figure serving them.

CHAPTER XIII

ROBERT SAYS "NO"

" OH, laws me, Bob, thee's as damp as a fish," said Jonathan, when Robert came in, " you mind me of the old rhyme."

" What was that, my dear? " said Mrs. Makepeace cheerfully, though she knew quite well.

> "' Soggin' wet:
> Where yo bin ? '
> ' I've bin a-souling
> In the Lost Land o' Lleyn.'

You mun know as the Land o' Lleyn was covered by the tide amany years ago, though you can hear the bells a-ringing. So them as goes theer singing for soul-cakes, if any such there be, canna look to be dry."

" Oh, well, I reckon I've been there then," said Robert.

" You'd best change, lad," said his mother.

" Ah." He turned at the stairfoot. " And I'd be glad of a bite and sup, Mother, for I'm taking the day off to-morrow, and I'm starting to-night. I'm off to the Keep after supper."

" Lord love ye ! dog's leave agen," said Jonathan. " What a lad ! "

" There, my dear, you leave un be," said Mrs. Makepeace. " He's werritting about summat. I wonder what ails un ? "

" It's young blood and the pride o' life ails un, I know. I was like it myself onst," said Jonathan daringly.

" Ah, I'm sure you were, my dear," soothed his wife.

"And mind what you're doing with that knife, or you'll cut yourself."

She would have liked to blunt all knives, razors, brummocks and brushing hooks before letting Jonathan touch them.

She bustled about, getting something hot for Robert, drawing beer, blacking his best boots. "Though dear knows, they'll be all of a muck in three strides," she said. "But I'll know as he started clean."

Robert came down in his Sunday clothes, Jonathan chuckled.

"It's a runaway match, that's what he's a-playing truant for—a runaway match," said he. "Did ye ever hear tell o' Lord Meldrum of the Gorsty Bank? Now there's a tale! Lord Meldrum fell in love with Squire Lineacre's wife, and she with him, but not with *all* of her mind, seemingly. Well, Lord Meldrum's fetched the longest ladder—the harvesting ladder from under the rick—and he's up at Mistress Lineacre's windy, while the Squire was sleeping off a Wake Day supper. So Mistress Lineacre looks at the Squire, and the Squire was red and breathing heavy. And she looks at Meldrum. Meldrum 'ud got his best plush coat on—and he was a Lord into the bargain. So she slips on her hood, and away. But they hadna gone a mile afore she turns her ankle—her shoes being her pride and that small as never was, but very treacherous—so they was forced to wait at the nighest inn while Lord Meldrum sent a lad to the place where his coach was waiting. And it happened as the lad met a poacher by Squire Lineacre's brook. And he ups and tells him what's the news. And the poacher thinks to himself,' Seven good trout, two brace of pheasants, and a tidy few mixed game I've got off Squire Lineacre this night. And, dear to goodness! Lineacre shall have his missus back.' So off he goes to Squire's, and drums him up and tells him, and Squire's away-to-go in a minute on his hunter. And just as Meldrum's coach drives up in a lather, Squire comes pounding up in a lather as well. Says Meldrum : ' Pursued, by God ! ' The lady stops with one foot on the coach step,

and she looks at 'em both. ' Come, love of my life,' says
Meldrum, ' I'll gie you the world to walk on ! ' ' Meg,'
says the Squire, ' I canna fancy my porridge unless you
cook it.' And with that Mistress Lineacre gives a sob and
runs to the Squire, and he swings her up and off whome
agen."

" She was a good ooman," said Mrs. Makepeace. " Not
but what she was a brazen piece to encourage the man !
But she did right at last, and the Lord 'ud reward her."

" I canna say as He did, for it was but two month
after as Squire Lineacre ran away with the Vicar's daughter,
and by then Lord Meldrum was away to the war—so she
hadna neither on 'em."

" Maybe," said Mrs. Makepeace dryly, " maybe that
was the reward."

" To my seeing," remarked Robert, " they were a parcel
of fools."

" And why so ? " inquired Jonathan.

" ' Ifting ' and ' anding ' all the while, and too highful
to hunger after ought, with yer leave and by yer leave, in
and out like hares through a muse."

" Well, my dear," said his mother, " and what 'ud *you*
ha done ? "

Robert laughed.

" It dunna matter what cowman-shepherd does, Mother."

" Well, but what d'you think they ought to ha' done ? "

" Let 'em each give the lady a good smacking kiss, arms
round and no time to think of plush coats and lords.
And the one she misliked the kiss of, let that one give her
up."

" What ? If she was his married wife ? "

Jonathan's face was a study in amazement.

" My dear ! " cried his wife " look where you're going
with that knife ! "

" If she didna like the feller's kiss she wouldna *be* his
married wife," said Robert, " or maybe she'd a liked to
be kissed by the one, and make porridge for tother, and
I say—let 'er. And now I'm going to Maister to ask off."

" Laws ! The lad's peartening up cruel," said Jonathan.

And dreamily, as she shook out the supper cloth on the cobbles, Mrs. Makepeace said to herself, " He's getting the very moral of his dad."

The moral of his dad, meanwhile, felt rather sheepish as he took his cap off and walked into Isaiah's parlour.

" I'm after another day off, please, sir," said Robert.

" Another ? "

" Ah ! "

" Musicianing agen ? "

" No, sir."

" What then ? "

" A bit of business of my own."

" Oh ! "

Isaiah observed him.

" Not going to get wed ? "

" Not yet," said Robert composedly, adding in the secrecy of his own heart, " not till I wed your daughter, Mr. Lovekin."

" And what if I say no ? "

" Dog's leave," observed Robert.

" And if I give you warning for it ? "

" If you mun you mun. I reckon I can drive plough for others same as I've druv it for you."

" But go you will to-morrow ? "

" Ah."

And suddenly the irony of the situation came over Robert and made him laugh. Here was he, going to save Lovekin's daughter from what Lovekin would consider worse than death (" for she'll be on the streets in a week if she goes off to Lun'on the like o' that, poor little innocent," he thought) and Isaiah threatened him with " warning ! " And he could not say anything : firstly, because if Isaiah knew that his daughter had planned to deceive him he would never forgive her ; secondly, because Robert could not very well disclose his system of receiving private information.

" What be you laughing at ? Me ? " enquired Isaiah.

" Laws, no, sir ! "

" The randy you're set on ? "

" Ah, that's it," said Robert, rather grimly, knowing very well the dreadful " mouth-mauling " Gillian would give him, " it's the randy as I'm thinking on."

" Well, go if you must," said Isaiah, " you're as bad as you were when you were a lad—always neesening. And you might give the mare a hot mash. She's out of condition. Looks unkind."

" Right sir, and thank you."

Robert saw to the mare himself, though doing so robbed him of time he really needed. And as he tramped towards the Keep, and thence to the Junction (of happy memory) to catch the midnight train for Silverton, he began to feel that he was having rather a busy day. And seeing that he had received from Providence (and would, he judged, receive) more clouts than apples, he made it up to himself by thinking of a little song. But he did not sing it. Somehow he did not want even the moonstruck rabbits that loped across the road, or the weightless blur that was a questing owl, to hear this song. No one would ever hear it, not even Gillian. Least of all Gillian. Then why make it ?

" But if you begin to ask why, my lad," he adjured himself, " you'll be stepping out on the road of never-end."

But as he went splashing along the half-flooded roadways, with the waterdrops raining on him from every tree, and an occasional scud of rain hiding the moon, he said his little song over to himself.

> I amna going neesening !
> There's only one nest
> As I'd lief rob,
> And that's where Gillian do rest
> With a head like a brown fir-bob.
>
> I amna going to rob the skeps !
> There's no comb worth my money,
> Not even a fardin,
> Only the white virgin-'oney
> From Gillian's gyarden.

Reaching Silverton between twelve and one, Robert lay down on a bench on the platform and went to sleep.

At dawn, after a cup of coffee at a coffee-stall, he set out for Johnson's.

Johnson sat on the steps with the inevitable pipe.

" However did you hear tell of it all so quick ? " asked Robert.

" What I dunna know about this owd town inna worth knowing," said Johnson.

" But this was inside the house, like."

" There's the day-girl," said Johnson. " There's blotting paper. There's train guides. There's luggage. And she's bin at station."

" She met think of coming whome."

" She *says* she's going 'ome. But it wunna the Junction she asked for."

" What time ? " asked Robert.

" Twenty minutes past noon, it leaves, just while the funeral's on. A clever piece, she is, but not clever enough for Johnson."

" I'm much obleeged."

" You're welcome, Rideout. I reckon we'm lastin' friends."

" I reckon we are."

Nine o'clock by the gold and silver chimes.

Ten o'clock.

Eleven o'clock.

And all the half-hours and the quarter-hours between !

Never had time seemed so long to Robert.

Twelve o'clock !

He was on the London departure platform, just by the stairs, where she could not escape him.

From the far end, in a bay, the one o'clock train for the Junction would steam out. It was just coming in now.

Twelve-ten ! Twelve-fifteen !

Gillian !

" Oh laws, she's prettier than ever was ! " sighed Robert.

He waited.

His plan was to bide his time until just before the train started.

Twelve-twenty.

" Now or never," muttered Robert.

She had put her bag in, and was buying a bun.

" Gillian ! " said Robert, " I'm acome to take you whome, lass."

Gillian's face was quite white with consternation. She was trembling from the sudden onslaught of Robert's will. She could see from his face that it was to be a fight to the finish.

" I'm going on a visit elsewhere," she said defiantly.

" No ! "

Gillian stamped, and put one foot on the step. Robert's right hand was heavy on her shoulder. With the other he reached her bag.

" Will you come down the platform quiet to the Junction train ? " he said.

" Never—never—never will I ! " cried Gillian, bursting into tears.

The porters were shutting the doors. The guard was ready with his flag.

Without more ado, Robert picked her up.

" My missus is feeling fainty," he explained to the wondering porters. " She mun bide till the next. She's granny-reared, lukka ! and a bit nesh." And the cow-man-shepherd walked quietly down the long platform with his master's daughter and his master's daughter's bag in his arms ; deposited them in the waiting Junction train ; got in ; shut the door ; mopped his face, and prepared for the worst.

CHAPTER XIV

" DAGGLY WEATHER "

THERE was a long, bitter, tearful silence. At last the few passengers strayed down the platform, porters appeared, and Robert, who wished to have an immediate and complete explanation, leant out and whispered to one of them.

" Dunna let anybody in."

The porter peered at Gillian and looked suspicious.

Robert gave him a shilling, and breathed the word: " 'Oneymoon."

But not all the porters of Silverton could prevent the old lady with the two market baskets from coming in. The more Robert tried to keep her out, the more determined she was. It was useless for the porters to tell her in persuasive accents that there were carriages of extreme comfort further on. One porter, who had recently returned from his own honeymoon, even went so far as to hint that she might travel first.

None the less, she pushed Robert aside and climbed in. Once in, she perceived that something was wrong.

She offered Gillian a lozenge, that being the only sweet she had about her. Gillian, thinking of all the things she might so soon have been enjoying, refused it and cried more than ever. The old lady frowned at Robert.

Then she went and sat by Gillian.

" Now, my dear," she said, laying a large hand in a yellow worsted glove on Gillian's slatey dress, " you mun mind as it's what we all have to go through."

Gillian's scarlet cheeks took a deeper shade. Robert desperately said :

" Very daggly weather, missus."

" Daggly is it ? " said the old lady ferociously. " I take no count of what it is. But I know it's bad to leave your whome, and your father and mother and all that you have, and cleave to your 'usband."

Now it was Robert's turn to blush.

" And you mustn't be impatient and hurryful, young man, I say. You mun 'umour her. You've just said them blessed words : ' Love, honour and cherish ! ' remember that ! "

Robert, in scarlet wrath, yet wished with all his heart that he had.

" And you, my dear," continued the zealot, " you've just said : ' Love, honour and obey.' And obey him you must."

" I never, never will ! " said Gillian. " He's treated me shameful."

" I thought as much."

" He carried me down platform, and he wouldna leave me go to London—I hate un ! "

" Dear, dear dear ! " said the old lady, very much perturbed. " What a union ! "

" Hark ye ! " said Robert. " If you dunna hush I'll throw you out of window."

It was now the old lady's turn to be taken aback. She looked at Robert with her spectacles, and without them. Slowly, dreadfully, she came to the conclusion that they were both mad, and as the train opportunely drew up at a station she hastily got out.

" Now," said Robert, " you mun explain it all, Gillian."

" I'd thank you to call me Miss Lovekin from this day on."

" Miss Lovekin ! What for did you think of doing such a soft thing ? "

" I *will* do it yet."

" No."

" I'm free."

" You're not free to get alost."

" You're a spoil-sport and a tell-tale and a sneak."

" What's this about Mr. Gentle ? "

" I hate Mr. Gentle."

" Sh !   He's dead, Gillian."

" Miss Lovekin ! "

" Miss Lovekin."

" Could I help it if his lungs was bad.   Could I ? "

" No, I dunna see as you could."

" They say's I 'ticed him to death.   Aunt Fanteague called me—called me—called me——"

" Well, what did she call you ? "

" A murderess ! "

" Poor little thing."

Robert patted her shoulder.

" Dunna touch me, Mr. Rideout ! "

" And then ? " asked Robert.

" Then Aunt Emily went mad."

" Mercy me ! "

" She screamed and screamed.   She said she was a widow, and she's bought the weeds."

Gillian gave a hysterical giggle.

" And she said she'd kill me."

" Lord love us ! "

" So Aunt Fanteague says : ' Go home,' and you wrote and says : ' It's very quiet,' and I made out to go to London."

" I see."

" And I canna hear nought but Mr. Gentle's voice a-singing ' Queen of the Earth,' and I canna see nought but the bald spot on his yead when he bowed Good-evening. And it inna fair.   It wunna my fault.   I only wanted a bit of fun.   Say it wunna my fault, Robert !   Say it ! "

" I shall be obliged to think it over a bit afore I says that," answered Robert.   " Did you tell your dad you were coming whome ? "

" Yes."

" How'd he ha' felt when you didna come and was alost ? "

" I dunna know. I dunna care. He wouldna mind."

" He 'ould mind, Gillian."

" Miss Lovekin ! "

" Maybe Miss Lovekin to-morrow, but Gillian now. And did you tell Mrs. Fanteague you were coming back to the Gwlfas ? "

" Yes."

" How'd she ha' felt when you went out of her house into silence and never heard tell of agen ? "

" She wouldna care. She called me murderess."

" You've told two lies, Gillian. You've rode rough-shod over a sight of people. Did Mr. Gentle take kindly to coming on the water ? "

" No."

" But you made un come ? "

" Made un ? "

" Now, Gillian ! You and me knows how you goes on when you're set on your own way. Tantrums ! Worse'n a pig drove the wrong road from market."

" I wunna be called a pig ! "

" You'll harken to me."

She stopped her ears.

He dragged her hands away.

" Now, Gillian ! If I liked I could go straight to Maister and tell un."

" But you wouldna ! "

" Not if you behave decent. So you made out to go to London by your lonesome ? "

" Ah."

" Well, you've got to give me your bounden word never to do it agen. Not wi'out telling your dad."

" Why ? "

" Because I say so. Promise or I tell your dad."

" I promise. I never could a-bear you ! "

" You mun write to your Aunt Emily, poor thing. You've took her lover away. He met not be what you'd choose for a lover, but he was Miss Emily's choice, and you'd no cause to draw un away."

" Aunt Emily's old and ugly."

"She inna ugly. She met be a bit old. But he found no fault till you tempted un."

" I didna ! "

" Gillian, it's no use for to deny it. I know your ways. Now you mun write a long letter—dust and ashes—to your Aunt Emily. And another to Mrs. Fanteague. And you mun make a cross for Mr. Gentle's grave."

" What mun I make it with ? " Gillian was still defiant, but curious. " There's nought in blow."

" Blackthorn and gorst be in blow ; you mun make it of blackthorn and gorst, and no gloves on, Gillian. And when the blood runs down your hands, you mun say : ' I helped to kill Mr. Gentle the same as I killed the slatey drake—for my adorning.' "

" But only a little wreath ? " she pleaded.

" No. A big un. I'll make the groundwork for it. and you'll cover it. And there's a posy knot of snowdrops in our gyarden ; you can put 'em in. Now that's done with."

" It'll never be done with, Robert Rideout ! I'll hate you to my dying day ! "

" Can you make shift to walk from the Keep ? "

" Ah, but I'd liefer walk alone."

" You shall have a sup of tea at the public and then we'll start."

It was a very different tea from the one at the Junction, but Robert was glad of it, after yesterday, and last night, and to-day's tension.

" I'm ready for a drop of summat heartening," he said. It was his only comment on his own feelings.

Early in the afternoon they set out.

When, at last, after an almost silent walk, they sighted the fire-lit windows of the " Mermaid's Rest," Gillian said :

" The new folks be come then ? "

" Yes, dang it," said Robert.

" What's the family ? "

" Two men and a woman."

As they passed the open door, Elmer spied Robert,

for the light had not yet faded, and from where he sat he could see the road.

" Come in, oot ? " he said.   " The young lady as well."

" Not to-night, Elmer, thank you kindly," replied Robert, and walked on.

Ralph laughed.

" Two's company !   Good luck ! " he shouted.

" What's that name ? " asked Gillian.

" Ralph Elmer."

" A tidy sounding name."

" Ugly, I call it," said Robert.

Why would everybody conspire to accuse him of his dearest, most impossible, dream ? he wondered.

His face looked older.   He always seemed older than he was.   For original thought, like running water, leaves its mark.

They came to the meadows of Dysgwlfas, to the wicket of the farm.

" Good night," said Robert wistfully.   " I'll watch you in."

Gillian took her bag.

" It's good-bye forever, Robert Rideout," said she.

" Not yet !   There's the cross."

" Get the gorst an' blackthorn for me, oot, Robert ? You've got your hedging gloves, and there's none nigher than the little gyland."

" No, you mun get it yourself."

" But I can't abide the little gyland : you said yourself it was unket."

" It *is* unket.   I dunna mind giving a hand with the gathering."

" To-morrow ? "

" Ah.   And maybe you wunna hear Mr. Gentle singing ' Queen of the Earth ' so much when you've made it."

CHAPTER XV

ISAIAH HEARS A BELOWNDER

GILLIAN felt both relieved and bored as she realized that her father expected her—at least, that he expected her soon, if not this evening. Instead of the wild dismay, the searchings and enquiries, the mystery that she had planned, here she was, home again as punctually, as unemotionally, as Mrs. Makepeace from market. Still, she would " best " Robert yet. She would coax and cajole her father. She would go out into the world by hook or by crook.

Isaiah was doing accounts by the fire.

" Well, father ! "

" Well, I never ! Why didna you tell me the train ? Where's luggage ? "

" I met Robert, and he carried it."

" Well, that was a bit o' luck, for the mare's not up to much. So you're whome agen. How bin 'e, my dear ? "

" I'm a'right, dad. Had tea ? "

" No. It's only just on six."

" I'll get it. I'm as hungry as a ratling."

" All well at Sil'erton ? "

" Not to say very well, Father."

" Oh ? "

" Aunt Fanteague's well."

" Not poor Emily ? "

" Aunt Emily's met trouble."

" Oh ? "

" Mr. Gentle's dead."

" Ha ! I thought as much. He'd no business to die. He'd ought to ha' married the girl."

" Girl, Dad ? "

" Girl to me. She's younger than me, you mind."

" Aunt Fanteague kept on about him having no business to die. First she'd say that. Then she'd say : ' You'd no business to 'tice him on the water.' It was fair like a cuckoo dinning."

" Did you 'tice 'un ? "

" Dad ! I couldna bide in the house all day. And if a fellow says : ' Come on Severn ? ' what's a girl to say ? "

" Very true."

Gillian suddenly set the tray on the table with a bang, and put her arms round her father's neck.

" I like you, Dad ! " she said.

" Obleeged, I'm sure."

" Dad ! "

" Well ? "

" Seeing I've been deceived in my visit to A'ntie, will you let me go and learn to sing ? "

" I don't see as I very well can, just now."

" In a bit, then ? "

" Maybe in a bit. Did you hear tell of the new folks at the ' Mermaid's Rest ' ? "

" Only just. What like are they ? "

" There's a queer fellow called Fringal, as is the odd man. And there's a housekeeper, a wild-looking, ill-favoured wench, and there's Mr. Ralph Elmer."

" A housekeeper ? "

" Ah. Seeing there's no missus, there's bound to be a housekeeper, inna there ? "

" Ralph's a nice name."

" I don't mind Elmer, neither."

" What does he do, Father ? "

" Buys to sell agen, and breeds sheep, and now he's doing a bit in the publican line."

" Seems a lively chap, Dad."

" Middling lively. There's nought made of horseflesh as he canna ride."

" Inna there ? "

" Quite the gentleman. Makes Robert look very rough."

" But Robert *is* rough, Dad."

" Ha ! "

" What ? "

" Nought. Ralph Elmer's bin to dinner here."

" Maybe he'd like to come agen ? "

" Maybe he'd 'ould."

" It's awful quiet, Dad."

" What ? Tired of your native afore you're properly back ? "

" Why not ask him next Sunday ? "

" I see nought in particular agen it."

" Will you send Jonathan with an invite ? "

" Maybe I will."

Gillian lost no time in seeing that the note was written. Then, after tea, she ran across the fold and the orchard to the cottage.

" Why, Miss Gillian ! " cried Mrs. Makepeace. " You *be* a stranger ! Come your ways in."

But Gillian saw that Robert, in the corner of the settle by the fire, was already busy on the cross.

" No thank you, Mrs. Makepeace. I only came to ask Jonathan to take a letter to Mr. Elmer."

Robert looked up, then hastily looked down again.

" Ralph Elmer's a nice name, inna-d-it ? " she observed to people in general, and was gone.

Sadly, ruminatively, Mrs. Makepeace looked at the bent head of her son, and almost echoed the words of Jonathan :

" Oh, what a silly, kimet lad ! "

Meanwhile, Gillian made a happy tour of the farm. For now that there was a prospect of a little excitement, she was very glad to be home. She was heartily sick of her aunt's prim house ; and the sweeping lines of moor, the cowhouse with its warm fragrance and sound of low, deep breathing, the rushing fowls that came at her feeding-call, the one hatch of early chickens—of the colour of rich sponge-cake—had a new delight for her. She found three snow-drops in the long border under the orchard hedge—so white, so radiantly green, that she picked them and pinned them into her dress, defiantly, because she knew she ought to have kept them for Mr. Gentle's cross.

Quite early next morning she slipped out of the house and whistled for Robert with the long shrill whistle they both knew.

"'Oh, that we two were Maying!'" sang Gillian, as they swung out across the frosty fields; but she stopped suddenly as she remembered that it was one of Mr. Gentle's songs.

It must be confessed that Gillian shirked her thorn-gathering.

"You can reach ever so far above what I can," she said. And Robert gathered a great many branches, not because he was taken in, but because he hated to see Gillian's hands pricked. Gillian set her anger aside for this morning, and became her old self.

"It inna so unket here, with you, Robert," she said. "Still on, I'm not going to give you more than a 'good-morning' and 'good-evening,' forever and ever, and you know why."

"I'd like to keep trouble off you allus, Gillian, and not only in the little gyland," said Robert, hacking at a bough of blackthorn, so that Gillian did not see the blaze of love in his eyes.

"I'm a child of sin," she said lightly. "They turned me out of my cradle; likely they'll get me agen."

"I wunna let 'em, Gillian."

"There's no charm to keep 'em off."

"Ah! there is."

"Tell!"

"No. That is, maybe one day."

"When?"

"When I'm a rich farmer and you're hoeing turmits barefoot," said Robert.

"That'll never be."

" There's no mortal man can say what'll be. When I'm high and you're low, I'll tell you. And this very day there's a bit of a charm for you."

" What ? "

" Making the cross. It'll keep harm from you, Gillian."

" It'll only prick me."

" A prick to the body oftentimes 'ull heal the soul."

" Oh, look ! There's Jonathan gone to Ralph Elmer's."

" Dang it ! "

" Why, ' dang it ' ? "

" I dunna like the fellow. There's summat ill-favoured about the folks."

" He looked well-favoured enough."

" To look at ? Ah ! But you wait till you've been there. You wait till you've seen that poor wench."

" But he inna married ? "

" No," replied Robert slowly, " no. He says he inna married."

" What's amiss, then ? She could leave if she'd a mind."

" All's amiss. She's a foundling. And she's dumb ! "

" Dumb ! "

" Ah ! "

" Oh, I wouldna like to be dumb ! "

" Surelie you wouldna ! You're as good as a nest of seven-coloured linnets, Gillian."

" Canna she say ought—not at all ? "

" Nowt."

" Nor write ? "

" I didna ask. Maybe she can. That 'ud be summat."

" It must be so cruel hard," mused Gillian, " never to be able to answer back."

In his mirth over this, Robert forgot the woes of Rwth for a time.

When they reached the farm again, Gillian said, " Help me with the cross ! "

" No ; you mun do it by your lonesome. I'm going to lock you in calfskit."

" Robert Rideout ! You darstna ! "

" I'll show you if I darst," said Robert, and having gently pushed her in, he turned the key in the padlock.

" Now I'll bring you the frame and the wire and the snowdrops, and when you've used up all the thorn and all the gorst, I'll let you out."

So it was that Isaiah, wanting a button sewn on to his coat, shouted for Gillian until Mrs. Makepeace said to Jonathan : " Hark at Maister bellowing ! I'll go and see what's to do."

Mrs. Makepeace having sewn on the button, Isaiah wandered up to the attic to see if Gillian was there. It was a favourite haunt of hers in autumn and spring, when she would sit in the sunshine that streamed through the one window, in her mother's old rocking-chair, munching a carefully chosen selection of Ribstone Pippins, Pearmains, and Blenheim Oranges, while she read the dusty, mouse-gnawed, strangely illustrated romances of Aunt Emily's girlhood.

Once in the attic, Isaiah could not resist picking-over all the apples. Then he stood in the window and surveyed his garden, the road, the fields, the pale blur that was blackthorn blossom in the little gyland, the fair spring sky. His hedges were all in good order, the work well forward, the sheep prospering. Gillian was back, and was probably even now getting his tea. The sun was warm. He leant on the high window-sill, drowsy and contented. Suddenly he started.

" What a belownder ! " he said, and peered out to see what caused the thunder of hoofs, the rattling of stones.

It was Ralph Elmer, galloping past the farm like a man possessed, stooping forward, slim and eager, flogging till the very limit of speed was reached. Watching him disappear down the road, Isaiah saw that he was riding bareback. Suddenly the interpretation of the exhibition came to Isaiah. He was overcome with silent, delighted mirth.

" What a caution ! Well, I never did ! Tuthree words from me, and all that belownder ! Showing off, that's what he is. Laws ! If he dunna break his neck ten times over, he's the very son-in-law for me. To think as my few words—well, well ! Seed fallen on good ground ! That poor cob thinks he's going to stable in hell this night ! What a pity—what a pity ! Gillian ought to ha' been here. Fall in love ! Well, if I'd 'abin able to ride the like of that, I wouldna have wasted two year wiling her mother to church. Well ! the young devil can ride, whatsoever else he canna do. I'll take sixpence a head off them lambs for this bit of entertainment. If he does it often, I shouldn't wonder if he gets everything a bargain. If he comes back the like of that, I'll take another sixpence off. Danged if I won't ! "

Elmer did come back, rather more recklessly than he had gone. Isaiah chuckled.

" But most a pity, Gillian's not seed it ! " he mourned.

None the less, Gillian *had* seen it. For hearing a great commotion, she peered through the calfskit window, which looked on the road, and she beheld Elmer, straight as a dart, red with fresh air, endowed by her eyes with the eternal youth of the heroes of romance, flash past her dark strawy prison.

She heard the rumour of his return in time to get a longer look. And exactly what Ralph Elmer intended came to pass. She was dazzled, stormed, inebriated with his recklessness, his pride of life, the hard physical beauty of him. She fell into a dream about next Sunday. It was lucky that she had finished the cross, for her thoughts were at the " Mermaid's Rest " till Robert came to release her.

" Did you see ? " she asked.

" See what ? "

" Why, Ralph Elmer, galloping down the lane like a cowboy from the west."

" Ah, I saw un. I didna think much of un."

" You couldn't do it yourself."

" Couldna I ? "

" Will the cross do now ?   I canna do it any better."

" Well, I think you've done pretty fair," said Robert, his eyes on Gillian's red scratched hands.   An unbearable longing to kiss them made him abrupt.   But when Gillian had gone, he gathered up some of the fallen flowers of thorn and gorse and put them in his pocket.   And when Isaiah went round the orchard after tea, he suddenly heard beyond the thick bounding hedge, another belownder.   He peered through a gap.

" Well, blast me ! " he muttered, checking a great roar of laughter.   For there was Robert, on the unbroken three-year-old cart-horse, riding bareback as Elmer had ridden and galloping as if a fiend pursued him.

" Well, he's got as good a nerve as the other !   What's took the fellers ?   Spring !   Well, well, we know it burns in the blood.   I mind when I'd 'a done the same if I'd 'a thought of it.   Lukka !   There 'e comes.   Round agen ! Lord, Lord !   If he brings that colt down, I'll make un pay.   Every farthing I will.   Round agen !   If he works as hard as what he plays, I shall be a rich man in no time. I'd like to see the two of 'em at it.   Well, well !   I dunna say as Bob inna the best of the two.   But it wouldna do for Gillian to know it."

He walked away stealthily that Robert might not know he had been watched.   Later, in the stable, he came on Robert grooming the colt.

" Looks warm ! " he observed.   " Sweating ? "

" A bit," said Robert.

" Dog in the field ? "

" Not as I know-to."

" Must ha' galloped like mad to sweat so."

" They do, these spring evenings," said Robert.

" They do ! " assented his master.   And as he went across the yard, he gave a great roar of laughter and repeated :   " They do !   They do ! "

So that Jonathan, at his tea, observed : " Maister's merry."

" Ah, I've not heard him laugh so lungeous this long while," said his wife.

"Minds me of the tale of Farmer Knighton and his brother," said Jonathan. "Never laughed, Farmer Knighton didn't. Not if it was ever so. So his brother bet him half the farm (they went shares, seesta) ! as he'd make him laugh. So in case he lost the bet, and in case his brother died first, Farmer Knighton insured him for five hunderd pound. So young Knighton tried and tried to make his brother laugh. And one day he was foolin' about on top of the hay waggon and he fell off and broke his back, poor fellow. And he died. And Knighton hadna' laughed. So he got all the farm, and because his brother was dead he got the five hunderd as well. And when he come back from the funeral it come o'er him sudden, and he laughed. And out of the chimley corner, where young Knighton was used to sit, came his brother's voice. ' You laughed ! ' he says. ' You've lost ! ' he says. ' I claim the farm.' And he haunted the farm from that day, and there was no prosperation in beast nor in meadow ; and it went back into the moor, and Knighton died."

Robert came in while the story was in progress, and his mother looked concernedly at his damp face and hair.

"You *be* hot ! " she said as soon as Blossom was safely disposed of. "Whatever's been after ? "

"The colt inna very easy to ketch, these days," said Robert meekly. But his heart was not meek. It was insolently gay. Let Elmer gallop past the farm as often as he pleased, Robert Rideout was ready to gallop also. He might not be able to make love to Gillian, as he knew with bitter rebellion that Elmer would, but anyway he could gallop. And when Gillian tried him past bearing, he could go away into the far meadow and ride the colt till he was too tired to feel anything. Also, he would begin to compose his long poem about Dysgwlfas—a poem in which Gillian did not appear until the very end—a poem of rock and rugged vistas, of savage winds and wide spaces and dark weather—the expression of Robert's philosophy as he had hammered it out under winter skies. Its unemotionalism would comfort him. Brooding on it,

he would attain some kind of detachment.   And perhaps
he would find out what it was that the moor wanted of
him ; why it gripped him so in snow-time ; what prophecy
lowered upon him so strangely in the little gyland—the
unket place.

CHAPTER XVI

RALPH ELMER COMES TO DINNER

ELMER came next day to accept the invitation in person.
Gillian was practising a new way of doing her hair, and
a new song she had heard in Silverton. The afternoon
sun was warm ; the air was keen and gay ; she leant
from her window with a long plait held between her teeth
while she tied a bit of bootlace round it to keep it firm.
And looking up from her absorbing task, she saw Elmer
sitting easily in the saddle with his hat pushed back and
his left hand idle on the bridle reins, staring up at her
window, at her pink blouse, her half-done hair, her blushes.

"Miss Lovekin!" he called. "Come down, Miss
Lovekin!"

Gillian withdrew.

He laughed softly, keeping his eyes on the window. He
could see her at the glass, hurriedly putting in pins.

He whistled the tune she had been singing.

"Lord! What a time to keep a fellow waiting!" he
observed. Then, aware that Isaiah was at a sale and Mrs.
Makepeace at market, he sang :

> " The lily's white,
> The violet's blue ;
> The rose is sweet,
> And so are you."

"Oh, dear now! What a roaring!" giggled Gillian.

Robert heard it from the cowhouse, and began to hate
Ralph Elmer unreasonably.

" Miss Lovekin ! Are you coming down, or——? "

" Or what, Mr. Elmer ? You are Mr. Elmer, I suppose ? "

Gillian's face looked out roguishly.

" Or—shall I come and fetch you ? "

Gillian laughed uproariously.

This was really amusing.

" Oh, dear now, Mr. Elmer, you are a caution ! "

" Are you coming down ? " said Elmer softly.

Gillian decided to go down. She put on her best hat.

" Well, Mr. Elmer, pleased to meet you, I'm sure," said she, standing under the green archway by the wicket. " But why didna you come yesterday when you went by like a storm of thunder ? "

" Because, if I had, I couldn't have come and talked to you to-day. So you saw me ? "

" Ah, I saw you."

" Where were you ? "

" In the calfskit."

" Do they put you there when you're naughty ? "

This came so near the truth that Gillian was on her dignity in a moment. She was angry, not with Elmer but with Robert.

" I'm not a chyild, Mr. Elmer."

" What are you, then ? "

" A grown-up lady."

Elmer laughed.

" Shall I tell you what I think you are ? "

" I dunna mind if you do."

" A little devil."

" Oh, Mr. Elmer ! "

" She's a lot prettier than her father said," thought Elmer. " Bit o' colour ! I should say so ! Waist ! About eighteen inches, it looks. My two hands ud go round it."

He held his hands out.

" Would they go round, Miss Lovekin ? " he inquired slily.

" Go round what, Mr. Elmer ? "

" I said, ' Would they go round Miss Lovekin ? ' "

Gillian did not know whether to laugh or to blush or to pretend she didn't understand.

She decided on all three.

" Oh, dear now, Mr. Elmer. How can I guess your riddle-me-ree ? "

" Shall I tell you the answer ? "

" Oh, no ! no ! "

" Shall I show you the answer ? "

" I'm agoing in, Mr. Elmer."

" And me ? "

" You've no call to come in, seeing father's at Weeping Cross."

" And long may he bide. Is he going agen next week ? "

" He's going to Mid-Lent Fair, Friday's a week. He's going to bring me a Simnel cake."

" Will you come to the Mermaid to tea and I'll give you a Simnel cake as big as a wedding cake ? "

" Laws ! Will you ? Will the girl as canna say ought be there ? "

" Yes. She's my housekeeper."

" Then I'll come."

" You'll come to see her, but you won't come to see me."

" That's the size of it."

" No," said Elmer reflectively, holding out his two hands to form a ring, " *that's* the size of it."

" I'm going in."

" I'm coming to dinner, day after to-morrow."

" Shall you come galloping ? "

" If you like."

" You'll break your neck one of these days."

" I don't care. If you like to see me gallop, I'll risk it."

" Father, he did laugh ! Talking about the lungeous way you came down our lane, I thought he'd burst with laughing."

" Laugh and grow fat ! I'll make your father as fat as a pig, Miss Lovekin. I'll give him something to laugh at every day of his life."

" Miss Gillian ! "

Robert stood in the porch.

" The milk's cooling. Be you coming to sieve it and scald the pails, or mun I ? "

" I'll come, Robert. Good-evening, Mr. Elmer."

" Good evening, Miss Lovekin."

Elmer dug his heels into the cob and was away.

" Goes like a flash of lightning, dunna he ? " said Gillian, watching him race across the moor.

" If I had the say, he'd go faster than a flash o' lightning and he wouldna come back ! " said Robert, very sulkily.

They sieved the milk in an aloof silence.

Robert turned to the door.

" I suppose you wunna think of coming neesening this year," he observed.

" I'm grown-up now, Robert."

" I know to three or four in the making. And I shouldna wonder if there'll be a canbottlin's in our gyarden a bit later on."

" Well—I met think about it—early in the morning sometime."

" And if I was you, Gillian—Miss Gillian—I'd give Ralph Elmer a ' go-thy-ways ' oftener than I'd give him a welcome."

" Oh, you would ? "

" Ah. And I wouldna get made into a nay-word for a jill-flirt, if I was you."

" Oh, you would, would you, Robert ? And suppose I give you a goose-apple ? I must go in now. If I stay coddling about in the dairy with you, I'll be called a jill-flirt. Good-evening, Mr. Rideout. Ketch of frost ! "

While Gillian laid tea for her father, she felt rather sorry for Robert. He had no money, no rambling inn, no sheep—nothing. He was just a landless man. And yet—would Mr. Elmer be such a good companion, such a faithful friend ? Would she enjoy tea with him as much as she had enjoyed it at the Junction ? Still, Ralph Elmer made her laugh. What with his jokes and his

galloping, time fled faster with him than with Robert.
Perhaps she mistook Robert's self-control for dullness.

" It's like as if all Mr. Elmer's goods was in the window,
father," she said later. " With Robert you canna tell
what's in the shop ; he keeps the window so sparse."

"Robert's neither here nor there. Elmer's a gentleman—very nigh."

" What makes a gentleman, father ? "

" Well, my dear, it isna hardly easy to say. But you
can see. Look's Elmer, look's Robert. One's got a good
coat and a bankbook ; the other hanna. Ha ! that's it.
A good coat and a bankbook. That's a gentleman."

" Then you're one, father ? "

" Oh, I wouldn't like to go so far as that. I'm only a
poor lost and forgotten working-man."

Isaiah, with a great laugh, lit his pipe and subsided into
the weekly county newspaper.

On Sunday, Gillian got up very early, and would not
let Mrs. Makepeace help with the dinner. Mrs. Makepeace
was very glad not to help, for she knew who was the invited guest and that her dreams were probably to be
destroyed by that guest.

Gillian made a tart of bottled damsons, horseradish
sauce, custard , there were the usual liberal vegetables
and the usual mountain of beef. It was all cooked to a
turn when Isaiah came back from church. He always
drove across the moor to Sunday morning service. Soon
afterwards, Elmer came cantering into the yard, turning
his cob into a spare stable, and came in.

As he watched Gillian bring in the various dishes, he
began to be afraid he was going to fall in love with her.
Few girls had ever attracted him as much. Femininity
had very little power over him. Women mean much less
to men than men do to women. Most men would be
content to go through their day's work and even their
leisure without any feminine influence whatever. They
are sufficient to themselves. If woman did not invade
their aloofness, they would still be perfectly happy. But
woman does invade it. She is driven to attract, to invite,

to entrance, by a deep instinct that is often at variance
with her psychic self. Only very exceptional women can
live contentedly outside the masculine atmosphere :
but the man who cannot live the greater proportion of
his life without woman is the exception. This is, of course,
apart from love ; for real love between the sexes is an
exceptional thing. So when Elmer thought of " falling
in love " with Gillian, it was not real love he meant,
but the curious unreal " false dawn " that is often mis-
taken for it. Yet even this he mistrusted. He had seen
it weaken men's hands so that their purses slipped from
their control. He had seen it diminish their flocks and
herds, curtail their lands, make them a bye-word. It
would not do. He was getting on so well. He had his
life mapped out. He had his household, well-chosen,
inexpensive. He had his amusements, interests. And
Gillian Lovekin was outside them all. She would disturb
his nicely adjusted existence. She would cost a great
deal. If he flirted with her, he would have to take her
about. He would have to give her presents. If he fell
in love with her, she would break into his thoughts and
disturb his concentration on business. Instead of remembering the precise shilling, penny, farthing at which some
other bidder at a fair usually stopped, he would remember
Gillian's smile. Instead of being punctual to the moment,
as he was famed for being, he would be always rushing
over to the farm, or meeting Gillian in lanes or lost dimples
of the moor. It would not do. Yet here she was, bright
as a geranium, eager, shy, attracting and repelling at
once. No greater contrast could have been found to Rwth.

When he thought of Rwth, he frowned. Then there was
the old man—Lovekin. He would not tolerate a flirta-
tion that did not end in marriage. If a young woman
walked out with an " acquaintance," she must very soon
walk to church with him or be disgraced. No. It would
not do.

" Sauce, Mr. Elmer ? I made it."

There she was in that lavender-blue dress that made
her look so richly-coloured, blushing, laughing, leaning

over him with her round breast, her soft shoulder, the
scent of violets that she seemed to breathe. She had
bought a bottle of violet scent in Silverton, but how was
a man to think of that, when the only women he had
known intimately had been his mother, who was an
earnest Methodist and eschewed all the wiles of woman,
and Rwth, to imagine whom with a bottle of scent was
a thing to beggar reason. That was why he considered
her such a suitable housekeeper for a man who wanted
to get on. She had a woman's usefulness without a
woman's wiles.

"Oh! if you made it, Miss Lovekin, I should like
buckets full," said his voice. His eyes said, "I should
like your lips better." His reason said, "You're a fool,
my lad."

"No need for such an arglin' over the girl's name,
Elmer," said Isaiah. "You met as well call her Gillian
as not."

"Gillian," said Elmer. "Why, it's like gillie-flowers!"

"And so are you!" said his eyes to his hostess.

"I like a gillie-flower," said Isaiah, packing beef into
his mouth and talking round it. "A good, dark, hand-
some gillie-flower beats a rose."

"It'll beat anything," said Elmer, with his eyes fast in
Gillian's.

Isaiah had not observed the allegory. He was busy
with his dinner, and he relegated allegories to church and
the Bible.

"I seed a red one, rosy-red it was, at the show at
Weeping Cross last year," said Isaiah.

"I've seen a red one, too," said Elmer, staring very
hard at Gillian's scarlet cheeks.

"Where?"

Elmer's eyes said, "Here!"

"I forget," said his mouth.

"You're a fool, Ralph Elmer," said his mind.

"It was as soft as a good fleece," said Isaiah. "Sauce,
Gillian!"

"The one I saw was as soft as a fleece, too," said Elmer.

" And it was rosy-red, and sweet, and enough to drive anybody mad. Sauce for me, too—Gillian."

" Why ' drive anybody mad ' ? " inquired Isaiah. " Where's the girl gone ? What are ye grinning at ? "

" Drive you mad to grow it ; it's nigh on impossible to get 'em that colour," said Elmer glibly.

" She's gone to fetch some more gravy, maybe," said Isaiah. " I said, what were you grinning at ? "

" Only a tale of a barmaid I heard tell of. She'd got such a complexion as never was. It drove the fellers silly. So one day a chap I knew bet the rest as it wasn't real. (Because he knew it wasn't. His sister'd found the rouge on her dressing-table, see ?) So he puts his arm round her very loving and he dips his other hand in the beer and he draws it down her cheek, and all the colour came off and the fellows roared."

Isaiah laughed.

" Serve the hussy right. Brassy, I call it, daubing her face with raddle the like o' that ! "

" Oh, father, I think the feller was a beast," said Gillian. " I'd have given him a clout on the ear."

Elmer laughed.

" Should you give anybody a clout if he kissed you, Gillian ? "

Gillian went to fetch more potatoes.

" Why, where's the wench agen ? What ails her ? It's everything by fits and gurds seemingly to-day."

" More potatoes, father ? Mr. Elmer ? "

Gillian had regained her composure. But when Isaiah settled himself for his nap, Elmer suggested that he and Gillian should " look the farm," and Gillian lost her composure and Ralph his cool-headed foresight, and the walk ended in a struggle and an attempted kiss behind the haystack, which was unwillingly observed by Robert as he brought the cows in. He clenched his hands and passed them with averted head. And all evening he could think of nothing but the intense rapture it would be to murder Ralph Elmer.

CHAPTER XVII

TEA FOR FOUR AT THE " MERMAID'S REST "

IT was on a green March evening that Gillian set out for her tea at the " Mermaid's Rest." Her father had started early in the morning. Mrs. Makepeace was doing a day's washing at her own cottage ; Robert had gone to fetch the cows in. Away went Gillian, with a posy of golden hazel catkins in her frock, and an anticipatory blush in her cheeks. Mr. Elmer did say such things ! He was much more amusing than Robert. Of course Robert was a necessity, like bread ; one could not contemplate the farm without Robert. But bread, she thought, was improved by a relish. Mr. Elmer was that relish, highly spiced, perhaps (Mrs. Fanteague would have said undoubtedly) not very wholesome, but pleasant. The cornelian heart shone in the sun. The yellow catkins swung. A thrush sang loud and sweet from a brown-budded chestnut in the hedge of the far pasture. There was the inn. They had put a coat of whitewash on it, and it looked clean and romantic in the afternoon sun. Elmer's sheep, with their black-faced lambs, contemplated her from the gate of his croft. She came to the door. It was bright with new paint. The windows were clean. Fringal had tidied the flower-bed. Gillian thought it was charming. She knocked. Would Mr. Elmer come ? She wondered. But Elmer was awaiting her in the parlour ; and as he was tired after galloping to Weeping Cross and back to attend an auction which usually took up the whole day, he had fallen into a doze.

Fringal came to the door. He knew she had been invited, and he strongly disapproved. He had his reasons for this. He had not intended to come to the door at all, only Gillian was early, and he thought it might be a customer.

He stood and looked at her with a face of goblin mockery.

" Good evening," said Gillian.

" Evening," replied Fringal, and doubled-up with silent mirth.

" I'm Miss Lovekin."

" Oh! Miss Lovekin? Ah! I dunna just mind who you be."

" Yes, you do! I'm Farmer Lovekin's daughter."

" Oh, Farmer Lovekin's daughter. I thought maybe you was travelling in cottons and laces."

Gillian was furious. She stamped.

" I'm asked to tea! " she said.

" Beg pardin? "

" I've had an invite to tea! "

" I be getting very hard of hearing," said Fringal.

" You heard as well as well."

" What bell? "

" I didna say ' bell,' I said—oh, ha' done with your nonsense, you silly old man, and leave me come in! "

" Magpies, magpies, oh! it's like a nest of magpies in a tree, it is," remarked Fringal, and he doubled up again.

He stood crushed between the door-post and the door, which he held open only just wide enough for himself.

" I tell you I'm Miss Juliana Lovekin, and I've had an invite to tea! "

" Not from me."

" From you! No. From Mr. Elmer—your master."

" Mr. Elmer? Oh, theer's amany bidden to this old public by Mr. Elmer," said Fringal, suddenly losing his deafness. " Theer's such a mort o' young women bidden to this public as keeps me all my time finding glasses for 'em."

" I don't care who else comes. I'm coming in."

" Like tom-titmice to a bone they come," mused Fringal.
" He bids 'em and then forget's 'em.   He's forgot you."

" You're a wicked old man ! "

" He's forgot you, and he's gone to sleep."

" Wake him up, then.   I'm going to have tea with him."

" 'Ow can you take tea with Mr. Elmer when Mr. Elmer's
in bed ?   If that's in your mind, you inna no better than
what you should be."

He laughed again.

Gillian realized defeat and resolved on *finesse*.   She
remembered the back door and the existence of Rwth.

" Well, good-day to you," she said, and walked away.
But no sooner had Fringal shut the door than she ran
round the house and into the back kitchen, where Rwth
was mangling.   Rwth turned her lustrous eyes upon the
intruder, not in surprise but in reverie.   She always gave
the impression of being impervious to surprise, beyond
tears, beyond pain.   Her riven young face looked into
Gillian's across the mangle.   Her spare figure, clad in
her usual dust-coloured raiment, with a big sacking apron,
her dishevelled hair and arms wrinkled from the wash-
tub, would have made her an arresting picture of loveless
toil even if she could have spoken.   But the fact that she
could not speak invested her with tragedy.   Even to
Gillian's unsympathetic, superficial gaze this was obvious.
She stood darkly against the whitewashed wall, with the
sun smiting across her tired face, and her beautiful eyes
dwelt on Gillian's vivid colours.   Gillian was in sunlight
also.   The sun seemed to caress her, though it had no
caress for Rwth.   With her angry flaming cheeks and
eyes bright grey with rage, with her richly-tinted dress,
her catkins and her red heart, she quite shone against the
pale wall.   Rwth's eyes lingered on her, accepted her,
loved her.   Gillian's eyes pitied, Rwth's adored.

She smiled.

" Is Mr. Elmer in ? " asked Gillian quickly, smiling also.

Rwth nodded.   And there was something in the nod
that said how sadly and heavily she was aware of Mr.
Elmer's presence.

" The old man said he was in bed. Is he ? " asked Gillian.

Rwth shook her head.

" Where then ? "

Rwth wiped her arms on her apron ; came and took Gillian by the hand and led her along the passage, avoiding the kitchen where Fringal was, and brought her to the second door of the parlour. They stood before it, looking at its dark panels, like figures of day and night, or life and death.

Then Rwth went up the three steps and lifted her hand to the latch. But before she opened the door she turned once more and looked down into Gillian's eager, vivid face. There was interrogation in her look, and tolerance and tenderness, and was it pity ? A fleeting expression, as of a vast motherly compassion, seemed to tenant the large eyes for a moment. It was almost as if she said, from a vantage height of many sorrows :

" What do you want with this man ? What is he to you, beautiful creature ? Is it wise to go up those three dark steps in through that dark door ? I could stop you. Even now I could catch you by the arm and drag you into the kitchen where Fringal is. I could save you, for an hour—a day. Save you from what ? How do I know ? Do you come to disturb my peace ? Have I any peace to disturb ? Will you become like me if you go in at that door ? Will your face be granite and your shoulders bowed, and dumbness freeze your days ? Maybe not, for I am here. I will be your saviour. I had no saviour."

Gillian trembled beneath her gaze. Why, she could not explain to herself or anyone else all the days of her life. She could not explain that she had, standing at the foot of the parlour steps at the " Mermaid's Rest," suffered the impact of that dumb creation which groaneth and travaileth in pain, that creation which, once to see, to hear, to realize, turns the hair of youth white, and numbs the heart ; for this is Calvary.

It was as if there lay across the face of Rwth the perpetual Shadow of the Cross. It was as if, losing oneself

in her eyes, one saw the rocky, dripping caverns leading
through the jagged flinty ways of agony down to death.

She felt very small and helpless with those eyes upon
her, frightened and yet consoled.

Suddenly, as if at the beckoning of Destiny, Rwth laid
her thumb on the latch, smiled, opened the door, stood
aside for Gillian to enter, and went away.

The room was comfortable and even gay. It reassured
Gillian. There were red curtains. There was a glass-
fronted corner cupboard full of bright china; two armchairs; a blue tablecloth; brasses on the mantelpiece;
a dresser full of plates; pipes, and riding-whips and
spurs; a hearthrug with a tabby cat on it, and in the
largest armchair, fast asleep, the master of the house.

Like a nymph gazing on the sleep of a satyr, Gillian
looked at him; tiptoed nearer; put her head on one
side and looked at him again.

"He's real well-favoured," she thought. His hair,
roughened by his ride and his sleep, suited him better
than in its usual sleek condition. His relaxed brow, the
eyelashes on the cheek, the mouth less hard than it was
in its firm waking lines, the flush, made of him a picture
that his mother would have liked to see, sent him back to
his boyhood. His long nervous hands lay on the arms of
the chair. His long legs were stretched towards the fire.
Close beside his feet the cat, humped in content, purred.

"The cat inna afeard of him. Why me?" thought
Gillian. Now what should she do? Go out and come in
again? But then that horrible old man might see her.
Cough? He would be startled then, and cross. He
sighed in his sleep. Sighed! This great, hard-riding,
hard-bargaining, hard-staring man sighed like an old, old
woman or a little child.

"Now what be troublin' thee?" whispered Gillian, in
the words of one of Robert's rhymes.

> "Now what be troublin' thee?
> Now what old ancient sorrow
> Stands up like a tree over yesterday
> And shadows to-morrow?"

Why she thought of this rhyme, why this strange pity held her, Gillian could not have said. She was impervious to sympathy as a rule. She had no more pity for the world in general than the hungry young bird has for its over-driven parents. She stood close beside his chair. It was strange that he slept so soundly, she thought, and as a matter of fact, it was only because he had treated and been treated by so many friends at the " Drovers' Rest " that he did. Gillian was tired of this silent host. What with him, and the dumb girl and the forbidding Fringal, she felt that the house was too welcomeless. Even the cat had purred itself into quiet.

" Now I'll end it ! " whispered Gillian. With a silent laugh and a blush she stooped over and lightly brushed her bunch of catkins across his mouth.

" Hey ! " cried Elmer. " Hullo ! What the devil ? Who kissed me ? "

This sudden angry vitality in a person who had been so passive alarmed Gillian. She stood with clasped hands, very red, not finding a word to say.

Elmer got up ; yawned ; stretched.

" Bless me ! I must ha' been asleep ! " he said. " How did you get in all on the quiet ? How long since did you come ? What was that—— ? " He stopped, staring down at his guest. " You did ! It's no manner use saying you didn't ! "

" I never, never did, Mr. Elmer ! "

" I swear you did. I felt it." He laughed suddenly. " You can do it agen if you've a mind."

" Oh, ha' done, Mr. Elmer. It wur only these lambstails. I just brushed 'em across."

" Did you unpin 'em ? "

" No. Whatever difference ? "

It made a good deal of difference to Elmer.

So that soft, round breast had been near enough for its posy to brush his lips !

And he asleep ! A sudden intense wish not to have been asleep made him say, " Do it agen ! "

Gillian laughed.

" No danger ! You're awake now."

He sat down, closed his eyes, snored.

" Now, Gillian ! You can't have yer tea till you wake the master. Just once across ! If you will I'll bring you a piece of music next fair I go to."

She hesitated. He looked very harmless.

She came nearer ; stooped over him ; the catkins just touched his mouth.

" Oh ! " cried Gillian. " Oh, dont'ee ! Dont'ee ! "

For suddenly Elmer's foresight, his business faculty, had gone to the winds. He had seldom so much wanted anything as he wanted to lay his head against the slatey frock. His arms went round her ; his face was hard-pressed between her breasts amid the catkins ; she was breathless and terrified.

" Oh, Mr. Elmer, the old man's coming ! " she cried ; and she did hear his step somewhere along the stone passage.

" Yo mun loose me ! "

But the tense, the almost agonized grasp, did not relax. The pillow was so soft, the violet scent so sweet. He had given so little time to romance, and here was romance in essence. He took no notice of her pleading, which grew more imploring as the steps came nearer. He just sat there, holding her uncomfortably bent above him, and went on pressing his face into her breast and his hands into her back till she was breathless and faint.

Another moment, and Fringal would come in. But suddenly on the other door—the door she had come in at—sounded a loud anxious knocking. Elmer heard it and set her free. The door opened slowly and Rwth came in. Just afterwards came Fringal. He started at sight of Gillian. Stared. Coughed. Went into a fit of laughter.

Rwth held a tea-tray, and putting a cloth on the table she laid tea. She looked at her master, and then pointed enquiringly at Fringal.

" No. In the kitchen with you," said Elmer.

Evidently they all three had meals together as a rule.

" I want Rwth to have tea with us ! " said Gillian.

" No ! By God ! "

" If you dunna let Rwth sit down along of us, I'm off."

Gillian was redder than any rose, and there were tears in her eyes. Looking at her, Rwth nodded softly three times. Yes ! she would sit down with them, whatever happened afterwards.

" I say no ! " said Elmer.

" I say good-evening to you ! " said Gillian.

Fringal hurried to usher her out.

" Oh, bide ! Bide ! " said Elmer irritably. " Fetch two more cups, wench. But after tea they'll go," he finished.

" And me—in a bit after."

" A bit after. Not when they do."

Rwth returned with two kitchen cups and a pot of inferior tea for herself and Fringal.

" You pour out," said Elmer.

" Not Rwth ? "

" I'll not hear you say the name again. Here's your chair. Now then ! "

Very nervously Gillian did so.

" Sugar, Mr. Fringal ? Sugar, Rwth ? "

It seemed so strange. She was using the same phrases as her Aunt Fanteague used. Yet here they echoed hollowly. It seemed even to her untrained imagination that these people were outside the ordinary give and take of life. Rwth drank her tea as if it were a witch-broth. Fringal ate his bread-and-butter as if he were a shipwrecked mariner with his last biscuit. Elmer simply stared at her, wondered at her, drank nothing, ate nothing, but sent Rwth into the kitchen four times for different things he imagined Gillian might like.

Fringal eyed him ; frowned ; drank his tea at a gulp, and said without apparent reason, " A dog-bee ! "

No one took any notice. Gillian, anxious to be courteous, said :

" What was that, Mr. Fringal ? "

"A dog-bee," repeated Fringal sullenly, "a dog-bee, and a queen-bee and two workers."

"Kennel!" said Elmer, comprehending and quelling immediately.

Gillian was more puzzled than ever.

"Yo bein' the queen," he explained, "and him the dog-bee, which is to say, the drone."

Gillian blushed more than ever. A country girl could not fail to see the interpretation.

"You'd best feed the pigs," said Elmer.

"When I've done me tea."

"Look sharp, then!"

Fringal swallowed a few more ship's biscuits and departed in a silent paroxysm.

Elmer glanced at Rwth, who had not finished her tea, having been cutting bread-and-butter.

"Out!" he said.

She got up and went towards the door.

"She hanna finished her tea!" cried Gillian. "And what for d'you speak to her like that?"

Elmer's eyes looked angrily into Gillian's; lingered; melted.

"Finish!" he commanded Rwth.

He seemed unable to speak to her except in single words and the imperative.

She sat down and gulped her tea and bread-and-butter very much as the Israelites must have eaten the Passover. Gillian, her egotism penetrated by curiosity, watched her and noticed the sweat beading her forehead. Before she had finished the last mouthful Rwth got up and made for the door, as if thankful to escape from Elmer's glowering eyes. Elmer came and sat down by Gillian.

"What for do you speak to Rwth like that?" she repeated.

"That's not your business, Gillian."

"If I want to know, it's my business."

"If I tell you, will you give me another kiss with the catkins?"

Gillian considered. She had not liked his face being

pressed against her breast. It made her feel hot and awkward. She wondered if she would have disliked it as much if it had been Robert's face instead of Elmer's. But it was difficult to imagine Robert, the composed and chilly, in such a position.

Still, the embrace had stirred curiosity. And Gillian really wanted to know more about Rwth, who awakened in her the same shivering wonder as the old terrible tales of Faery—such as Jack the Giant-killer—stir in the mind of a child.

" I'll draw the lambs' tails across your face, Mr. Elmer, if that's what you mean ; and now tell ! "

" Well, if you want to know why I speak to her like I do, it's because she wouldn't understand anything else. She's got no soul."

" No soul ! Laws ! Is she a child of sin like me ? "

" Child of sin ? You ? "

He was half-way between awe and laughter.

" Ah ! They got in when I was a baby. They came round like wasps and put a mark on me. Look yer ! "

She lifted her hair.

" Only Robert Rideout can save me," she added.

Elmer gave a kind of half-groan, half-laugh ; and stooping, kissed the scar. " He couldn't save you : but you're no child of sin," he said, and laughed.

" I doubt I've got no soul," said Gillian.

" I don't care whether you've got a soul or not."

" But if I hadna, I'd be only like that Mermaid— wandering and wailing and leaving a bit of money here and a bit there, and yet she couldna buy love——"

" You mean the one outside—the Naked Maiden ? "

Under his look Gillian blushed ; then she dropped her lashes ; blushed deeper ; bit her lip and tried to get to the door.

But his arms were round her again. He lifted her face to see its confusion.

" Robert Rideout can have your soul and welcome," he laughed, " if I can have——" He left the sentence unfinished.

" Shall you be awake early to-morrow ? " he asked.

" I dunno."

" Well, mind you are. There'll be something you'll like to see. Look out at six."

" Oh ! "

" And I'll take you to the May Fair at Weeping Cross if you like."

" Maybe : but I'll be going now. Good evening to you, Mr. Elmer."

He let her go. As he watched her pass the window he drew his sleeve across his hot face and said to himself :

" She's got you, Ralph, lad."

Again the dark, gloomy look came over him. " If only——" he muttered. And again : " If only——"

Rwth came in to clear the table. Suddenly Elmer snatched up the riding-whip.

" Get out ! " he shouted, threatening her with it. " Get out, you slut ! "

When she had gone, with the same submissive apathetic obedience as always, he flung himself into the armchair.

" The old man won't like it," he thought. " He's the sort to be roaring-mad if his gal's made into a nay-word. But still ! And there's Fringal. . . . What about Fringal ? "

As if in answer to his question the knowing face of that gentleman peered obliquely through a crack of the door. Fringal never opened a door wide. To see him open one was like watching a man with a closely-guarded secret.

" What d'you want ? " queried Elmer.

" A rise."

" Oh. That's the tune of it."

Fringal gave his reedy wheeze of a laugh.

" How much ? "

" Five shilling a week."

" Robbery."

" I canna be sure of my tongue under five shilling."

" But if I give that ? "

" Mum. Mum as a mole six foot under. Mum as a shell-bound chick. Mum as a fish in a frozen pond. . . ."

" Mum. That'll do."

Fringal gazed into the fire regretfully, as if he saw there all the picturesque illustrations of mumness he was forbidden to use.

Elmer pulled out the washleather bag that was his purse.

" There ! " he said. " The first week."

" Thank you kindly, sir."

Fringal pocketed the money, nodded, creased up with laughter, turned to go.

" Fringal ! "

" Ay, sir ? "

" Take the white hen and her clutch of chickens in the morning, early, to old Lovekin's. Get there at six."

" What's he give you for 'em ? "

Fringal spoke jealously. He had set the clutch of eggs, and tended the hen, and fed the chicks with soft food many times a day. He would miss them.

" That's my business."

" Oh, that's your business, be it ? Did you gather the eggs, and set 'em, and coax un on, and coddle with un, and wire 'em in from rats, and help out the chicks, and all ? Did yer ? And now it's your business ! "

" I'm satisfied with what I get."

" Where be I to put 'em ? "

" You can take 'em inside the garden wicket and turn 'em abroad on the grass. At six. Then come away."

" Nought said ? "

" Nought."

" Mum's the word, then, chicks, or——"

Fringal nodded softly ; made his mouth like the slit in a small country letter-box, winked, wheezed, opened the door charily and was gone.

CHAPTER XVIII

THE GIFTS OF RALPH ELMER TO GILLIAN LOVEKIN

In the grey dusk of morning Fringal knelt beside the coop of the white hen, and by the light of a lantern lifted her into a basket.

" I'll miss yer," he observed to the furious, clucking, pecking white bundle of motherhood.

As he placed each chick beneath her calming feathers he sighed, lingering over the job. Then he set out across the dawn-cold moor, to carry Ralph Elmer's first love-gift to Gillian. He went in at the wicket according to orders and emptied his basket on the wet grey lawn. Whereat the contents divided like quicksilver into twelve small yellow bits and one large white bit, and were seriously disturbed. At the clucking, Gillian, just out of bed, came to the window.

" Why, dear to goodness, Mr. Fringal, what'n you doing upsetting Mr. Elmer's clutch o' chickens in our garden ? "

" Orders is orders," replied Fringal, " but if I 'ad my way I'd lug 'em back. They'd be better at our place, a power."

" But they inna for us, Mr. Fringal ! Father hanna bought 'em. It was only yesterday as he said we'd got too many broodies, and he said there'd be such a sight of chickens as it ud be fowl every day of the week on our table."

" Orders is orders."

" Did Mr. Elmer tell you to bring 'em ? "

" Should I bring my best clutch to this God-'elp place if he didna ? "

" And to empty 'em just there ? "

" Should I play such a fool's game if I was left to meself ? "

" It must be a mistake, Mr. Fringal."

" Shall I tell un you dunna want 'em ? " asked Fringal persuasively.

Something in his expression, in his way of appealing to her, conveyed the truth to Gillian. The hen and chickens were a gift for her. That was why she was to look out at six.

She was pleased and she was afraid. Robert had never given her such a present. Her lips turned downwards scornfully. Robert was only a cowman shepherd. Why must she always think of Robert ? Didn't her father forbid it ? Didn't her aunt forbid it ? Hadn't Robert brought her home by force and ordered her to make a prickly cross ?

" It was like Bob's owdaciousness," she thought. And because Ralph was not Robert, she was suddenly angry with Robert. She leant out in the pink dressing-jacket, given her by Aunt Emily. She had been shocked one day to find Gillian doing her hair in her chemise, and had said :

" Even if the folk in the street can't see you, Gillian, there's always the angels."

" Mr. Fringal ! " she said, looking like a rose.

" Ah ? " said Fringal. To himself he added : " A brazen piece ! "

" Tell 'im, Mr. Fringal, please, as it's the best clutch ever I see. And as soon as I come down I'll kiss the chicks every one as quick as I can ketch 'em. And tell 'im they're like yellow catkins. And there's a shilling for yerself."

Blushing very much, Gillian withdrew.

Fringal picked up the shilling—remembered that this would all happen again—remembered also the five shilling rise—and decided to give the message.

Once outside the wicket in the shelter of the privet hedge, he doubled up with long-suppressed laughter. Jonathan, taking swedes to the sheep, saw him, watching and appraising him with curiosity.

" Colic or rheumatics ? " he asked.

" Eh ? "

" What ails you, two-double the like o' that'n ? "

" I was a-laughing."

" What at ? "

" A five shilling rise."

" Oh, well, you didna look so much like a rise as a twinge, to me. You mind me of the Ghost of Little Endor as took 'er sister's lover, and the sister said : ' Your laughter shall turn to wailing.' And sure enough, when they come to the church door, and he says summat a bit lively in her ear, she means to give a laugh, but what she did give was a long, fearsome wail, like an owl, as echoed and echoed and froze the marrow. And when the bride was abed and the bridegroom comes into the chamber and whispers summat to make 'er colour up and laugh, what did she do but give that awful skrike agen. And it come to pass as whenever he was nigh, and she should ha' been merry, she wailed. So 'e tired of it, and left 'er, and went to the South Seas and married a black ooman. But the lady of Little Endor died, and every year, when the wedding night comes round, you can hear un wailing. So when I sees you all two-double, I says : ' Maybe he comes from Little Endor.' "

A spasm went across Fringal's face, and he said hurriedly :

" I've nought to hide."

" Yo mind me of the man as stole the sacrament cup for the glitter of it," said Jonathan. " Between sacrament and locking up he took it, and they seed him running away with it acrost the meadows. He wunna his own man, like, a bit of a ratling 'e allus was."

" A near relation of yourn ? " queried Fringal, but the satire was lost on Jonathan, who was sublimely unaware of his own fame as a buffoon, and always told

stories about people exactly like himself, to the delight of
the countryside.

" No relation at all," he answered. " So he put it under
the pillow and went to bed, and when the constable come
in, he says : ' I've nowt to hide ! ' he says, all of a twitter,
' I've nowt to hide, but I'm took ill,' he says, ' and I munna
be moved.' So then o' course the constable knowed."

" Your tales," said Fringal glumly, " bin lies, I do
believe. They inna true tales. You maken 'em up,
old man. They'm lies—lies—lies."

With a defiant stare he dodged past Jonathan and set
off home. Not only had he lost his clutch of chickens,
but Jonathan, the fool of the country, had probed his
soul, had ventured into those recesses where the notices
against trespass were plain to be seen. He was very much
out of temper.

" Well ? " asked Ralph on his return.

" Er says they're like nowt but yaller catkins," said
Fringal insultingly, and was surprised to hear a shout of
laughter from his master.

" To-morrow," said Ralph, " you can take the two
Aylesbury ducks. She admired 'em."

" To-morrow ! "

" And the next day, and the day after, and on and on
till——"

Ralph smiled.

" There's one thing I know about women," he said,
" though I've had nought to do with 'em, and that is,
you must hurry 'em."

" Nought to do with 'em—saving one," said Fringal
gloomily. " I reckon you mean no good to that young
woman yonder——"

" I'm not going to marry her, as you know very well."

Fringal went into a fit of laughter.

" Every day at six you've got to be there. I'll tell you
each day what to take. Turn 'em abroad, call out something so's she'll hear, and come away."

" You wunna get 'er."

" Oh ! "

"I heerd that old foolish man, Makepeace, talking in the bar one day, and he says she's sweet on young Rideout. And he makes up songs and rhymes about 'er. You canna make 'em."

Elmer mused.

"I can't make 'em, that's true," he said. "And maybe she'll get tired of 'The lily's white, the violet blue.' But I can buy 'em."

Fringal laughed long and silently.

"A five shilling rise for me. The fowl yard for Gwlfas farm. Money for songs to Rideout. Laws me, Maister! You'll come to the House yet!"

Fringal walked away with dignity.

"I've gi'ed un one for 'isself," he thought. "And I gi'ed old Makepeace one for 'isself too." Which was precisely the phrase Jonathan used when describing the interview to his wife.

"I gi'ed old Fringal one for 'isself," said he.

"I'm sure you did, my dear," said she soothingly.

The scene was re-enacted next day.

"Oh! Oh! Oh!" cried Fringal, drearily, beneath Gillian's window.

Two white ducks greeted her.

Fringal departed, and met Jonathan outside, ready for conflict.

On the third day, when Fringal's "Oh! Oh! Oh!" sounded, there was a turkey. On the fourth, a lamb. On the fifth, two little pigs. On the sixth, a yearling calf.

"Dear soul," said Jonathan, in the kindly, protecting voice he used towards the Mallard's Keep idiot, "dear soul, hold your hand a bit! We'm used up our thankyers. You mind me of the tale o' 'Give-and-it-shall-be-given.' There was a very ancient lady, and she was a miser. So the vicar took a vow as he'd make her give in the collection, which she wouldn't never do. And he laboured terrible over the sermon. Well, she got to hear of it. And she was one as liked a joke. So she says: 'Give, shall I? Give I will!' she says. 'The sermons be long,' she says, 'the giving shall be long, too.' And when Sunday

came, she walks up the church with two great bags o'
brown linen, as she'd set the maid to sew.   And what
d'you think was in 'em ? "

"I'm sure I dunna know, old man.   But you're keeping
me a tedious time," grumbled Fringal.

"Fardens !   They was chock-full o' fardens ! " said
Jonathan.   "And she kept the congregation two mortal
hours, and the band playing every tune they could mind
(for there was no organs then) while she doled them fardens
into the gathering-bag.   Bag I says !   But a-many and a-
many bags it was, and such a to-and-agen for the wardens,
and such a tittering !   The vicar never preached ' Give-
and-it-shall-be-given,' agen."

"If you'd bin born an 'oney-fly," said Fringal, "yer
tongue wouldna ha' bin longer, but it would ha' bin more
useful, a power."

"Take a rest, Lord's Day ! " said Jonathan.

"That'll be as the fool I work for chooses," replied
Fringal.

But on Sunday, just as Isaiah and Gillian sat down to
breakfast, Fringal appeared again, leading a little hill
pony brought back by Ralph on Friday.   It had a side-
saddle, and a bridle with silver fittings.

"Ha ! " said Isaiah on the doorstep.

Each day he had said " Ha ! " but this was beyond all
expectations, and he said it so loudly that the pony
lifted liquid, startled eyes.

"Tell 'im—" said Gillian, trembling a little, "tell
'im——"

She stopped, for Robert was coming across from the
fold.   Robert was looking at her with dark eyes, hard
and steely with pain.

"What be I to tell 'im, missus ? " asked Fringal.

Robert was near.   He was looking down at her.   His
eyes were shining with anger.   And as Isaiah stooped
over the pony, his mouth, his beautiful, slow-smiling
mouth said very low :

"Bought !   A bought woman !   Gillian, you dunna
love the man.   Send it back ! "

Isaiah was in ecstasies, looking into the pony's eyes, into her mouth, running his hands up and down her hocks.

"A right good un!" he said. "Pedigree! That's what she is! Good enough for stud."

Robert's eyes were compelling.

"Send it back. Now!" he said. Then, since he saw that it was the deciding moment between himself and Elmer, he added:

"Gillian! He dunna mean marrying you. Shall I tell you what kind o' woman you'll be if you keep this pony?"

Gillian stamped.

"Husht! Husht!" she said. "You forget yer place, Robert Rideout."

Robert turned his back on her and walked away.

"Please to take the pony round, Robert!" said she.

He took no notice.

"Robert!"

This was Isaiah.

"Sir!"

"Take the pony, oot?"

"I wunna, sir, and that's flat."

"What? Not take the pony?"

"I'll never have nowt to do with it, sir; I'll neither harness it nor water it, nor litter it down, nor take no notice of it. Step-father mun do it. You can give me notice if you've a mind."

"No."

"Thank you, sir. Tell the old man as step-father 'll see to it."

There were tears in Gillian's eyes as they re-entered the house.

Isaiah looked at her archly.

"Seems like as if Elmer's moving house to the Gwlfas," he remarked. "Very like it, it seems." And, thinking of the aggrandisement of the Gwlfas during the last seven days, he gave his great comfortable laugh. He rose and went to the old dilapidated bureau with its doors of small, greenish panes set in with lead. From a small drawer he took a magnet ; from Gillian's workbox he fetched a needle, and he proceeded to demonstrate with them.

"That's how it is with our neighbour, I'm thinking," he said, "you being the magnet. Dunna go to think of what a cowman-shepherd says. Many's the ride you'll go on that nice little pony. We'll ask Elmer to eat a bit of dinner with us, come next Sunday."

Gillian tried to put away her uneasiness. But Robert's eyes, Robert's prophetic words, remained in her memory all day.

Ralph was awaiting Fringal as usual.

"Well ? " he asked.

"Young Rideout towd 'er to send it back," said Fringal.

"But she didn't."

"Would any woman in this mortal world send back a thing as meant good money ? She says : ' Take it to stable,' 'er says. And Rideout says ' No,' and 'e giv her a talking-to, and he says very nigh straight out as you'd make her a w'ore."

"Damn the fellow ! He can't know ? "

"He knows nowt. But there's so many words in his yead with this old poetry as he does maken, that it makes 'im frangy."

"What did she say ? "

"Oh, she looked very old-fashioned, and went as red as a peony, and cried."

"Oh, damn ! "

"And he says he wunna take no notice o' the beasts as you send. Not if it's ever so. He took on awful."

"And she cried ? She must like the fellow."

"It's them rhymes, I reckon."

Ralph pondered. His pondering resulted in his arriving, at a thundering gallop, at the gate of the Gwlfas late in the day when everyone was out except Robert.

"Evening, Rideout."

"Evening."

"Bin making any poetry lately, Rideout ? "

"How d'you know I make it ? "

" Fringal heard Jonathan say so in the bar."

" Oh, step-father ! He's a silly old man with a maggot
of story-telling in brain. He makes things up faster than
a child can make a tossy-ball."

" And I asked yer mother."

Robert sighed.

" Oh, well, if mother told you——"

" Do yer make love poems, Bob ? "

" Love poems ? "

" Ah ! Look you, Bob. Lend me half-a-dozen of 'em,
as short as you like—and I'll give you ten pound."

" Lord love you ! " said Robert, laughing, " they inna
worth a farden."

" Lend 'em to me ? "

" Be you in love ? "

" Ah."

" Who with ? "

" You know."

" If you're in love and I'm not, you'd ought to be able
to write love-poems."

" But I can't. I have to keep on at ' The lily's white,
the violet's blue ! ' And she'll tire of that."

" Look you ! " said Robert. " When you go to the
forge of Trewern Coed and you say to Gruffydd Conwy,
' Shoe my cob ! ' and you go away, and folks say : ' Where
did you get your nag shod ? ' you'd answer ' Gruffydd
Conwy, of the Smithy of Trewern Coed, shod my nag.'
And whether they liked the plating or whether they didna,
it ud be the same. And so it is with the bits of things
I put together in my head. For a man's work is the man,
if it's made of iron with an 'ammer, or if it's made of words.
He sweats for it, and it's hisn. And what's the man—or
woman either—without the work ? I'd sell you my pennillions if they were in a book, for you to read if you wanted
to : but I wunna sell 'em for 'em to be yours. Suppose
the Squire came to Gruffydd and says : ' Conwy, I'm a
do-nought. I'll pay you a hundred pound to say I make
your horse-shoes.' And suppose Conwy took it ? What'd
he be then ? He wouldna be Squire. He wouldna be

smith. He'd be a man of nought. And if I sold you my
pennillions, what ud I be ? And what ud you be ? She
wouldna like you the better for being mommocked up with
another chap's thinking. If she likes you, she likes you
because of the things you canna do, as much as for the
things you can. But I hope she dunna like you."

Their eyes met, stilly, but none the less savagely.

In Ralph's was passion, mingled with defiance and
devilry. In Robert's was passion also, and defiance and
devilry, but there was also the poet's intuitive knowledge.

" There's summat dark in your life, Elmer," he said.
" Take thought if you'd ought to come nigh anything so
bright as Gillian Lovekin."

" Let Gillian decide."

At his mention of her name Robert ground his heel
into the path, so that a large stone beneath it burst into
fragments.

" Let the best man win," added Elmer.

" I dunna set up to be the best. And in this world the
best dunna often win. But I'll say, ' Let the man as ud
do most for 'er win—in the long run.' "

" How d'you mean ? "

" I mean as it isn't to day, nor to morrow, nor in a
year as the truth comes out and the metal's tried. Jacob
worked seven year for Rachel and counted it nought.
You canna tire love. You canna tire life. You canna
escape the words you've set ringing and the deeds as you've
set blazing."

" You're in love with the girl, Rideout."

" And if I *was* in love," said Robert, a spasm of acute
pain passing across his face, " if I was in love, must I
mouth it to you, Elmer ? If I was in love, and she wi'
me and all well, dun you think I'd stand here argling the
like of this ? "

" You are in love ; I know. I've got it bad myself.
Now fair and square, Rideout ! What'll you take to give
me first chance ? "

" First chance and last chance and all—they're yours,"
said Robert, with intense bitterness. " Amna I cowman-

shepherd ? Inna you a moneyed man ? I'm not entered
for this 'ere race. All I says is, let the child be, Elmer."

" But supposing as she's sweet on me, what then ? "

" If so be she was sweet on you, Elmer, though I canna
say as I like you, there's nought in the world I wouldna
do for you—that is "—he gave a little awkward laugh—
" that is, if I could keep my fists off you."

" What sort o' things ud you do for me ? "

" Dig yer garden, plough yer land ; I shouldna wonder
if I'd pretty well kill myself for a chap she was set on—
if so be I was in love with 'er."

" She's set on me. I'll tell you something—she kissed
me of her own accord——"

Hatred, stifled but violent, blazed in Robert's face.
And though Elmer was the taller man, he flinched before
the savage intensity of Robert's spirit, which seemed to
give more breadth to his broad shoulders, more muscle to
his strong clenched hands.

Urgently, almost pleadingly, Robert motioned him to
be gone. Hoarsely, almost in a whisper, he besought
Ralph not to make of him a murderer.

"Out of my sight, man ! Out of my sight ! " he
implored. " I canna answer for myself. I said ' If I could
keep my fists off you ! ' "

Elmer, astonished and offended, departed.

So this was what the men that made up songs were like.
He had imagined them quiet and peaceable, and had never
dreamt that Robert would refuse good money for a few
bits of paper.

" Dang me ! What a temper ! All of a blaze before
you could say ' Jack Spratt ! ' I'd as lief not meet him
in a lonely place after Gillian——" He fell into a medi-
tation ; began to whistle, " The Lily's White," squared
his shoulders ; said, " What a pother about a girl ! " and
strolled home.

Robert, meanwhile, was thundering round the far
pasture, " taking the devil out," as he said. This he did
to such good effect that when he and the young horse
returned they were both dripping with sweat, and neither

of them wanted anything in the world but a long drink and a long sleep.

"I reckon," observed Robert in an interval of vigorous grooming, "as you'll do a many of these gallops in the next few weeks, my bird!"

And it was so.

CHAPTER XIX

BLOOM IN THE ORCHARD

ROBERT flung himself into his work and his poem about the Gwlfas. And, because he was so determined not to notice Gillian and Ralph, he did not notice, either, Gillian's wistful glances in his direction. She rode her new pony. She fed her chickens and all her other living toys. The gifts went on. But, having culminated in Fringal's beloved little cush-cow—the hornless cow that is regarded as a special favourite on farms—they took the form of furniture. Whether Elmer had sufficient irony in his composition to think that he might get all these things back again, with Gillian included—as people put water into a pump to fetch up more—is doubtful. He was not a complex person. He wanted Gillian's favour. Concrete things seemed to him desirable, especially to woman : therefore he sent them to her. Being in love and in suspense were irksome. He was quite genuinely and completely in love. When he was with Gillian he felt as the passionate lover of flowers and leaves sometimes feels— in despair at the impossibility of wholly possessing the beloved creature. Whether the creature be a flower or a human being it is the same longing, the same despair. " Touch not, taste not, handle not," is no text for lovers or mystics. The mystic, if his way to God lies through nature, is not content with looking. He wants the nearer, the dearer, the more primitive and spiritual senses. He must kneel down and gather beauty ; grasp it ; embrace it. He must even eat of it and drink of it. He must

absorb it, be nourished upon it. So Robert began by
grasping Gillian's spirit, and Elmer caught her hands ;
flung himself on the floor and held her feet in his grasp ;
wound her hair about his fingers ; kissed her, and still
implored with thirsty eyes. And Gillian being already
in love with Robert, now fell in love with passion. What
woman, who is a woman at all, does not do so at some
time in her life ? What woman is not glad and glorified
to be made sister of the silken narcissus, the delicate
anemone—to be desired ? For a woman's greatest career
is love—spiritual and physical (and the two are one),
and the crown of her career is a child. And whatever else
she may be, and obtain, and create, she will if she misses
these die with the knowledge of defeat. For a man it is
not always so. A man's genius is ego-centric—a woman's
altruistic—sacrificial. A man is himself whether he loves
or not. A woman who has not supremely given herself
is not supremely herself. Her work is halt and blind.
She has not lost her life ; so she has not found it. Robert
could still make his poem about Dysgwlfas, though his
heart was riven for Gillian. But Gillian had no more
interest in her singing since she fell in love with Robert—
which happened while she made the thorny cross, and of
which she knew nothing. Her subconscious self perhaps
knew, but she would not listen to it. There was a hunger
in her heart. Elmer assuaged it. Robert absolutely
ignored her. Therefore being a vivid and eager creature,
she took the brightest path. But every time when, as
she parted from Elmer, he kissed her so wildly, she, with
shut eyes and soul gathered inwards, said, " It's Robert !
It's Robert ! "

And every night when she closed her eyes in her little
room at the Gwlfas she entranced herself by remembering Elmer's kisses in conjunction with Robert's eyes.
She always saw Robert angry, with eyes that flashed fire,
and it was a triumphant moment of the imagination
when she had conjured into unity Elmer's hot love and
the angry eyes of Robert. Whatever she may have
thought or guessed in the past, she did not now think

that Robert loved her. Like most women, she was a
creature of actualities. If Robert loved her, he would
give her presents, live creatures, things of solid wood
or metal, something she could see. Besides—she could
never marry Robert. How could she call Mrs. Makepeace who was beginning to call her " Miss," " Mother ? "
How silly ! And Jonathan ! And she would have to
live always here in the manner of a humble cottager's
wife. No. She had been denied the joys she craved for,
and she was quite as ambitious, in her humble way, as
Cleopatra—and quite as savage.

" If so be I get married to Ralph Elmer," she reflected
through the days of April, " I shall know I'm alive,
anyway."

That was it She must know she was alive. She
must, at all costs, escape the fate of Emily. And with
the rather pitiful illogicalness of woman in all times and
in all places she would have been willing (if she had thought
of it) to risk death in order to know she was alive.

So she remained in love with passion, and Elmer was
its exponent. Strange glories, strange despairs and
wonders dazzled her through the wild, chilly April days.
For at Dysgwlfas April is cold as a snowflake. No blossom
comes upon the trees, no pale light of primroses lies along
the sparse woods until May. Then, one morning, behold !
a white cloud is fallen on the damson tree, and soon in the
little orchard, where the trees are all bent away from the
west and so it seems there is always a great west wind
blowing, soon, there come in the apple tree pink, close-
fisted buds, like babies' hands folded close on treasure.
And late come the swallows, the blackcap and the willow-
wren. Late sound the cuckoo's two mellow bells. The
Lent lilies in the far pasture shiver in the chill air long
after Easter, and often on the red flowering currant and
the wreathed orange of the berberis by the dove-cote falls
in May a white layer of snow colder than the damson
blossom. The fruit sets at the Gwlfas in no easy South
Country way. There are the plum winds and the cherry
frosts, and wild rains to smite the pear blossom, and a

last frost for the apple. And no sooner are these over than it is thunder time. For the high lands draw the storms; night after night on the young green apples descend rains that are like thick, permanent wires taut between heaven and earth.

But whether the blossom fell or the snow fell Elmer courted Gillian Lovekin—in the pastures, in the woods, on the moor, at the inn or at the farm. With his purpose flaming in his eyes so that she caught her breath with the fear of her half-comprehension, he strode through April—through her girlish shyness and angers and retreats, that were like April, towards May Day.

For it was May Day that he had fixed in his own mind as the limit of his patience.

So every lengthening day Fringal cried, "Oh! Oh! Oh!" beneath Gillian's window; and the whole country-side stood amazed before the scriptural splendour of this wooing, which set the distant markets aflame with its expensiveness, brought old sunbonneted heads close together over garden hedges, and set the young men in a roar as they lounged on village bridges, or took their quart mugs in lonely inns. But those that drank at the "Mermaid's Rest" were mute, eyeing Elmer with mingled amusement and reverence. They appreciated the poetry of his courtship, for country people are never blind to poetry when it is real, whether it is expressed in words or action. It is no uncommon sight, on the Welsh border, to see an old ploughman turned preacher for the Sabbath moved even to tears at the beauty of the Psalms or Isaiah. This was Elmer's one poetic inspiration, and they accounted it to him for righteousness. One young farmer, generally considered "near," did say it was a fool's game, and that Elmer could have had Jane Chips for a brace of pheasants. But he was quickly taken up by another, who said:

"Eh! But what's Jane Chips? That pitcher's been to the well too often! A poor creature! Now Miss Lovekin—well, I'd half a mind myself—plenty of good red blood and a gallus laugh and innocent as a child."

" You couldna afford it, me lad."

" I met and I metna. But it's no use to think on it, seemingly."

Meanwhile, Isaiah said " Ha ! " at sight of the gifts ; Jonathan jested with Fringal at the entering in of the wicket ; Mrs. Makepeace sighed for her son ; Gillian's heart fluttered, rejoiced ·and boded ; Elmer, without saddle or stirrups, but with red-tinted spurs, his knees gripping his horse's panting sides, thundered down the lane, and Robert, without spurs, but with a more furious speed (though the thunder of his going was muffled), strove with his love and hate in the far pasture. And through all these spring days, in the strangest and most mysterious way, invisible threads spun themselves between the Unket Place and four very different people. One thread reached out to Gillian Lovekin, so that when she passed the Unket Place on her visits to the " Mermaid's Rest," or with Elmer's arm about her, wandering on the moor, looking at its straight, dark line above the pale water, she would shiver. One thread reached out to the dumb girl and made her tremble as she gathered sticks there—for there was nowhere else to gather them—and as she wandered on strange, secret ploys of which there is more to hear. One thread held Elmer, so that he loathed the place, as he had loathed it upon the evening of his first coming—loathed and yet was drawn there by a darting curiosity. And one thread, taut and steady, held Robert Rideout, awoke in him again the knowledge that something awaited him there—there, in the little Gyland, where the blackthorn wove her crown of thorns, where the water moaned and the snow lay long. Something, some great decision, a thing that would make him for ever a god or a poor, mean creature, was preparing for him in the Unket Place. There, like a dark jester through a paper-covered hoop, evil would leap out. There, as in his dreams, Gillian would be saved or lost, saved or lost for ever by some sacrificial deed that he must do. It would not be in summer. No. In summer the Unket Place seemed almost kind. The sleepy hemlock stood so high about it, hazy and foamy and pale ; the white wild roses with blood-red thorns made impenetrable thickets ; the stunted fir trees gave, though charily, their brown cones to the brown, loose, sandy soil. A magpie's nest was in the tallest tree, and one magpie would sit all day above the low singing water, dreaming and for ever dreaming, as though he knew Gillian's magpie song, and was cogitating about the secret that has never been told. The bracken grew stealthily and exquisitely taller and taller, until it was as high as Robert's shoulder. Bittersweet wreathed the hedges, and garlic mingled its biting scent with the slumbrous hemlock. Beneath the dark-leaved sloes and the dog-berry bushes were to be found here and there among the pine needles small neat plants of sanicle, with its gracious ivy-shaped leaves and its tall buds that flower in foaming white in May—the sanicle that, so the old books say, heals all outward hurts and inward wounds, and is the emblem, lovely, ephemeral, hardy, of love.

And now, as April drew on to May, it was as though, in silence and in patience, invisible hands began to prepare a stage for some drama. The young pine needles pushed out ; the elm leaves and alder leaves uncurled ; the sloe had flowered ; the white campion shot up ; the larch set out her roses. These roses would be cones, the campion broken, the elm and alder leaves spread amid the old pine needles, dark fruit hung thinly on the bare sloe, when that snow-weather came which was boded in Robert's soul.

CHAPTER XX

ROBERT PLEACHES THE THORN HEDGE

On May morning, ever since Robert had come to the farm, he and Gillian had gone "neesening." So, because he wanted to forget that he was not going neesening to-day, Robert got up very early, and went off to pleach the big hedge at the foot of the far pasture. It was certainly a young man's job. Every muscle of his shoulders and arms and back was called into play. Jonathan could never have done it. It was composed of huge may-trees, now set with green, bursting buds. Their thick trunks had to be felled like forest trees. Their huge intermingled branches had to be sawn off one by one with infinite labour. It was a twenty-foot hedge, and so old that even the topmost boughs were thick and tough. At ordinary times Robert would have been annoyed with Isaiah for ordering the destruction of so much beauty. For the poet in him had loved this great wall of living green, all frothed with fragrant creamy flowers. But now he was glad when each blow sent a shock up his arms ; when, with the final blow, the crash came ; when the ivy-wreathed branches groaned under the saw. In a few hours he was surrounded by débris ; the boughs lay in confusion ; the rubbish of years—old nests, old leaves, dead twigs—fell out in clouds, was dust in his nostrils.

"Well !" he observed satirically, as he sat down on a fallen trunk to eat his "ten o'clock," "if I amna maying along with Gillian, I *be* maying."

And rising up in a little while, he set about the largest trunk he could find.

He was so absorbed that he did not hear the voice of Gillian Lovekin sounding over the meadows from the fold. Thin and wistful as the voice of a lost fairy it came—three times.

"Robert Rideout! Robert Rideout! Robert Rideout!" Then it ceased. There was an urgency in it which came across the distance. But amid the echoing thuds of his axe, with a crackling of twigs and a smother of dust about him, Robert heard nothing, and, as no one knew where he was, no one came to disturb him, until, two hours later, a voice on the other side of the hedge observed :

"Late for pleaching."

It was Gipsy Johnson. He stood there looking up at Robert with his chocolate eyes like a faithful dog.

"Ah!" assented Robert without surprise, for it was Johnson's time for going into Wales, and besides, he was seldom surprised at anything.

"Ah! That's gospel. It be late, but Maister would have it done. So you see I'm busy at it."

"By the looks you've bin at it for days."

"Only this morning."

"Dear 'eart! You're a powerful good worker, Rideout."

"Come over," said Robert. "There's a drop of beer. Come over and sit you down."

"Well, lad," observed Johnson when he had climbed over and taken off his hat so that the wind could play in his long grey hair. "Well, we stopped her."

"Ah!" Robert spoke without enthusiasm.

He felt the irony of the fact that he had brought Gillian back just in time for Elmer.

"Ah! I was in a pother when I found out what she was after," said Johnson, chuckling as he filled and lit his clay. Then a sad and gloomy look came over his face and he said :

"It met ha' bin my own, my little dark-eyed Ailse."

"Who was that? "

"My little girl as disappeared."

" She'd got black eyes ? "

" Ah. Like her mother. I told ye about Esmeralda ? "

" Ah. I know about Esmeralda."

" Well, I took Esmeralda whome to my new caravan one Lammastide. And in early May the little un was born. And Esmeralda sends the old ooman for me so soon as she was lighted of the child, and she looks up at me with that smile, and she says : ' At last ! At last ! ' ' Why,' says the old ooman, ' you couldna ha' given him a little un much quicker, lass.' And she beckons the old ooman out (oh ! she'd a proud way time and agen, had Esmeralda) and she whispers ' At last the hunger's better.' And I didna understand. So she says ' Since I seed ye, I've hungered and thirsted to go to hell for ye,' she says. ' And now I've been. And eh ! But I'm glad ! ' Rideout, would any other woman say that ? "

" Maybe—one or two."

Robert thought of one who would not—yet. Would she ever cease to be a frozen fairy and ask to go to hell for a man ? What man ?

" Lad ! dunna grind yer teeth the like of that'n. It's unlucky," said Johnson. " Well, so the child grew and got plump and her was the spit and image of Esmeralda. My Lord ! Johnson was a gay man them days. Work ! You couldna tire me. Come back in the evening and there they was. Like birds in a nest. She nursed the child— our folk think it sin not to. And she'd sing to it. And she took and sewed all my gold buttons on its little gown. And some necklaces as I'd took for a nag in lieu of money she put round its neck, and gold buckles on its shoes. And one time when we went through Sil'erton, nought would do but I must buy the child a coral rattle like what the little lords and ladies have. For she said : ' Gipsy Johnson's the Lord of Creation for me.' Laws ! The things she'd say. Well, the long and the short is, one day the child went."

" Went ? "

" Ah. Just went. Esmeralda left her in cradle by the caravan while she fetched the water. And when she come back, the child was gone. Her said it was the fairies, and sure enough I dunna see who else it was."

" Didn't you ever find her ? "

" We didn't never—we looked high and we looked low, but never—never—did we find 'er."

" Could she walk ? "

" No."

" Somebody stole her."

" But it was such a lonesome place."

" Somebody *must* ha' stole her."

" If I could find that man," said Johnson with the whole savagery of his furthest ancestry in his quiet voice, " if I could only find 'im—" and gently, lovingly, he made the gesture of cutting his throat.

" And watch 'im bleed ! " he said savouringly. " Esmeralda went mad." Robert bent his head before this old bitter sorrow.

" Went mad, and died. I never heard tell of the child."

" What would she have bin like ? "

" You couldna tell, not well. But she'd ha' bin summat like Esmeralda ; she'd got the same dark hair and eyes."

" Clear black eyes ? "

" Ah. But they met alter."

" Could she talk ? "

" She could say bits o' words. Not many. She was but five."

" How many years ago ? "

" Twenty three. I was seven and twenty then."

A strange, triumphant look came into Robert's face. Then he said :

" But she could talk ? "

" I said as she could talk."

The triumphant look faded.

" Ah ! It was long ago," said the gipsy, " very long ago, and it's all gone over. But I'd lief find the child."

" If there's ought I can do," said Robert, " you know where to come."

His eyes flashed. Johnson observed it. He knew the sign. That look came only when Robert loved or hated.

Two very strong and dirty hands met in a grip that neither noticed particularly, though it would have made a townsman shout.

"Lovekin's got a new trap, seemingly," observed Johnson. "And a new friend."

"Who d'you mean ? "

"I seed your girl driving away with a big darkish chap in a bran new gig."

"That's Mr. Elmer of the ' Mermaid.' "

"A new chap ? "

"Ah ! Thatcher's left."

"I thought the girl was yours."

"Oh, laws no ! She took up with the new chap," said Robert shortly. " I shouldna be surprised if he's her acquaintance by now."

"Why dunna you kill 'im ? "

Johnson spoke with great simplicity.

Robert laughed.

"Well, we may be a bit rough in these parts," he said, " but we dunna go as far as that."

"It's what them black cattle do up in the mountains if they canna agree."

Robert felt that the black cattle had not grown up, and he had. He was too old for this infantile whimsey of hatred.

"If it was me, I'd fight 'im."

"If she likes 'im best, let 'im take 'er ! " said Robert. "I amna a murderer."

"You're a queer 'un," said Johnson, preparing to depart. "If it was me and I was a young chap like you, I'd have the wench in my caravan before nightfall. Well, goodbye to ye, Bob. See yer in the back-end."

"What did you say the little un's name was ? " asked Robert.

"We called her Ailse."

"Ailse ? That's what townfolk calls ' Alice,' inna it ? "

"Ah. Well, that's what we called 'er. You should 'a heard Esmeralda crooning it over in the twilight— ' Ailse—Ailse—Ailse ! ' She learned her to say it and to say, ' Gipsy Johnson ' and ' Dad,' and ' Esmeralda ' and the names of the places we camped in.   Well, I mun be going."

" Goodbye, Johnson, and good luck."

" I've no reason for such, for Esmeralda's gone, and there's no woman for me but Esmeralda."

Late in the evening, with aching back, Robert trudged home.   And the result of his day's cogitations was that Rwth must be taught to write.   She must be taught in secret, by Gillian.   Neither Elmer nor Fringal must know. And when she had learnt, he himself must question her. He must probe into her soul and see if it was gipsy.   He must ask if she remembered jewels and golden buckles. He would ask Gillian the moment she came home.

CHAPTER XXI

BRIAR ROSES

WHEN Gillian awoke on that bright May morning, she suddenly wanted to go to the Fair at Weeping Cross with Robert; but yesterday she had finally promised to go with Elmer. This did not trouble her. Elmer would get over it. She had dreamt of Robert. In her dream Robert had been standing knee-deep in snow. His face was sad and wild. The cold wind blew about his dark hair. His hands were clenched. At his feet lay a dead lamb. Why should Robert be so miserable over a dead lamb? Then Mr. Gentle came and touched him on the shoulder, and Mr. Gentle's eyes were streaming with tears. Robert turned unwillingly and went away with Mr. Gentle, who carried the prickly cross. And Gillian awoke crying out to Robert not to go with Mr. Gentle. There was something so grey and clammy and dreadful about him; if Robert went with him he would be changed. His hands would be no more the hard brown hands she knew. His face would not be weather-fresh, sunburnt and lean with health. He would become like Mr. Gentle. It was horrible. After she woke she still remembered it all and was urgent to find Robert, to tell him. Tell him what? How he would laugh! Still, she must find him.

So she ran from fold to rickyard, from stable to shippen, but she could not find him. And then came Elmer, all impatience to be gone.

But even as they drove away, she in all the pride of conscious beauty and admiration, he gay with the cer-

tainty of attainment, a foreboding of disaster was upon
her. She struggled with it, and after a few miles of keen
blue air it vanished.

" I've ne'er been to this Fair afore," she said. "There'll
be a power of folks, likely ? "

" I've never been neither. But I reckon there will.
I shouldn't care if there wasn't anybody."

" Oh ! What's a Fair with nobody at it ? "

" There'd be you."

" Can I buy and sell and all ? "

" You can."

" Dear sakes, I've no money."

" You've got what money can't buy."

" And what met that be ? "

" Love."

The word rang like a shot—like a gun-shot in a silent
shelving wood.

" But, what'll love buy ? "

" All I've got ! "

" Oh ! Mr. Elmer ! "

" You're a flower ! You're a bird ! You're a butter-
fly ! " said Elmer, unevenly, and he kissed her. So, with
kisses and sudden embraces, with badinage and long
urgent silences they came over the lovely levels, the
steep descents of the moor. They came through the
green places and the brown ; they traversed the near
and attained the far purple distance, and it melted before
them and became the near. Then they saw a long way
off, in a veil of rain, the small shining steeple, the low
shining roofs—red and brown and blue—the clustered
trees, half in leaf, the nestling ricks, the apple-green
fields of Weeping Cross. They gazed on it. To her it
was the site of a day's revelry. It was a place to laugh
in, to dine in, to shy at cocoanuts and look at fat oxen,
buy a fairing and come away. It was a place she would
have most liked to see in company with Robert ; but as she
could not, she liked almost as much to see it with Elmer.

To Elmer it was a place utterly uninteresting until
nightfall, although his whole life centred round such

places on such days. He cared not a rap though he lost as many good bargains as there were minutes in the day, so long as the day soon went. Fringal had said he must bring back a cow. The milk was sinking. A good cow. He could get one cheap. Had he not given the best to old Lovekin ? " If you wait about a bit, you'll likely get one cheap," said Fringal. Good Lord ! was he never to enjoy himself ? Must he always keep his nose to the grindstone ? How the road glistened ! What a merry sound the ringing hoofs made ! God ! How green the honeysuckle hedges were ! How many miles from home ? How many miles from Isaiah ? He laughed to himself.

Gillian should come to the "Mermaid's Rest." She should have the best room. Rwth should wait on her. Oh ! she should wait on her hand and foot like a slave in the Bible waiting on an Eastern Queen.

" You're a flower ! You're a bird ! You're a butter-fly ! " said he again, far too much in love to be original. And Gillian laughed—much too gay and happy to be critical. She was looking almost beautiful, for she had magnetism, as Isaiah divined, and all her magnetism was alight. It beautified her as a veil often beautifies a plain woman. It gave her magic and romance and femininity. It set roses in her cheeks and blue lights in her eyes, it made her smile scarlet, sweet and lavish.

They came quietly down the steep main street of Weep-ing Cross, where the shops had, like Jonah's whale, given up that which they contained, and had spread it on trestles and booths. There were gay flowered chintzes and flannels, scarlet and white, and prints for summer frocks and sunbonnets and corduroys outside the drapers' ; and wonderful bowls and tea-sets and coloured glass vases outside the china shop ; and great leather boots for ploughmen, and elastic-sided cashmere boots for people of eighty, and tiny white or red boots for people of one ; there were sticks of pink rock and bulls-eyes and jumbles that reminded Gillian of the Junction ; there were shining black collars with silver or brass hames for carthorses, and brown harness for the ponies of farmers' wives, and

reins and riding-whips and spurs; even the furniture
shop was a whale, and its Jonah was a lady's antique
dressing-table inlaid with shells on a green ground, with a
mirror and little brackets.

" Oh ! Look's that ! " cried Gillian.

" You like that, do you ? "

" Ah ! "

" It's yours."

" Oh, Mr. Elmer ! You've given me too much ! Besides
it's too big for my room."

" Change your room."

" They're all little in our house ! "

" Change your house."

Gillian's simple yet subtle mind was much disturbed.
Did he mean this to be a proposal or did he not ? She
changed the subject.

" Oh ! Look's that trestle with lemonade and beer. I
be so thirsty."

They pulled up and had some refreshment, served by
an ancient dame in a white cap and check apron and
fringed shawl, who smiled at everything they said and
murmured : " You're welcome ! You're welcome ! " but
all the while gazed at them gravely over her spectacles,
as if she were reserving her judgment. As if, thought
Gillian, she was made up of two people, one merry and
one strict, and they never agreed.

Elmer had a striped blue and white mug of frothing ale,
and they continued on their way in company with other
gigs and late arrivals for the Fair ground in the shape of
a drove of sheep and a great mud-bespattered sow with
eight pale pink, silky piglets.

They drove into the yard of the inn, and Elmer sent
Gillian to inquire what time the Farmer's Ordinary was,
and if they might sit down to the first table. Then he
unharnessed the cob and led him into the great stable
where only a faint green light came in from a high, ivy-
covered window, and where the silence was full of the rust-
lings of hay being pulled down from cratches, and stamping
and pawings of shod hoofs on the stone floor, and the deep

breathing and sighing of horses. Elmer tied up the cob, rubbed him down, pulled a pair of pincers out of his pocket, took the cob's near forefoot between his knees and wrenched off the shoe. Then he went out, shut the stable door, threw the horse-shoe on to the mixen, and joined Gillian in the hall where she was talking to the landlady. The lady of the inn was a person of so much self-respect that it was impossible to imagine her in any situation that was not supremely dignified. To think of her taking a bath was sheer irreverence. To imagine her being rocked in her cradle, being born, was impossible. If she could not exist without being born then she did not exist. And she would never die, because it was impossible to imagine her laid low, unstarched, and without the slight flush of conscious rectitude. Her right hand lay on an oak table on which were a row of bedroom candlesticks with very white candles, and the impression was given that these candles were the landlady's Vigilance Committee, virginal and austere, who would see that nothing but what was absolutely correct went on in the mahogany-furnished and very highly-polished bedrooms.

There were no rugs or carpets in the hall, or the smoking room, or the dining room. By the end of the day of the Fair the reason for this became apparent. A thick layer of straw and farmyard manure covered the floors in true Arthurian manner. For it is obviously impossible, when in the throes of bargaining or when meeting a rival from across the border (border feuds are by no means dead), to remember the mat and the scraper. The Fair ground lay at the back of the inn, the street lay in front, and by the end of the day it was not easy, by simply looking down, to tell where you were. The Farmers' Ordinary was already in progress, so Elmer and Gillian went into the dining room and found two seats at one end of the long table.

It was a huge repast. People such as Isaiah, riding and driving in all weathers, wrestling with great beasts, having huge thews and sinews to keep up, take a great

deal of feeding. The landlady was aware of it. Her
sirloins were the largest, the juiciest, the fleshiest in the
town. Her fowls were heavy-weights and went in couples,
her tarts were each the sepulchre of a whole tree of
gooseberries. Only on this day they were bottled—bottled
last year with rectitude and competence, and made into
tarts yesterday in the same atmosphere, so that each
gooseberry seemed to swell and bristle with acidulated
righteousness. Everything, from the baskets of bread
to the lakes of sauce and gravy, in old-fashioned tureens,
was generous and hospitable. There was a mingled scent
of underdone meat, pepper, hair oil, hot fruit, mezereon
(with which the table was decorated) and manure. There
were a great many farmers, and a few farmers' wives.
There were plenty of wild and rugged faces, faces used to
fronting the eternal grandeur of the hills, faces becalmed
from long gazing into the brown waters of mountain
pools. There were a few beautiful faces. Ruddy com-
plexions prevailed, and the eyes of the company were
mostly the dark and brooding ones of border-Welsh or
the rather choleric blue ones of border-English. The
women looked at Gillian kindly. She was obviously out
for the day with her lover—either just married, or just
going to be, they opined as they glanced at Elmer's face.
It would have been difficult to say, as they consumed
their large platefuls with their splendid teeth, whether
they knew that they were the backbone of England. But
they were conscious, as they took their well-earned holiday,
which was only business in a new dress, of the wide ploughed
acres, the well-got hay, the snug corn-ricks and pruned
orchards, the clean floors and the cradles full of babies
at home. They liked strong food, broad jokes, primitive
justice, safe politics and solid religion.

Elmer whispered to Gillian that it was like a wedding
breakfast.

Nobody knew Gillian. Isaiah had steadfastly refused to
bring her to fairs, and, on those rare occasions when he took
her to Weeping Cross, he had not taken her to the "Drover's
Arms" but to a small, demure tea-shop further up the street.

They knew Elmer by sight, and supposed she was his wife or his betrothed.

Dinner over, they went out to the Fair, where the damp soil sent up a sweet scent in the sunshine, and the fragrant breath of cattle, the hot woolly smell of sheep, the fœtid panting of dogs, mingled with tar, oil from the merry-go-round, corduroy, horses, leather, and the ever-present manure, made one great bouquet sweetened by the fresh, eager country air.

A man was sticking bills on the smooth tight bodies of the pigs. He slapped a wet brush on to their sides, clapped down the bill, smoothed it and passed on, leaving the animal self-conscious and puzzled. The sale began, but Elmer forgot his cow. They went on the merry-go-round. They saw the fat woman. They had their fortunes told. Johnson's clan was here, but Johnson himself never came to fairs now. They shied at cocoanuts ; they patronized a thimble-rigger. They watched the young men putting the weight, and Elmer tried his hand and did very well. At that, Gillian completely shelved Robert for the day. She decided that she was in love with Elmer. As they stood with the crowd and watched two heavyweight policemen boxing, she saw Elmer as the winner and Robert as the loser.

The auctioneer was making the walls of the houses ring with his voice.

" Now, ladies and gentlemen, I'm here to *sell* 'em ! They're here to be *sooold*. Now's your chance ! Take it or leave it ! I tell you this "—(he lowered his voice to a penetrating whisper)—" it'll never happen again ! Lose your chance now—you won't get it again ! I'm here to *sell* 'em. Not next week ! Not to-morrow ! *Now !* "

" Now ! " To Elmer his raving was as the voice of a prophet, prophesying smooth things. He smiled to think how well he had made his plans.

He decided not to tell her about the shoe until just as they were preparing to start for home. Meanwhile he suggested that they should go to the dance which was always held in a large room in the town on the night of the

May Fair. And while Gillian tidied her hair and borrowed a blouse from the landlady's friendly daughter for the festive occasion, Elmer took the opportunity of bespeaking the room.

" Juliana and I," said he, " like a bit of a dance. Maybe the time will fly. We'd best stop the night over."

" What's she done with her ring ? " enquired the lady with a lynx look.

" Left it on the sink when she was washing up," said Elmer, and oil was poured upon the waters.

At Dysgwlfas, Johnson had passed the inn, had seen in the distance a girl gathering sticks in the gyland, and had gone on. Robert had finished his hedge and had his supper ; Isaiah sat in his parlour. All the creatures of the farm, furred and feathered, had gone to sleep.

At the " Mermaid's Rest " Fringal had settled his depleted live stock and had demanded his supper—beer and bread and cheese—which Rwth brought to him, afterwards going up the shallow creaking stairs to her attic under the gable, where she took the pins from her thick, lustreless hair, washed her face, put on her unbleached calico nightdress and knelt down. But the rite she was absorbed in was not that of prayer. Rather it might be called ecstasy. On the bed she had spread out a large red cotton handkerchief of Robert's which he had dropped when helping with the move. She had washed it, ironed it, folded it with sprigs of southernwood and laid it in a drawer.

Every night she took it out and laid her face upon it, kneeling by the bed. Her dark eyelashes lay on cheeks flushed with a passion as spiritual and intense as it was unconscious.

She looked almost beautiful (she could never be pretty or " nice-looking," but just ugly or beautiful) as she knelt so, shaken and flushed with love that was anguish because it had no relief. She could not even speak his name. She could only, with a tenderness that ravaged her face, and yet glorified it, press her cheek hard upon the scarlet cotton decorated with white horse-shoes which Mr. Makepeace

thought so delightful a pattern, and which Rwth regarded
as a mystic regards his altar draperies—as something that
had known the sacred presence of the God of Love.

For to Rwth, who knew nothing of either God or her
fellows—except the harsh things she had observed from
watching Elmer and Fringal—Robert had become as a
God—to sit and look at him was heaven. To hear his
voice was health and joy. To suffer for him—that was, all
unknown to herself, the ultimate purpose of her life. Once
he had come to the inn with a long red briar-scratch on his
cheek, and had chanced to say that the old dog-roses by
the rick-yard wanted lopping, only he'd have to wait till
he got some new hedging gloves.

Next morning, mysteriously, uncannily, the dog-rose
briars were neatly cut and the cut branches burnt in a little
bonfire outside the gate. And had anyone at the " Mermaid " observed anything about Rwth they would have
seen that her hands were a mass of wounds, and they would
have seen, as she plunged them into the bucket of soda and
water to scrub the floor, the smile on her sad face, uplifted, ecstatic as that of a martyred saint.

CHAPTER XXII

WEEPING CROSS

INTO the large upper room throbbing with sound went Gillian and Elmer. And there they danced with the rest, oblivious of heavy country boots and the stifling air, until ten o'clock, when some of the men were drunk and some of the women a good deal dishevelled. Now Gillian had given her solemn word to be home at ten. So, when the leisured silver chime crept out from the church spire into the dark blue night, she judged it time to go home. They walked down the narrow street with its cobbled pavements, where the shadows of the gables and chimneys on one side touched the doorsteps on the other side.

In the inky shade of a yew tree Elmer suddenly snatched Gillian and kissed her, holding her close against him so that he could feel the crushed softness of her breast. It was by no means the first kiss of passion, but it was the first nearness of their bodies, and it terrified and intoxicated Gillian. She was wax in his hands after that, prisoner not only to the sudden physical love that his passion awoke, but to her own vitality and to unassuaged but completely awakened curiosity. With something between reverence and ferocity he set both hands on her shoulders and slipped the loose round blouse and the bodice beneath down to her elbows so that she gleamed palely in the darkness. Then, as she pleaded and struggled, he kissed each shoulder and slipped her blouse on again.

With his arm about her they came to the inn. Everyone was asleep, except the daughter who had been to the dance.

and whose candle still burnt in an attic. The great hollow
hall, still carpetless, was all in darkness. Only a faint
distillation of moonlight from an upper window showed the
large curve of the stone staircase, unenclosed and baronial,
sweeping up to the railed gallery above the hall—which
gallery served as the landing. It was like a picture of a
mediæval inn, only there the open courtyard took the place
of the hall. On the table stood only one vestal candlestick, and beside it a little placard with the number of the
room assigned to Elmer and a request that he would fasten
the bolt.

" The cob cast a shoe," he said. " I saw we couldn't go
home. We'll be bound to stop the night over."

In Gillian's mind adventure struggled with fear of her
father. Still, the adventure was now, the anger to-morrow.

" A' right," she said.

" There's only one room—my dear."

In the sifting moonlight brilliant eye met brilliant eye.
A vitality greater than their own rushed through their
veins and pounded in their breasts. They could no more
help themselves than slaves bound for sacrifice on Druidical
altars. They were bound for sacrifice on an altar older than
mythology : the altar of one who reigns in fold and field,
in town and village, in the castle and the hut, who is merciless and arrogant ; at once lovely and hideous ; who wears
the garb of every creed and sect, but belongs to none ; who
hates virginity ; who will be worshipped as long as there
remain in the world maids and men ; but whose worship
is mysterious as the forest, and whose name is unacclaimed
of any worshipper—for her name is unknown. She has
lust in her treasury as well as love ; yet, because of her
deathless, keen, miraculous vitality, she is clean. And
such is her witchery that those who have lived and loved
without having known her feel cheated. But those who
die in her arms are content as if they already lived in
Paradise.

Elmer and Gillian looked on each other as the clear-eyed
deer in the forest look—thrilled, yet loveless. Thrilled in
every nerve, trembling under the hand of the merciless one,

they stood. And white, virginal, the landlady's unlit candle stood. It was to remain unlit. Suddenly Elmer snatched the number of the room, swept Gillian into his arms, and went up the shallow stairs as if he had tasted the elixir of immortal youth. He had no remembrance of yesterday, no thought of to-morrow. An air, eager and sweet and maddening as the wild air of early morning on a mountain, blew about him—the same that ruffled the hair of Antony in the arms of Cleopatra, of the lovers of Thais, of Paris, and Tristan and many long-forgotten in desert and in forest.

Gillian lay still in his arms, brown lashes on flushed cheeks, passive in a spell she could not break, gripped by a sudden agony of desire. Her heart raced in the silence like a doe pursued through a dark forest. That it was Robert to whom she desired to give herself, she did not remember.

But through the long night, as she lay in the arms of Elmer, faint and weeping, ecstatic, afraid, she would see at intervals against the lightening grey of the window Robert's deep-set eyes, full of anger ; Robert's curving mouth, set in wrath. Robert was awake, she knew, awake at the Gwlfas, thinking of her. He was angry because he was robbed. Was it fair that he should be angry at losing what he had not asked for ? She was bitter at the thought of it. As the lines of light at the sides of the blind became golden and she knew that morning had come and that she must go back and face Robert, she had the lethargic feeling of those who wake on a day of expected bitterness. And when Ralph woke from a short and restless sleep and took her in his arms again, she was angry and ashamed and scornful. So this was all that lay behind the locked and guarded door that the matrons kept so carefully ! This was the secret she had given her maidenhood to discover ! No, this was not all. There was no love in it, and so it was a lamp unlit. If Robert had awakened by her side——

At the thought floods of shame overwhelmed her ; she lay and sobbed. It was useless for Elmer to kiss her bare shoulders, to let his hands stray up and down her smooth body. The more he caressed her the more she cried. With the wisdom of awakened sex she knew that she loved Robert, that she adored him, because he *was* Robert, that she would rather have his anger than all the gifts and kisses of Elmer.

So, as day strode over the purple-shadowed moor and looked upon the sleepless, haggard face of Robert Rideout in his attic, Gillian lay and cried as many another has cried—because she had just found out that she had awakened by the side of the wrong man.

She supposed she would have to marry Elmer now, and Robert would never speak to her, and perhaps he would marry someone else.

" If he do," she said to herself with sudden rage, " I'll kill her and myself as well ! "

As if in reminder of the steadfast commonplace that, like Juliet's nurse, is always with us whether we laugh or cry, there was a knock and an uplifted voice without, announcing breakfast.

The carpet was being put down in the hall as they went into the dining-room. The Fair was over till another year. Then once more the carpets would be rolled up, other lovers would dance in the upper room, and lie in the antique bedrooms. Other candles would watch over them or be ignored. Once more, then, the great joints would sizzle in the oven, the tarts and pies be made, the casks of home-brewed broached, the sheep go by through dust or mud with a leafy rustling, the bargains be driven, the purchases made. But now the Fair was over. The shops had withdrawn within their windows ; the hobby-horses were packed on their waggon ; Johnson's clan had set out for the mountains, not to return until the autumn ; the little old woman with the striped blue and white mugs and the spectacles, who was half merry and half strict, had withdrawn into mystery for another year. And everything was the same as it had been the day before yesterday. Only Gillian Lovekin had awakened beside the wrong man. And what, in the sum of things, did Gillian Lovekin matter ?

Southward, across the moor, two men were driving, and to this question they might both have answered : " What dun Gillian matter ? Gillian Lovekin's all the world to me ! "

But as they drove with dogged faces not a word did they say. Isaiah flogged the mare, and the purple moor sprang to meet them, the far hills ran towards them, tree after tree leapt on them. The steeple of Weeping Cross came to them discreetly, but very fast.

Robert, sitting with his arms folded, without a hat (having forgotten it), was glad of the speed. Though he knew what they would find, he was glad to be going to find it soon. It was better to know the worst. Especially was it necessary to know whether this had happened with Gillian's consent or not : because, if not, he was going to kill Elmer, and he would rather kill him while he was angry. He hated killing things. He knew exactly how he would do it—choking the life out of the man with his powerful hands. His brown hair lifted in the wind ; his brow was lined beneath it ; his eyes weary. It is unpleasant for a man not to know if he is to be hanged or not, and Robert did not know.

So he was almost absent-minded when Isaiah, pointing with his whip to some winter wheat, said : " 'Ealthy ! " And he was intensely glad when the long high street closed up like a telescope before the mare's reckless canter. They pulled up with a slide before the " Drover's Arms," and Isaiah went in. He stood in the dining-room door.

" Ha ! " he said.

The culprits said nothing. Isaiah pointed to the door.

" Leave me and Elmer to talk," said he.

Gillian went into the hall.

" Gillian ! " said Robert softly.

So Robert was here ! This was cruel. She trembled and was white as the landlady's newly-stoned doorstep. She stood shrinking against the wall and did not answer.

" Gillian ! "

Oh, that kind voice ! Oh, that voice so full of tenderness and strength ! It drew her as the shepherd's voice

the sheep—as cooing dove draws dove—as the deep
murmur of the sea draws the sailor.

" Gillian ! "

Across the hall, down the six white steps, over the
cobbles, it drew her. She stood beside the cart. She
laid her small hand as if for comfort on the mare's panting,
shining flank.

Robert was looking at her. He was going to make her
look at him. Oh, grief ! Oh, bitter pain !

Slowly she lifted her face, her eyes. There he was—
Robert, the man she loved. With shoulders a little
stooping, with hand quiet on the reins, with mouth for
once grim and forbidding, with deep-set eyes gazing,
probing, seeing through and through her very being.
Love met love. Love forsworn and deserted met love
the wanderer, the forlorn, all dim with tears.

He had seen all. He knew of the kisses, of the naked
shoulders, the marriage of loveless bodies, the shame.

With a cry of anguish she covered her face and turned
to run away.

" Nay, Gillian. You mun answer first."

Obediently she waited.

" Did Elmer make ye stay ? "

There was a long silence. Little breezes lifted and
sank in the half-unfurled leaves of the chestnut tree in
the garden of the "Drover's Arms." In its top bough
a blackbird sang musingly. It was as though he passed
the whole of life through the crucible of his song and
turned it to sweetness. The drone of voices came through
the window. The mare stirred and sighed. From far
away came the rumble of the receding gipsy wagons.
The ivy lisped upon the house. Earth and air seemed to
be waiting for a verdict. And with the swift intuition of
love Gillian saw Robert's purpose. If she said Elmer
had made her stay, she would be uttering the death
sentence of both men. If she said she wished to stay—
what ? Only that for ever and ever Robert would think
she loved Elmer, would never speak to her or look at
her. She would be married to Elmer. Even now, if she

told the truth, she might be saved. But that look!
That dreadful look in Robert's face!

She gazed up at him as a seamaiden might look at a
sailor lover when she heard the call of the Merman King
and sank into deep water. One look, and all was over.

" I stayed because I'd lief stay, Robert," she said.
" And you munna lay hand on him."

Then, with a gasping sob, she fled into the house.

CHAPTER XXIII

ISAIAH SAYS "HA!"

" I'LL thank ye to tell me," said Isaiah, as soon as Gillian had gone, " what ye mean, lugging my girl off from whome, stopping the night over, making her a nay-word, and fetching me out o' my bed and my farm all of a lantern-puff, with never so much as bite or sup? A pretty courant you've gid me ! "

The sentence rose to cumulative heights and the voice rose with it.

Elmer poured out a cup of tea, buttered some toast, and took it across to him. Isaiah was speechless with rage.

" No need to be so angered, Mr. Lovekin. I'll make everything all right."

" Then it's true ? "

" It's true as the cob cast a shoe."

" Dunna I see the blacksmith's pincers sticking out o' your pocket this very minute ? Oh, you black son of Satan ! "

" Now, Mr. Lovekin ! "

" Did ye or did ye not ? "

" I dunno what you mean."

" Liar ! "

Isaiah rang the bell. It sounded somewhere in the great empty house, and after a long time the landlady entered.

" How many rooms did ye keep for this gentleman ? " queried Isaiah.

" One, sir. We hadn't no more." She was on fire with curiosity.

" Oh! what a fool the fellow is! " thought Elmer.

But Isaiah was no fool.

" Then if I'd come after all, I'd 'a had to sleep on the floor! A pretty friend! " shouted Isaiah.

" We didn't know you thought of coming, Mr. Lovekin, nor that you knew this gentleman," soothed the landlady.

" That's the last arrand I'll give to you, young man! " said Isaiah. " Thank you, ma'am, that was all I wanted to know."

" Any time, Mr. Lovekin, if you'd write," she murmured, and withdrew, knowing nothing.

" Would a thousand pound—— ? " began Elmer.

" A thousand pound? For my girl's good name? And you've got the impidence! " Isaiah was speechless with a spate of confused words that struggled for utterance.

" Two thousand? "

" Now, silence! Husht! You dunna want to fight an old man, do ye? Then listen what I'll tell ye. There's no cure for this but banns up next Sunday as ever is. And no more to be said."

" But—— "

" It's no use ifting and anding. I'll tell ye what'll come to pass if you marry my girl—and if you dunna. Marry her. I'll settle ten thousand on her. The farm she'll have when I go. And there'll be a tidy bit o' money, all willed to her and you. I'll learn you all I know. I'll make ye rich, respected, a churchwarden, if ye like; a magistrate if ye like. You can join the Silverton Hunt if ye like. If you want a better house I'll build one. If you want a better nag, I'll buy one."

" It isn't that, Mr. Lovekin. I don't need bribery."

" Well, what in God's name is it, then? "

" I—I just can't, Mr. Lovekin."

" You just can't! Dear to goodness! That Lovekin of the Gwlfas should come to this! Down on his kneecaps pleading with a young wastrel to marry his girl. Now I'll tell ye what'll come to pass if you dunna."

He stood up, his silver hair and beard shining against the dark high mantelpiece, with its carving of a stag hunt. He spoke quite softly, even persuasively.

" If you dunna," he said, " I'll make you a bye-word. I'll make you like one of them men as was excommunicated in the old times. I'll make you an Esau among your kind. I'll drain yer money from ye, shilling by shilling, farden by farden. I'll spoil yer credit. I'll set the police on ye. I'll set all men agen ye. Yer ricks 'll ketch fire, and none'll know why nor how. Yer beasts'll sicken, and none'll come to cure 'em. I'll outbid ye at fairs. And when you've ought to sell I'll cheapen the market. I'll set the gipsies on ye——"

Elmer visibly started.

" If ye leave the place—I'll foller. It'll be all to do over agen, but I've a-many years afore me yet and a-plenty of money. Wherever ye go Isaiah Lovekin'll be with ye. And which d'ye think folk'll believe—a young wastrel like you or an old ancient white-'eaded man as is respected ? And when I've made ye the laugh and the nay-word of every fair and every public, and yer bones stand out, I shanna ha' done with ye. No. When you're broke "—he snatched the poker in his great hands, snapped it and flung it into the fender—" like that—*then* I wunna kill ye. You'll want to die, but you shanna. You shall go to the Asylum. You shall be drove along the roads like a silly sheep, and my girl shall come in a kerridge and laugh to see ye. You wunna be mad, but I'll make every man think you're mad, until you be— until you slaver like a mad dog and none to pity."

Suddenly Isaiah sat down, exhausted by his hatred.

" That's what Isaiah Lovekin'll do to the man as made his girl a nay-word," he said. " Choose."

Elmer, pale beneath the tan, experienced the most appalling moment of his life so far. He could not marry the girl, and Fringal knew he could not. Yet he must. He was quite aware that Isaiah could do exactly what he said. A man with so tremendous a reputation, of an old, known family, of almost fabulous wealth—for Dysgwlfas measures wealth by its own standards—revered to idolatry, could smash him as easily as he could smash a wasp on the window. Or he could make him. It was an instance of the reversal of reward and punishment. If he did right he would not only lose Gillian, but spend his life in hell and end in madness. If he did wrong, he would have not only everything he had ever wanted, but Gillian as well. If he did wrong he would never be found out. There was only Fringal, and Fringal was open to bribes. Also Fringal was old. Rwth was dumb. Providence was kind. And Isaiah waited.

The light shone full on Elmer and revealed in his face the marks of his struggle. Isaiah was puzzled. Here was a young man with no ties, very much in love with Gillian, and he had offered him not only Gillian, but all he had as well. What could be the matter? What was it? The arrogance of youth overcame Isaiah. He could have wept.

"She's as white as snow!" he said.

"I know—I know."

"And if it inna enough, I could put my money out better, I make no doubt, so it 'ud bring in more."

This was intolerable. After last night Ralph wanted to fling himself and all that he had at Gillian's feet. And here was this terrible old man bargaining and offering him this and that.

"It's enough and more than enough," he said. "I want no better than to marry your girl and work for 'er."

"You do?" Isaiah was almost in tears from the great shock of joy. "You do? Then what in hell—— ?"

"It was just—I thought she was in love with Rideout."

"Rideout! Dear to goodness, man, d'ye think Miss Lovekin of the Gwlfas is going to marry a barn-door savage? She'd scorn to let the fellow kiss her feet."

Flushed and triumphant, remembering his own kisses, Elmer went across to the old man, holding out his hand.

"Sir!" he said, "will ye take it? I'll swear to do my best for Gillian, the prettiest girl in the county."

Isaiah put his great paw into the outstretched hand.

" Now you're talking sense, my lad ! " said he. " Then you'll be axed in church Sunday ? "

" Ah."

" Likely you'll want to drive Gillian back in your gig, eh ? " Isaiah was full of laughter now.

" Thank you kindly, Mr. Lovekin."

" And seeing as nobody knows the girl in Weeping Cross, nobody'll be any the wiser if you keep away for a bit. They wunna put two and two together, being busy-like. And now I'll be going. Will ye send Gillian to me ? "

Gillian came, pale and tearful.

" Now, my dear," said Isaiah, " I shanna chide ye. That's the mother's place if she was in life, poor soul. I say nought. But here's fifty pound to go on with for ribbons and rubbitch, and plenty more where that came from. And the banns'll be up Sunday."

" Oh, Father ! "

" It's no manner use saying, ' Oh, Father ! ' You've stopped the night over with the man. You best know why. No argling, now. Buy what ye like. Ask for as much as ye like. But you've got to be Mrs. Elmer Monday three weeks."

" Oh, I canna—I canna ! "

" You know better. You dunna want a barley-child, do ye ? " *

" Father, I dunna love him."

" Then what for did ye lose yer maiden'ead, you nasty baigle ? " Isaiah turned to the door. " With yer leave or without it," said he. " So ye'd better put a good face on it and buy some fal-lals. And to-morrow I'll take ye to Silverton to buy the bride cake and the wedding dress : but no more hiver-hover. See ? "

Gillian did see. She saw where curiosity and youth and vitality had brought her, and she stood like a drooping flower, while Isaiah got into the trap and drove away,

---

* Barley-child—a child born within a few months of marriage, in the time that elapses between the sowing and the harvest of barley.

Elmer having promised to follow very shortly. Faintly, when he came in and snatched her into his arms ; when he kissed her feet, her ankles, her knees, held her close against him by the waist and pressed back her head to kiss her beneath the chin till she felt as if her back would break—faintly and palely she suffered it. Robert had given her no glance as he drove away. Stern, remote, he had looked into the distance. She was the chattel of Ralph Elmer. She had no refuge. For three weeks she could stay at home, but after that he would take her to the inn, and nobody—not her father, nor her Aunt Fanteague, nor the Rector, nor Robert—would stir a finger to help her. And, as Elmer helped her into the gig and drove away, whistling as they went along the fresh morning roads, the bitterness of her soul could have been gauged by the fact that she wished she was back at Aunt Fanteague's, yes, even with Mr. Gentle for her only lover, and Aunt Emily talking for ever of her dreams of angels.

"Well," remarked Elmer, with the crassness of self-absorbed happiness, "well, my dear, it's all over, and nobody any the worse. Everything all right, the banns up, and you at the ' Mermaid ' afore we know where we are." He stifled a foreboding.

All right, was it ? Gillian listened in silence. For, ah ! had not the man she wanted to be with driven off without her ? Wasn't she in the wrong gig ? Hadn't she awakened beside the wrong man ?

She wondered if Aunt Emily had felt, when death robbed her of Mr. Gentle, the same as she herself felt when life stole from her Robert Rideout. She even began to wonder if the slatey drake minded when she rent its life and its feathers away, if the rabbits minded when she bought music with their lives. She understood why Robert had told her to make the thorny cross. She felt as if she was going to make one for the rest of her life. In fact, Gillian Lovekin began to grow up, began to grow wiser, for she began to suffer. And to suffer is to be sensitized to the cosmos and to everything within it, from a grain of dust to the soul of a poet.

CHAPTER XXIV

A HANK OF FAERY WOOL

DURING the next three weeks Gillian entrenched herself behind mountains of clothes, which Isaiah rejoiced to see her buy, and she would have nothing to say to Elmer. She had deferred her wedding to the last possible day allowed by her father—the 25th of May. Isaiah drove her to the Keep, to Silverton, to the Keep again, wrote cheques, sent off invitations, saw the Rector, had the farm smartened up for the wedding, mentioned Elmer as being more suitable than himself for the post of churchwarden, and ordered a large consignment of champagne, which he told Robert to fetch on the first spare day. Whereupon Robert wrote a letter, and had a large packing-case to bring as well as the champagne. Even Mrs. Makepeace was won over by the sight of so much fine linen, and the immediate thought of baby linen which it brought to her mind. She flung herself into the preparations with all her might.

At the inn Fringal and Rwth worked from morning till night, and Elmer went to and fro in a frenzy. Jonathan came back with tales of the great supper that was to be given free when the bride was brought home, and of the casks of ale and wine to be broached.

" It's to be hoped we'll live to eat it and drink it," he said; " there's over a fortnit. A'most anything could come to pass in a fortnit. Why, the world could come to an end in that tuthree days if it ud pleased the Lord to plan it so from time everlasting."

"Well, my dear," said his wife, and if He'd planned it so, it ud be best so. And you wouldna be werritting about a drop of liquor then."

"Well, but I do hope the Lord hanna planned it the like of that, Mother!" and he worried himself and everybody else so much about it that they could scarcely bear to hear the wedding mentioned at all. He gave so many instances of weddings that were never solemnized, and told so many stories about feasts that were never eaten, that Gillian built up a specious happiness upon his prophecies of disaster.

She sat all day in the parlour, and as she had intuitively found it an anodyne to live on the surface, she did so. Her slim fingers lovingly caressed the fine linen, and tied and untied the pretty ribbons with which her beauty was to be clad when she gave herself to Elmer for ever. Though she knew he did not love her as she wanted to be loved, it was her nature to enjoy her power over him. She picked up the foamy garments one by one, and sighed. There came a day when the postman brought cardboard boxes, large and heavy, and behold! on her bed lay the wedding dress, with its misty moonlight look, and the veil and the wreath. Everything was to be done in the best manner, according to Isaiah's decree, just as if she were a Squire's daughter.

"Oh, Robert!" breathed Gillian, and two tears fell upon the spotless beauty of the white-ribboned wedding nightdress. "Oh, Robert, Robert, my dear!"

But not even Mrs. Makepeace, affectionate and inquisitive, not even Aunt Fanteague, with her piercing eye and her leading questions, found out about the two tears or what caused them.

Though she must always keep a niche in her heart for Elmer, because he was the first man to initiate her into the meaning of passion, yet it was Robert's glance, the touch of Robert's hand, as he helped her into the trap or out of it that threw her into a faintness so sweet that she wished she could have died then and never awakened to the common day. Her step, which had always been

haughty, faltered when Robert was near ; her lashes
swept her cheeks, her deliberate cool hands shook. And
if, while she spoke to Elmer at the gate, she heard Robert's
step, immediately she was an image carved out of snow.
She was sitting by the parlour window one showery
evening, and the early Gloire de Dijon roses were sending
out great rushes of sweetness in the rainy warmth, when
a slight, dark-clad figure came in at the wicket, and Rwth
stood hesitatingly at the door. Gillian, with her new
vision of sadness, ran to let her in, put the kettle on for
tea, treated her not as her future servant, but as a friend.
The lucent black eyes shone, Rwth's whole face lit up
with tenderness, with a mysterious sacrificial love. She
had come to bring a wedding gift—a work basket woven
of rushes, such as gipsies sell, at the making of which she
was very clever. Her hands were deft at all kinds of
work, and once she had learnt a thing she never forgot it.
She proffered the basket with a little deprecating smile,
and Gillian went into raptures over it, stowed away her
thimble and scissors in it, and made much of Rwth. But
this was not all. From her pocket Rwth drew out a
photograph of Elmer. She held it in her hands, nodded,
showed it, clasped it again, as if to say : " It is mine."

Then she got up, placed it in Gillian's hands, looking
questioningly in her face, closed them over it and made
a motion of discarding it, of utter renunciation. Then
she once more looked questioningly at Gillian, who was
puzzled, received the photograph very coolly and offered
it to her again. Rwth took it, but not as if she wanted
it. They continued their tea, and Gillian picked a bunch
of roses for Rwth, who went away smiling.

Soon after she had gone, there was a sound of heavy
wheels, and Robert stopped outside the wicket, standing
in the waggon, calling for Jonathan to come and help
him. Besides Isaiah's packets and boxes there was the
large packing case which they carried in, and which revealed, when they had opened it, a rosewood cottage
piano. Jonathan departed, and Robert knelt down to
pick up the straw.

A Hank of Faery Wool

"Bob ! " said Gillian, ignoring the piano, "what for do you treat me as if I was a leper ? "

" I dunna. If there's any leper, it's me. And the leprosy's called poverty, and it's the hot-bed of pride."

" Speak kind, Robert ! "

" I never did no other."

" Who's the little piano from, Robert ? "

" How should I know ? Be it my place to ask ? What am I ? " said Robert with great bitterness.

" What are you ? You're Robert Rideout, and there inna your like the world over—for a sharp temper," she hastily added. " And I'd thank you to look for the label, Bob, so's I can tell who to write to."

Robert made a great show of looking for the label. But suddenly as he was kneeling there, Gillian came and stood close to him.

" Now look at me, Bob ! " she said.

He lifted his clear dark eyes.

She laid her hands lightly on his shoulders.

" Now Robert ! It's from you ! You canna say no to it ! Look at me and say no ! I dare you ! "

In the aching silence he looked at her, and the truth was plain to see, in his eyes, in the slow red that came under the tan.

" Why did ye think—it was from me ? " he whispered.

" Because nobody else in all the world 'ud think of it, Robert. And I canna thank you, Robert ! "

" I dunna want thanks."

" Robert ! You've spent every penny you've saved ever since you were twelve ! "

Suddenly she stooped, and very lightly and softly kissed him on the brow. He sprang to his feet and said hoarsely :

" You're very kindly welcome—Mrs. Elmer ! " and staggered to the door.

And Gillian with her hands clasping the polished wood of the piano, sobbed until it grew dark, and her father came in, and she ran away to wash her face that he might not see the traces of tears.

"And that's got to last for all our lives!" she said to herself. "It's got to last a hundred thousand years!"

Robert, quite mazed with the sweetness of it, said to himself: "She did it for fun: she dunna care for me. She dunna know as I care for her. She canna know," he added simply, "because I hanna said a word. Nor yet I hanna showed her the pennillions and the poetry. She did it because she's a little flirt and she wanted to see what I'd say."

Oh, sad and cruel jest of life, that a gay laugh, a smile of lip or eye can deceive even a lover, when the heart is dying within; that, when we are making our last frantic attempt to grasp that which is our very life, we are thought to be in jest—as one might say to the wretched fish gasping and leaping on the hook, dying for water—"Ha! What a merry dance you are giving us! You are the best of jesters, fish!"

It was not until the very eve of her wedding that she ventured to speak to Robert again. She had played on his piano, and sung to it, and she had sometimes heard his steps pause a moment on the path outside. But they had neither of them said anything, until this evening when they met by chance in the rickyard, when Gillian was gathering butter-leaves from the old sycamore tree so that she could pack the butter for market before the wedding day.

It was a calm and delicious evening, laced with a hundred scents—may and buttercups, appleblossom and chestnut, lilac and the dry sweetness of hay.

"Robert!" said Gillian. "Oh, Robert!"

He stopped by the orchard fence.

"Robert, I love the piano. I wish there was anything as I could do to thank you——"

Robert remembered Rwth and the writing lessons.

"There's something you can do for somebody else, and yet it'll be for me," said he. "Will you learn Rwth of the 'Mermaid' to write, Gillian?"

Gillian was amazed.

" But why ever ? "

" Because I ask you to. There's a reason for why, but
I canna tell you. Learn her quick. I'll buy the copybooks."

" But suppose she canna learn."

" She can. She's right down clever with her fingers.
You see ! But——" he hesitated.

" Well ? "

" Well you see, it's the like of this. Mr. Elmer dunna
much want Rwth to learn things."

" Oh ! "

" Would it be, like, agen your duty to keep it from him ? "

" No ! "

" A'right then. Thank you kindly."

" Robert ! "

Ah, how she adored his name ! How she loved his
mother and his cottage and his ploughman's boots, his
rough hands, the bit of grass he was twisting in his fingers,
the cade lambs waiting for him in the orchard. Every
day he caught those lambs in his hands. Every day
their close stiff wool felt the caress of his fingers—and
would. But she ; she must be content with a little
clasp of the fingers, and perhaps a word now and again,
and the sound of his laugh or his step. And that was
all. She held out her hand now.

" Good-bye, Robert ! " she said.

And Robert knew that if he waited another moment
he should simply pick her up and walk away—over the
moor—over the hills—over the world's rim.

He put his hands on the fence and vaulted over.

" Good-neet," he said. " Good-neet, Gillian Lovekin
—and—bless you ! "

He was gone.

In the cottage Jonathan still laboured over the mystery
of the piano.

" It bodes no good," he said, " a present from a person
unknown, to a bride. Now listen. A long while ago
there was a lady, and she loved a lord. But a prince out
of fairyland seed her one day picking red currants in the

garden. And he said, ' her mouth be as red as the currants,
I'll have her for myself.' So he takes and sends her a
wedding present of a hank of white fairy wool for spinning.
Now she was a very industrious lady, and though the wedding was nigh, she took and spun the wool. But when
she'd spun it, the end went wafting out of the window,
and the more she spun the more went out, stretching
along in the breeze. "So when she'd finished it, she
keeps the end as she's got, and begins to wind it up on
an ivory spool. For she says : ' It's blowing up for
tempest, and the wool munna be rained on.' But when
she pulled, summat else pulled, quiet but very obstinate,
and it pulled her acrost the room, out o' window, into
the garden and the lane, and away-to-go over the fields ;
and it lugged her right into fairyland, so the fairy got her
after all."

What a strange faint clamour as of many distant bells
woke in Robert's mind at those four plain words : " Got
her after all." Did he ? But then—he was a fairy.
He was not just Bob o' the Gwlfas, clad in corduroy and
a patched coat, helpless in the grasp of circumstance. But
was he helpless ? Suppose that leaping suspicion about
Rwth were correct ? What then ? Why, then, the man
who stood between himself and Gillian Lovekin was in
his hands. One word to Johnson. After so many years
of grief, after such a tragedy, would Johnson forgive ?
Robert knew he would not. Maybe, if the more dazzling
presence of Elmer were removed, Gillian would turn to
him. And Johnson would reward him. Johnson was
rich. Nobody seeing him would ever have believed it,
but he was. Or he might make Elmer pay him for his
silence—unless that would injure his friend. He might
also lay the case before Elmer, demand the inn in return
for letting him go, and wait to tell Johnson till Elmer
was across the sea. But then Gillian would still be
married—unless——. And her father would not allow
her to live with him. Every avenue was shut. And
above all, greater than all, was the fact (of which he
was nearly sure) that Gillian loved Elmer.

"I mun bide as I be," he thought. "It's wormwood in the mouth, but there's nought else to do. I mun go childless to the grave, for take any other but Gillian, I never will. The cradle 'll rock in Elmer's kitchen. It wunna rock in mine.

"Well, Mother!" he said, as he got up to go to bed, "I'm off to Gruffydd Conwy's to-morrow. I'll take bite and sup with me if you've a mind."

"What?" cried Jonathan so loudly that the cat leapt right across the kitchen. "What? Not go to the wedding? Not go to the supper? Laws! Laws! What's come to thy poor head? Why, man, there'll be yer bellyfull three times over! At Lovekin's in the morning; agen at Lovekin's for tea; and then at the 'Naked Wench' for supper. Beef and mutton and good ale, and plenty of old tales—for there's nought like a drop of beer to loosen the tales in the old men's heads—out they come like birds from cages!"

"Now, my dear!" Mrs. Makepeace stemmed the tide of words. "Now you leave Robert be. Robert dunna like old tales like you do. Robert likes the music. Everybody's going to keep holiday in their own way. Why shouldna Robert keep it in his'n?"

She gave Robert a shy little pat on the shoulder, and took out of Jonathan's hand the knife which, in his surprise about Robert, he had forgotten, and which had pointed itself straight at his eye.

At the "Mermaid's Rest" the bridal chamber was ready, sweet and clean as Rwth's quick hands could make it. Its long, low window looked towards Dysgwlfas, and Gillian had been glad when she had seen it. For sometimes in the early morning in the pasture that sloped up to the moor, when it was not misty, she would see a dark slim pencil on the bright green field. And that would be Robert.

As Rwth smoothed the white sheet and shut the window for the night, and turned to go, she was sorry for Gillian. As she climbed the attic stairs she was glad for herself, glad with the wild intuitive joy of a bird. For no more

would she have to come trembling down the attic stairs
in the dark, and go to Elmer's room. Forever she would
be able now to go through the calm rite of her worship
of Robert.

The irony of things did not, of course, strike her—the
strange irony of the fact that two women who loved
with all their hearts and souls the man of Dysgwlfas
Cottage, should be living with the man of the " Mermaid's
Rest." But irony was never lost upon Fringal. He never
missed anything, and the Sardonic Jester found in him
the perfect audience.

He sat on his bed in the dark, tired, but not too tired
to laugh ; he let the curious situation soak into his mind
—every detail, every queer twist (and he knew more of
the situation than anybody, even the protagonists).
And then, in silence, because his master slept beneath,
he laughed. He rocked with laughter. He slapped his
thigh (still silently) and rocked again. And the old house
seemed to listen in its silence, seemed to watch and wait,
and to culminate in him. Beneath was Elmer, lying
awake, in an anguish of physical desire. Close by was
Rwth, kneeling in an ecstasy of spiritual love. Round
the three, in the hush of night, the house wove minute
sounds—the gnawing of a rat in an empty room ; the
rustle of a bat's wings in the passage ; the faint rasping
of the feet of a daddy-long-legs, advancing upon Fringal
with its extraordinary ghoulish clownishness ; the hoot
of an owl in the unket place ; and the everlasting whisper
of the moor which changed into a roar in winter, but never
died, and which was, even at its quietest, like the lisp of
one destined to become a conqueror.

CHAPTER XXV

THE BRIDE COMES HOME

THE wedding was precisely like all other well arranged weddings. Everything was as it should be. Everyone was punctual. Everything went smoothly as Severn in July. The Rector had a very white surplice and a very bright smile. The bride's father was the very pattern of a father. The Bridegroom was presentable, and his long three weeks of waiting had given to his expression an eagerness which simulated real love very nicely. The ringers were refreshed with beer from the " Mermaid," and they pulled the bell-ropes lustily. Aunt Fanteague had a new dress, so stiff that her own stiffness was as nothing. Aunt Emily, dosed with bromide for the occasion, and imbued with the idea that she and Mr. Gentle were going to be married to-morrow, looked very sweet in lavender. Jonathan had a flower in his buttonhole, and a story ready to burst from his lips the moment they were out of the Church. Mrs. Makepeace was in her best dress and tears. And the bride was " the very moral of a bride," as the wife of the people's warden said. " And if when you come to the altar, you come like her," she remarked to her young daughter, " you'll do well."

Whereat the daughter smiled satirically, for the young are desperately clear-sighted. Fringal was there in a controlled paroxysm. Afterwards, the breakfast was all a breakfast ought to be. Merriment ran high. For when Isaiah chose to jest, Olympus was shaken. He jested. Even the Rector jested. The wedding presents were

viewed ; the mystery of the piano was a mystery still.
Elmer was seen to kiss his wife behind the dovecote, and
as nobody knew that she had been very cross, everybody
thought it very delightful. Jonathan and Fringal, in
wonderful Sunday suits and cuffs of which they were as
ashamed as if they were handcuffs, waited to the best
of their ability. Fringal and the cold dishes on the side-
board had a good many quiet jokes. And Jonathan's
feud with inanimate matter reached an acute stage.
For having been requested to remove the cake to a side-
table for greater convenience in cutting it, he dropped
it flat on the floor, and there was no need to cut any of
the sugar, but only to gather up the fragments.

As soon as they had digested dinner, if not before, they
had tea. And when tea was over, Elmer's patience was
over too.

" The cob, Fringal," said he.

" Sir-to-you ! " said Fringal. And in a trice the cob
and the gig were there, and Gillian was in, and Elmer was
in, and Fringal leapt in like a chaffinch leaping at a tall
dandelion, and they were off at full gallop. There stood
the proud father at the door, with the Church to back him
up. And Elmer waved his hat, and Fringal clung on for
dear life and laughed till he cried, and the cob leapt over
the stony road till the gig rocked, for he had had his
share of the stinging rice, and he was exceedingly angry.

And so the Bride was brought home. Then all the
revellings began again. All the people who had not yet
feasted (and a good many who had) took their fill. Some
of them had, as they said, " clemmed all day to do it
justice." The ringers came ; the ploughmen and shepherds
and their wives from far and near ; the young man from
Silverton who had taken photographs of everybody and
everything. The oldest woman in the village came, and
her children and grandchildren, and great-grandchildren.
The youngest baby in the village came in its mother's
arms, and howled very lustily. The ministers of two
chapels, the butcher who drove round the country once
a week, the postman, all Gillian's schoolfellows, the young

farmers who were Elmer's friends, all came, and the stout village midwife with her mystic smile as though to say : "My time will come." They came and they stayed. They sang uproariously. They made broad jokes. They said all the things that are so sweet to lovers, and so bitter to the loveless. Last of all, when the May night grew dark and the indigo of the sky merged in the violet of the moor, came a stray gipsy woman of Johnson's clan, detained at the Keep by the sickness of her baby and now benighted. And she said :

" The flower's plucked too soon. . . . I hear the drip o' tears. . . . There's one in this place wunna see the year out. . . . There's one over the mountains should be in this place. . . . I hear a cradle rocking—but not in this house—not in this house ! "

As she said these words, Rwth rose and came towards her, looking at her strangely. The gipsy said a few words quickly, in the lingo of her people, but Rwth shook her head and showed by a gesture that she could not answer.

The gipsy feasted with the rest and departed. Gradually the guests went their ways, and at last Rwth and Fringal finished washing-up the glasses and went to bed. The bride and bridegroom were alone. Then they too climbed the stairs, and Gillian ran to the window and saw a star hang above Dysgwlfas Farm, where the cottage was, and the orchard, with those lambs—blest above all creatures—who were handled by Robert every morning and every evening. She remembered Robert's request, touched with some of the pathos of the requests of the dying, for she thought Robert could scarcely be more removed from her if she lay in her grave.

" I must just go an' speak to Rwth a minute," she said.

" To Rwth ? "

" Ah."

" Whatever for ? "

" Oh men, men, men ! " said Gillian in a very good imitation of the manner of the Squire's wife. " You think there's nought in the world but you ! "

"Well, don't be long."

She was gone, climbing the attic stairs softly, tapping softly at Rwth's door. But Rwth was wrapt in worship. She did not hear. Gillian went in and saw a picture she never forgot. The casement was open and the Dysgwlfas star was in it. On the blue and white check quilt lay Robert's handkerchief, and Rwth's brown cheek lay caressingly upon it.

"Rwth! Be you took bad?"

Rwth sprang up defensively, crumpling the handkerchief into a ball. But fortunately Gillian had not noticed it.

She shook her head to show nothing was wrong.

"Saying your prayers, was you?"

She nodded. If she had been able to read the Bible, she might have remembered the text : "Ye shall draw them with cords of a man, even with cords of love."

They looked at each other softly—the bride, still in her wedding-dress in the country manner, her bright colour and vivid grey eyes lighted into beauty by the mingled grief and triumph of the day ; and the little handmaid, locked away from human intercourse, with her pale, swart face and strange luminous eyes, and her dignity of sorrow. The bright star, raying out into the blue night, shone on both, and shone also on Robert as he passed by, all unknown, wearily covered the distance between the inn and his home, and flung himself upon his bed.

"Rwth, Robert asked me to learn you to write. Would you like it?"

Would she? Ah! What a smile, with all rapture in it !

"Robert wants you to learn quick. Can ye?"

She nodded vigorously.

"We'll start to-morrow."

Another nod.

"And, Rwth!"

Rwth waited.

"He dunna want the Master nor Fringal to know.

And I was thinking there inna no place safe from 'em but here, because my room——"

She faltered.

But Rwth looked complete comprehension.

" So shall I come up here, after you've washed up dinner ? You can take a bit of time off then. If he says anything I'll say you're sewing for me. Now mind you come to-morrow. I'll come at one. You'll ha' done by then."

Suddenly, she did not know why, she bent forward and sealed the compact with a kiss.

Then she returned to Elmer. Once more darkness and silence were upon the house. Once more Fringal laughed in his attic. The moor whispered. Time and space wove their strange tapestries across eternity. And at the cottage under the star Robert made a little song.

> " I heard a clary* in the wood ;
> I went to see, and there she stood.
> The song was like a charm o' birds.
> I lost my heart, I lost my words.
> A roaring sea was in my ears ;
> Her clary filled my eyes with tears.
> My soul was bantered down with grief,
> For she was like a tree in leaf
> And bright as calaminca.†
>
> " I'd lief as I could make a bower
> Of briar roses all in flower,
> With scarlet rose mops set between
> And crimson thorns among the green.
> My naked hands with blood should run,
> To ease my pain. And when I'd done
> I'd closem her within my breast,
> For she's my clary and my rest
> And bright as calaminca ! "

* Clary—A ringing song.   † Calaminca—Red shale.

CHAPTER XXVI

A.B.C. AT THE SIGN OF THE MAIDEN

SUMMER drooped warm wings over the moor. The blossom fell, the fruit set. The grass lengthened, grew silken, rippled, lay in brown and green confusion when the rain came, and arose softly and rippled again. Haying began. In the early mornings Gillian could see her father's machine going round the big meadow, and she knew that Robert was driving it. The roses bloomed and faded. The fruit ripened, and Gillian and Rwth picked it and made jam under the mocking eyes of Fringal. But, whatever they were doing, they always disappeared as soon as the dinner was cleared away. They said nothing ; simply, like swallows in December, they were not there. They evaded questions and, with the quiet obstinacy of bees—who at one time will be outside the hive in spite of all efforts to get them in, and at another will be in, whatever may be done to get them out—continued to meet in Rwth's attic room. The fresh summer breezes came in, laden with hay and moss and bracken scents. Dysgwlfas Farm, miniature but clear, met their eyes when they looked up from their work. And sometimes, when the wind was in the right quarter, they could hear the pleasant high note of the machine, and the shouts, made soft and short by distance, of Jonathan and Robert and their helpers as they lugged the hay. Then the fields lay like pieces of jade against the dark moor. Red and white cattle dotted them, and sheep, white from the shearing. The blackbirds grew silent. The whimbrels rang their elfin

peals less often, and their pencilled chickens ran among
the heather near the springs. The whimberries ripened,
and higglers, starting off with their empty carts or returning with full ones, would stop outside the inn and shout
for Fringal to bring them a quart of ale.

Elmer was away a great deal. He and Isaiah went
to fairs and auctions together now, and the mantle of
Elijah descended upon Elisha. Elmer was tasting the
promised success. Young men of his own age deferred
to him. He was credited with some of Isaiah's omniscience.
There had been a vestry meeting, and upon Isaiah's
representations he had been made churchwarden in Isaiah's
place. So Gillian sat in the second pew close to the
Rector's wife, to the exceeding content of Isaiah. Sometimes in the evening Gillian played her piano, and if, by
any chance, Robert passed with the farm cart or the trap,
he would wait under the shelter of the hedge at the side
of the house and listen for a little while. Isaiah came to
tea in state, and Gillian and Elmer returned his visit.
Often in the afternoon, towards tea-time, she would put
on her best dress, which was covered with pink roses and
had pink ribbons, and go across the fields to see her father.
Sometimes she went with Elmer to see her friends among
the other farmers' wives and daughters. Or she and
Rwth would go " berrying " out on the moor. But
whatever they were doing, they always met for the writing
lesson in the bare little attic. And Gillian, in whom an
unaccustomed softness and perceptiveness had begun to
appear, would try to make these hours a delight to the
little maid-of-all-work. She would tell Rwth to put the
kettle on, and as soon as the men had gone out she would
set the tray with the pretty cups, painted with violets,
given her by Aunt Fanteague, and then she would make
tea and they would put the tray in the attic window-sill and
draw their chairs close together like children with a stolen
feast. If Rwth's energy slackened, Gillian had only to
remind her that Robert wanted her to learn quickly, and
the dark face would flush, the coarse, knotted hands fly
over the paper. Sometimes they spent whole afternoons

at it. Sometimes Gillian went to bed early and then stole up to Rwth's room to continue the lessons by moonlight. Once, on a wonderful and memorable day, Robert had come to thatch the stack. Elmer could not thatch, and Fringal was very lazy and had suggested that Robert should do it. So Robert had his dinner and his tea at the inn. And as a newly-bought flock of sheep had strayed away, and Elmer and Fringal had to go and look for them, they carried the tea out on to the moor, and had a merry time. Robert asked how the lessons were going on. So he had to be shown how well Rwth could write her own name. And he was very much surprised, and perhaps he evinced even more surprise than he felt, when the four large, square, drunken letters sprawled out across the page—" R W T H."

" Now that's a right good name," said Robert in his kindly, jesting, paternal way. " What else, Rwth ? "

She looked at the paper, she looked at Gillian, she looked at Robert. No help came. She did not know what else.

" She can't do things of herself, yet," explained Gillian, anxious as a mother with a backward child. " She can't remember things and put 'em down. She can only put down what I say."

" Well, afore I come agen," said Robert, " teach her Esmeralda."

" Esmeralda ? "

" Ah. Rwth, do ye know that name—Esmeralda ? "

Was that a flicker in the large dark eyes ? Or was it just friendship, gratitude and trust ?

" Ne'er mind. Just go on," said Robert.

Ah, what an evening ! How the gold ran over out of the sunset sky into their hearts. How the two lovers, neither knowing of the other's love, and the waif who loved them both, revelled in the clear rapture of comradeship, of being together. How marvellously good the bread and butter tasted, cut by Robert's hands, which, truth to tell, were not very clean, for he had carried the kettle. And what a drink for gods was the tea made by Gillian !

And how happily Rwth ran to and fro, collecting sticks for the fire ! And how glad Robert and Gillian were of her presence, for how could Mrs. Elmer of the Mermaid and her father's cowman have picnicked on the moor unless she had been there to make it look like an ordinary berry-picking ? And how sad, when that low obdurate baaing, which heralds the homecoming of strayed sheep, sounded faintly over the heather, to have to gather the tea things together and say good-bye.

But the day gave a tremendous impetus to the writing, and very soon Rwth could write " Esmeralda."

And then, towards the end of August, came Gillian's triumph. For suddenly, one Sunday evening, when Elmer was at church and Gillian had pleaded a headache, Rwth, after writing Esmeralda three times, suddenly wrote " Als " without any help from Gillian. First she wrote " Als." Then, not satisfied, she added an " e." Then Gillian, who had been teaching her the sounds of double vowels, said : " Is there any other letter in it ? " And Rwth wrote it again with the " i " in it. So it stood— " Ailse."

Gillian folded up the paper, put it in an envelope, and sent Rwth to the farm cottage where only Robert was in. It brought Robert hotfoot over the fields.

" I didna tell you that name, did I ? " he asked.

" Why ever should you ? " Gillian answered. " I never knew anyone of the name. Did you ? "

Robert was awed by the strangeness of destiny. For this was the memory of a bird, of a squirrel, memory untaught and expressing itself with the utmost difficulty. The name Esmeralda had not directly illuminated Rwth, but it had touched a chord which had sounded another name.

" Now," said Robert, " you mun just work with the two names. I tell you nought. First, because I munna tell a soul. Second, because you met put things in her mind. And what I want is just what's there already. I want the truth. And, by gum, it looks like getting it."

He gazed and gazed upon the impassive face of Rwth,

who was Ailse—of Rwth the maid-of-all-work who was
the daughter of a kind of gipsy-king—of Ailse who had
prattled in gipsy merriment and who was now Rwth the
dumb girl—of Ailse the child of sweet love, the child of a
woman like a star, who was, or had been till Gillian's
advent, the dumb foundling dependent on Elmer's charity,
the creature that, Robert shrewdly suspected, knew
what it was to be beaten.

" You know what you've got to do ? " he asked, as he
went away, and Gillian dwelt in a maze of sweetness all
evening at having received a command from Robert.
And in a few days she received another. Jonathan, on
his way to Weeping Cross, brought a few words written
in haste on a scrap of paper, thrust into an old envelope
that had contained advertisements of sheep dip, and
fastened with a bit of cobbler's wax. She laughed to
herself as she opened it. Then, very shyly and suddenly,
she kissed it. He said : " Get to know some bits of
gipsy songs and play 'em and see what she writes."

But Gillian did not know any gipsy songs, and had to
write to Silverton for them, and there were none in Silverton. So Robert wrote to Johnson, and at long last received
a letter telling him of a man who could not only sing
them but write them down. But before the gipsy songs
came, Gillian was away in Silverton, so the testing of
Rwth's memory in this was deferred for some months,
and they went on with the writing.

Meanwhile the corn ripened, and everyone was soon
too busy to think of anything but the harvest. Rwth-who-
was-Ailse laboured in the brewhouse, and Gillian very
often put her big apron on and worked with her. Fringal
drove off almost every day with barrels of beer for this
farm and that farm, and returned sometimes with money
and sometimes with a quarter of mutton or a few score
of eggs or a sack of early-lifted potatoes. And gently,
a shilling at a time, his wages went on rising. Once,
when Ralph was obdurate for some time, he chose a moment
when Gillian was in the room and observed gently with a
sideways nod towards Rwth : " The missus 'ere."

Gillian did not notice. It was quite enough for Ralph, though. He was angry, but helpless, and he paid the money. Fringal was exactly the sort of sardonic, heartless, intelligent yet ignoble person to levy blackmail successfully.

Robert did not come to the inn till the harvest was " saved : " or at least until the last was in stook. The only young man on a farm always has plenty of work to do, all the early jobs and the hard jobs and the risky jobs. And Jonathan had been getting more feeble very gently for years. Nobody noticed it because they saw him every day, but insensibly more and more things were left to Robert. So the mystery at the Mermaid was left for the time, and not only Ailse, but Gillian herself had a very small place in Robert's thoughts—intent on the all-important harvest. But after harvest Robert promised himself to go thoroughly into the matter. There was no hurry, because Johnson was not returning until November, being laid up with rheumatism in a small Welsh town, and not able to travel. So an absolute peace lay upon the inn and the moor and the farm. Ralph and Fringal and Rwth had been absorbed into the life of the place, and the ripples of their advent had subsided. Ralph already saw himself as a second Isaiah, laying down the law, treating people to drinks, tolerant yet just, popular with gentry and cottagers, with his pretty Gillian waiting for him at home, with so much money coming in that Fringal's paltry demands were as nothing, and with Rwth— as ever—cowed, submissive, dumb. Never, for a single instant, did he dream that the man with the curiously intent grey eyes who trudged to fairs with the sheep while he and Isaiah drove, the man with the quiet, curving mouth which could so suddenly become set and relentless, knew any more about him than the bleating flocks he led. That this man had pieced together a part of his own history which he believed unknown to any but Fringal the bribable and Rwth the incurably dumb ; that he had summed up his character to a nicety ; and that he was silently but quite mercilessly watching him, giving

him room to commit himself, and all the while only waiting to put him to the test—was as far from Elmer's happy,
successful thoughts as were those long-forgotten threats
of Isaiah's at the Drover's Arms. Would he have been
afraid if he had known about Johnson being Robert's
friend, and had guessed that the only thing that withheld Robert from confronting him with the gipsy was
Gillian's love of him, and that Robert watched and
listened for the undercurrents beneath their lives to
find out if that love still existed ? Would he have continued his happy life with no guilty secret to make him
afraid, or would he have left his inn and his flocks and
Gillian, and fled ? Then the things that afterwards
happened at the Inn of the Maiden would not have happened, and the spirit of evil which was to leap out of the
solid earth like a devastating flame and threaten Gillian's
very soul, would perhaps never have heard, in its quiescence
beneath the things that are, the sound that was to awaken
it—the stealthy footfall of Ralph Elmer in the unket
place.

CHAPTER XXVII

" IN A DREAM SHE CRADLED ME "

At last the corn was all carried, even to the thin rakings. The fowls had pecked the corn out of these ; the turkeys had gone to the stubble ; potatoes were being lifted ; the hum of the threshing had already begun ; soon Robert would be driving straight reddish-brown furrows in the pale stubble. The autumn sheep sales were going on up in the hills. The ewes that had feasted all summer on the sweet herbage of valley and summit were brought down before the hard weather should set in, only a small flock being kept by each of the hill commoners. Isaiah always took Robert to these fairs, for it is customary for the shepherd to advise his master on such occasions. So Isaiah and Ralph had the front seat and Robert had the back, returning on foot with the sheep. Sometimes, when Ralph laughed his secure, careless laugh, a contraction of the muscles in Robert's hands would occur, and Robert would have a sudden desire to throw Ralph out of the trap—why, he could not tell, for he knew nothing whatever about him. The fact that Rwth was Johnson's daughter need not necessarily mean that Elmer was a villain. But it probably meant that somebody was, and Robert intended to find out the mystery.

It was mid-October and the day of a sheep sale. Ralph was waiting in the kitchen, which was both hall and bar, until Isaiah and Robert should appear. Gillian leant

against the table, dutifully brushing Ralph's hat, but,
as the brush went industriously round and round, she was
planning a day's festivity for herself and Rwth—a day
which was to begin with a long, secret, satisfying gaze
at Robert during the fuss of Ralph's getting off, a look
at Robert in his best suit (which she liked, not because it
was his best, but because its grey accentuated the grey
fire in his eyes) and the hat with plaited cord round the
crown, and the home-made pen (which had now written
several important letters) stuck through the cord at the
side, in case it should be necessary to sign his name
during any business transaction.   There was also the
fellow to Rwth's handkerchief in his breast pocket, and
there were his best boots, a thought less thick and weighty
than the others, and not quite so heavily shod with iron.
Then, of course, there was Robert's face—the brown face
with its economy of flesh, its lines of humour and thought
and labour, the sweeping brows with their look of almost
lifting into wings, the heavy lashes whence the eyes looked
out like creatures from an ambush—tameless, mysterious,
intensely alive and full of questions and demands and
gifts which his mouth (by nature) continually assented
to in every curve, but (by the decree of Robert's will) at
the same time continually denied.   There was his way
of sitting there on the back seat with his arms properly
folded like a groom and the correct biddable manner
of a groom—and yet making even Isaiah's pomp look
foolish.   And there was the tacit understanding that
Robert would conform to all the usual standards—with a
reservation.   Then there was his voice, which had the
same natural warmth and acquired severity.   To hear
him say " Mrs. Elmer " was a pain that she dreaded yet
desired.   She persisted in bringing it on herself.   She
also tried to cause him to give her some order, such as :
" Mind the wheel, Mrs. Elmer ! "   Once she had even had
to stand on the felly of the wheel with her feet between
the spokes almost until Isaiah said : " Tabor on ! " to
the mare.   Robert had seen her quite well : but he made
his mouth into a line and remained silent, giving her to

understand that her own commonsense, her father, or
her husband should guard her from her childish foolish-
ness. So Gillian said to herself with a kind of petulant
ecstasy : " I'll stay on this old wheel till my legs are
broke, but I'll make Robert speak."

She saw (and Robert knew) when Isaiah drew up the
rug, settled the reins more comfortably, grunted, took
up the whip and prepared to say " Tabor on ! " Then
Robert looked at Gillian. Obstinacy veiling passion
met obstinacy veiling deeper passion. Wrath in Robert's
eye met rebellion in Gillian's, and before the first syllable
of " Tabor " was out, Robert said : " Please to gerroff
that wheel, Mrs. Elmer ! " But by the end of the sentence
the words were so frozen that the delight of the order
was rather dashed.

Lately the writing had provided a real reason for
orders, and when Robert, after enquiries, said : " Well,
get on with it ! " there was such a spirit of delight at the
Mermaid that the very cat became intoxicated and played
with pens and copybooks and ink to the destruction of
all three. If the vast, vague Someone who created Robert
and Gillian and Rwth has in Itself anything ironical (and
this must be so, because It created Fringal and all the
Fringalism in the world), It must have felt gratified at
the pleasant irony of these departures. For there was the
Toy-in-Chief, Isaiah, the omniscient, hoodwinked and
befooled by his own child and everybody else. And there
was the Successful Toy with his fruit of happiness which
had been nourished on some evil thing, but which looked
deliciously ripe and sweet—and was quite dry and hollow
within. And there were Gillian and Rwth, both living
with the man of the Mermaid and both in love with the
man of the farm. And Rwth, the little maid-of-all-work,
had begun life covered with gold and silver, while Gillian,
the child of a rich father, the mistress of the Inn, might
hear at any moment those words of Fringal accompanied
by a nod to Rwth : " the missus 'ere." And there was
Robert, grim and gruff, with enough passionate love-
poems under his pen-decked hat to conquer the hearts

of half-a-dozen women, and because one very ordinary little country girl did not tell him she loved him these songs would never be seen nor heard by anybody. There had been Fringal himself on that May Day, sitting on his bed, laughing over his " rise," while the man who might kill him if Robert gave him a hint (granted that Robert found out anything to his disadvantage) passed within a few yards of him, unconscious. It must all have provided Providence with some very pleasant cogitation, if Providence ever has time to look down on Dysgwlfas. If He looks at Dysgwlfas now—but we must get back to our satire.

On the floor knelt Rwth, blacking Ralph's boots. Ralph was counting money and notes, and the safe stood on the table. Gillian wished she could fling it and herself at Robert's solidly shod feet. But when the sound of wheels came, there was another little irony—for Robert was not there.

" I'm sorry, Ralph, I canna go to the sale," called Isaiah.

He came in.

" Your poor A'nt Emily's worse," he said. " She's heard a cradle rocking for a week or more, and now she says there's hundreds of little angels with no bodies, like on Christmas cards, filling the place so as she can't breathe. And she wants a butterfly net. So your A'nt Fanteague she's sent for me. Poor Emily ! That's what comes of being childless."

He gave the young couple an admonitory look. Jonathan, from the trap just outside, said :

" It minds me of the tale of Melchisedech Barrows, the silent man. If there was a thing in life that chap wanted, 'twas a son. And the young woman he fancied was terrible fond of children. But they never had none because he wouldna spend the words to ax her to wed. Between whiles he thought of what he'd say. But when he was with the girl no words 'ud come. So when she'd waited about ten years, she took and died of a decline. And after about ten year more he began to go very simple.

And a pity it was, for they met 'a reared a nice family
and been remembered."

" Well, the long and the short of it is, Jonathan and
me's off to Silverton," said Isaiah. " You mun go to the
sale alone, Ralph. We'll be back to-morrow night."

So they drove away. But it was many a long day
before Isaiah came home, and poor Jonathan had told
his last story and he never came back at all. Nobody
knew quite what happened ; but on the evening of their
return, just outside Silverton, Jonathan must by mistake
have pulled the correct rein. According to her usual
custom, the mare going in exactly the opposite way, the
long-expected disaster of Jonathan's life occurred, and
when the remnants of the trap and harness were picked
up, Jonathan was past all Abigail's care forever. Almost
there could be read on the still, passive, fatalistic face,
the poignant regret that he had not lived to eat his own
funeral feast. But whether Isaiah " fell soft," or whether
he simply lifted up his great voice and said " Ha ! " to
Death, as he had to Dosset's bull, and scared away the
king of terror, at any rate Isaiah was alive when they
found him. And alive he remained. He was taken
back to his sister's, where Emily had not ceased her
dreaming, and Mrs. Fanteague at last had almost enough
to do. For not only was there Emily with her entourage
of cherubic heads, but there was Isaiah, who was so offended
at being laid low that he " grumped " all the time and
would have nobody but his sister in the room. Then
there was Gillian, who came to help and really hindered,
for there was still very little abnegation in Gillian's nature.
There was also Abigail Makepeace, who came for her
husband's funeral and was like a bird lost in a great waste
now that she had no one to manage. She sat in the
kitchen with the day-girl and wept, talking intermittently
through her apron. And her mind was so distraught
with the lack of Jonathan's distraughtness that she talked
about both husbands impartially and without differentia-
tion, so that the day-girl never knew whether it was
John Rideout who " a'most needed a bib and bottle,

the poor dear man," or whether it was Jonathan Makepeace with whom it was "one word, and that the right
word, and no more said." And she (the day-girl) became
quite useless to Mrs. Fanteague because her mind was
full of Jonathan-John, whose huge, confused, conflicting
personality she was unable to grasp. It was really the
great hour of Mrs. Fanteague's life. Her gifts of being
prop and stay were called into full use at last. And it
was such a joy to be able quite conscientiously to tell
the Vicar's wife that there was nobody to do a hand's
turn but herself. She even mourned for Jonathan better
than his wife did. She knew what text Jonathan would
have liked on his headstone—or if she did not, she at least
chose a suitable one—"As a tale that is told." She could
face Isaiah's icy misery of sickness with a very blaze of
cheerfulness. When Gillian hinted that she wanted to
go home (only Gillian knowing that it was Robert and
not Ralph that drew her), Mrs. Fanteague said that a
sick father came before a healthy husband and that she
was surprised at such lovesickness after over four months
of marriage. To which Gillian composedly replied :
"So am I." When Emily fought the cherubs, Mrs.
Fanteague fetched a feather duster and swept them away,
and Emily was pacified.

Meanwhile, at Dysgwlfas, Robert went on with the
writing lessons on the rare occasions when Ralph was away,
Fringal busy out of doors, and he himself free of work.
It was on one of these occasions that Rwth wrote something which startled him very much. It even made him
pause in the lessons on the very verge of discovery. It
was a cold, wet evening, settling into a dreary night.
Ralph and Fringal were at Weeping Cross. No customers
were in the bar. Only Rwth and Robert sat by the
fire. Robert was smoking, wondering when he would
try his great experiment on Ralph. He bent forward to
see how Rwth was getting on. She was writing on a
stray sheet and not in the copybook. She had written
"Gillian loves Maister, Ailse loves Robert." She was
not aware that Robert had seen it.

With a flush in his face he quietly leant back, watching her with half-closed lids guarding his already deep and guarded eyes, while she secretly looked at what she had written and slipped it into her pocket.

Strange ! Here was this forlorn creature who had never received love since she could remember, pouring out her love for him. He knew, now, the meaning of those liquid dark looks, those silences full of the wing-beats of the spirit—for he was intensely sensitive (as all poets are) to silence. The quality of a person's silence was his measure of the person. He knew Gruffydd for a more complete personality than himself because his silence was of more dimensions than his own. The silence of many people is quite flat and thin, meaningless. Those people are to be avoided, not because they are evil, but because they have not enough life in their souls to be either evil or good. Now Robert had observed the silences of Rwth, and that they were richer, thicker, as it were, than those of most of the people he knew—far richer than Gillian's. Gillian's was of one dimension only ; in it she dreamed herself—the dream of the world of suffering and ecstasy was not in her silence. It was in Rwth's. Strange, and very strange, that the woman to whom his love was irrevocably given should not have this quality, while this waif had it ! Curious, that when he looked into the lake of her mind he should see not only the misted, enormous reflections of existence, but also—himself. Himself exactly as he was, and not in the least as Gillian saw him—and all this without so much as a " with your leave " to him, and without a glimmer of understanding from Rwth's everyday self. Yet, though she could never have put the thing into words, she understood him. He knew, as he sat there with his eyes shut, that she could never misconstrue any motive of his, though his mother might. She could never accidentally wound him, as Gillian did. She, who toiled weekdays and Sundays, was his rest. She, who was dumb, spoke with the tongue of silence. So it happened to Robert, as to many, that the woman who

held his soul like a babe in her arms was not the woman
he would have chosen to mother his children, was not the
woman he loved, in whose presence time flowed by un-
heard, and whose gift was eternity. It was Gillian who
took his breath so that often he could not speak to her
at all. But it was Rwth who knew, very far down in her
soul, all about this breathless wonder of his, who wondered with him, pitied, understood.

There and then, as men have done in all time, Robert
turned Rwth into the Madonna-woman. In ignorance
of what his secret self was doing, he set up a little shrine
and put her there—womanhood etherealized, with a
grieved, unprovocative beauty. He felt that he could
quite easily have told her about that unlucky business
of the girl at Shepcot when he was eighteen. Only it
was not necessary. She understood the wildness that
was in him, she knew how the pulses hammered in your
ears, how the savage yearning seized you, how the cleaner
you lived and the healthier you were, the madder was
desire when it came. Gillian would not have known.
Shame seized him at the very idea of Gillian in connection with this old episode in his life. Gillian herself
awoke these savage yearnings, she was fuel for that fire
as well as he. It is almost impossible for the same woman
to stir and be stirred by passion and to feel maternal
towards the man who has roused it. Exceptional women
might, by the strength of their spirits, by the splendour
of love and abnegation, achieve it ; but Gillian was not
exceptional. She would probably never attain the detachment necessary. The man she loved would always
remain for her the lover, the mate, the ruler, the
giver of children and of daily bread, the comforter.
To her children she would be, perhaps, maternal.
But she would never find in any corner of her lover's
personality (even if that lover were the right one and
not Elmer) the little weeping lad who is somewhere
in every man.

Robert decided that the writing lessons must stop,
not because there was anything wrong in this relationship,

but because he felt it a kind of disloyalty to Gillian to
be understood so well by another woman. He felt precisely as the lover in the old tale must have felt when the
Madonna, on whose finger he had thoughtlessly slipped
his bride's ring, softly stepped between them on their
wedding night. But the depth of her immortal understanding of desire was no comfort to the young bridegroom all on fire for the bride in her sweet mortality.
It is useless to tell a child all about a flower when what
it wants is just the flower—to pluck it and to wear it.
So the Madonnas must always be content to give and to
receive nothing, to see the eyes of men ever on the pink
rose waving above the hedge, and to comfort them when
the thorns have been sharp.

Robert was not picking roses, but he was dreaming of
one, and there was a sense of discomfort in his mind at
the idea of sharing his dream, even in this vague, half-
conscious way. And all the while he was full of wonder
that a being so crushed and so like the dumb, driven
creatures of the fields, should give him this extraordinary
sense of rest. Again and again he looked at her search-
ingly, marvelling at it. " Ailse loves Robert." How
simple ! Yet how piercing the three words were ! For
a moment her sincerity made Gillian seem almost uninteresting. Supposing he had first met this girl as a
young gipsy, gay and proud, the daughter of the chief of
the tribe ? Would he have given her the love he had
given to Gillian ? He could not tell. But in the light of
her love he saw that she was not ugly. Success and joy
and a measure of ease might have made her almost beautiful in a strange untamed way. He knocked his pipe
out and got up to go.

" Well, good-night, Rwth. Get on with it ; I shanna
be able to come for a bit," he said.

Rwth smiled in her usual way. And that was all.
Why, then, were Robert's eyes full of tears as he tramped
away to his lonely supper at the cottage, where no more
his stepfather told stories in an atmosphere of danger,
where he had to fend for himself during his mother's

absence. Was he to know that, every time he went to a fair or a sale, a small, thin, dark-clad figure stole over from the inn and scrubbed his floors ? He wrote to his mother that he was proud of keeping the place so clean, and that he hardly ever had to wash the floors. His mother smiled.

" I doubt I'll find a pigstye when I've raught back," she said, not knowing of the elf who scrubbed and polished, always very careful to have finished long before Robert should return—so that all should be dry. Robert found it very quiet on the farm without the loud voice of Isaiah, but his time was full, and he had not much leisure for thought. His time, apparently, would always be full, for he heard that Isaiah would never again be strong enough for an ordinary farmer's life, and Robert did not intend to desert him. He only hoped that Elmer and Gillian would not come to live here, for he did not feel that he could stand receiving orders from Elmer.

" Well, we mun grin and abide and see what comes," he observed, as he drove his plough through the reeking wet soil under the low brooding clouds that always haunt Dysgwlfas in the dark months. And while the silver plough-share cut into the stiff soil, his spirit drove its way into the heart of the moor and left on its stern beauty the long shining fruitful furrows of the imagination. He wrapped himself in the moor, and he attained a beauty he could not have won in a town. Little by little he made his poem—rugged, sweet and wild—and when he sat alone by the fire in the evenings, he was comforted by this unifying of himself with the beauty of the earth, by this caging and taming of remote loveliness, by the welding of phrases and the ripple of metres and the mysterious mingling of his soul with the sweeping dark expanses with their grey roofing cloud. And the vast moor, seamed and chasmed with streams, the immense heaven, veiled and feathered with cloud, were like his own personality—large and vital, passionate and stormy, yet veined with melancholy and brooded over by philosophy.

And this is the song that Robert made for Ailse, though she never saw it nor heard it.

> She inna like a woman fair,
> She inna like a little child.
> But she is like the evening mild,
> And like the wide and quiet air.
> Not as a golden star is she,
> But like dim sky where stars can shine.
> She's not my love (oh, love o' mine !)
> But in a dream she cradled me.

CHAPTER XXVIII

FRINGAL FORGETS TO LAUGH

As the November evenings drew in Ralph began to miss
Gillian more and more. He wrote demanding that she
should come back, and as Isaiah was out of danger and
Mrs. Makepeace willing to stay, Gillian decided to go
home.

Ralph met her at the Keep on a cold blue afternoon
with the first powder of snow on the hills. She was glad
to be back. It was very sweet to see her old home in
its hollow, and the cottage, and Robert leaning over the
yard gate of the inn, come to give her a welcome and
enquire after Isaiah. It was a joy to think that the
writing lessons would begin again and that Robert would
again say: "Well, get on with it!" The two young
men would have to attend fairs alone now, and she
hoped they would not quarrel.

"Ralph's so aggravating, times," she thought, "and
Robert's tempersome now and agen." She was very glad
to see Rwth, too, for the girls were fond of each other,
and the shared secret of the writing, as well as the un-
shared secret of their love, drew them together. And
oh! joy of joys! When they were up in Rwth's attic
looking over the winterly country, Rwth gave her a
slip of a note from Robert.

Robert was coming on Friday evening. Gillian was to
have the songs ready to play, and to arrange that Ralph
and Fringal should both be there when she played them,
and Rwth was to have the old blackboard from the farm,

on which Mrs. Fanteague and Isaiah and Emily had learnt their lessons long ago. It was to be covered with a cloth until the moment came. And Rwth was to write on the board anything the music made her think of. There was to be a big fire, and there were to be both lamps—kitchen and sitting-room. And if Mrs. Elmer would be so kind, Robert would take a cup of tea with them.

Gillian was in an ecstasy. The idea of tea occurred to Robert as a means of getting everybody together and being able to choose his seat. Also, he wanted Ralph, Rwth and Fringal in one room, and Gillian in the other. This could easily be managed if Gillian played her piano while the others were at tea. During the hour before Gillian's arrival he had taught Rwth exactly what she was to do. She was first to write all she had previously written— her name, and Esmeralda, and other things she had remembered. Then she was to write the names of the places up in Wales where she had lived, and various stray names and words that he could not identify or get into connection with the rest. Lastly, she was to write anything the music made her think of, and, if her own name and others occurred in connection with newly remembered names, then she was to put those down too.

Gillian was afraid, as she remembered Ralph's black looks whenever Rwth showed any new intelligence. What would he and Fringal do when they discovered all this? Still, Robert would be there. All would be well. Even now she could see him, down in the meadow that stretched out long and narrow from the farm fields to the Unket Place. He was rounding up the sheep (which always lay in this meadow in November) in case there should be snow. Now he was gone into the twilight with his pattering flock. The air was cold and glassy, and everything presaged snow within a few days. The far hills, where the sunset had been, floated on the purple darkness of the moor cut out of palest sapphire, and on their pointed or rounded tops the blurs of snow faded in the white sunset clouds. The Unket Place lay darkly by the water ; as Gillian looked at it she suddenly said :

" I'm a child of sin, Rwth ! "

As Rwth looked at it her black eyes grew blacker, sorrow and trembling seized her heart. But then she remembered the altar that was there, the woodland altar she had set up little by little as she gathered sticks, the altar decked with fir cones and consecrated to him who was as her god, and also as an infant gathered to her breast. A smile, wild and dazzling, flashed over the swart face, and in the glory of her love she was suddenly Ailse, the gipsy queen, Ailse rare and rich and alluring, Ailse lifted from all the troubles of the children of men by her love— lifted even beyond fear of the King of Fear. And Robert, glancing at the Unket Place as he led away his flock, knew that the hour was coming soon when his presage would be fulfilled, when evil would leap out and there would be none to wrestle with it but himself, when the snow would fall and muffle Dysgwlfas, and somewhere in the snow he must fight blindly with his own impulses, his own desires, to save his love—to keep the spring for Gillian, and Gillian for the spring.

Only a little snow had fallen by Friday, and Rwth had been busy each morning gathering sticks in the gyland ready for the hard weather. Lower and lower drooped the soft, grey, massy clouds, as if to shut Dysgwlfas away from the world, so that the drama that was preparing there should be undisturbed. Wilder cried the peewits across the mangold field, and the notes of the owls shuddered through the little wood half the night—for the moon was at the full and the hunt was fierce and easy.

And away over the dark hills Johnson was travelling, unknown to Robert, towards the inn of The Mermaid, for the gipsy woman had told him of a girl there who, though she could not speak, seemed to know the gipsy speech, and whose eyes were large and black and clear.

All Friday morning Gillian and Rwth prepared for the

feast. They made a cake. They cut mountains of bread
and butter, and Rwth put off her daily gathering of sticks
till to-morrow, when she could, unless the snow came
sooner than it was expected, gather all day. But now
there was such an infinity of things to do ! Every
chair and table had to be polished. The floor must be
washed with milk and water to make it shine. The best
china must be dusted. Not one of these things would
be noticed by Robert, but what did that matter ? Do
those dear and simple souls who go to church across the
fields every Sunday, scrupulously clad in their best, with
a sprig of southernwood in their prayer-books, really
think that God notices whether they have on the best
black coat or only the second best grey one with the
frayed sleeve ? Do they really believe He smells the
southernwood ? The point is that the best coat is on and
the southernwood there—for that is part of the revel
of worship. Thus the best china and the polish on the
chairs were essential both to Gillian and Rwth. Rwth
did not know the songs that Gillian was going to sing.
It all added to the thrill of the day.

"Well ! " (Fringal inserted himself in the door).
"There's to be a feast of fat things, seemingly."

An overwhelming gust of laughter drowned his words,
for the excitement of the two girls, being mysterious,
seemed to him exceedingly funny. Everything Fringal
could not understand, from mother-love to the structure
of a threshing machine, seemed inexhaustibly comical
to him.

"It's for you too, Fringal ! " said Gillian, with
unexpected geniality. She disliked Fringal. He always
made her feel as if she was not really the mistress of the
house at all. " You're to come in to your five o'clock in the
bar (they usually called the kitchen the bar), and Robert's
coming too, to see the Master, and Rwth's going to sit
down with us, and I'm going to play. "

"What a joke ! O what an overpoweringly funny
joke ! " Fringal was in agonies of mirth. To play ! To
draw sounds out of that curious invention of wood and

wire, and then to lift up her voice and (as Fringal put it)
to caterwaul. Well! it promised to be a very enjoyable
evening. Plenty to eat and plenty to laugh at. That
had always been Fringal's motto. The only trouble was
that it was always " at " and never " with " that Fringal
laughed. The only creature he might have been sufficiently
detached from self to laugh with was the little cush-
cow—and the little cush-cow (which had returned with
Gillian on her marriage) had no sense of humour.

Ralph had gone to Dosset's, but was to be back before
teatime. At three o'clock Gillian disappeared. She was
going to put on a new winter dress—slatey like the old
one, but grander, made of rippling silk—and she was
going to wave her hair. For the interest of the afternoon
for her, as for Fringal, centred in herself—only she had
given her soul into Robert's keeping, so her absorption
included Robert. But it was not Robert's experiment,
the mysterious idea he was working out, that interested
her. It was simply the knowledge that those dark eyes
would look at her. Their light would play over her.
She would let fall every pretence and simply rest in them.
And she would play upon his heart-strings with her voice.
Long and long ago she had told him that she wanted to
make folk cry. She had longed to make them remember
her, love her, rue her. She would make Robert love her
to-day. She would fill those grey eyes with tears. She
would awake desire. For in that moment when, in the
shadows at Weeping Cross, brilliant eye met brilliant eye,
she had learnt what desire was. She thought that if ever
Robert looked at her as Ralph had done she would die
of sheer joy. She knew what the song was, the first
song she must sing. And oh! the name she would think
while her voice spoke across the kitchen from the little
parlour, the name she would conjure and adore, was the
name of Robert Rideout!

" Robert Rideout O!" she murmured as she fluffed
her hair to make it look prettier, " It's the name of
names! "

She floated down. Rwth held up admiring hands.

They waited—the young mistress, assured and sweet, in the hyacinthine gown of lights and shadows, and the little maid, in her old black dress and a clean apron, with the new cap Gillian had bought her.   They sat by the fire, only one dumb in reality, but both dumb with love. A sound! Is it he? No. On the pale sky beyond the window moves Fringal's head, like a gargoyle set up on a church.

" Be I to come now, missus ? "

" Ah."

Fringal sat down at a judicious distance from the mistress.

Quick feet on the hard ground! Is it he? No. It is Ralph come back from the farm.

" Is tea ready ? " said he.

" Everything's been ready and waiting this long while past," replied Gillian, unconscious of the double meaning of her words.   But something in the room seemed to hansel her words and give them another meaning—something that was akin to the faint soughing of the snow wind in the chimney, and the pale, deathly colour of the sky.

Another sound! The two girls became still, intent, watching the door.

" Oh, please God, let him have the grey suit on ! "

This was Gillian, in the depths of her silence.

There were no words in Rwth's silence.

Robert knocked the soil from his boots and came in.

Both girls softly rose.   So might two queens of Faery arise in their places to greet a visitant from earth.

Then Rwth went into the back kitchen and made the tea, and the meal began.

" Closing in early," said Ralph.

" Ah !   I reckon there'll be a downfall soon," replied Robert.

" Snow, Robert ? "

" Ah ; snow, Mrs. Elmer," said Robert.

" Why dunna you say ' Gillian,' like you was used to ? "

" You're a married lady now, Mrs. Elmer."

Robert's eyes rested on Ralph for a moment.

" Yes, yes ! you're married now," assented Ralph.

There was a sound from the other side of the table like a cat sneezing. It could hardly have been Fringal laughing, because when Gillian looked at him he was quite solemn.

" I canna see why, because I'm married, you should give me the cold shoulder," complained Gillian, and her eyes appealed and lured him. But Robert thought : " She's more in love with Elmer than ever."

And because that look of hers made him confused and hoarse he deliberately turned away—and there was Rwth, there was Ailse-who-loved-Robert, softly looking upon him with her dwelling eyes. Had Robert been of a cynical turn of mind he would have been amused : but he had nothing of the cynic in him. It only struck him as rather pathetic that this child should feel thus towards himself and that he should be hopelessly in love with Gillian. He had heard Fringal's little sneeze of laughter. And again suspicion awoke in him—suspicion that hurt him abominably because it affected Gillian. He looked straight across at Ralph, who was in the full lamplight, and said :

" Be you in agreement with marrying twice, Elmer ? "

Why did Ralph's eyes fly to Fringal's face so suddenly ? What was that expression ? Nothing, surely nothing.

" No," said Ralph loudly. " No." He turned away from Rwth towards Gillian: " Once married, married for good."

" Or ill," put in Fringal softly, and laughed the shadow of a laugh.

" And suppose you'd got married to one and then you got to like another as didn't rightly belong to you, would you leave the one an' go to the other ? "

" No, no ! " Elmer spoke hastily, irritably. " No. Better a slut of your own than share a queen."

Rwth's gaze moved away from Robert, and lit on Ralph.
The change in it was the change from a caress to a sword-
gleam.

The room had become curiously electric—like the
atmosphere before a contest. And it was Robert, not
the master of the house, who dominated it.

He turned to Gillian, and the firelight caressed his face,
showed the lines of thought and care and love. Tenderness lit his eyes, but under the tenderness they were
stern.

" Sing, Gillian, oot ? " he said.

Whether he did it purposely or not, his calling her by
her Christian name was fire in her veins. She forgot
Ralph, she forgot the sneering Fringal, where she was
and what she was. She even forgot why she was to sing.
Why ? Ah, she knew very well why she was to sing !
She was going to sing her heart out, in a gipsy song, to
Robert Rideout. She was going to make him, *make* him
see. She was going to sing him out of the dream of fact
into the reality of love. Her fault ? It was not. He
had planned it. He had given her the piano. He had
told her to sing. He had sent to Johnson's friend for the
song that Esmeralda, taught by her mother and her
grandmother—for the song had come down the genera-
tions—had sung to Ailse by the quiet waters of Fairy
Dingle. Not that Gillian knew this. She only knew it
was a song that made her tremble, that made her afraid,
that rang in her mind bells that she had never yet heard.
If she could sing the song to Robert as she wanted to
sing it, surely—surely—Robert would understand ?
Surely he would see at last that she loved him, and not
Ralph, that she longed and longed——

With a queenly air, her head high, the firelight making
a glory of her dress, she walked across the kitchen and
disappeared in the little parlour.

Robert glanced at Rwth, and she quietly rose and sat
down near the blackboard. Robert shifted his position
so that he could see Ralph and Fringal as well as the
board.

And this is the song that Gillian, wife of Ralph, sang in the dusk to Robert Rideout, her father's shepherd :

" O littlest one !
  Only a spring, a fall o' leaf, a winter fled
  Since I did mock my mother when she said
  Some day I'd love.
  O thou !
  Little and small upon my breast,
  Taking thy ease, taking thy rest——
  Thou littlest one !
  See, see, what thee hast done !
  Wasna I crazed enough with love afore—
  Feeling that little head nestling at last
  Upon my breast, those little fingers fast
  In mine : but thee has found a new surprise
  Smiling upon me with thy father's eyes ! "

Robert was dazed, blinded to what was going on by the voice of Gillian, always beautiful to him, but now full of some new glory, something that dazzled him, fired him, set him groping for some way—any way by which he might put his arms round Gillian and never let her go.

When the song was over he sat with bowed head, then suddenly started up to go to her, and as suddenly sat down again. He had forgotten—forgotten——

He looked across at Rwth, she had uncovered the blackboard. She was writing. What had she written, what was she writing now ? One glance at the white chalk moving slowly and relentlessly like Fate, and he fixed his eyes first on the face of Fringal, then on that of Ralph. With jaw dropped, stark as a dead man, Fringal sat. For the first time in his life he had forgotten to laugh. Ralph was almost as pale as the chalk, only not white, but of a sickly grey.

Neither of them seemed able to move nor to speak. They were like two paralysed men looking on while all their worldly possessions were flung into the sea. It was impossible to say, from the expression of Rwth's face, whether she understood the gravity of what she was doing. But whether she did or not she intended to go through with it. It was Robert's wish. That was enough.

The white letters shone relentlessly from the board.

Esmeralda. Mother. Fairy Dingle. Fringal beat Ailse.
Mister Elmer.

Elmer gave an audible groan ; but still he did not
seem able to get up and end it. Gillian, obedient to a
word from Robert, was playing again. The writing
went on :

All Saints' Church. Black Mountain. Mrs. Rwth
Elmer. A baby. Fringal took it away. Rwth forgot her
words. . . . Dysgwlfas. . . .
Here the busy chalk stopped, snapped. Rwth flung
the pieces on the floor.

The silence ached. The music in the other room had
ceased. On the black window one snowflake flattened
itself enquiringly. There was a sound in the parlour.
Gillian was coming.

" Go on playing, Gillian," said Robert. His voice was
harsh and imperious. She wondered at it, but she played
again.

Robert was as pale as Ralph now. His eyes stared
fiercely at his rival. This was what he had sacrificed
himself for ! So that Gillian should be made a mock of !
He started forward with such ferocity in his look that
Ralph almost cowered.

" Is it true ? " he said. " Is it true ? "

He spoke very low, so that Gillian should not hear.

He had got Ralph by the collar. He was almost drunk
with rage. But all Ralph could say was :

" How did she learn ? Oh, how did she learn ? " He
was stupefied with wonder.

Rwth sat huddled beneath the blackboard. It was
Fringal who recovered first. He intervened between
Robert and Ralph.

" Canna you see," he said, " she's mad. She can write,
but she's mad. She mun go to the asylum."

Ralph sighed like one coming to life again after a swoon.

That was it ! She was mad. They must say that, and
nobody would believe her. Besides—Robert could not

piece those words together. He had not the clue. It was dangerous enough, especially as Rwth mentioned gipsies, but it was curable. She must go at once—he would have to get her certified—that could be done in a few days, and then ! Fringal was worth his salt, after all.

The music stopped. Gillian was coming. Robert sprang up and drew his sleeve across the board, and whispered to Rwth, " Dunna let Gillian know you're Elmer's wife. If she didna love you," he muttered to Elmer as he went back to his seat, " I'd nigh kill you."

And there she stood, very pale in the lamplight, very still. She had heard. She looked at the board for enlightenment, but there was nothing. She looked at the four faces. There also was nothing. She could see that something had happened ; but the only sign of it was in their expressions and in those muttered words of Robert's. There had been something fierce and dreadful in the room. She shivered. It had left a shadow here, but what it was she could not guess.

The boding wind was louder in the chimney. Robert's face was stern and set.

" I'm going now," he said. He turned to Gillian. " A word with you, Gillian," he said.

Silent, wondering, she followed him. He stood on the doorstep, his outline almost lost in the soft, smothering blackness of the night, which was invisibly astir with falling snow. She stood on the step above, her figure very sharp and definite against the bright ruddy glow of the bar. Their eyes were almost level.

" No offence meant," said Robert, " but I'd be glad if you'd tell me summat. Do ye love Ralph Elmer or don't ye ? "

A flake of snow lit softly on his brow, just where she had kissed him. The wind sighed in the old dry grasses round the door.

" If she didna love you I'd nigh kill ye."

The words rang in her brain, echoed and rang again. If she said " Yes," Robert was safe, for he would not touch Ralph then. But if she said " Yes " her fate was sealed. She would have to live with Ralph for ever. It was the old struggle over again. If she said " No," would he take her in his arms ? Would he take her back to that cottage of his, the door of which was the door of heaven ?

She must not think of that.

She gazed into the dark wells of his eyes, and clearly, very softly, she said " Yes ! "

Robert nodded and went away without another word.

When Gillian went back into the room, Rwth had a look of being at bay ; both Ralph and Fringal seemed to be questioning her, but she wrote no answer to their questions, and when Fringal put a piece of chalk in her hand she flung it at her feet and trod on it.

Ralph turned to Gillian.

" She's gone mad," he said. " She's going to be shut up."

" Mad, is she ? " Gillian laughed, and Ralph was afraid at her laughter. " She inna mad, Ralph Elmer. And what's more, I'll find out what she wrote on that board."

" She's mad, and she's going."

" She inna, and she's going to stop. And I'll tell everybody as she inna mad. And to-morrow she'll write agen for me, wunna you, Rwth ? "

Rwth nodded.

" You've got a tidy bit to hide, seemingly," said Gillian in a steely voice, " if you're so terrified of what poor Rwth writes."

All night, while Gillian and Rwth were asleep, Ralph and Fringal consulted as to what they should do.

" It's the gipsies—it's me having stolen all that gold, and us burying that child and the girl going dumb when she found out—them's the things I canna smooth away," said Fringal.

" And only this very day," Ralph said, " as I was coming away from Dosset's Farm a gipsy-looking fellow was loitering about, and he says, ' Is this the place where there's a wench with big black eyes like clear water ? "

" Laws ! "

" It must have been that woman that came on the wedding day as talked about her," said Ralph. " But it shows we've got to be careful."

" What did you say ? "

" Told him she'd gone to the Keep."

" You're a clever un, maister."

At that moment Gipsy Johnson, having passed the inn while the playing was going on, and not stopping because of his anxiety to get to the Keep before the snow came, was well on his way. He had knocked at Robert's door, but finding him out, had decided to return to-morrow if the snow held off. If it did not he was going to send a younger man to find out where the girl was, and to haunt the place until he could come himself.

Ah ! how the moor sighed all night, under the fitful wind, as though it cried : " What matters it ? Soon I return, covering all with a sea of heather. What matters it ? Trouble not your midget lives with midget griefs ! See ! Even now my tide rolls on, like the tide of Time. What matters it ? "

In the cottage by the moaning orchard Robert fought down the desire to destroy his enemy. He fell asleep at last in the armchair that had belonged to Jonathan, and heard like the songs of sea maidens sounding in the wind, the song he had made for Ailse : " In a dream she cradled me," and the voice of Gillian, perilously sweet, singing the antique song of motherhood.

But he would never have believed, even in a dream, that the reason Gillian sang like that, with such piercing sweetness, was that there, in the little dark parlour of the " Mermaid's Rest " she had seen a vision, as she sang the song of Esmeralda, of the child of her desire, and that the child had eyes dark and dreamy and well warded by lashes —eyes of such a blazing vitality that the colour could scarcely be seen—and the smile of Robert Rideout.

CHAPTER XXIX

SNOW IN THE LITTLE GYLAND

STORM sank to calm on Saturday morning, for the snow was falling quicker than it thawed, and Ralph and Fringal had to go out on the moor to bring in the sheep. Before he started Ralph caught Rwth by the arm and said: " If you dare to write any more I'll pretty nigh kill ye ! "

But Rwth looked defiance. She would write just as much or as little as Robert liked. This Ralph was not the man she loved. Robert had told her not to write about her marriage with Ralph, not to let Gillian know of it, so she would not. But all the rest she would write if Gillian told her.

" And the aggravating part of it is," said Fringal, as they tramped through the heather, " as I ne'er meant to take the little vixen. I only meant to take the gold, but I heard a noise afore I'd done, so I was bound to take un."

He spoke as if the gold were his right, and his sin only the stupid mistake of being found out.

" You're a very cunning old man," said Ralph. " I dunna forget as it was you that made me marry the nasty little thing."

" You was quite content till the t'other turned up."

" I made the best of it."

" But it were a pity we didna get a doctor when the brat was born. And then you clouting the girl just after, and telling her too soon about it being dead——"

" She wore me out, moaning for it."

" It was a pity. It's that as ud make the gipsies mad.

261

And now's the other's took on so obstinate you canna get Rwth into any asylum. But maybe she'll catch summat and die."

" She never will. She's too strong."

" If the Lord ud be pleased to take er——"

" Oh, drop that, Fringal. It's no joke to me."

" Nor me. If I was you——"

" Well ? "

No words. Only a long look into each other's faces, and a thought leaping like a sword from eye to eye.

Ralph turned away.

" No more o' that, Fringal," he said. But the thought was in his mind. They rounded up the sheep and returned. On the blackboard, re-written, was most of the writing of the night before.

Ralph, coming into the kitchen to fetch his gun and snatch a hasty meal before going round the fields to get the Sunday dinner, as was his custom on a Saturday, saw it and was furious.

" Where's Rwth ? " he said.

" I dunno. Maybe she's gone for a few more sticks afore the snow comes proper," said Gillian indifferently.

Ralph went out, beginning the long detour of enclosed moor and field, which usually resulted in rabbits, a hare or a pheasant.

Fringal went to the stable with broom and shovel, as he always did on Saturday. Gillian lit the parlour fire and sat down to play over last night's songs. She alone was undisturbed by Rwth's writing. What did it matter to the daughter of Isaiah Lovekin, the wife of Ralph Elmer, that a certain gipsy girl called Rwth had once been Ailse ? What did it matter that Fringal had found her, and that she was now servant to Ralph ?

Nothing, nothing at all.

She sang the song of Esmeralda.

She did not know that the young gipsy runner who had once brought a letter peered in through the kitchen window, saw the blackboard, on which the writing remained (for to rub it out would be an admission on the part of Ralph), looked into the parlour, recognized her for Lovekin's daughter, whom he had seen once when with Johnson, and went away, only to return, stealing about the house and fields like a ghost.

The afternoon wore on.

Meanwhile Ralph had got a couple of rabbits and a partridge, and was on his way home. He was walking along the thick holly hedge that bounded the last field belonging to the farm and ended in the gyland. He did not see Robert in the field below. Robert had just been to the inn to ask Gillian where Isaiah kept some special recipe for a drench, as one of the cows was sick. As he had turned away from the door she had said wistfully : " I'm all alone."

" Why, where's Rwth ? " he asked.

" Gathering sticks. She went out after dinner and she hanna come in yet."

" She'll be in the orchard," thought Robert. " The snow's too deep in the gyland."

In order to cross the bridge to the field that led up to the inn Ralph had to go through the gyland. Twilight had fallen. Before he was half-way through he saw Rwth, kneeling before a kind of bower of branches. This was the shrine where she worshipped her god. Every treasure she had gathered—the handkerchief, a pencil, a flower Robert had once given her—was hoarded here, buried under fir needles in an old tin box. And on festivals she came and took them out and adored them. Her lifted face was enraptured. She was saying her Name of Names.

" Robert Rideout ! Robert Rideout ! "

And then :

" Ailse loves Robert ! Oh, Ailse loves Robert ! "

Then she would kiss the old red handkerchief and hold it to her heart.

" She never did have any soul," said Ralph. " And now she's mad."

He saw only, in that pathetic picture amid the falling snow, soullessness and madness. And did it matter what he saw? Does it ever matter what the fools of the world understand? And certainly Ralph, for all his cleverness, was a fool.

As he stood there, that which Robert had so long fore-seen came to pass. From somewhere, from nowhere, out of the earth or the pallid sky, or out of Fringal's bleak mind burst the spirit of evil. It tore through the shreds and patches of good in Ralph Elmer; it laid hold of the kindness in him with tooth and claw, and rent it; it whispered and whispered and whispered. So did the snow. So did the sere larch needles. So did the water. The whole world seemed to be whispering round the whispering girl.

Hoarsely, with blood-shot eyes, Ralph whispered also.

" Who's that? " he breathed. " Who spoke to me? "

There she was, a worthless, soulless creature, and she was going to ruin him. And someone had said—someone had hinted—someone was saying it now, close in his ear :

" Suppose she was out of the way? "

Out of the way! Under the snow! The snow was falling now, thick and fast. She had only to stay here, and it would cover her. But she never would stay. She was so full of life. So *damnably* full of life. Back she would go—and write. She would write that she was his wife, and Gillian would leave him. Gillian would be the creature of his passion no more. She had striven for freedom before, half-heartedly. She had almost told him she did not love him. He knew why. He knew whose arms would be round that smooth body if his were not. And this mad woman here, kneeling in the snow, was the cause of it all. It was because she was so full of life. The spirit of evil stressed that very heavily. Well, so had these rabbits, limp in his hand, been full of life an hour ago. Just a shot—one painless shot—and the life was out of them; they could never eat his winter broccoli again. And now here was Rwth—with no more soul than the rabbits—and here was kind twilight, and snow for a covering—and silence and utter loneliness and oblivion.

The white spirit of Ralph, that his mother had loved, that Gillian had sometimes seen, moaned, "No!" But the spirit of evil silenced it. What use was Rwth to herself or anyone else? The voices went on, the busy snowflakes whispered on. They were shutting him away from the world. They were making sure that nobody would ever know. The sudden ungovernable impulse that causes more crime than anything in the world, came upon Ralph Elmer.

He lifted the gun to his shoulder and fired. Rwth fell forward without a sound. She slipped into eternity within the globing peace of her love, as the chrysalis of a dragon-fly might go down-stream in a water-lily. Certainly to her the Unket Place had not been unket, but kind.

As Ralph looked round it had the air of content which some places seem to wear when that which was foreboded, which had to happen there, has happened at last.

Ralph was suddenly collected, cool, detached. He did not feel at all as if he had done it. But somehow he did not feel like going home quite yet. He picked up the rabbits and got over into the sheep field. Robert, who had stood still at the shot, came across the field. Ralph was genial, unusually so. He was gay. And it seemed to Robert curious that a man with sweat running down his face (which he could see by the light of the climbing moon) —sweat which, in such weather, in itself needed explanation—should have this bland, affectionate manner.

Usually they hardly spoke to each other. As if at an order from some hidden self far down, Robert suddenly said :

" Where's Rwth ? "

" Oh," said Ralph gaily, " I've sent her across to Dosset's. Their girl's run away. She's town-bred, and she's afraid of the winter."

" What time did she go ? "

" Oh, early. About mid-day."

Now why such a lie? For Gillian had just said she was gathering sticks, and if Rwth had started, she would have taken some luggage, and Gillian would have known.

" What did ye get then ? "

" This coney."

" Stiffens very quick. A'most as stiff as the others."

" I shot the others but now."

" I've been in this field a good hour, looking the sheep," thought Robert, " and there's been no shot. So that's his second lie."

" Well, you must come and see us soon," Ralph observed, still with his rather hectic cordiality.

" Maybe. If the snow inna too deep."

" When it goes, then. Yes, it's going to be deep. A heavy fall ! "

He was evidently pleased with the snow. He turned away.

" Pity you taught Rwth to write," he said. " It's addled her brain. But no offence. You meant well. And it makes no manner difference to me. It was all lies."

Robert felt embarrassed at this outpouring—embarrassed and troubled. All the way home he thought about it. Why doubt the man ? What an evil mind he must have ! Why, when the fellow said he'd just shot a rabbit, didn't he believe him ? What did he believe ? What premonition was it that laid an icy hand on him, that urged him, with a strange and dreadful voice, to go once more to the sheep meadow ? It was very late before he obeyed this voice, and it was no pleasant journey, for the snow was falling fast and softly piling itself up over the fields. Fitful moonlight shone between the clouds. When he reached the gyland he heard a sound of digging. Frantic, hurried, yet careful digging. But before he had time to go over it stopped. He waited. Not a sound. Had the person who was digging heard him ? Was he waiting for him to go ? He intended to wait and see what was to be seen. He was certain no one had left the gyland. To do so they must cross the bridge and be clearly outlined against the water. For the bridge was so near that even if the moon was behind a cloud, Robert could see it plainly. He waited. An hour went by—more. Not till two hours had gone was there any sound. Then across the bridge, very stealthily, went Ralph.   And as if in an ironic jest the moon swam out and revealed every feature —every haunted, terrified feature of his face.

And Robert knew, as surely as he had ever known anything in his life, that Ralph had murdered Rwth, had crept here to bury her, and had waited afterwards till enough snow had fallen to conceal his work.

CHAPTER XXX

ROBERT AWAITS THE DAWN

IT was the hour Robert had seen with prophetic vision—the hour that had waited for him from all time—the aching, dreadful hour, filled full of smothering snow as he had always known it would be, which would decide his destiny and that of the woman he loved.

Tears were in his eyes for the dead woman, the poor, forlorn child sleeping like a frozen bird in the snow.

But the living waited. Gillian, whom he loved, waited. And the man he hated was in his power. He had only to will, and his enemy would be gone like autumn thistledown, swept away for ever.

As he plunged homewards in the snow, the life he might lead if this happened swam up before him like a promised land. Isaiah would be glad of any son-in-law after this false alliance with a murderer—glad of a strong young fellow to run the farm, too. And Gillian? Robert did not think, after the look she had given him on the threshold, that she would be very hard to win, if Ralph was destroyed in her mind by what he had done. Surely he could make her love him? He would show her his passion as well as his love, and she would, after a time, being lonely, give herself to him.

But if Ralph were saved, then she would stay with Ralph, because she loved him. Had she not told him so? That was the trouble. She loved Ralph. To make her happy he must save Ralph. But how? It would be discovered as soon as the thaw set in. There was no possibility of its not being discovered. And as he realized this, and realized the thing he must do if he would fulfil his love for Gillian, he cried out in the muffling silence :

" Oh, God ! I canna do it ! "

Ah, no ! He could not, could not die. He had so much to do, so much to see, so many poems to make. All life's experience lay before him. The love of woman, the triumphant joy of the bridegroom, the long, sweet days and nights of love—fatherhood. To hear the laughter of boys in the orchard—his boys, with Gillian's smile ; to see girls sitting on little stools by the winter fire earnestly stitching, with Gillian's puckered brow. To see Gillian with a baby, tiny and helpless and unutterably dear, at her breast.

The young man's heart went almost faint within him at these pictures. And the gipsy had said—for Jonathan had told him—that she heard a cradle rocking, but not in Ralph's house. In whose, then ? In his ? In Robert Rideout's ? It should rock on the uneven floor of his mother's cottage, and he would make it himself. He would create it out of good seasoned oak, and love and toil. And he would create the babe that should lie within it. By his will, with or without Gillian's, she should attain perfection ; she should have the gift of gifts ; she should live and give life. And with the haughtiness without which no young man's character is perfect, he knew that it was not Gillian, rich woman though she might be, who would be the creditor in that bargain. He, Robert the shepherd, would be the giver, giving her his kingly gift of children. Although humility was his usual mental garb when thinking of Gillian, he knew that, ultimately, this was how things were, and must always be.

He was back in the kitchen now. It was as if he could hear the rockers, could see Gillian with her hair sweeping across the scar, with her haughty nose and sweet mouth and the challenging eyes into which never, never could he look long enough. He could see the dark brown cradle, low on the floor, with its large rockers. He could see the

little face within it, with the same sweet mouth, the same
challenging eyes.

And all the while he knew he was only playing with Fate.
He was only putting off the moment when he must face
things. And what he must face was this. Gillian loved
Ralph Elmer. And there was no other way to save Ralph
than by someone else taking upon himself the guilt.
Fringal? Well, but why? Fringal had not done it.
It was not fair to try and force the guilt upon an
unwilling victim. Besides, no doubt Fringal could prove
an alibi.

Two men only had no alibi. And one of those was himself. He had been present at the murder and at the
burying.

And Gillian loved Ralph Elmer.

She might turn to him if Ralph were gone, but it was
Ralph she loved. She had told him so twice, and Rwth
had known it, for she had written it. All night, while the
snow softly enclosed him from action, he wrestled with
himself. And in the morning, when he woke from a
troubled sleep, he had conquered.

" You needna wrostle with me any more," he said
to himself or someone unseen. " I've said I'll do it. It's
as good as done."

And in the peace of this thought he threw some brush-
wood on the fire and made himself a cup of tea.

He could do nothing till the thaw set in, for if he shot
himself now (and it was that way he intended to go) he
would leave the poor creatures of the farm to starve. He
must wait till the thaw had set in, till he was sure someone
would come to the farm quite soon. On Wednesday the
butcher came round. If it had thawed by then——
Yes, that was it, Wednesday. Nobody would ever know
about his pennillions, nor his poem of the moor. It was
agonizing in its negation of all he was and all he had
hoped to be. He felt he *could* not do it. His poems had
beauty; Gruffydd had told him so. They were the
very best of himself—the long one of the moor especially.

They had cost him so much. For the words and the metre of a poem—the mere making of it—are in such small proportion to all that went before. It is the capacity for suffering and joy, and the hard-won knowledge of life and mankind that make a poet. It is generally easy to distinguish a poet from a mere versifier by the lines of sorrow round his eyes and mouth or on his forehead. To write one small lyric—if it is real poetry—a man must give a lifetime of pain. And, after that, to be wiped off the face of the earth, with none to remember him, with not a line of his poetry to remain, and to go to his grave branded as a murderer! What would Gipsy Johnson think of the friend who had murdered his girl? What would his poor mother think when she saw the letter he must write? He could not! No. He would not!

And Gillian? Gillian, the bloom of the moor, the sweetly, darkly-tinted flower, creature of sudden dewy gleams and glances, quite incomprehensible to him; of rippled laughter and those sullen moods that most stirred passion in him, when he could have snatched her and set his mouth hard on hers and (as he said to himself) " learnt her better manners."

Yes! That mischievous naughtiness, that unconquerable pride were what made it hardest to leave her and die for her.

Yes! It was because he sometimes wanted to say, " You little devil! " that he so wildly loved her, wanted her, startled and angry and provocative, in his arms. He would never have wanted to say " Little devil! " to Rwth. So he would never have wanted to marry her.

O God! How he desired Gillian! Through the snowy hours he would suddenly start up to go to her—just to go to her. Yet it was Rwth that had, in his dream, cradled him. Rwth would not have made it so hard to die—poor Rwth who lay beneath the snow. It was not tenderness that made it hard, nor love. It was passion. There is a melancholy sweetness in leaving for ever some dear garden in the hush of evening, when dreaming birds no longer flute, and the colours are washed away, and the sweet of the day is over and has become a part of experience. But to leave it all in the unravished wonder of dawn! Oh, no, no! God of youth and manhood, no!

" I've said it. It's as good as done," repeated Robert Rideout. And he walked heavily across the kitchen to look on the dresser for the pen. The letter must be final and conclusive. It must damn him past argument. And he must write it now.

To die for a man he detested!

Yet Gillian loved the man.

When rebellion fired his mind he remembered this. He dipped his pen in the ink and began. He must set his death at the door of conscience. That was it! He had murdered Ailse Johnson in the little gyland, and then he could not bear it, because she haunted him. He forced his imagination into the recesses of a murderer's mind. A murderer, quite alone near the scene of his crime, practically snowed up, might very easily be haunted by his crime until he became almost insane and was driven to suicide. It nauseated Robert to be mixed up with such morbid, deathly things. But there was worse to follow.

Why did Robert Rideout murder Ailse Johnson?

" Well now, that's a poser, that is! " observed Robert.

He looked at the window, drifted with snow. At the clock. At the fire.

" Oh, dang it! Why did I? " he asked of things in general.

And the only answer, the horrible, disgusting answer was—lust. There was no other possible answer to the question of motive.

" Now that's too much, that is! " he said. He had always lived so cleanly. He was no saint, but he was not sensual. He did not lust after women : he fell in love with them. He had " got into trouble," as the charitable country speech expresses it, once. But there had been romance and delight and beauty in it—something very different from mere lust. And now——

He put his head down on his arms and groaned. Then, with a wild, drawn face, he wrote the letter. He called

to his aid the impersonal artist in him, and he made the
letter a masterpiece of remorse and self-revelation, fear
and cunning. It made him feel debased. When he had
finished the letter he went out into the welter of snow,
and put his head under the icy water of the pump.

The snow stopped on Tuesday morning. On Tuesday
night the wind veered to the south. A sweet damp
air blew from the inn to the farm. The late chrysan-
themums in his mother's little plot freed their faces of
snow. Black pits and crevasses began to show on the
moor. The rustling thunder of snow sliding from the
roofs sounded at short intervals with the imperious tumult
of a landslip.

The thaw had come. Reprieve was over. With flap-
ping silver flight the plovers went to the dark, rich plough-
lands. The roads, Robert judged, would be passable to-
morrow. The gun stood ready in a corner. The letter
lay on the table.

After the feeding and littering-up were done Robert
sat down with a pipe to watch for the lights at the
Mermaid's Rest. He had not been able to see them
before, but now it was clear weather again. There they
were ! Calm, golden lights, beaming on others, not on him.
Tender lights of a home that was not his ! Well, they
beamed. That was something. Into the drear night of
hatred and pain they gleamed, and it was he that was
going to keep them alight.

So, with lamp and fire for company, he sat all night,
waiting for his last dawn.

CHAPTER XXXI

" NOW WHAT BE TROUBLING THEE ? "

WHILE Robert made for her the sacrifice that is greater than any, what were the thoughts of Gillian Lovekin at the sign of the Maiden where the yellow lamps were shining, but not love ? Was her heart blind and deaf that she did not see and hear afar the agony of the man who loved her ? Was the dream of self so drowsy on her that, straitened within her own being, she was losing the glory of life ? Hark, oh ! hark how the hours toll ! Slowly time drops away. Slowly above the dark head she loves opens Eternity. It is five o'clock in the morning, and already, away at the Keep, the wife of the butcher who travels the Dysgwlfas road to-day looks out of her window into the wild, dark, rainy morning and goes downstairs to get her husband's breakfast. And as soon as his cart comes in at the farm gate, Robert goes out through the gate of silence.

Is Gillian Lovekin asleep ? The inn is dark and still. Only the mice nibble. Only the bats squeak. The windlestraws whisper sadly by the door, and what is Gillian's life but a windlestraw with no sap of love in it ? Down in the gyland the south wind laments, and from the hidden moorland comes a ceaseless roar like the roar of the sea.

Poor child, are you still asleep while the best of life goes by ? Have you forgotten Mr. Gentle ? Have you had no intuition of your share in the crime of Ralph Elmer—the crime which began long before he ever saw

the unket place ; which began when he took a woman
for his mate out of fear of Fringal and of gossip, which
continued when he took another woman at the com-
pulsion of Isaiah, mingling deceit and cupidity and passion ?
And in that crime, as in her dealings with Emily and Mr.
Gentle and the conies, Gillian Lovekin's share was that
she thought only of herself. She married for self. She
lay in Ralph's arms for self. She denied Robert for
self. She was so drugged with self that while she
could have held in her breast, like a nestling bird
with pinions folded, the real breathing soul of a man,
she never knew it, but filled her hands with useless gifts
instead.

Gillian ! Do you hear the shot which will sound in so
few hours from Dysgwlfas cottage ? The shot which,
for you, should be sounding now, since a woman is a
foolish creature indeed if love does not make her a
prophetess. Lovers can hear forwards as well as backwards. If the women of the world always heard forwards
in this way, they would hear the bruit of war in time to
stop it. A lover feels the weight of sorrow that lies
upon her distant love, feels his spirit, in pain, urgent
upon hers. For surely it is unnatural and horrible for a
woman to give herself to one whose personality is not
large enough and strong enough to dominate her. And if
it dominates her, she must feel the grief and joy of that
mind in absence as well as in bodily presence.

Could Gillian sleep on this last morning on earth of the
man she loved ? The dreaming house, and the bats and
mice within it, knew that she could not. The south wind,
that raced by the open window of Rwth's empty attic,
knew that she could not, for it lifted her hair and tore at
the shawl she had put on over her nightdress. And the
white star knew, which hung in the north just above the
faint yellow radiance of Robert's window, for it dazzled
in her eyes and showed the love there. That yellow
radiance had been in the cottage window all night, she
knew, for she had watched it. Awakening from a strange
dream soon after two, in that hour of visions and portents,

when vitality is lowest and the dying slip away, she had heard Robert's voice quite clearly saying :

" Gillian Rideout ! "

Not Elmer. Not Lovekin. Rideout.

In the dream she had seen herself lying at Robert's feet in his cottage. Robert was speaking kindly to her, and was offering her—holding it in both hands—his mother's large, heavy bread-dish of old Salopian ware with the wreath of green leaves and yellow ears of corn in high relief.

" See, Gillian ! " he was saying. " Take this. I must go away with Mr. Gentle now : but take this, because I love you. It's my heart, Gillian Rideout."

And looking at the dish she saw that it was so, and woke with a cry. And now, there was the light. It was a thing unknown at Dysgwlfas, to burn a light till daybreak. Robert must be ill. She leaned from the window in an agony. Robert ill, and she not there ! Oh, no ! It must not be. She sobbed. She wrung her hands. For it had come to pass as Robert had said in one of his poems. He had loved her until she was blind and deaf to herself, until she " couldna abear herself."

She went down to the room where Ralph tossed and muttered. She dressed quickly, not waiting to do up her hair, but tying it with a ribbon. She could hear the wind driving on the southerly window of the passage till the small panes seemed to crackle with its onslaught. Rain washed on the glass. The snow was gone, except under northern and eastern hedges, and on the highest points of the moor, and in the unket place. But the road to the farm was a river. And though, if it had been straight, the wind would have blown her there, as the way was a winding one she would often meet the storm or half meet it, and would be buffeted and breathless and drenched before she arrived. She made some tea and threw dry furze on the fire to make a blaze, for she was very cold after her vigil. Then, with the shawl pinned closely round her, she started. It was not a day on which even a ploughman, who will face almost any weather, would

have chosen to be out. When she was half-way there
she saw a thin spire of smoke from Robert's chimney,
and decided to go back. But something within drove
her on. The ends of the shawl lashed her eyes. She was
wet through and exhausted. But she went on. She
came to the farm, to the yard gate, to the wicket of the
cottage. She knocked softly. There was no reply.
She looked through the window. There was Robert,
in the arm-chair, very still.

His eyes were shut.

Asleep, or—— ?

She went in. How like and yet unlike that day of
spring when she awakened Ralph Elmer with a catkin
kiss ! She was not going to awaken Robert in any such
way, because she dared not. She was only going to see if
he was ill or well. She tip-toed across the little kitchen,
dim in the early light, with its one window sheeted in
rain. His head was sunk a little forward. The broad,
beautiful brow looked weary. The long lashes that had
never made him look womanish lay on cheeks grown
thinner in the last year, where the fine, clean bone showed
more than it used to do. His hands were lightly laid on
the arms of the chair, and he had taken off his boots and
sat in stockinged feet, for he and Jonathan would have
thought slippers very womanish.

She stood there, awed by his grave beauty, and she saw
with a rush of gratitude that he breathed regularly. He
was not ill, then ; only very tired. Something must
have been troubling him to make him sit up all night
like that.

" Now what be troublin' thee ? " she whispered. And,
as her high-handed manner was, she began to rove round
the little room. She did not mean to pry, only she must
find out, before she went back, if it was anything serious.
She dared not wake him to ask, for she knew he would be
angry, and his anger she could not bear. He might even
tell her what sort of a woman he thought her to come thus
to the house of a man not her husband. If he did, she
thought she would die of shame. But suppose his mother

was dead, and he very miserable, with no one to comfort
him ? Suppose he had found that the sick cow had
anthrax, and that he had caught it ? Then she wanted
to catch it too. She must know. She looked round.
Nothing. Her glance went indifferently past the gun.
It is such a usual thing to see a gun leaning against the
wall of a country kitchen. But it is not so common a
thing to see a long letter on the table—and a letter in the
writing of Robert himself was a very rare thing indeed.
Was it a letter to herself ? To some girl he was going to
marry ?

Ah ! ah ! She must know. She must know that
girl's name ! She would hate her. She would destroy
her. Oh, no, no ! If Robert loved her, Robert should
have her. Yes, he should—only she must and would
know. She reached across the tablecloth and picked up
the letter. Then, standing rigid on the opposite side of
the hearthrug, she read it. Line by dreadful line she
read it, and Robert's firmly made letters danced before
her eyes like elves that have drunk too deeply of metheglin.
She knew it was not true that he had murdered Rwth.
She would have known it if Rwth had lain dead in this
very room. That Rwth was dead she did not doubt,
if Robert said so ; but when Robert accused himself he
was denying his own nature, and so he was lying. And
as he did not like lying he must be doing it for some great
reason. To shield—whom ? Fringal ? But why should
he ? There was another—there was one who had muttered in his sleep, who had told her Rwth was at Dosset's
when Rwth was dead, who had spoken to her of Rwth
as if she had no soul, who had been angry at the writing,
who had been out all afternoon—all evening, with a gun.

" I shot Rwth in the little gyland."

" 'Twas Ralph ! " whispered Gillian. " 'Twas Ralph !
Oh, my soul ! "

She returned to her reasoning. The clock with the pale
golden voice chimed the quarter to seven very sweetly.
But Robert was too deeply asleep to hear it.

" Keep asleep ! Oh, keep asleep ! " she whispered.

It was like an incantation. He might have been some
young mariner under the green water, and she the veritable
mermaid of the legend, charming him to slumber.

Yes ! That was it ! That must be it ! Ralph had some
reason for hating Rwth. He spoke to her as if he hated
her. Ralph had come upon Rwth in the little gyland.
He had had the gun in his hand, and he had been tempted
and had shot her. And now here was Robert, evidently
after long, anguished thought, going to kill himself and
take the blame. At the reason given in the letter for the
crime Gillian drew down the corners of her mouth scornfully. " Another lie ! " she thought. " I make no
doubt there's been a tidy few girls in love with ye, and
you've kissed here and there—and there was the Shepcot
girl. But never *this*, Bob ! No ! "

But what a complicated tale, all made up for his own
destruction. Why had he—— ?

Like a bell, deep and beautiful and far away, she heard
Robert's voice :

" Do ye love Ralph Elmer, or do ye not ? "

And she had said : " Yes."

And now, she knew ! Now with one hand pressed to her
racing heart, with a face white from the stress of her
emotion, she knew !

Robert loved her. Robert had planned for himself
this dreadful death, this dishonour and utter annihilation
from the love of everyone he knew, simply for her—
simply because he thought she loved Ralph Elmer, and
what she loved she must have.

As a kind father gives his child a toy deeply desired,
so Robert had planned to give her Ralph Elmer. Quietly
and without any hope of gratitude or love in return, he
had arranged to give up his life, so that she might keep
Ralph Elmer ! It was all as simple, as eloquent, as the
grave silence of the sleeping man.

Earth and Heaven broke up round Gillian Lovekin.
Her spirit melted ; her pride was a snowflake of yesterday.
Herself ? Where and what was herself ? Once there had
been a person called Gillian Lovekin, who had loved her-

self so much that she was hard to everyone else ; who had
thought of the universe as it affected Gillian ; who had
said, " I *will* have this *!* I *will* be loved and admired. I
am Gillian Lovekin ! " Then she had changed a little.
She had wanted Robert's love. She had been Gillian
Lovekin, wanting him to love her. Not now, not now !
Now it did not matter whether he loved her or not, if
only she might love him.

Everything had melted away. It was as if the cottage
and the farm, the moor and the inn, were all part of the
thaw, were all flowing, flowing down to the sea. And she ?
She was melting away, too ; there was hardly any Gillian
left, nothing but tears ! Oh, tears, that would not fall,
that choked her and blinded her ! Nothing in all the
world was left but Robert's face—asleep in this tempest
that raged about her. And suddenly she thought of a
picture of Christ walking on the sea, and of Peter, poor
wave-devoured Peter, clinging to His feet.

She flung herself at Robert's feet. She laid her wet
cheek on the coarse hand-knitted sock of her father's
shepherd, and clasped his ankles with her hands. Her
damp hair lay along the floor ; sobs tore her ; the tears
came at last.

It seemed that even on Juliana Lovekin the south wind
had blown. Even to Juliana Lovekin the thaw had
come.

Robert, in his exhausted slumber, became vaguely conscious of unrest. He had fallen asleep with his purpose
so keenly in his mind that the first thing he thought was
that someone was awakening him because the moment had
come. He thought of his mother, and how she used
to awaken him on days of childish sorrow—when he was
to go to the doctor to have a burn dressed, or to have
a tooth out. He had the same sinking of the heart now.
But his mother would not fumble about his feet like a small
lost creature. Something damp was pressed against his
sock. A frantic clasp was about his ankles. What was
it ? Had he died, and was this warm peace with seven
pale golden chimes in it Heaven ? But surely there were no

woollen stockings in Heaven, nor damp, sobbing creatures clinging to them ! He dragged himself into wakefulness. With a great effort he opened his eyes.

Gillian ! Gillian as he had once prophetically seen her and written of her Gillian, the rich farmer's daughter, all bedraggled with tears, fumbling at his feet, kissing his socks.

Oh ! he *must* be dead, and this a dream of Heaven. But why was the poor child crying so ? Where was his letter ? This was not at all as he had planned it. And Gillian never spoke. It was most strange.

" Why, Gillian ! "

He stooped and touched her hair. It was wet. His socks were wet. What with the rain and the tears, no mermaid could have been much damper than Gillian.

And still she clung to him. Never had he seen a creature in such an abandonment of woe. He was shocked ; it was dreadful to see this lovely haughty Juliana lying there like a forgotten penitent.

" Mrs. Elmer ! " he said, " you've forgotten yerself."

She caught his hand and pulled herself on to her knees at that. With a face streaming with tears she looked up at him. She was like a child saying its prayers.

" I love ye, Robert ! " she said. " I know it all, and I love ye ! I read the letter. Please to let me love ye, Robert Rideout ! "

Robert lifted her face and looked into her eyes. And because he was very near crying himself, he took refuge in a kind of desperate mirth, and with a look half-way between reckless triumph and demure jest, he said :

" What, marry cowman-shepherd ? "

" I wish I could ! Oh, I wish I could ! But I'll never go away unless you send me, Robert."

" What ! Live along of cowman, and you a married lady ? Make yerself a nayword ; you that was the pattern of a rich woman ? "

No words. Only that frantic grip, those kisses on his hands, those sobs.

" My dear ! " he said. " Rwth was Elmer's missus."

" Rwth ? "

" Ah ! "

" Then I'm—— ? "

" You be Miss Lovekin agen, and we mun find a remedy for it. Why, you're lying right across the ' Welcome ' on the rug ! That'll never do ! "

With a laugh that had in it the merriment of a hundred boys, all taking " dogs' leave " and all neesening, he stooped and gathered up the sobbing little creature who was the heiress of the countryside.

Soon he must think about all sorts of things—about Rwth lying lonely in the gyland, and Elmer and Johnson. But they must wait.

He smoothed the damp and tangled hair from her brow.

" Will ye like doing what cowman-shepherd tells ye ? " he asked, with a tenderly malicious smile.

Silence. Only the busy, comfortable ticking of the clock, the sigh and wash of the rain.

" Will ye sing Esmeralda's song agen—some day— Gillian Rideout ? "

No answer. Only the rain, lisping on the window.

" Why, Gillian ! You've lost your words ! " said Robert.

Bending his head he set his mouth on hers. Ages upon ages went by. There was time in that kiss for the world to dispart itself from a blazing meteor, and cool, and gather moisture, and bring forth grass and trees, and deck itself with orchards and gardens. There was time for it to create for itself denizens, creatures terrible and beautiful ; time for the roar of the mastodon to echo and diminish and fail, for fish to become beasts ; for beasts to take wing ; for mankind to appear—there was even time for humanity to find, in the windy darkness of evolution, its soul.

A hundred thousand ages fled. Time was left far back on the road like a hobbling ancient. Eternity flowered in every crevice. And yet, when Robert Rideout came to himself after that kiss, and slackened the grip that had almost crushed her, the hands of the respectable eight-day

clock, which seemed to be observing him with astonish-
ment, pointed precisely to five minutes past seven.

" Oh, Robert ! " whispered Gillian, " Robert ! The
powers of darkness have loosed their hold, and I'm not
a child of sin any more."

And it seemed to Robert, as he looked at the high brow
he loved, with all the disordered hair swept away from
it, that there was no scar there at all.

CHAPTER XXXII

"SEVEN FOR A SECRET THAT'S NEVER BEEN TOLD"

BUT the reader must by this time be indignant. What is the explanation of the title? Why has everything gone to pieces like this? Why are Robert and Gillian sitting all alone in Robert's cottage at half-past seven in the morning? What has happened to Johnson and Elmer and Fringal? Has nobody missed Rwth? Where are the police? Has not Robert remembered that it is past milking time and that the fowls are still shut up and complaining bitterly? Did the butcher come? Did it go on raining always? Did the thaw last? Did not Isaiah and Mrs. Makepeace ever return to their respective homes? Who has, in this uncalled-for manner, let eternity into the cottage and spoilt the plot? Reader, that is how things happen! When Love, the scarlet-mantled, comes in, can the author help being dazzled?

But things did happen almost as they should in a well-regulated novel. Johnson had found out everything, and he went to the Mermaid's Rest that very morning, only to see an empty stable, an empty cash-box and signs of hurried departure. Ralph and Fringal had disappeared for ever. The whole story came out. Isaiah and Mrs. Makepeace returned in great agitation. Poor Ailse was buried in the churchyard. Nobody would live at the Mermaid's Rest, so the moor began to flow back over it, covering its sorrow with beauty. The sign of the Mermaid swung creaking in the wind, and as no-one renewed her,

284

the lady was at last quite obliterated. But the children
who rove about the deserted and silent place, unafraid in
their innocence, call the buttercups " Mermaid's Money."
And the story has made for itself a place in the annals
of the country, and has become as one of Jonathan's
tales, which the other Jonathans will tell in rosy bar-par-
lours, or in the brindled shadow of blossoming trees, while
the years roll their purple over the moor.

And on a summer day, when the deserted doorstep of
the Mermaid's Rest is blue with birdseye, a boy with eyes
so bright and dark with vitality that you cannot tell the
colour of them says : " A long time ago, when our dad
was a cowman, mother lived there." And a younger lad,
with solid shoulders and a masterful air, asks : " Why
dunna she live there now ? " " Oh ! Father fetched her
away," says Bob ; " ye see, he wanted her for himself
and us. He was nobut a cowman then, our dad wasn't."

But the eldest, whose hands are full of summer flowers,
and who is like her mother, says : " How durst you say
our dad was a cowman, Bob ! " For she is a true
descendant of Isaiah and Juliana Lovekin, and she thinks
it kinder not to mention her father's humble birth. Does
she not go to tea at the Vicarage ?

" It dunna matter, so long as he was a good cowman,"
says Bob.

There is a shout of naughty laughter from the younger
one. " He wasna ! He forgot to milk one day till it
ud gone nine ! "

But the reader wants to know about the title of the
book, and about the secret. Was it Robert's love for
Gillian, or Gillian's for him, or Ailse's, or her hidden story ?
But all these have been told. Is there more ? Out in the
early summer morning, listening to the silence, you know
that there is more, that in and beyond the purple earth
and silver sky there is a mystery so great that the knowledge of it would be intolerable, so sweet that the very
intuition of its nearness brings tears. Every sigh of the
mystic, every new word of science, is fraught with it.
Yet its haunts are further away than time or space or

consciousness. It may be that death reveals it. Certainly life cannot, for if we learnt that secret, such is its glory and piercing beauty that it would kill us.

Maybe it was not Gillian, in all the tremulous yet triumphant beauty of wifehood and motherhood, not even Robert in the glory of manhood and poetry and courageous love that came nearest to this mystery, which decrees that those who are all love, as Ailse was, must suffer, while those who are selfish, like Gillian, are redeemed. Perhaps it was Ailse's compensation, as she floated down-stream to eternity in the water-lily of a pure and unrewarded love, that she understood before them all the secret that's never been told.

THE END

Other VIRAGO MODERN CLASSICS

EMILY EDEN
The Semi-Attached House &
   The Semi-Detached Couple

MILES FRANKLIN
My Brilliant Career
My Career Goes Bung

GEORGE GISSING
The Odd Women

ELLEN GLASGOW
The Sheltered Life
Virginia

SARAH GRAND
The Beth Book

RADCLYFFE HALL
The Well of Loneliness
The Unlit Lamp

WINIFRED HOLTBY
Anderby Wold
The Crowded Street

MARGARET KENNEDY
The Ladies of Lyndon
Together and Apart

F. M. MAYOR
The Third Miss Symons

GEORGE MEREDITH
Diana of the Crossways

EDITH OLIVIER
The Love Child

CHARLOTTE PERKINS
GILMAN
The Yellow Wallpaper

DOROTHY RICHARDSON
Pilgrimage (4 volumes)

HENRY HANDEL
RICHARDSON
The Getting of Wisdom
Maurice Guest

BERNARD SHAW
An Unsocial Socialist

MAY SINCLAIR
Life & Death of Harriett Frean
Mary Olivier
The Three Sisters

F. TENNYSON JESSE
A Pin to See The Peepshow
The Lacquer Lady
Moonraker

MARY WEBB
Gone to Earth
The House in Dormer Forest
Precious Bane

H. G. WELLS
Ann Veronica

REBECCA WEST
Harriet Hume
The Judge
The Return of the Soldier

ANTONIA WHITE
Frost in May
The Lost Traveller
The Sugar House
Beyond the Glass
Strangers

If you would like to know more about Virago books, write to us at Ely House, 37 Dover Street, London W1X 4HS for a full catalogue.

Please send a stamped addressed envelope

Book Tokens

Give them the pleasure of choosing

Book Tokens can be bought and exchanged at most bookshops